STAR WARS

AFTERMATH

EMPIRE'S END

STAR WARS

AFTERMATH

EMPIRE'S END

Book Three of The Aftermath Trilogy

CHUCK WENDIG

DEL REY • NEW YORK

2017 Del Rey Mass Market Edition

Published in the United States by Del Rey, an imprint of Random House, a division of Penguin Random House LLC, New York.

DEL REY and the HOUSE colophon are registered trademarks of Penguin Random House LLC.

Originally published in hardcover in the United States by Del Rey, an imprint of Random House, a division of Penguin Random House LLC, in 2017.

"Blade Squadron: Jakku" by David J. Williams and Mark S. Williams was originally published in *Star Wars Insider* magazine issue #172, in 2017.

ISBN 978-1-101-96698-3
Ebook ISBN 978-1-101-96697-6

Printed in the United States of America

randomhousebooks.com

9

Del Rey mass market edition: September 2017

To Luke S.,
wherever you are

THE DEL REY
STAR WARS
TIMELINE

THE DEL REY STAR WARS TIMELINE

A long time ago in a galaxy far, far away. . . .

For the first time in a generation, democracy has been restored to the galaxy. Although reeling from a crippling Imperial attack, the New Republic has managed to drive the remnants of the Empire into hiding. Still, the threat of continued violence will always remain while the war persists.

On the remote planet of Jakku, far from Republic eyes, the once-secretive Gallius Rax strives to rebuild the crumbling Empire in his own image. But his plans may soon be challenged by former Grand Admiral Rae Sloane who seeks to destroy Rax and reclaim her Empire from his dark machinations.

Unaware of Rax's plot, Norra Wexley and her crew continue to pursue any information that could lead them to the fugitive Sloane. Convinced that Sloane holds the key to the Empire's defeat, Norra's search brings her closer and closer to Rax's hidden army. For on Jakku, the Empire prepares to make its last stand where the fate of the galaxy will be decided.

PRELUDE

THE SECOND DEATH STAR OVER ENDOR

THE ARCHITECTURE OF the Death Star, even in its unfinished reconstruction, brings awe to Admiral Gallius Rax. It is a world unto itself, and as he walks the hallway toward the turbolift, shepherded by a pair of red-helmeted guardsmen, he notices that the battle station hums and thrums all around him—a subtle vibration in which Rax hears a mad song. It is a song of might, of potency, of destruction. An Imperial opera in timbre and tremor.

He never set foot on the first incarnation of the Death Star. He wasn't allowed to—it was his role to be kept at the margins, waiting for a destiny he was sure would never come. And yet now, here he is. Invited on board to see. Which suggests to him he is either soon to fulfill that destiny, or even sooner to die as his destiny withers on the vine.

The guards step forward, summoning a lift lit with red and white light, its black floor so smooth and so dark it's like a mirror cast in obsidian and stained with moral decay. They usher Rax into it, but do not follow.

He goes up alone.

The turbolift opens.

There waits the Emperor at the far end of the throne room. The old man in his black cloak sits regarding the soft glowing curve of the Endor moon that lies beyond the radial viewport. Slowly, the chair spins.

Only half the man's face can be seen. The lines in it have deepened considerably. Flesh sags from the jaw and the jowls, and his mouth is cast in a feral grimace that is somehow also a troubling smile. That face with that mouth is like a rotten piece of bag-cloth with a knife-slash cut in the fabric. The rest of his countenance is hidden in the shadow of the black hood.

It has been many years since Rax has seen Palpatine up close. The awfulness he once saw cast upon the man's face has been carved into his skin and made flesh.

The sight of the Emperor robs him of breath. It steals from him a measure of strength, and his knees nearly give out. Palpatine has the presence of a collapsing star and the consumptive void that results from it. It draws you in. It takes something from you. It is a flensing, frightening force.

But Rax stands tall, as he once did on Jakku.

"Come," Palpatine says, a rigor mortis claw summoning him.

Rax does as commanded. "My Emperor." He bows his head.

"A shuttle has landed on the Sanctuary Moon," the old man says. Rax doesn't know how to answer this— the words come almost as an accusation, though not necessarily aimed at him. "Destiny accompanies that *ship*. There is one on board who challenges the course of fate as I have seen it."

"I shall have the shuttle destroyed."

"No, my boy. I have greater plans for the one on the shuttle—whether he will be a demonstration of my power or a slave to replace the one who has failed me, I cannot say. That remains unclear. But we are led to a moment in time, a moment of grave uncertainty. All things flow toward this moment." His voice goes soft and his head eases back into his hood. "I sense . . . chaos. Weakness. I sense a shatterpoint."

Rax thrusts out his chin and puffs up his chest. "Just tell me whatever it is you need, my lord."

"I need you to be ready."

"I am always ready."

"It may soon be time for the Contingency."

At that, Rax's throat tightens. *My destiny . . .*

Palpatine continues: "You will go far away from here. You will take the *Ravager* and hide in the Vulpinus Nebula until the events of this shatterpoint resolve."

"How will I know?"

"You will know. I will send a sentinel."

Rax nods. "Yes, my lord."

Palpatine regards him. Rax cannot see the Emperor's eyes, but he can certainly *feel* them. Sticking him like pins. Dissecting him to see what he's made of. "My boy. My *precious* boy. Are you ready to be the Outcast? Are you prepared to become the Contingency should it come to that? There will be others you must call to your side."

"I know. And I am ready." *I am ready to go home.* Because that's what this means, does it not? It means one day soon returning to the sands of Jakku. To the Observatory. To everything he hates, and yet to the place that harbors his destiny—and the destiny of the galaxy as a whole.

"Then go. Time is precious. A battle will soon be upon us."

"You will win it, most assuredly."

Another vicious smile. "One way or another, I will."

PART ONE

CHAPTER ONE

THIS PART OF Taris is a wasteland, and Mercurial Swift moves through it like a rat slipping through bolt-holes. The bounty hunter clambers through the wreckage of an old habitation building, its apartments long shattered, the walls torn open to expose the mess of collapsed urban sprawl. Through the broken world, life tries to grow: creeping three-fingered vines and twisting spirals of slime-slick fungus. And though the ruination conceals it, people live here: They dwell, huddled up together in shipping containers and through crumbling hallways, hidden under the fractured streets and atop buildings so weakened they sway like sleepy drunks in even the softest wind.

His prey is here. *Somewhere.*

Vazeen Mordraw, a wilder girl who stole a caseload of ID cards from the Gindar Gang—cards that were themselves stolen from New Republic dignitaries. Cards that would allow anyone easy passage through the known worlds without triggering a closer look. The Gindar want the cards back. And as a special bonus, they want the girl, too.

Preferably alive. Dead if necessary.

Mercurial plans on the former. If only because it'll be a lot easier to extract someone who can move around on her own two feet—carting a corpse over the wreckage of Taris sounds like a damn fine way to snap an ankle. And that would make this job unnecessarily harder.

There. Up ahead. Some scum-farmer kid stands in the shadow of a shattered wall, scraping sponge-moss off the stone, maybe to feed his family, maybe to sell. The boy—head shaved, dirt on his cheeks, his lower lip split as a scarmark indicating that he is an owned boy—startles and turns to run. But Swift calls after.

"Hey! Slow down, kid." He shakes a small satchel at him. Credits *tink* as they jostle together. "I'm looking for someone."

The kid doesn't say anything, but he stops running, at least. Wary, he arches an eyebrow, and Mercurial takes that as a sign of interest. The bounty hunter taps the gauntlet at his wrist, and a hologram glimmers suddenly in the air above his arm. It's an image of the girl, Vazeen.

"Seen her?"

"Maybe."

"Don't be cagey." Again he shakes the credit bag. "Yes or no."

The boy hesitates. "Yes."

"Where?"

"Close."

Yes. Mercurial knew she had to be here. The old Ithorian at the spaceport crawled out of his spice-sodden haze long enough to confirm that he knew the girl *and* that she would go to ground near her family. Her uncle lives here in the remains of the old Talinn district. (Swift is suddenly glad she doesn't have family on the far side of the planet—there the wealthy live in massive towers, hypersecure, guarded by armies of private security.)

"*How* close?"

The boy's eyes flit left and right. Like he's not sure

how to answer. Which leads Mercurial to suspect that the boy actually knows her. "I . . ."

"Kid. I'm going to either give you these credits, or I'm going to throw you out the hole in that wall over there. You can leave here with some extra currency in your pocket, or with two broken legs. Maybe even two broken arms." Mercurial flashes his teeth in a sharp grin. "It's a long way down."

And *still* the boy hesitates. He's chewing over his options. A heady, swamp-stink wind whips and whistles through the shattered hallway.

"I'm not going to hurt her," Mercurial assures him. It's mostly true. In his experience, people *want* to be selfish, but they need to feel like they're being selfless while doing it. They want an *excuse*. He's happy to help the boy feel good about doing bad if that's what it takes. "Better I find her than someone else, trust me."

There it is. The moment of acquiescence. The boy closes his eyes gently, a decision having been made. Finally he says: "She's one building over. The old Palmyra foundry. Vazeen has a little . . . cubbyhole up there. A hiding place."

"Congrats," Mercurial says, flipping the satchel into the kid's open palm. The boy stares down at it, greedy and eager. Too bad he doesn't realize that the credits are barely worth their metal. Imperial currency has crashed hard, cratering with meteoric impact. Everyone knows that soon the Empire will be stardust—and then what?

That is a worry for another time.

The boy runs off.

Mercurial hunts.

Hours later, the bounty hunter lies flat on his belly and brings the quadnocs up—he stares through them, flicking the zoom forward click by click until his view is zeroed in enough to make out just enough detail. The roof of the foundry is flat and, like everything else here, broken. A vent stack tower from the next factory over fell across the foundry, connecting the two ruined buildings—and Mercurial decides that will serve as his extraction point if everything goes sideways. Though he's hard-pressed to imagine how collecting this simple bounty could go wrong . . .

He spies sudden movement on the roof. Swift focuses in on it, and sees a small sheet of tin move aside—and a brush of pink hair catches the fading light of day.

Target acquired.

A little part of him is thrilled to find her, but at the same time, his heart sinks. The future plays out in his mind, and at its end waits a worthless payout. He'll nab her. He'll take her to the Gindar prigs. They'll give him a meager stash of chits—not Imperial credits, not anymore, but chits that he can take to *certain* merchants on *certain* worlds and cash in for gear or ammo or a meal, but of course they won't work *everywhere,* and what one chit is worth now will fluctuate wildly depending on who owns the currency. In this case, the Gindars are owned by the Frillian Confederacy, and the Frillians are owned by Black Sun. And nobody owns Black Sun. Not yet. But that day may be coming—with the Empire waning and the New Republic rising, the syndicates know that opportunity waits for those willing to seize the galaxy during this time of chaos. But who? Who gets to exploit that opportunity first? It's led to infighting. The syndicates are aiming to one-up each other, trying to establish supremacy. A shadow war is just getting started. They want to own the currency *and* set the criminal destiny for the entirety of the galaxy. Black Sun. Shadow Syndicate. The Hutts. Red Key. The Crymorah. The Sovereign Latitudes of Maracavanya. *What a bloody mess.*

Eventually, Mercurial knows that someone will try to own *him,* too. But he has no intention of being a kept boy.

The bounty hunter stands and emerges from the bent, dented hull of an old freighter—one that must've crashed on the habitation roof eons ago and is now just a sculpture of rusted beams. Swift pulls his batons and moves fast: He runs and leaps off the lip of the building, giving his jetpack two quick pulses. The crackle of energy fills the air behind him, propelling him forward as the foundry roof comes up fast. Swift tucks and rolls, and when he returns to his feet, he spins his batons and runs straight to the ramshackle lean-to where Vazeen has been hiding.

She steps out. She sees him. He *sees* that she sees him, and yet his target stands there, unmoving. At first Swift thinks, *The girl knows the game is over,* but that doesn't track. This is a girl on the run. This is her planet. She should spook. She should run. *Everyone* runs.

And yet she remains, staring right at him.

The realization sticks Mercurial like a knife:

She's not running. Because she's bait.

Damnit!

He drops down again into a roll just as the stun blast fills the air above his head in a warbling scream. Swift leaps to his feet and expects to see someone he knows coming for him: an old enemy, a betrayed friend, an ex-girlfriend with a broken heart and a blaster rifle. But instead, he sees some *other* woman coming for him. Older. Silver hair moved by the wind. Whoever she is, she looks familiar to him, but he doesn't have time to sort through all the faces he's met, because she's got a pistol pointed right at him and another stun bolt comes—

But he's fast: a coiled spring, suddenly unsprung. He deftly pivots on the ball of his right foot, and as he spins around he has one of his batons up and flung—it leaves his fingers and whistles through open air.

Clack! His baton clips the front of her blaster. She cries out as the gun tumbles away, clattering onto the rooftop. The woman shakes her hand—the vibration surely stung her mitt, and now she's trying to soothe it—but still she keeps on coming, her face a grim rictus of determination.

Good for her. But she's still not going to get him.

He flexes his hand, fingers pressing into the button in the center of his palm. The extensor pads at the tips of his fingers suddenly buzz, and his one flung baton jumps up off the ground—

And surfs the air currents back into his grip.

The older woman skids to a halt, throwing a punch as she does—it's a good punch, solid, but the bounty hunter knows it's coming because her body language telegraphs the attack. Mercurial sidesteps, her fist catching open air, and it gives him an opportunity to jab his baton up under her arm. Electricity courses through her. Her teeth clamp together and her eyes open wide as every centimeter of her seizes up. When she drops, he hears the scuff of a boot behind him, and he thinks: *I'm too damn distracted.* This job made him too comfortable, *too complacent,* and now someone's hammering a fist into his kidneys, dropping him down to one knee.

He cries out and goes low with the next attack—his baton whips around, catching the second attacker behind the knee. His foe, a tall man with a hawk's-beak nose and dark eyes, curses and drops hard on his tailbone. He recognizes this one, doesn't he? Imperial. *No.*

Ex-Imperial. Working for the New Republic now—now he wonders, *Is this about the Perwin Gedde job?* It's coming back to him now. He stole their target right out from under them. What do they want? Credits? Revenge? Is he on their list?

Doesn't matter. *I have no time for whatever this is.* The girl isn't worth it. The payout is garbage. It's time to go. The fallen vent stack tower is his escape route, so he leaps to his feet and bolts fast across the roof-top. Another stun blast warps the air around him (the older woman reclaimed her weapon), but he leaps and slides onto the crumpled tower now serving as a bridge. He rights himself and runs, feet banging on the metal. The vented durasteel provides texture that helps him keep his footing, and he charges down the bridge and toward a break in the factory wall next door. Nobody follows. His assailants are slow, *too slow.* Because, he reminds himself, *nobody is as fast as me.* Mercurial Swift, triumphant again.

He leaps across the gap—

And an arm extends across the open space and slams hard across his trachea. His heels skid out and Mercurial drops onto his back, the air blasting out of his chest as his lungs collapse like clapped hands.

"Hi," says a voice. Another woman. *This* voice, he knows.

A fellow hunter, a bounty killer and skip-tracer like him: the Zabrak, Jas Emari. She steps over him, and as his eyes adjust he sees her juggling a toothpick on her tongue and between her teeth. She cocks her head, a flip of hair going from one side of her spike-laden scalp to the other.

"Emari," he wheezes, air finally returning to his re-inflating lungs.

He wastes no time. He brings one of his batons up fast—

But she is faster. A small blaster in her hand screams. And all goes dark.

It has taken them months to capture Swift.

Months to set up a false sting—*months* to steal ID cards from the Gindar Gang, to pin it on a young woman (who blessedly was happy to do her part in seeing the Empire take its licks), to falsify a bounty on behalf of the Gindars (one they had no choice but to pretend they initiated when hunters came knocking at their door to accept the bounty). They had to make it look good, make it look *tantalizing* to a bounty hunter like Swift—but not *too* tantalizing, because Jas assured them that when a job looked too good, too easy, it set one's teeth on edge. Nobody wanted to spook him, so it had to be done gently, slowly, with great caution and care. And all the while, Norra's guts twisted in her belly like a breeding knot of Akivan vipers, the nasty thought haunting her head again and again: *While we waste time, Rae Sloane drifts farther and farther away.* And so did their chance at justice.

It feels good to have caught Mercurial Swift in their little trap—he's the one bounty hunter known to interface exclusively with Sloane. But it's bitter candy, because they have bigger prey. He's just one rung in the ladder.

Please, Norra thinks. *Let it be the final rung.*

She's tired, and she's coasting on the fumes of anger. It's burning her out, stripping her down, leaving her feeling raw inside her heart.

But at least they have him.

Mercurial Swift hangs from a bent pipe here in the old munitions factory, his arms extended above him, his wrists cuffed. Night has fallen on Taris. Outside, vapor lightning colors the dark clouds ocher, while down below snorting scutjumpers click and scurry amid the wreckage of this world, hunting for bugs to eat.

"I hate him," Sinjir Rath Velus says, leaning in and staring at their prey. His nose wrinkles as if he's smelling something foul. "Even unconscious the man looks so bloody *smug*. And trust me: I know smugness well."

Jas twirls one of Swift's batons in her hand. She jabs it in the air. "He's smug but crafty. These batons are practically art. One end is concussive. The other end, electric. Kill or stun. And the second baton can be modified with a hypoinjector for poison."

"Let's wake him up," Norra says, suddenly impatient. "I want answers and I'm tired of waiting."

"We've waited this long," Jas says. "We can wait a little longer."

"I want Sloane. I want justice."

"You want revenge," Jas says. It's a conversation they've had before. Many times, as a matter of fact. Round and round they go. Sinjir just sighs and shakes his head as Norra responds:

"Revenge and justice are two sides of the same coin."

"I don't know if you would've said that before Chandrila."

"It's a little galling that you're the one judging me," Norra snaps.

Jas holds up surrendering hands. "No judgment. I far prefer revenge as a motive. Justice is a jumping bull's-eye. Revenge sits still right here." She taps the center of her chest. "I admire revenge. It's pure. It also happens to be the thing that pays me most of the time. I just think it's valuable to know which one is which, and why we're doing what we're doing."

She's wrong, Norra thinks. That day on Chandrila

was a nightmare: her own husband joining the rest of the mind-controlled captives from Kashyyyk to sweep across the stage and plaza in a wave of assassinations. The funerals went on for days. The mourning *still* continues, months later. This is one of those times when the needs of justice and the urge for vengeance line up neatly, like the metal sights at the end of a scatterblaster. And isn't justice really just a name for institutional revenge? Commit a crime, pay for the crime. Castigation arrives regardless of whether it's at the hand of a governmental body or a lone soldier.

At least, that's what Norra tells herself. And she's about to tell them all the same thing when Sinjir moans and interjects: "Both of you, please stop droning on about this. It's giving me a brain-ache. Let us wake up our *new friend*, if only so I can stop listening to *you* and start listening to *him*."

With that, Sinjir reaches up and plunges the tips of two fingers into the unconscious bounty hunter's nostrils. He tugs upward, hard. Mercurial's eyes jolt open and he sucks in a hissing breath.

"Wakey-wakey," Sinjir says all too cheerfully. "Time to *move* and time to *shake-y*." As an aside, he says: "My mother used to say that. Sweet woman. If I didn't get out of bed fast enough, her sweetness turned rather sour, though, and she would whip me with a broom." Now, back to Mercurial: "I don't need to hit you with a broom, do I? Are we awake?"

"I'm awake, I'm awake," the bounty hunter says, wrenching his head away from Sinjir's nose-probing fingers. His eyes focus on Jas. "You."

"Hello, Mercurial."

He laughs, a small, sad sound.

"What's funny?" Jas asks.

"Something someone said to me once. Dengar, actually." He flashes a smile. "He said the day would come.

'*Bounties on the bounty hunters.*' Seems today is that day, hm?"

"Dengar," she says, the words sounding to Norra like they're spoken around a mouthful of something spoiled, something foul. "I hate to admit it, but that slovenly lump of congealed sweat could be right: I have a bounty on me, after all."

"That's right. I remember Rynscar saying Boss Gyuti had put a number on your head. That number doubled, recently, didn't it?"

"Tripled," Jas says. Like she's proud. *Maybe she is.* "It's a big bounty. You, however, are surprisingly without one."

His eyebrow arches sharply. "Then why am I here?"

"Because we have questions," Norra says.

"Is this about that mess on Vorlag? I thought I recognized you up on the foundry roof. Gedde was all too easy, you know."

Jas says, "I *knew* that had to be your handiwork. The mycotoxin gave you away."

"I wasn't trying to hide it."

"We don't care about Vorlag," Norra says. Extracting Gedde—only to have him die in their care thanks to a slow-acting poison hidden in his spice—feels like a lifetime ago. So much has changed since then. "We care about the one who paid you to take him out. We care about *Sloane.* Grand admiral of the Galactic Empire, and now—out there somewhere. In the wind. In the stars."

"Don't know a '*Sloane,*'" he says, but the way the corner of his mouth tugs upward, as if on an angler's hook, is telling. "Sorry."

Sinjir gives Norra a look.

Norra gives Sinjir a nod.

With that, Jas eases aside, and Sinjir formally takes up her position in front of the dangling Mercurial

Swift. The ex-Imperial clucks his tongue as he starts in on Swift. "If I asked you the question, *What is the most important part of your body,* you would—as the ego-fed narcissist that you are—say . . ."

"My mind," Swift answers.

"Your *mind,*" Sinjir says, simultaneous with Swift. "Yes. And then I'd roll my eyes like I am now—here, look, I'm rolling them." He does indeed roll them. "I'd say, *No, no, silly, I need your mind keen and sharp, fully aware of what is about to be done and what is happening as it happens.* I'd note that what's precious to you is your *hands.* Your fast hands, spinning those nifty little batons around like a man from the Nal Hutta circus, and I would note that the hand has so many tiny bones, none so strong as your batons, and it would be dreadfully easy to break each of them, one after the other, as if I were playing the keys of a melodium. And you'd bluster—"

"Break my hands," Swift hisses. "Do it. Cut them off for all I care. I can afford their replacements. Metal machine hands would—"

"Help you do your job better, yes. I know. And how right you are. The bones in your hand are such small thinking. All of your body is! It's *amateur hour* interrogation, really. Ah. Time then to go deeper. More aspirational. Forget flesh and bones and blood. Well. Hold on now. *Blood.* That's interesting." He leans in, practically nose-to-nose with the bounty hunter. Swift struggles. Norra wants to warn Sinjir to be cautious, but he's like a hypnotizing serpent—Mercurial won't do anything. Not yet. Not now. He's rapt. The mystery of the threat to be revealed has been fitted around his neck like leash-and-collar, tugging him forward. "Your name, your *true* name, is not Mercurial Swift. Is it, Geb? Geb Teldar. Right?"

A flinch as Mercurial retreats from that name like a

buzzing fly. "I don't know that name," he says. But he does. Even Norra can see that.

"It's not really as *snazzy* as 'Mercurial Swift,'" Sinjir says, making a pouty face. "I mean, is it? Geb Teldar." When he says those words, he deepens his voice, flattens his lips, makes his accent sound common and muddy. "*Oy, my name's Geb Teldar. I'm a pipe fitter from Avast. I'm Geb Teldar, fathier stallmucker. I'm Geb Teldar, droid-scrubber extraordinaire*. It's really very . . . bleh, isn't it?"

"Go to hell."

"Thing is, Geb? Once we knew your real name, it was easy to find out *other* things, as well. You're from Corellia, aren't you?"

Swift—or, rather, Teldar—says nothing. His eyes shine with what Norra believes may very well be fear.

In the palm of Sinjir's hand is a flat disk—a holoprojector. He taps the side, and a single image shines in the space above it: a nice house in the Vrenian style, square and boxy but with climbing flowers up its corners and a lace-metal trachyte fence surrounding it. The door is tall and narrow—and by the door stands a droid familiar to most of them standing there.

Mercurial's cheek twitches. "Is that—"

"A B1 battle droid," Sinjir answers, "it is, indeed. I'm sure he had a proper designation at some point, but *we* call him Mister Bones, in part because he's very good at pulling the bones out of people's bodies. Oh. Perhaps you were instead asking a different question, and to that the answer is: *Yes*, Geb Teldar, that is the house of Tabba Teldar, and if I read the intel correctly, she is . . . your mother?"

The captive bounty hunter's face twists up like a juiced fruit. He bares his teeth in a feral display as he seethes: "How did you find her?"

"It was an ordeal," Norra interjects. "But less than

you'd think. You're arrogant and people don't like you. All it took was one bouncer in one seedy club to tell us that *he* heard sometimes you send an infusion of credits to someone living in Coronet City. Cross-referenced with the ever-growing New Republic database, which ties in now with CCPS records. And so it revealed Tabba Teldar to us. Which was enough."

"You're New Republic," Swift says, suddenly smug. He winces as his arms strain above his head. "You wouldn't do anything to her. You've got a code. You have to follow the *law*."

Sinjir looks to Jas, then the two of them erupt into laughter. Norra doesn't, because she's not in the mood, not even for the pretense of this faux-amusement acted out. But they sell it, and Sinjir—when he's done laughing and wiping tears of hilarity from his eyes—says with sudden, dire seriousness: "This is all very off-the-books, Gebbo, my friend. The NR doesn't even know we're *out* here. We're like a proton torpedo without guidance—just launching through space, rogue as anything. Jas, as you know, is a bounty hunter. As for me—oh, my name is Sinjir, by the way, Sinjir Rath Velus—I was once an Imperial loyalty officer, which meant I secured and tested the loyalty of my fellow grayshirts in *whatever way* was most motivating for them and me."

"We follow no law but our own," Jas says.

Mercurial visibly swallows. "Don't hurt her."

"We won't," Norra interjects, "as long as you tell us what we need."

The dam of his resolve cracks, shudders, then breaks, and the words come gushing out of him fast and desperate—gone is the pretense of ego and arrogance, gone is his preening self-confidence. "I haven't spoken to Sloane in months. Last time was just a transmission. She was looking for a ship on Quantxi. The *Im-*

perialis. Coordinates on that ship were tied to a, uh, an Imperial officer, a high-ranking admiral named Rax. Gallius Rax. She wanted to know the coordinates—where he was from, what system, what world."

Sinjir grabs his jaw and squeezes. "Tell us, what world?"

"Jakku."

The three of them all share looks. In their eyes: confusion. Norra's never heard of it. Not that she's some kind of galactic cartographer—out there in the black are thousands of systems and millions of worlds. Swift fills in more information: "It's in the Western Reaches. I don't know any more than that because I never had reason to care."

"Did she go there?" Norra asks.

"I . . . I think so. I don't know."

"There's more," Sinjir hisses. "I can see it on your face. Something else you're not telling us, Gebby. Don't make me call our droid."

"Sloane wasn't alone," Swift says.

"Do tell."

"She was . . . injured, and in a ship, I think some kind of stolen Chandrilan cargo cruiser. There was a man with her. I didn't get his name. I could barely see him."

"Imperial?" Sinjir asks.

"I swear, I don't know."

Norra to Sinjir: "Do you believe him?"

"I do."

"Then we're done here. I'll call in Temmin." The younger Wexley, her son, is in orbit above Taris, piloting the *Moth* with his battle droid B1 bodyguard, Bones.

"We could haul Swift back to Chandrila," Jas offers. "He's worked for the Empire. Maybe he knows more than we know to ask."

"No. No time for that," Norra says.

"No time? We'll be headed that way anyway—"

"We will not. We're headed to Jakku straightaway."

Jas scowls. "We're not ready for whatever's there. We don't even know where it *is*. Norra, we need to take the time, plan this out—"

"No!" she barks. "No more planning. No more *time*. We've wasted enough already on this one—" She jabs a thumb against Swift's breastbone for emphasis. "And I will waste no more. We don't even know that Sloane is still on Jakku—so we need to pick up whatever trail is there before it goes so cold we can't find it."

"Fine," Jas says, her voice stiff. A voice inside Norra's head presents a warning: *Ease off, Norra. Jas might be right, and even if she's not, you don't need to bark orders at her. This isn't who you are.* But every part of her feels like a sparking wire. Like she can't control it or contain it. Jas asks: "What do we do about Swift, then? I could . . . dispatch him."

"Emari," Swift pleads, "there's no bounty, there's no value in killing me, it's just not worth it—"

Norra sees her opportunity. She yanks one of Swift's batons from Jas's grip and spins it around. With a quick slide of her thumb she brings the electro-stun end to life: The tip of it crackles like static, and a blue elemental spark dances between two prongs.

She sticks it in Swift's side.

He makes a stuttering sound as the electricity ravages him. Then his head falls, chin dipping to his chest. A low, sleepy moan gurgles from the back of his throat. "There," Norra says. "Let's go."

Morning comes to Taris, and with it, Mercurial comes to life just as much of the planet—its scavengers and scutjumpers and its clouds of sedge-flies—goes back to hiding from the encroaching light of day.

The bounty hunter takes some time, then eventually flips his body up so that his legs wrap around the pipe married to his cuffed hands. He hangs there, then jostles his body, slamming it down again and again until the plastocrete at the far end cracks and breaks free, the pipe crashing down—and him crashing down with it.

His muscles aching, Mercurial scoots free of the pipe. He calls upon his body's memory of a different life as a young dancer in a Corellian troupe and leaps backward over the loop of his cuffed wrists.

He tries to find his batons—one of the concussive ends will make short work of these magnacuffs—but Emari must've taken them.

Fine. He'll head back to his ship and use the cutters there. But before that happens—he extends his thumb, opening up a comm channel to make a call to Under-boss Rynscar of the Black Sun. The face that appears is her true face, the one Rynscar keeps behind that rusted demon's mask. Her true face is pale, with dark eyes. Her lips are painted the color of dirty emeralds.

She sneers. "What is it, Swift?"

"Jas Emari."

"You say that name like it is a key unlocking a door. What of her?"

"Is it true? There's a bounty on her head?"

Rynscar lifts her brow. "It is true."

"What'd she do?"

"She did nothing. Which is quite the problem. She has debts. More now than when she started, given Nar Shaddaa."

"Gyuti wants her head?" Mercurial asks.

"He does."

"And he'll pay handsomely for it?"

"He will. Fifty thousand credits."

"I don't want credits."

She hesitates. "Are you saying you have Emari?"

Not yet. "I will."

"Let's say you do. What do you want in return?"

He grins. A cocky, lopsided smirk. "A case of nova crystals."

"A dozen," she counters.

"Twice that." When she doesn't answer, he says: "I know Gyuti, and I know for him this is personal. It burns him that she keeps slipping the leash. Makes him look bad in front of the Hutts and everyone. I know where she's going, so I'll get her, but I need real currency."

"Why that much?"

Again Dengar's words echo: *We gotta band together. Form a proper union.* "I need a crew to get this done."

Finally she says: "Then get it done."

"I'll get my crystals?"

"You'll get your crystals."

Mercurial ends the call and cackles. Time to get paid, because he knows where Jas Emari is going:

The nowhere sandswept deadlands of Jakku.

CHAPTER TWO

LEIA STARTLES AT the sound of a furious pounding on the door, her knee banging into the table above which a glittering star map is projected. The map flickers, and when the voice comes through the door—"Leia! *Leia!*"—she struggles to stand swiftly, almost forgetting the tremendous living weight around her midsection. The child inside her kicks and tumbles as she endeavors to get upright. *Calm down, little angel. You'll be free soon enough.*

"Mum," says her protocol droid, T-2LC. "It appears as if someone is at the door."

"Yes, I hear that, Elsie." She winces as she moves out from around the couch. That couch was supposed to be comfortable—but all it does is swallow her up like a devouring sarlacc. "It's just Han."

"Is he in danger, mum? He sounds like he's in danger. Should I open the door? I don't want to let the danger in, *but*—"

"Leia, damnit, the door," Han says from the other side. His voice is followed swiftly by more thumps and thuds. *He's kicking the door,* she realizes.

"I'm coming!" she yells back. To the droid she says: "I'll get it."

"But your condition, mum—"

"I'm not dying, I'm pregnant," she snaps back, then

opens the door. Han wastes no time in almost falling through it, his arm cradling a lumpy, uneven bag of *something*.

"Took you long enough," he says, smirking as he juggles his footing and skirts past her, giving her a quick kiss on the cheek as he does.

"Don't you know," she says, shooting T-2LC a dubious look, "I have a *condition*."

"Elsie, I told you, Leia doesn't have a damn condition." But then, more seriously and in a lower register, he says to her: "You do need to slow it down a little bit." He gestures toward the star map. "For instance."

"I am in command of my own body, thank you very much."

"Tell that to the little bandit," he says, dropping the sack of whatever down on the counter in the kitchen. *The little bandit* is what he's taken to calling the child currently wrestling inside her belly.

"You mean the little *angel*." She follows him into the kitchen, and T-2LC's whining servomotors behind her indicate he's following closely behind because *someone* (Han) told the droid to keep close to her in case she falls. Never mind the fact the droid stays *so* close to her, she's nearly tripped on his metal feet half a dozen times already. "What did you bring?"

Han winks, thrusts his hand down into the bag, and pulls it out gripping a jogan fruit. "Look." He gives it a lascivious squeeze.

She sighs, crestfallen. "Is that . . . whole bag full of jogan fruit?"

"Yeah. Why?"

"I cannot possibly eat that much jogan fruit."

"Sure you can."

"Let me rephrase: I don't *want* to eat that much jogan fruit."

"It's good for you."

"Not *that* good."

"The doctors—"

"Dr. Kalonia said to incorporate jogan into my diet, not to replace everything with jogan fruit."

He sweeps up on her, cradling her face with his rough hand. He strokes her cheek gently. "All right, all right. I'm just trying to do right by you two."

"I know, Han."

"If I think I can help, I'll always help. With whatever you or our son needs. You know that, right?"

She laughs. "I know."

It's been hard for Han. He won't say it out loud, but she can see it on his face. Her husband needs something to do. He's *bored*. Chewbacca's back home, looking for his family. Luke's searching the galaxy for old Jedi teachings. Han Solo's got nothing to smuggle, nowhere to gamble, no foolish Rebellion to fight for.

He's like the *Falcon*: retired to a hangar somewhere, waiting for something, *anything*, to happen.

So he buys fruit.

Lots and lots of fruit.

And, of course, he worries about her. He turns her toward the table and the star map. "You're not still on this, are you?"

"What?"

"Leia, Kashyyyk was a fluke. We got lucky."

"I'm always lucky with you by my side, scoundrel."

He shakes his head. "You joke, but this is nuts."

"It's *not* nuts," she says, suddenly irritated. "What we did on Kashyyyk was the right thing to do, and you know it. If we could formalize that process, if we could target other worlds that the Senate is too cowardly to liberate, then maybe we could—with the unofficial sanction of our friendly chancellor—find a way to do right by those worlds. Which means not only do we save whole systems, but those systems might swing our way and join the chorus of voices here in the New Republic."

He sighs. "I dunno. Can't somebody else handle this? Just for now . . ."

"Look," she says, heading over to the star map. "Tatooine. Kerev Doi. Demesel. Horuz. All worlds still in thrall either to some Imperial remnant or to criminal syndicates or gangs. Rebellions work. We've seen it. We've helped make it happen."

"You know Mon's not going to go for that."

"She already has. In a way."

In the aftermath of the attack on Chandrila, the New Republic was left reeling. Already the whispers arose: *The New Republic cannot protect itself, how can it protect us?* Already the accusations have been aimed at Mon Mothma's head like turning rifles: *She is weak on military presence and now she's injured, how can she truly lead us?* Leia and Han came back bringing a much-needed—if illegal and unexpected—victory for the New Republic at a time when it badly needed it. Yes, Chandrila was attacked. But they saved Kashyyyk. They ran off the Empire and liberated the Wookiees. It was a win. And it stopped the Senate from hemorrhaging loyal senators.

She starts to say, "If we could aid rebels on each of these worlds—"

"Mum," T-2LC chimes in, literally thrusting his copper-shine protocol droid head in front of her. "You have a call."

"I'll take it here." She settles back down into the couch, then swipes the star map off the projector. A new image replaces it: the face of Norra Wexley. Once a pilot for the Rebellion, and recently the leader of a team of "Imperial hunters," tracking down the Empire's many war criminals when they fled to various corners of the galaxy to hide. She had helped Leia in a different capacity, finding her missing husband and helping Han free Chewbacca and his planet from the Empire. Now, though? Norra is out there looking for prey most elusive: Grand Admiral Rae Sloane.

Sloane is a mystery—like a seed between the teeth that Leia cannot work free. First, the self-proclaimed grand admiral went and admitted that she was in fact "the Operator," a high-level, confidential informant who had helped the New Republic win vital battles against the crumbling Empire. Then Sloane offered to talk peace, and so she asked to come to Chandrila for that very purpose. And while she was present, those captives freed from the prison ship that had held Chewbacca turned on the New Republic, assassinating various high-level figures and injuring many others. The tally of the dead is too long. Senators, diplomats, advisers, generals, admirals.

Was I on the list of targets? Leia wonders that even still. If a twist in fate—Han going off half-cocked to save a whole planet all by his lonesome—hadn't set her on the path she took, would she have been standing there on the stage that Liberation Day?

No way to know. The list of targets remained embedded in minuscule control chips planted at the brain stem of each returning captive. Too easy to miss on a general scan, and too sinister to even consider real until it was far too late. By the time they discovered the chips—weeks after Liberation Day was already over and the blood had been scrubbed from the plaza stone—they had fritzed out, malfunctioned in some kind of planned degradation. Leia's own payroll slicer, Conder Kyl, wasn't able to find anything, either. If Conder can't find it, then there's nothing to find.

Point is, Sloane fled Chandrila. An act that coincided with the Empire going dark. Outside a few splinter remnants, the enemy has gone silent.

Which disturbs Leia considerably.

"Norra," Leia says. She owes this woman a debt. Norra's own husband was one of the assassins, and Leia tries to imagine what that must do to a person's own heart and mind. Even more, what that must do to a wife and mother's heart and mind. (Motherhood has been on Leia's mind a lot recently, unsurprisingly. What Norra has gone through for the Rebellion and for her family is both admirable and harrowing. Could Leia do the same? Could she walk that line? And then a troubling question she's almost afraid to answer: Where do her true allegiances lie? She has a family to raise, but a galaxy to help lead . . .) "Tell me some good news, please."

"We found Swift."

"The bounty hunter. Good. Did he give you anything?"

"He did. He said Sloane went to a planet in the Western Reaches called Jakku. Know anything about it?"

Leia does not. She gives a look to Han, who clears his throat and waves to the hologram. "Hey, Norra. Jakku, huh? I know it. Been there once, years ago. You know, the usual: bringing bad things to bad people. There's nothing there. Miners, scavengers, dirt merchants. They got some kinda hokey religion there in the south, and there's the Wheel Races in the north. Otherwise—c'mon, it's a wasteland. Makes Tatooine look lively."

"Why would Sloane go there?" Leia asks.

"Beats me," Han says. "Maybe she's looking to get away. Run and hide. Nobody would look for her on Jakku."

Norra says, "Swift thought it had something to do with another Imperial. Someone named Gallius Rax."

That name isn't familiar to Leia, and she says as much. Something about all this feels *wrong*. A feeling of worry has burrowed under her skin. "Norra, come home. Perhaps it's time we present this to the chancellor—"

"Respectfully," Norra says, "I'd like to scout the planet first. Time is slipping through our hands like so much rope, and I'd rather not lose any more of it. After what happened on Chandrila, we need to report more to the chancellor than just the word of some bounty hunter. At least let us take a pass, see if we can't uncover . . . something."

Leia gives Han a look. He twists his mouth into a lopsided grin. "Hey, don't look at me. You know what I'd do."

"Yes, you'd run off like a madman, right into danger."

He shrugs. "A smart bet."

All the more reason to warn Norra away from that course of action. Any plan whose best endorsement is a thumbs-up from Han Solo is trouble. Still, Norra isn't Han. She's smarter than that. Isn't she?

"Go," Leia says, finally. "See what you find out, and then we'll have something to bring to Mon."

"How is the chancellor? Her injuries?"

"They're healed, mostly." Though far deeper injuries remain: injuries to the woman's spirit and to her career. "She's fine, I'll tell her you were asking. And eventually, we can tell her what we've been up to."

"Thanks, Leia. I appreciate your help in all this."

"It's you who's helping me, Norra. You're helping me *and* the whole of the galaxy if you can find Sloane's scent out there. Just be careful. If you see the Empire, do not engage. Do you understand?"

"I hear you loud and clear," Norra says. "I'll see you soon."

And then she's gone.

CHAPTER THREE

THE *MOTH* FLOATS above Taris.

The long-legged Sinjir Rath Velus sits on the lower bed in the back bunk, the hilt of a vibroknife flipping between his fingers, over his knuckles, and from one hand to the other. Back and forth, the blade dances. Around him, the ship is alive with activity: Norra off talking to Leia, updating her on their progress ("We found Swift"); Jas shuttling from room to room, looking for her ammo belt ("I swear, if that droid misplaced it, I'm going to turn *him* into ammunition"); Temmin stalking the hallways, moaning again about how his mother keeps him in the ship and out of danger ("I'm an adult now, you know, *basically,* and I can handle myself"); Mister Bones humming along, tapping and whirling about, singing some song in Huttese:

LA YAMA BEESTOO, LA YAMA BEESTOO
CHEESKAR GOO, CHEESKAR GOO
WOMPITY DU WERMO, WOMPITY DU WERMO
MI KILLIE, MI KILLIE . . .

Sinjir remains sitting and silent. The knife hilt rolls and turns. Sometimes he looks down and sees blood on his hands. Real, fresh blood: the fingertips wet and greasy with it. He thinks: *I cut myself. The blade is out and I am injured.* But then the blood is gone again. An illusion. A dream. Real until it's not.

Eventually, Jas moves past the bunkroom, the ammo belt slung over her shoulder, and she reverses and storms up to Sinjir and says, "It was in the kitchen. Why was it in the kitchen?"

He has no answer, so he shrugs, the blade still dancing.

She narrows her eyes. "What's your problem?"

"I have no problem. I am a man unburdened by conflict."

"Sure, and I'm a baby Hutt-slug."

"You're slimy, but not *that* slimy."

She kicks him in the knee. Not hard.

"Ow."

"No, really, what's your malfunction?"

"For starters, I don't have anything to drink."

She sits down next to him. "Thought you quit drinking."

"Hardly. I quit drinking Kowakian rum, because even though it tastes like the sweet, syrupy glow of pure liquid stardust, it invokes the kind of hangover that makes you feel as if you've been romanced by an irascible rancor. It is the kind of hangover that makes you plead for death while hiding in the darkness under your bedcovers or even under the bed itself. No more Kowakian rum for me." He sniffs. "Everything else is fair game."

"You're doing that thing."

"What thing?"

"That thing where you use mockery, sarcasm, and derision to deflect a sincere question."

"Ah, *that* thing. It's a very good thing."

"I'm not going to pull teeth. If you don't want to tell me what's going on with you, I won't pry—"

"*Takask wallask ti dan,*" he says. "Do you remember telling me that phrase? On Kashyyyk after our work was done?"

"I didn't just tell it to you. I called you that. *A man without a star.*"

He finally stops moving the blade between his hands and stoops over, rubbing his eyes. "I feel like you were wrong."

"I'm not wrong often, so okay, lay it out for me."

He turns to her. "*This* is my star. Not this ship, but this life. A life where I threaten people and make them do things. I tell them I will break their hands, kill their mothers, ruin all that they hold dear. I know how to find weakness. I know how to exploit it. And . . ." His voice drifts and he almost fails to summon the next part. "I think I enjoy it."

"If you enjoyed it, you wouldn't be telling me this."

"Perhaps."

"Besides, you could've actually chosen to hurt Swift. I wouldn't have stood in your way. But you didn't. You did it with words, not violence."

"Words can be violence."

Jas shrugs. "Sinjir, you need to think less. That brain of yours is a whole lot of trouble."

"Now you know why I drink."

"You ready for what's on Jakku?" she asks, changing the subject. He knows the subject at hand bothers her. Jas cares little for self-reflection in herself or others. She is not only a woman *with* a star—he suspects she is the star itself. Implacable, serving itself, disinterested in debating right or wrong. She doesn't orbit you—*you* orbit *her.*

He plays along, letting the current of the conversational river take him where she wants it to go. "If I overheard the conversation right, it sounds like what's on Jakku isn't much at all."

"It's not Jakku. I'm worried about Norra."

"Norra will be fine."

"She's on edge."

"Who isn't?"

Jas drives the point home further: "She's becoming like me."

"Nobody could become like you, dear heart. Besides, I noticed *you* were the one advising caution down there."

"Someone has to be a voice of sanity, and I choose me. Norra's pushing herself hard. Not physically. Emotionally. Her husband is in the wind again, our quarry is a grand admiral she failed to dispatch above Akiva, her son is here and theoretically in danger . . . guilt and anger are driving her. She thinks this is all her fault." Jas gnaws at her lower lip, hard enough that Sinjir is surprised she hasn't drawn blood. "I just worry."

He shrugs and sighs. "See, you're a good person because you worry about others. And I'm a good person because I didn't actually hurt Geb Teldar. And Norra's a good mother and Temmin is a good son and Mister Bones is a very good murder-droid, and we're all *good* people doing a *good* thing and let's just shut up and get it done, hm?"

"You mean to be sarcastic, but really, that's damn sensible." She pats his knee. "You might be right about all that."

"Like you, it is rare that I am wrong, Jas Emari."

"Let's hope Jakku has no surprises for us," she says as she stands.

"Oh, I wouldn't count on that. The galaxy seems quite fond of surprising us, I'm afraid."

"I can handle myself," Temmin says to his mother. He waits till she's done talking to Leia, at least, before he begins his objection. But the moment she ends the call, he springs on her like a jaw trap. "You know I can."

Norra, seemingly startled by his presence, looks back. "What?"

"You *know* what." Temmin plunks down in the copilot's seat and straps in. "Yet again you went planet-side without me. Yet *again* you left me and Bones on the ship. It started on Kashyyyk, and it's only gotten worse: Ord Mantell, Corellia, Jindau Station—"

"Tem, we don't have time for this." Norra's fingers move across the controls as she enters coordinates for this planet in the Western Reaches: Jakku. Wherever that is. Some dirtball planet that he won't get to see because *yet again* she'll make him stay in the *Moth*. Ugh. "Someone needs to stay with the ship and make sure it's ready to fly."

"Bones can do that. Let me come with you. On Jakku."

"No."

"Mom—"

"I said *no*." She gives him a stern look. "Hyper-space cross-checks?"

He rolls his eyes and scans the data. "Everything looks good." He admits to himself that it's a pretty cursory glance: Navigation is totally boring. Piloting is where the fun is. The MK-4 freighter is leaner than most and has a ton of aftermarket mods that keep it nimble—but it's still nothing like flying Jas's gunship, the *Halo*. Or better yet: an X-wing. He *dreams* of flying those.

Norra engages the hyperspace drive. The stars stretch into lines and his stomach tightens as the ship lurches to lightspeed. They sit in silence for a while, watching the starlines pass. Eventually, Temmin looks over to his mother, scowling. "This is what you do, isn't it? This is just *you*."

"Going to hyperspace? What are you talking about?"

"You think you have to do it all by yourself. It's like when you joined the Rebellion. You left me behind to go off on some crusade to find Dad."

"We're not looking for your father." She speaks those words quietly, so quietly he almost doesn't hear them over the thrum of the ship. "This is about something else, Tem."

"I know, I know. We're looking for Sloane. But it's because of Dad, isn't it? What he did. What *she* did. And you think she can help you find him. Which is great! It's smart. But don't leave me out of it. I want in. I want to be with you on this. *I wanna help*."

"I AM VERY HELPFUL," Bones chimes in from behind them, whirling past with clanking, dancing feet.

"See? We can help."

He knows this is hard on her. He knows that she wakes up at night, crying out for him or his father—nightmares, he guesses, though she won't say. Because of that, she sometimes chooses not to sleep. It's like she's standing vigil over the console, like at some point Brentin Wexley will just appear over the comms, and tell them he's sorry, and that everything will be okay. It wasn't even Dad's fault. They said he had something in his head—a control bio-chip like the ones in the Wookiees on Kashyyyk, except more advanced. These chips didn't just prevent behavior: They programmed it.

They turned captives into killers. Good people, made bad.

"I was there, too," he says softly. "I saw what Dad did." He thinks, but doesn't say: *He tried to kill himself*. Only after trying to kill Temmin. In fact, if Temmin hadn't intervened, his father would've ended it right there. Was that part of the programming? Or was that Dad resisting it?

"I can't lose you, too," Norra says.

"You won't lose me. Okay? Let me be a part of this."

"I . . ." But her words die on her lips. Instead she straightens up and gives a small shake to her head. "This is it. Jakku. Coming up out of hyperspace. Ready?"

"Mom—"

"Not now, Tem. Later. Are we good?"

"Fine. Yes. Whatever. Out of hyperspace in mark—three."

"Two," she says.

"One."

They drop out of hyperspace.

And that's when everything goes wrong.

CHAPTER FOUR

As SOON AS the *Moth* drops out of lightspeed, system alarms start going off—the cockpit fills with pulsing red light, and as the klaxons shriek, the screens start lighting up. But Norra doesn't need the screens to see what's out there. No way to miss what they just fell into.

After Chandrila, the Empire fell off the map. It was like one day they existed, and the next they were gone.

But the Empire isn't gone at all.

The Empire came *here*.

No. What is this? It can't be . . .

Her gaze casts across the span of space above the rawbones planet of Jakku. Hanging there are a dozen star Destroyers, maybe more. And farther out, the massive spear-tip shape of an Executor-class dreadnought. New alarms warn that Imperial weapons systems are spinning up and targeting them. Worse, new ships ping the *Moth*'s sensors:

TIE fighters. There's a swarm of them, coming in fast.

Even as Temmin is yelling at her, even as she hears Sinjir calling forward to find out what's going on, Norra does not hesitate. She's dancing on a tripwire, and no part of her can trigger the trap of indecision.

No time for questions. No time for uncertainty.

Instantly she focuses on the cockpit console, locking in the coordinates that will take the *Moth* and its crew to Chandrila. As her fingers work as fast as they're able, she barks an order to her son: "Keep us afloat, point the ship clear. Hyperspace in two minutes."

Then she unstraps and gets out of her chair.

He calls after her: "Where are you going?"

But she has no time to explain.

And he wouldn't like the answer anyway.

The TIEs are fast. They rush forward in a nest formation, then break apart around the *Moth*—the freighter rocks with laser blasts peppering the front shields, and Temmin cries out and jams the flight stick down as far as it'll go. The ship plunges toward the planet as one word whirls through his head on a repeating loop: *Evade, evade, evade.*

Flashes of laser light punctuate the dark around the MK-4; the craft shakes like a kicked can as Temmin puts a corkscrew spin on it, pulling back out of the dive, pointing both away from the planet and away from the fleet.

The Imperial fleet is here.

The. Whole. Damn. Fleet.

He's not ready for this. Suddenly his desire to be in the middle of the action seems like a child's plea— begging to be in on the adventure and then discovering it's far scarier than he ever imagined. Temmin doesn't want to be an adult, he doesn't want to grow up, he damn sure doesn't want to be a single ship caught in the middle of *the entirety of the Imperial remnant.*

Someone slams into the back of his chair. Sinjir's cry of alarm reaches his ears: "What the bloody hell is this? Where are we? Where is Norra?"

"I don't know!" Temmin bites the inside of his cheek as he desperately tries to point the ship at open space—but Imperial ships are everywhere. *So many ships*. TIE fighters fill the void. Star Destroyers line the sky like the jagged fangs of a monster's closing maw. The sensors start blinking faster, and on the screen he sees worse news: The SSD out there just launched a trio of torpedoes. *I can't outfly torpedoes. I'm not that good. I'm not ready.* To Sinjir he screams: "I need a gunner! Sit down and start shooting!"

Sinjir drops into the pilot's seat like a clumsy pile of broken sticks. He stares at the controls as if he's looking at an instruction manual written in Wookiee claw marks. "I don't know how to do this!"

"Join the club!" Temmin screams for his mother: "Mom? *Mom!*" Where did she go? What is happening?

Above his head, a light blinks on. Yellow, then green.

It's a signal.

One of the escape pods just went active.

Oh, no.

She's doing it again.

There. The clack-and-clatter of someone grabbing a gun off one of the rack mounts along the hallway reaches Jas's ears—she turns toward the sound, sees Norra moving past. Blaster rifle in hand. Leather go-bag over her shoulder.

"What is going on?" Jas asks—just as the ship takes a hit and she staggers hard into the wall. Pain blooms in her shoulder, but she shakes it off and hurries after Norra.

"The Empire. They're here."

"Who? Sloane?"

"All of them."

Norra jabs her heel into a metal button—a door slides open with a plume of steam. It's one of the escape pods.

"What are you *doing*? We're not abandoning ship. Are we abandoning ship? Norra, hold on—"

Norra starts buckling herself into the escape pod. "Keep them safe. Temmin especially. That's on you."

Norra's leaving. Doesn't take a scientist to figure that out. The burden of it all has pressed Norra down so far it's broken her. Now she thinks to go at this all by herself: a rogue element. *Like you, Jas.*

Jas can handle that life. But the same life will get Norra killed.

As soon as the pod door starts to close, Jas jabs her hand against the button and it reopens. The ship takes another hard hit from laserfire, causing Jas to tumble into the pod itself, crashing bodily into Norra. A tangle of limbs. Scrabbling, struggling. Norra elbows her in the side. "Get out!" she seethes in Jas's ear. "Get back to the ship. That's an order."

"You're not my mother."

"I'm your commander! Or whatever!"

Jas's fingers fumble for Norra's straps and she furiously starts to undo them. The plan is to haul Norra out by whatever part the bounty hunter can grab: neck, ears, ankle, doesn't matter.

Problem, though: Norra's stronger than Jas realizes. She's lean and she's tough and she's not just some soft-around-the-middle pilot content to stay buckled into a flight chair. Norra's hard like a stone, and she roots herself to the pod, kneeing the other woman in the stomach.

Norra grits her teeth, and Jas sees a grim determination take hold in the woman's eyes. "I'm going down there. I'm going for Sloane. You can either get *out* of this pod or you can stay in and take the ride."

For Jas, the choice is no choice at all. No hesitation marks the moment. She reaches back and slaps the red button to the right of the door.

"I'm with you, Norra."

The lights dim. The door starts to close. The escape pod rocks free of the *Moth*, jettisoning itself into space, carrying the two of them through chaos toward the planet's surface.

She's leaving me behind again, she's going off by herself and this time she's going to get herself killed. Temmin frantically works to get himself up out of the chair—even as he sees the hyperspace computer furiously conjuring a navigational path one digit at a time, even as a trio of torpedoes zero in on their position.

The light above his head goes red.

The pod is gone.

It shows on his scopes—a faint blurry line. Just a blip in a screen full of red. He cries out, a wordless sound.

Sinjir growls at him: "Sit down! We're about to leap."

Furiously, Temmin reaches to the hyperspace navigation system, tries to turn it off—but it's locked. *Damnit, Mom.* She did that on purpose, and he doesn't know the passcode to get it to stop. Wait. A new idea hits him. *There's a second pod.* If he could make it fast enough, if he could run through the ship and launch . . .

But Sinjir can't fly this ship. Bones can't, either.

Every cell inside his body wants to abandon this ship and go after his mother. But his mind is clear and he knows the score: Someone has to get back to Chandrila. Someone has to *tell* Leia: The Empire is here.

Temmin punches the back of the seat and slides back into it. He grabs the flight stick with one hand

and brings his other to his mouth, yelling into his comlink: "Bones! Can you get to the second pod?"

The droid's distorted voice crackles over the link.

"ROGER-ROGER, MASTER TEMMIN."

"Go. *Now*. I'll buy us a minute," Temmin says. Sinjir gives him a look, but Temmin keeps talking to his droid over his wrist comm: "Launch and get to Jakku. Find Mom. *Protect Mom*. At any cost!"

"ROGER-ROGER. NONE SHALL HARM HER OR THEY WILL BE CONVERTED TO A PLEAS-ING BLOOD MIST."

"*Go!*"

Temmin grits his teeth so hard he's pretty sure they start to crack. He whips the freighter back and forth even as his bewildered ex-Imperial gunner fires fruit-lessly at the swooping TIEs. New alarms start kicking off, the sounds coming faster and faster, indicating that the torpedoes are closing in—sizzling blue arrows of vicious energy aiming to blow the *Moth* clean in half. *And they might if I can't manage some fancy fly-ing.*

He looks at the light above his head.

Still dark. Still dark . . .

One of the torpedoes is on them, roaring up from behind. Temmin yells, "Hold on!" and does a hard inverted roll, bringing the ship up and back in a gut-churning loop. The torpedo passes by, and scanners show it and one of the TIEs going dark. One torpedo down, but two more are coming in heavy, and he sees them screwing through space right toward the *Moth*.

Bright-blue lights perforating the dark. Like the eyes of a terrible, vengeful thing, hungry for death.

Above his head, the light goes yellow.

Then green. *Go, Bones, go* . . .

Sinjir fires the *Moth*'s cannons at the torpedoes—

missing with every shot. The ex-Imperial winces and screams in ear-shattering frustration.

The light goes red.

Pod free.

Temmin launches to hyperspace, just as the torpedoes thread the spot where the *Moth* was half a second before.

CHAPTER FIVE

A RINGING SOUND in the back of the skull. A faint *beep beep beep*. Flashes in the black, memories like light pulsing in a dark room: a heel against a button; a shake and a bang as the pod unmoors from its socket in the freighter's side; a feeling of weightlessness as the whole thing drifts . . .

Then, light. Atmosphere. *Heat.* The pod shakes like a toy in the hand of an angry child. Everything feels like it's coming apart. Darkness goes to blue. Night to day. The weightlessness dissipates, stolen away by the feeling of falling—plummeting down, down, down. Someone screams. An elbow in a throat. A knee in an armpit.

A sudden lift from the repulsor-jets—a hard jarring motion.

The *whumpf* from a pair of parachutes.

Too late. Too fast.

Wham.

Darkness. Silence. The memory of it all threatens to crush her.

Norra gasps, fumbles for the door latch—she draws the lever down, a hard ratcheting mechanism. The door springs free and lands in sand: *thump.*

The light reflecting off the surface of Jakku blinds her. Everything is seared away in a burning wave of brightness. Her hands find hard rock and slippery sand.

Her guts are suddenly *weapons-free* and next thing she knows, she's puking up what little she had to eat today.

Behind her closed eyes, new memories flit past: the tangled pipes inside the resurrected Death Star, the battle above Akiva as she chases Sloane in a stolen TIE fighter, the shock as her husband lifts a blaster in the direction of Chancellor Mon Mothma . . .

Her eyes open again. Staring into her own ejecta.

This world before her is Akiva's opposite: dead and dry instead of damp and teeming with life. The only comparison is the heat, but here the heat is like the inside of a clay oven. It's drying her out. Baking her to a crispy blister. She coughs. She cries out. She thinks: *I am alone.*

Wait. No.

Not alone.

Jas!

She rolls over onto her bottom and sees the pod sitting askew in the mounding sand. Its door is open and off its fixture, and standing there, braced in the doorway with splayed-out arms and legs, is Jas Emari. A trail of blood snakes its way between her head horns, her lip is split, and her sneering mouth shows teeth wet with smears of red.

Norra starts to say something—some stammered greeting, some breathless entreaty about how she's glad Jas is okay—but the bounty hunter has only one response, and that's to pick Norra up out of the sand and slam her hard against the pod. Hard enough that Norra sees stars. Hard enough that the pod rocks on its axis, sending up a cloud of dust and scree.

"*Why?*" Jas asks. Her voice is raw and rough like it was run over coarse stone.

"We were under attack—the Empire—I had no time."

"No time," Jas says, repeating those words. She says them again and again, each time the phrase dissolving further into a mad cackle. "No *time*. No time! You keep saying those *words,* Norra Wexley. Like a mimic-bird, *No time, no time, raaaaawk, no time.* I had no time, either. No time to get my slugthrower. Or quad-nocs. Or a damn procarb bar! No time but to fall into an *escape pod* with you and plunge to a planet—*this* planet! This dead place about which we know *absolutely nothing.*" Her fist rears back and she pounds the side of the pod; the metal gongs like a bell. Then she slumps forward, her head pressing against the pod, her chin on Norra's shoulder.

The fight has left her. Norra pushes her away.

"I'm not sorry," Norra says.

"Of course you're not."

"I'm sorry you got dragged into it."

Jas sighs. "Save your half-hearted sorry for when I'm dead in the hot sand."

Norra's voice breaks as she says: "Liberation Day. My husband. I fought Sloane and . . . I have to do this."

"Fine," Jas says. "So let's do this. Where do we start?"

"You're hurt." She reaches for her friend, and after a gentle touch her fingers come away with blood. "The fall—"

"I'm fine."

"The pod has a kit. A medkit. I can—"

Jas pulls away. She says more sternly, and in her voice is the admonishment of a child to a parent, the way Temmin would say it: "I'm *fine.*"

Norra's mind goes to Temmin. *I hope he made it out okay . . .* that thought chased by another: *I've gone and abandoned him again, haven't I?*

Norra cranes her head back. Up there, in the broad blue, she sees the faint shapes of the Star Destroyers hanging in orbit. Diaphanous, almost as if they're not really there. Hallucinations. Or a vengeful ghost fleet, come to wreak their revenge.

"Looks like we found the Empire," Jas says, licking blood from her lip and scowling at the taste.

"But why? Why here?"

"That, I don't know. Hiding, maybe. We're pretty far from anything anyone would consider civilization. Far from any trading routes. Far from the known worlds. Close to the edge of the Unknown Regions. Maybe they're here, licking their wounds, hoping the NR won't notice."

"They'll notice now." *If Temmin made it away, that is . . .*

"What's the plan, Commander?" Jas throws her hands up. "I ask again, where do we start?"

"What?"

"You came down intending to be all by your lonesome, but now you have me. You're in charge of this little expedition. Do you have a plan?"

Norra sighs. All the anger she felt, all the panic—the noise has dulled now to a dim susurrus, and mostly she just wants to crawl back inside the pod and go to sleep. For days. For weeks. For all of forever.

"I don't have a plan," she confesses.

"Let me guess: no time to make one up?"

Norra barks a grim laugh. "Yeah. Well. I reckon the Empire will be looking for us before too long. TIE patrols, probably." Norra rubs her eyes with the heels of her hands. "We collect our gear. Then we walk."

"Any particular direction?"

"Just spin around, point your finger, and away we go."

"You got it, boss."

INTERLUDE

KASHYYYK

HERE ON THE slopes of Mount Arayakyak, the Cultivating Talon, the jungles once served as a rain-forest orchard, providing the Wookiees with an array of fruits, the shi-shok being most prized because its utility was wide—the pulpy fruit was delicious and vital, the hull was hard enough to withstand nearly any impact, and the vines of the tree made for the strongest binding and climbing ropes known.

But the child that lopes through the jungle now does not know these things. He does not know the world's history, for he barely even knows his own. He does not know that this rain forest was once lush and once gave his people life. All he knows now is that it is a scarred, carved-up place. Many trees are broken and collapsed against one another like campfire kindling. Others are sickened from the roots up—a poisonous black mold has taken them, rotting them, turning their fruits into hard, shriveled pods.

Lumpawaroo knows very few things. He knows his name. He knows that his mother was taken from him. He knows that his father has long been gone. He knows that he has been a slave for the *rrraugrah*— the hairless Imperial intruders—most of his life. But he also knows that recently, something has changed.

The bad song has ended. Each of the Wookiees had

a song in their head, a song of fire and terror, a song like the sound of the thrumming wings from a swarm of drriw-tcha blood-worm flies. The song made them do things. The song screamed louder whenever they defied the milk-skins. At its loudest, the song could kill them—Waroo remembers when one of his slave-mates tried to scale the walls of the daubcrete bunker, and the song in her head caused her such misery that her neck craned back far enough to snap.

But now the song is gone.

The *rrraugrah* locked them away. They brought out the old chains and collars. They now force the Wookiees to work again with shock-lance and blaster, with screams of rage and baleful threat. Things have gotten worse since the song died. But in that, they have also gotten better.

Many of the intruders at this settlement have fled. Others have doubled down, gone mad, locked themselves away. Sometimes the milk-skins are there behind their doors, yelling, smashing things, weeping. They've ceased cleaning themselves. They hide. They even attack one another, at times. All while claiming to wait for something, someone, anyone to come. They think they will be saved. That someone will come to bolster their forces, to bring them new food, to help return the song to the Wookiees' heads to control them once more.

Waroo feared that might be true, that someone might come, that the song might again be sung. So Waroo watched. And waited.

And soon the opportunity came.

One of the *rrraugrah* in a filthy gray officer's uniform began closing the pylon-gate. This was Commandant Dessard, a vicious little man with a greasy peak of dark hair. Waroo waited until Dessard had almost closed the gate . . .

Then he leapt for the opening. Though Waroo was weak and starving, he summoned everything he could to make it through that gap.

And make it, he did. Once out, he kicked backward with both legs, knocking Dessard through the gap. Waroo shouldered the gate closed, then howled to the other young slaves—for this is a child camp, where the young Wookiees are prized for their small hands and their ability to climb oh so high—that he would come back to free them all.

Then Waroo fled into the jungle, down the slopes of Arayakyak, the Cultivating Talon, through the broken trees, up into their diseased boughs, across old rotten bridges, and through shattered homes hanging from cratered bark. For a time, he was alone. Now, though, that too has changed.

Waroo is being hunted.

The stink of Dessard is carried on the wind: sweat and waste and his own hatred. Waroo knows now why the man comes for him: The loss of one Wookiee is of no consequence *except* to the man's own ego. He is angry to have lost one, to have been tricked and injured. That anger is a foul odor all its own, and Waroo can smell it. Worse, Dessard is not alone.

But Waroo is Wookiee. He is smart even though he is weak. He knows they cannot come for him up high, so he finds one of the diseased shi-shok trees, and Waroo ascends. He clambers from branch to branch, up a blackened vine that twists in on itself, through the sickened pleach. But his hand falls on something— a bulging fungal sac, one of the spore-pods that have helped to sicken the rain forest here. It erupts. From it comes a cloud of black spore, and Waroo inadvertently takes a deep sniff of it—

Everything goes white. He coughs, whimpering and bleating. Dizziness assails him; it feels like he's spin-

ning around and around, and his hands go slack and
the world rushes up past him—

Waroo falls. He hits branches. Rot-curled leaves whip
past him in a whirlwind. He bounces off a bough, and
before he knows it—

Wham. The air escapes his chest in a cannon blast.
He curls onto his side and tries to cough more, but
Waroo cannot find the breath. He wheezes and whim-
pers. Just as his breath returns to him, so does the
smell.

The stink of Dessard covers him like a tide of mud.

Dessard stands there, leering. His mouth is a vicious
sneer. He has a blaster in his hand—a grungy, rust-
rimed pistol. "You," he hisses. "You thought you could
get away. No one gets away. No one escapes. Not you.
Not my own troops. Any who flee die. And they die
very badly."

Other Imperials encroach, forming a half circle behind the commandant. Waroo tries to get himself upright, but his strength is sapped. The spore, the fall,
the fact he's already starving and weak . . .

But one thing that remains strong is his senses.

Waroo smells Dessard, yes. He smells the man's
sweat. He smells the Imperial's willingness—no, his
eagerness—to kill.

Then another scent.

A Wookiee scent.

A scent oddly familiar, one that stirs within Waroo
a sudden lift of his blood and spirits—

Dessard makes a sound—*grrk!*—and is yanked backward through the scrub and brush. Branches crackle
as he's whipped away. Then the air goes bright with
blasterfire. The other milk-skins are too slow. They're
cut apart. One is knocked back through the air so
hard, his feet whip above his head before he's slammed
into the trunk of the shi-shok. Dessard comes back,

crawling on hands and knees toward Waroo, his face
a simpering mask.

A shadow descends upon him.

And with it, a scent that says, *Father.*

A tall, shaggy Wookiee with a bandolier steps over
the commandant and plants a tree-trunk leg down on
Dessard's back, mashing him against the ground and
into the mud. Others emerge from the brush: a gray
Wookiee with one arm, another with a visor over one
eye, and several milk-skins in raggedy forest-green
camo, a firebird sigil on their arms. These others secure Dessard's arms behind his back, wrenching them
into a pair of looped cuffs.

The bandolier Wookiee sees Waroo and cocks his
head. He utters a soft purr before the strength seems to
go out of his legs. Waroo knows him. This is his father.
This is Chewbacca. They crash together, arms around
each other, the child's head buried in the father's chest.

Chewbacca lifts his head to the sky and ululates a
good song, a true song, a song of family, of lost love
found once more.

CHAPTER SIX

WHILE SENATORS ARGUE in her office, Chancellor Mon Mothma tries very hard to make a fist with her left hand. The hand rests on her knee under her desk, and she focuses on the act of pulling her fingers into the center of her palm. She can't do it, not yet, not quite. The fist she makes is less a fist and more a soft claw. Simply closing that hand feels like she's trying to move mountains, requiring an epic effort that she dearly hopes is not being shown on her face.

"Are you listening?"

She doesn't even know who asked the question. *Oops*, she thinks.

Looking up, she sees it's Senator Ashmin Ek from the Anthan Spire. His lips are twisted up in a sour knot. His silver hair is in a sharp, ostentatious peak above his head. Ek does not like being ignored. He says as much: "Chancellor, I get the feeling you're not entirely *with* us here today. You may see yourself as special, but I have taken precious time out of my schedule and put many meetings on hold for this committee . . ."

Some of the other senators gathered nod along with him: Bushar, Lorrin, and Rethalow. Next to them stands Jebel of Uyter—Minister of Finance for the New Republic. He docs not nod, but he strokes his beard and *hmms* and *ahhs,* continuing to serve as the pinnacle of ineffective neutrality. (Nower Jebel is always at his most comfortable when he is firmly in the middle—never extending himself, not even by a toe or a finger, toward one side or the other.) Others look embarrassed by Ek's outburst: Senator Oko-Po and Councilor Sondiv Sella in particular look on with disbelief.

"I apologize," Mon says, humbly. "I am feeling a little distracted today." *And why ever would that be?* she asks herself. *Could it be because this is the last week that the Senate will meet on Chandrila? Perhaps because of the rise of the New Separatist Union, or the Confederacy of Corporate Systems, or the pirates and their so-called Sovereign Latitudes? Maybe that horrid Senator Wartol has gotten under my skin. Or maybe, just maybe, it's because my left arm and the hand at the end of it barely operate as they should, thanks to the Empire's attack on Liberation Day.* "I fear it is best to end this meeting early and push it on to next month, once the Senate and my office have been moved to Nakadia. Will that do?"

"It will *not,*" Ek seethes. "The Committee for Imperial Reallocation is vital for distributing the resources of the fallen Empire—"

"It hasn't fallen yet," objects the broad-shouldered Sondiv Sella. He puffs out his chest as he talks— indicating that he's harboring some anger. "We have to be careful not to think we've seen the last of the Galactic Empire. It has a long and deep shadow."

"They have been beaten." Ek sniffs haughtily as he says it.

"Coruscant is still occupied."

"Coruscant is irrelevant! The Empire there is a *shadow.* They've no fleet. They've no weapons manufacturers or starship builders. Their bank has been plundered and those credits are now New Republic credits, which means they are ours to allot. The Senate elected me as head of this committee, so it is *our* time to do *our* job and not be held at arm's length by a distracted chancellor. My home, the Spire, is in need of funds *direly*—"

It's the Ithorian senator's turn to scoff. Oko-Po turns her big bright eyes toward Ek and shakes her bent, stooped head. Through the translation device around her neck, she says: "The Spire is a wealth factory. You're rolling in credits, Ek."

"The *illusion* of wealth!" Ek says, erupting. "We are trying to *demonstrate* and *project* financial strength, but I assure you we are weakened by the disruption this war has wreaked on the galaxy. And I'll remind you that just as you are Senator Oko-Po, I am *Senator* Ek."

Nower Jebel holds up both of his hands in a placating gesture. "Please, please, we should all endeavor to keep civil—"

"Stop."

That word comes from the mouth of the chancellor's Togruta adviser, Auxi Kray Korbin.

Everyone does as she commands. Auxi stands and puffs out her chest, her chin lifting so she can—even at her diminutive height—seem to be looking down on them. The adviser says: "The chancellor has made herself clear. This meeting is over. We will see you all on Nakadia."

She waves her hand dismissively—the gesture one makes when sweeping dust off a forgotten shelf.

As Ek leaves, he speaks loudly to the Abednedo, Senator Bushar. His words are meant to be heard, and he even looks over his shoulder as he says them: "I wonder if Tolwar Wartol would be so rude . . ."

His words linger like a bad smell as they all filter out the door.

All except for one.

Sondiv Sella.

The councilman represents Hosnian Prime. They have a senator, Yuprin Arlo, but Sella serves to help wrangle the different committees and subcommittees. He is new, but his help has been profound. Currently, he stands there, a small, strange smile on his face.

Auxi bites the air when she says: "I said the meeting was over."

He offers a self-effacing chuckle. "Oh. I—I just wanted to ask the chancellor how she was doing. I know she was in the medcenter for an extended critical care period and I thought—"

"I'm fine," Mon says, summoning a smile. "My arm is not yet at one hundred percent, but with my therapy exercises, it improves a little every day. They offered me a mechanical limb—but I said I wanted to try to keep mine for a little while longer." She thinks but does not say that she fears what it means to have a prosthesis. Mon knows it is an unfair assessment, but something about having a metal arm would make her feel less than she is, now. Inhuman. Unliving. Her mind conjures the implacable mask of the Empire's cruelest enforcer, Darth Vader, and she shudders. "But I am well. I appreciate you asking. You might be the only one who has."

"I know it's hard out there right now," Sella says, a little hesitant, as if he's sure he might at any moment overstep his bounds. He continues: "I was a cargo pilot, you know. For the Rebellion. I looked up to you as a leader then, and I don't blame you for Liberation Day now."

"I wish others shared that sentiment."

"They do. And they will." He nods, stiffly. "I don't

have a vote to give you, but Arlo does, and I agree with him. I'd like to offer my help to you in whatever way I can. I'll try to usher the committees along to fruition and say a few good words on your behalf. For the election."

"Oh," she chirps sardonically. "Is there an election coming up?"

He laughs, though a bit nervously as if he's not sure if this is a joke or not. As if maybe the attack those months ago did not merely injure her arm and shoulder but perhaps *scrambled her poor brain,* as well. "I . . ."

"I was making a joke. Something I'm not very good at."

"Of course." He forces an awkward smile.

"Thank you, Councilman."

"Thank *you,* Chancellor."

And with that, he's gone.

Auxi lets out a frustrated breath and pours two mugs of Deychin tea. Floral steam rises. Mon lets it bathe her chin and cheeks and closes her eyes for a moment, relishing the momentary peace.

"I could put brandy in it," Auxi says.

"Tempting. Sorely tempting. But no," Mon says with a sigh. "Last thing I need is for Ek to storm back in here and smell *that* on my breath."

"He's a pompous bombast. History will make him marginal."

Mon sips the tea. "He's hard in the bag for Senator Wartol."

"Don't worry about Wartol. In a few months, he, too, will be marginal."

"Oh, I rather doubt that. How are his numbers?"

Auxi gives her a look. No, not *a* look, but rather *the* look: a look dripping with such incredulity, it could fill a cup to overflowing. "You don't really want to play that game right now, do you?"

"I do."

"As your adviser, I strongly advise you to sit and drink your tea. And I also advise you to find a second adviser. Hostis . . ." Her words trail off, broken by a fracture of grief. The chancellor knows that her two advisers did not get along very well professionally, often fighting fiercely from two diametrically opposed points of view. But at the end of the day, they were friends. They drank together. They ate together. Their families did the same. Then his life was cut short by an assassin's blaster on that fate-dark day. "Hostis is gone, and we need someone like him. We need his voice."

"Yes." A pause. "That will come. For now: numbers."

"The numbers are sixty-one, thirty-nine."

"I assume I'm the *lower* number. Unless some grand inversion has happened and no one told me."

"Correct. You're at thirty-nine percent Senate approval at present polling. But polling is notoriously unreliable—"

"Senators are notoriously unreliable, too, and yet they form the bedrock of our democratic system. I will do better."

And yet how can she? She's losing. Day by day, her numbers wane, perhaps understandably. Liberation Day came and, with it, the attack on Chandrila. When the dust settled and the corpses were counted, she came out of surgery to find many friends and colleagues dead. And soon after began the accusations: She was too soft, militarily, and couldn't protect Chandrila when it needed to be defended. (Never mind the fact that the type of attack orchestrated against them was so far beyond comprehension and so subversive that *ten* navies couldn't have stopped it.) All that was made worse by the fact that *she* invited Grand Admiral Sloane planetside for the day's events. Which to many meant she was culpable in what happened.

Even still, the true shape of that plot against them is hard to see in full. Was Sloane a part of it, or just a pawn? Was Sloane really once the Operator? Did she betray them, or was she herself betrayed? Where did Tashu go? Where did *Sloane* go? Endless questions. Few answers.

It hardly matters, now.

The Empire has fled to some corner of the galaxy, and even with all her resources Mon hasn't been able to figure out where. And that makes her look weak. Her failures are a fattening meal for a hawk like her opponent in the coming election.

Tolwar Wartol: her opponent, and an Orishen. A tough, strange species, the Orishen. Two parents yield two children—one apiece—and upon giving birth, those parents die to give their progeny life, thus ensuring that the number of Orishen that exist now is a number that does not grow. (How they ever came to any number at all remains a mystery, one that none of the Orishen seem ready or able to answer.) They were a pacifistic species, once. Agricultural, mostly. Their world, Orish, was lush; though Mon has never been there, she's walked through virtual holoscapes serving as an archival memory of that world and found their planet to be a pastoral haven. At least, until the Empire came. The Empire enslaved the Orishen. They worked the inhabitants hard for food. Strip-mined the surface. Drained the soil of nutrients.

Then one day, the Orishen fought back. Over years they'd hoarded bits of pesticide and fertilizer.

They made a bomb. And they used it.

That bomb destroyed those Imperials on Orish. It

also poisoned the world: the ground, the water, even the atmosphere.

Now few Orishen are left. Thousands at best, no longer living on their world but above it, in a skeletal framework of tubes and stations.

Tolwar Wartol is one of those survivors. She's read his memoir. He was a chemist, once, and helped to make the chemical weapon that would destroy their world. In the book he tells stories of the beauty of his world, ruined. How the bodies clogged the streams. How they had to build massive tombs for those of their own they lost. And he also tells the story about the day that the Empire fled—they abandoned Orish and its people, because what was once of value to them had been ruined. Wartol described that day as a "triumph." And proof of what must be done to combat the Empire.

Wartol brings that survivor spirit to his politics: He offers the galaxy a well-earned assurance that *he* above others knows what sacrifice is and what must be done to preserve life and freedom.

He is charismatic. He is full of anger. His anger is righteous—

But is it *right*?

Either way, he commands every HoloNet news cycle. Attacking Mon at each turn. As he should, she supposes, if he really wants to win.

But she wants to win, too.

"I intend to continue on as chancellor," Mon says. "But I'm not yet sure how we win. So, adviser—advise me. Let's hear it. How do we win the election? How do I convince the Senate to vote for me over him?"

Auxi takes a seat on the other side of the desk. She purses her lips, *hmm*ing as she thinks out loud. "You're ostensibly doing the right things already. You're apportioning resources and infrastructure for worlds *af-*

flicted by the Empire—and afflicted by the vacuum of leadership now that the Empire has been pushed back. You've kept the military strong despite the loss of Imperial threat, but you've also made sure that the New Republic military isn't *too* strong, so it doesn't look like you're trying to enforce your will on a weakened galaxy. Kashyyyk—"

"Kashyyyk." Mon says that word with the weight of a heavy stone dropped into clear, still waters. "Kashyyyk is . . . complicated. The Senate resisted us getting involved there, and then Leia went and got us involved anyway. Given our friendship—"

"It looks like you approved the clandestine action."

"And because Leia's efforts there were a success, I cannot disavow."

Auxi thrusts up a finger as if testing the wind for its direction. "Do not be so quick to disavow. Yes, some within the Senate have naught good to say about that, but it *did* bump your approval rating—no small thing after Liberation Day. Kashyyyk was a win for us."

"A win earned by defying the will of the Senate."

"Leadership can mean defiance."

"Palpatine was defiant."

"So was Leia. And *you're not Palpatine.*"

Leia. Another complication. It's political, yes—her friend went against her explicitly, but of course that is a blade that cuts both ways, isn't it? Mon defied her, too. She couldn't get it done with Kashyyyk. Couldn't convince the Senate. Then again: Did she really try? She was hoping to handle the newly reformed Senate gently, *gingerly,* so as not to feel like she was pushing or pulling them. But perhaps leadership required a bit more of Leia's brand of defiance.

Leia. A political complication, but also an emotional one. They betrayed each other, a little at least. It hurts Mon's heart.

Auxi says, "We need to find an angle for you. Crime is an angle. The Empire goes away, and crime is up in its wake. The syndicates are struggling for dominance. We could go heavy on crime. Become the 'law-and-order' candidate without leaning too autocratic. Or if we played up the Kashyyyk angle with Leia by your side again . . ."

And then, as if on cue—

One of the chancellor's protocol droids pops its head in through the door. Metal face coated in white matte enamel. The droid, R-K77, chimes in a crisp Chandrilan accent:

"Chancellor, you have an urgent meeting request."

Of course. Everyone's desires are always urgent, aren't they?

"From whom?"

"Princess Leia Organa of the Alderaan sector."

Her ears must be burning.

Mon asks, "Did she say what it was regarding?"

"No, Chancellor," the droid says. "Only that it was of the utmost importance. She said to tell you it was a *Code K-One-Zero.*"

That was a Rebel Alliance code: Disengage and regroup. Last time they used that code, it was the signal that came out of Hoth when the Empire attacked their base.

"Send a reply. Tell her I'm on my way."

CHAPTER SEVEN

TEMMIN SITS ON a cushioned bench. Sinjir paces in front of him.

"She'll be fine," Sinjir is saying to Temmin. "Your mother has Jas with her. They're both tough. Tougher than you and me put together, boy. You needn't worry about her. They'll be *better* than fine. You watch—the two of them will tear the Empire out of the sky with their bare hands. I'm not worried and *you* should not be worried, either."

Sinjir is lying. The boy can tell that much. Usually, the ex-Imperial keeps all his emotions neatly vacu-sealed behind a cool, disdainful veneer. But that veneer is cracked. Worry bleeds out. A tremor of fear hums in his every word—each syllable like a nerve freshly plucked.

The two of them sit in a room. Only now does Temmin even realize what this room *is:* It's a nursery. Or the start of one. He's been staring at a round, white egglike orb against the far wall now for the better part of ten minutes, not even seeing it. More like seeing through it. But then it clicks that he's looking at an infancy cradle. That cradle will serve as a bubble of safety for the coming child. Above it is a holoport, ready to project—well, he guesses a mobile or other soothing images and sounds. An ocean lapping at the shore, or rain on a jungle canopy.

Princess Leia's baby, he knows, will have a good life. The *best* life. A family kept together, a father and mother who love him . . .

Temmin doesn't remember being a baby, but he remembers seeing his old crib in storage after Dad was captured and Mom left for the Rebellion. His cradle was in the old *unfancy* Akivan style: mesh sides, dark wood, curved slats at the bottom so it could rock back and forth. Netting over the top, too, to keep out the waves of ya-ya flies that came after every storm.

No ya-ya flies here. No old, creaky crib.

And no mother, either. No Norra.

"We have to go back for her," he says through gritted teeth. It's already been *eight hours*. *Eight hours* since Mom, Jas, and Bones jettisoned themselves toward Jakku. *Eight hours* since the *Moth* jumped into hyperspace, narrowly avoiding *death by torpedo*. Anything could happen in *eight hours*. The Empire may have shot them down. Or found and captured them. Or maybe they died on impact. Temmin bites his lip. He tastes blood.

"We will," Sinjir says. "We'll find a way."

But just as Temmin hears worry in his friend's voice—he also hears doubt. He's about to call that out when the door opens. A familiar face shows itself: Han Solo. Leia's husband. Captain of the infamous *Millennium Falcon*. Not long ago, Leia hired the crew to find Solo. They found him, all right, and ended up helping him get back his copilot, Chewbacca, on Kashyyyk.

Solo has a couple of fruits, one in each hand. He offers one to Sinjir, then tosses the other to Temmin. The boy catches it, just barely.

"Jogan fruit," Han says, looking uncomfortable. "I,

ahh, bought a bunch so it's fine. Eat 'em. I don't think Leia wants them." Moments like this, moments of real emotion, seem to bother the smuggler. He's like Sinjir that way. Most of him seems to be hidden away behind a wall of blustery ego and cocky pride. "Two of you don't look so good. If you need something, I can get the droid to—"

"What I need is my mother back," Temmin says, leaping to his feet. He gets in Solo's face. "I need you to take us back to Jakku. C'mon. Let's go. We get the *Falcon* and we charge in there, cannons blazing—"

"Whoa, kid, *whoa*. Cool your heels. I'm lucky, but I'm not that lucky. We go barreling in there, we're dead, all of us. Won't be any good to your mom if the *Falcon* is our casket."

"And what good is it if that planet becomes her tomb?"

Han's mouth works like he's going to say something but his brain can't figure out what. "I got a family coming. And there's a procedure here—"

"Procedure?" Temmin laughs, but it isn't a happy sound. "Where was your love of procedure when you went off trying to save Kashyyyk? When you got Chewbacca captured? And last I checked, my mom and the rest of us were more than happy to spit in the eye of the New Republic when it came to doing what you wanted to do."

Solo screws his face up. Like he's about to be angry. Then he says, suddenly:

"You want to do this, fine. Han Solo pays his debts."

"Helping *you* cost us a lot and I don't think you apprecia—wait, uh, what?" Temmin blinks. "What did you just say?"

Lowering his voice, Han answers, "I *said*, you're not wrong. I owe you. And . . . Leia's gonna kill me, but the *Falcon*'s the fastest ship I know, and maybe, just *maybe* if we hit that planet blockade hard, they won't even see us coming. I might be able to get us down to Jakku—we'll lose a couple tail feathers along the way, but nothing a bundle of bonding tape won't fix. The *Falcon*'s seen worse. If I could just get Chewie . . ."

"You're serious."

"Kid, I don't joke around about this kind of stuff."

Temmin's heart rises—then sinks just as fast. "You can't."

"Nobody tells Han Solo what he can't do."

"You're going to be a father. I can't . . . you can't." *A child needs his father, doesn't he?*

A battle unfolds on Solo's face. A whole *war*. Like he knows what Temmin's saying is true, but also like Solo knows who he is and what he does and for better or for worse, this is what he wants to do. "Leia will understand, she's like me, she does what—"

But whatever promise or plan Solo is poised to make, he loses the chance to say it when the door opens and Princess Leia comes into the room, flanked by the chancellor. They enter in a way that both fills the space with their presence and steals the oxygen at the same time. Even a cocky smuggler like Solo seems smaller, humbled in their shadow.

Senate Guards threaten to come in, as well, but the chancellor stops them short with a stiff shake of her head. "No. We will be alone."

Han takes the initiative and steps out of the room, pushing the guards back. His hand touches Leia's as he leaves—a sweet, lingering grip. Temmin remembers when his parents were like that. So long ago, now.

Mon Mothma closes the door as Han and the guards exit.

The chancellor's face is a strange thing. Temmin can't decipher what's going on there. Is that fear in her eyes? But a tug of a smile?

"Hello, Temmin Wexley," she says. "You will forgive me if I cut right to the chase, but time is precious. I want to know what you saw above Jakku. Tell me what you told Leia." Soon as they came off the *Moth* after landing on Chandrila, Leia was the first person they saw. And the only person, too—they went straight to her because who else would they tell? The princess has been their patron through all of this: Their hunt for Sloane was off the books, just like their hunt for Solo, just like freeing Kashyyyk. He's not sure he's really supposed to be talking to the chancellor about this stuff.

Mon Mothma is important. Her being here makes him feel very small. Temmin flashes a panicked glance to Sinjir, then to Leia. The ex-Imperial shrugs, and the princess gives a subtle nod indicating tacit approval.

"The Empire is on Jakku," he says, plain as he can make it.

"What does that mean?"

"I mean . . . there's a whole lot of ships there in orbit."

"How many and what kind?"

"At least one Super Star Destroyer. A couple dozen Star Destroyers, too, and that's just what we could see—the far side of the planet may have had more. TIE fighters were everywhere and . . ." A knot forms in his throat. He swallows it. "We got out but my mother is still there. And my droid!"

"Along with one of our crew," Sinjir interjects. "Jas Emari. A bounty hunter. I like very few people, but I quite like her and Norra, so we want to go and get them back, if you please." Under his breath, he says: "Though we don't have to bring the droid back, necessarily."

Shut up, Sinjir.

"This situation is . . . fraught," Mon Mothma says.

Sinjir scoffs. "Fraught? Yes, I bloody well imagine it *is* fraught. You've been looking for the Empire, haven't you? Well! Ta-da, we did it. We found them. And as a reward, I'd like you to send *all* your little ships and *all* your precious troops in to blow them into cinders and dust while me and the boy here rescue our crew. Correction: our *family*."

"Your presence there—your mission—was unauthorized."

Leia steps in, her chin up, her eyes flashing. "I already told you they were there on *my* authority."

"Your authority is not the Senate's authority," the chancellor retorts.

"Be glad it isn't, because presently the Senate is too timid to authorize a *handkerchief* for a noisy sneeze. Kashyyyk, I'll remind you, was a success, and we did it without your help."

"Hunting down Grand Admiral Sloane is the purview of the New Republic, not an Alderaanian princess and her friends—" The tension between the two of them is like a tightening cable. But suddenly the chancellor puts some slack in it. She lets out a deep breath when she says: "Leia. I'm sorry. You were right and you're *still* right. Freeing the Wookiees was the just thing to do. And if the Empire is really there on this planet . . ."

"This is what we've been waiting for," Leia asserts. Her tone, too, becomes more conciliatory, as if she's pleading with the chancellor. "This may be it. The end of the war. I know that you don't condone military action for the sake of it, but it was military action that destroyed *two* of their battle stations. It was our military that freed Akiva, and overtook Kuat. We have to take this seriously. If this is true, we have to attack."

"Wait," Temmin says. "Attack?" All of him tenses. Images from the space above Jakku flash inside his head once again: TIE fighters swarming everywhere, his innards gone cold, his blood gone hot, his mother rocketing away in an escape pod. If war comes to Jakku, she'll be even more vulnerable, even more in danger. War: That's what Sinjir meant—*Send all your little ships, all your precious troops*. Oh, no.

But no one answers his question. His fear lies unassuaged.

The chancellor nods to Leia. "Yes, but we have to do this right. We don't even know what *this* is yet. Why this planet? How much of a fight are we to expect? We want this to be the Empire's last stand. Not *ours*."

"Whatever we need to do, let us know," Leia says.

Sinjir adds: "Yes. We're ready."

The chancellor stiffens. Gone is the slack in her cable. Once more, the cold, undeterred mask settles over her face. "Good. Stay ready. This will need to pass muster with the Senate—I cannot authorize an action so consequential without their approval, but after Liberation Day I suspect they may be eager for a last taste of Imperial blood. Still—I must have data. I cannot take mere suspicions to them or they'll bury me. That is the primary mission: Get the facts. In the meantime: *Tell no one*. What we talked about here does not leave this room. Are we clear on that?"

Everyone nods except Temmin.

He stands there, shaking. His eyes wet. He wants to scream and yell and flail about. He wants to tell her, *My mother is there, and you don't need any more facts than that*. He wants to threaten her with: *If you don't go and save my mom right now, I'll go out there and tell everyone. I'll scream it so they can hear me as far as the Outer Rim*. But when the chancellor points her gaze at him, it's like being pinned by a set of cross-hairs.

Reluctantly, he nods.

Before exiting, Mon Mothma turns heel-to-toe with the precision of an old battle droid (*not* Bones, who would more likely do a plié and kick the door down). Leia says, "We will get Norra back, Temmin. I promise."

And then she's gone, too.

Once more, it's just Sinjir and Temmin.

"That's a promise she can't make," Temmin says, his voice quiet.

"True. Though I suspect she means it just the same."

"We can't count on her to get it done."

"Never count on a political machine to operate efficiently."

"So we do it ourselves?"

Sinjir claps a hand on the boy's shoulder. "We do it ourselves. And we call in our chip with Solo, too."

"Thanks, Sinjir."

"Don't thank me. I want them back as bad as you do. Now we just have to find a way to make it happen without, well, *dying* in the process."

CHAPTER EIGHT

NIGHT FALLS ON Jakku. With the darkness comes the cold. It leaches the heat out of the air, the sand, the stone.

In the distance, black shapes rise—shadows deeper than the dark of the sky. Plateaus and buttes like carbon anvils. It was Jas's idea to head in that direction. Not only would that get them out of the hellish heat of day, but she saw a flock of ax-beaked birds flying that way. "They're headed toward *something*," Jas said, then. "Don't know what. Food, hopefully. A settlement, maybe. Anywhere is better than nowhere."

And so, once they pilfered the pod of all its limited goods—medkit, blaster, a handful of rations—they started walking.

And walking. And walking some more. The sand is slippery beneath their feet. It's hard to find purchase, which works extra muscle groups—every time the sand shifts or she steps on a stone slippery with scree, Norra's muscles tighten further, and by now her legs feel as stretched out as the control belt on an old speeder.

Worse, Norra feels sick. The sun sucked everything out of her, siphoning her lifeforce away drop by bloody drop. Now, with night, the chill has crept under her skin and settled in those empty spaces like an infection.

But still, they trudge along.

To where, she doesn't know.

To what end, she cannot say.

This was a mistake.

Sloane is here. She knows that. She can *feel* that—not like she has the Force, but like it's something in the air, in the dust. Maybe she's just trying to convince herself that this is it, this is where it all ends. But even if Sloane *is* here, then what? Norra is on a dead-end, bone-dust world. The erstwhile grand admiral could be *anywhere,* in *any direction,* and Norra could spend the rest of her days wandering the burning dunes managing to find nothing or no one but her own foolhardy demise.

Perhaps the one advantage is that this *is* such a dead place. Someone like Sloane would stand out. Now if only they could find someone to whom that matters—someone with eyes to have seen Sloane in the first place.

She's about to say something to Jas—

But the bounty hunter now faces her with wide eyes. A hard finger mashes against Norra's lips. The Zabrak warns: "Shh."

Norra watches as the shape of Jas—her shadow, her silhouette—gestures toward her ear. A sign to listen, so Norra listens.

The few sounds of the planet crawl into her ear: the whisper of wind across the dunes, the distant ululation of some animal, the drum-pulsing of her own heartbeat behind it all. But then their ears pick up something else—a faint shudder and hiss. Like the sand moving. It's off to Norra's right. And then, again, to her left. The sounds come simultaneously.

And they're getting closer.

The noises stop as fast as they start. Once again

Norra and Jas are left with the wind, the faraway beasts, the pounding of blood in their own ears.

Norra thinks and is about to say: *We need to keep moving.*

She doesn't get that chance.

It happens quickly—from both sides, the sand erupts around them. The spray stings against Norra's cheek and she staggers back, her eyes burning. She swipes at her face, blinking back tears, and something crashes into her, roaring. Her shoulders hit the ground half a second before her tailbone. The wind is knocked out of her, leaving Norra gasping. Her attacker is on top of her, and as her vision clears she wishes it hadn't: The face leering down at her is far from human. Big black eyes, an insectile mandibular mouth, leathery flesh—

No. Not a face. A helmet. *A mask.*

"Sah-shee tah!" her foe barks at her, words gurgled around a hissing ventilator. A fist slams into her middle. Anger blooms in its wake.

Her adversary has his legs straddling her hips—but the ground beneath her shifts easily with the sand, and it takes little effort to wriggle free. She kicks out hard, pivoting her lower body as she does, and it gives her the opening she needs, crab-walking backward as her foe paws for something in the sand—a weapon. A *blade.*

Square at the top, bent in the middle. Like a machete. The metal is dark, maybe rusted, though it's hard to tell. He roars again and brings the blade down against her legs—but she scissors them apart, and the blade is buried in the sand with a coughing *cuff* sound.

Norra stabs out with her foot.

Her heel connects with his ventilator, and it starts squealing. Plumes of steam, white as a ghost, come free of his mask as he claws at his face.

Now, as he dances backward, Norra can see Jas—

Jas has her own enemy to deal with. The bounty hunter is still standing—and lashing out with a high kick. Her foe is bigger, heavier, with an upper torso like a handful of grain sacks strung together with heavy-gauge chain. She connects with the kick but it doesn't seem to faze him. The big monster bellows an incomprehensible cry, then catches Jas in a hard swing of his meaty fist. The bounty hunter topples, limp and lifeless.

No. Norra gets her legs under her and springs forward. She connects with his middle, tackling him, expecting her weight and momentum to knock him off balance. But the thug isn't going anywhere—he's like a pylon driven deep into the mantle. He doesn't budge.

Worse, he laughs.

A gross, mechanized chuckle erupts from his own ventilator, and both of his hands marry together into one hellacious mega-fist. He slams his hands down into the center of Norra's back. She hits ground once more. Air gone. Pain radiating. Blood in her mouth as her jaw snaps shut, teeth around the tip of her tongue. In the dark behind her eyes she sees streaks of white.

Someone grabs her ankle. Turns her over.

Her attacker is back. He adjusts something along the side of his head, and the jets of steam suddenly cease.

The thick sack-chested monster joins the other one. The two of them stand tall over her, talking, pointing.

"*Va-wey ko-yah,*" the littler one says.

"*Yash,*" the sack-chested monster says, agreeing, chuckling.

Then the little one shakes and shudders. His chin lifts and his head does this . . . *wobble* on his neck. Norra's face is suddenly wet, as if *misted.*

He hits the ground like a felled tree.

Sack-Chest grunts in confusion. Then his head tilts hard to his shoulder—this time, Norra sees a faint red flash along with it—and the monstrous thug pivots on one heel and lands hard atop the other.

We're saved, Norra thinks. Or, rather, Norra *hopes.* She stays still, though, just in case.

"Jas," she says in a loud whisper. Nearby, Jas groans.

Lights fill the air. Bright and bold. Not from one direction, either, but from three—all on at the same time, and Norra has to cover her eyes lest she go blind from it. Shadows emerge, light framing dark armor.

The crackle of static as a voice broadcasts:

"Don't move." As the shadows close in, Norra hears the faint jostling of jointed armor and blaster rifles in gloved hands. It's a familiar sound that means one thing: *stormtroopers.* The voice is quieter when it says: "We found them. We found the rebels."

From nearby, Jas curses under her breath.

Norra, though, smiles around her bloodied mouth. Because stormtroopers means Empire, and Empire means Sloane.

CHAPTER NINE

SLOANE KNEELS, BLIND and bound.

The ratty ribbon across her eyes is filthy and rough; it feels like it's abrading the skin off her face. This whole *planet* is like that, though: Everything is coarse-grained sandpaper wearing her down first to muscle, then to bone, then to the marrow beneath, and soon only to whatever passes for a soul or a spirit. A ghost left to wander these dust-choked deadlands.

Her wrists chafe, too: The rope binding them is raw and fibrous.

At least they haven't sealed her mouth or her ears.

What she hears: the *pad-pad-pad* of feet on stone. Not hers, but those who pull the cart in which she waits, drawing it deeper and deeper through the winding red cavern. The cart itself is old—stone-fiber boards lashed together with braids of tendon and not buoyed by hoverplanks or grav-plates but rather kept rolling by a pair of proper *wheels*. Wheels that clank and rattle as the cart is drawn over the hard rust-stone.

What she says: "We're almost there. The air is colder down here."

What he says: "I hope so. Everything of mine is . . . cramping up."

Those are the words of her traveling companion— a man named Brentin Wexley. She found him stowing away in her ship when she barely managed to escape Chandrila. Sloane was injured and drifting toward death, but he saved her life. Sometimes she's surprised he's still with her. But his purpose is her purpose, too: find Gallius Rax and end him.

Rax, who stole her Empire from her. Rax, who stuck a chip in this man's head and turned him into a killer. Vengeance drives the pair of them. It marries them, too, in a way. The oddest of couples, aren't they? She, the onetime grand admiral of the Empire (a title she cannot imagine matters anymore), and he, a former rebel spy turned programmed Imperial assassin. Neither of them wants to be here. But this is where they are.

And they've been here for months. Jakku is a decrepit wasteland, bleached to death by an unforgiving sun. And now, mysteriously, it hosts the largest remnant of the Empire—*her* remnant, as a matter of fact, a military faction she thought she controlled. But her control was an illusion. She was just another puppet dancing on the strings of Gallius Rax, a supposed war hero who came to serve the Empire at the urging of Palpatine himself.

None of it makes sense. Questions layer atop questions, and no answers are forthcoming. Why here? Why this place? It seems that Rax himself comes from this world, but why return? Jakku is no prize. It has few exports of note; kesium and bezorite have some value to the Empire, but only barely. Better resources exist, and they exist on worlds far livelier than this one. Why make an attack on Chandrila only to abandon the galaxy and come here? Why leave Sloane dangling on the hook? Why do any of it?

What is Rax's game? He has one—that much is clear.

He will tell her. One day soon, she will *make* him

tell her. At the end of a blaster, a blade, or her own choking hands.

But first, they must get to him.

Which is why they're here, right now, on this rolling cart. A cart pulled by men unclothed except for the skirts of threaded leather hanging from their waists— their chests, backs, arms, and shorn scalps are naked, painted with streaks of greasy red dust. Their mouths are closed with metal hooks—a hook in the top lip, a hook in the bottom, the two tugged together with a cinching knot. They can only murmur and mumble. They are servants and slaves—ardent operators and faithful lunatics giving their lives over to their mad desert mistress.

Next to her, Brentin grunts and growls as he shifts.

"I told you," she says to him. "Practice your breathing. Relax your limbs, a deep breath in, a deep breath out. Oxygenate your blood." Since leaving Ganthel, Sloane has lived her life on starships. In her earliest days, she flew patrols in TIE fighters and shuttles, and her very first job was as a signal hawk on an asteroid monitoring station in the Anoat sector. Those roles did not allow her the luxury of getting up and moving around easily, and so she learned ways to remain comfortable even in contortion.

"That only helps so much," he snaps, and she detects a surge of anger. He hates her, she believes, though he won't say as much. It stands to reason: His own wife, a rebel pilot, is the one who gave her the grievous wound he helped her to heal in the first place. She represents something he despises: the autocratic rule of a mad galaxy. He prefers that madness—the madness of rebellion. So be it. This alliance is built on anger and hatred, and that hatred is the glue that fixes Brentin to Sloane.

The cart stops short. Hard enough that she almost

loses her balance, which would mean pitching forward and smashing her face on the stone-fiber boards. Next to her, she hears Brentin do exactly that: He *oof*s as his head thuds against the floor of the cart.

Footsteps all around them. Hands grab at her face, tugging the blindfold off—hers is stubborn and fails to easily fall away, and she feels the cold metal of a crooked blade against her temple. Thankfully, the blade faces *away*, and with a quick pull the cloth is cut and falls.

It takes her vision a moment to adjust.

A massive impasse awaits: The cavern ends in a gargantuan, bulb-shaped chamber, its walls shot through with other smooth-walled tunnels—tunnels that are too high up for this cart to easily reach.

Next to her, she spies Brentin—his face and neck scrubby with beard, his forehead smudged with filth. He gasps as the slaves lift him up, rocking him back on his knees. They cut his blindfold free, too.

Red-streaked, dust-caked faces regard them with wide eyes. Hook-bound mouths murmur and hum. The servants perform one more action—cutting through the ropes that bind their wrists—before scampering off like animals. They clamber up the rocks, long fingernails mooring in the cracks. They pull themselves into the tunnels and scurry away.

Sloane and Brentin are alone.

He gives her a puzzled look. "Now what?"

Those two words echo, echo, echo in the bell-shaped cavern.

"I suppose we wait," she says.

"They don't want us to follow, do they?"

"I'm strong, but not strong enough to climb up into those tunnels." Still, maybe that's what these deviants expect. They seem hardly human. Sanity does not shine in their eyes—no, what lingers there in their stares is a special kind of derangement. The zeal of service, of having given your body and your mind over to someone else.

Sloane does not add that climbing into those tunnels would be difficult. Her side hurts today, a dread, deep ache from her injury—an injury that never really healed properly. Sometimes she lifts her shirt just to look at it—the skin there is puckered like the sealed, dry lips of a dead man. Were she still in civilization, it would have healed over well with bacta and mend-gel treatments. But Jakku is not civilization, and so her wound healed poorly. Every day it hurts, the pain lurking far deeper than the skin.

Brentin stands and stretches. He gingerly steps down off the cart, almost losing his footing. Sometimes Sloane looks at him and sees how much he's been stripped down. Again, the planet as an abrasive: He's gone from being a gangly, unruly branch to something leaner. A spear. A splinter.

Though she hasn't seen a mirror in months, Sloane assumes it's happened to her, too. Times like this she realizes nothing will ever be the same. She'll never have her Empire back. She'll never have her own starship. *I'm going to die on this planet.* That truth has settled into the well of her gut. That truth is a part of her now.

"I don't think—" Brentin starts to say.

But the sound of something coming through those tunnels cuts him off. It's a rasping sound. Something sliding along sandswept stone.

It's her. Their *mistress.*

The Hutt's face appears at the topmost chamber. Bruise-dark with red striations, the slug's face is not fat and thick as those of many Hutts, but narrower, like a slimy arrowhead. The mouth *is* wide, practically bisecting its whole head—the maw opens and a long, lashlike tongue licks the air, tasting it. The Hutt hisses. She blinks her one eye—the other is rheumy, the skin around it pocked and pitted with flecks of embedded metal, like a moon with glittering debris caught in its orbit.

The slug begins to slither. Up out of the chamber she comes, long arms pulling herself down from tunnel to tunnel. Sloane has met other Hutts: Jabba, for instance, was a fat, blubbery stump whose short tail was the most dexterous part of his corpulent body. A worm, a slug, a grub. *This* Hutt is longer, leaner, not like a slug at all, but like a *serpent*.

The Hutt slithers and wriggles down toward the ground, Sloane sees that behind the thing's head are a series of bulbous nodules and tumorlike protuberances. They hang bound together with filthy red ribbon— a strange accessory serving as an emblem of the creature's curious vanity.

As the Hutt nears the bottom of the hollow cavity, once more her servants emerge from the various tunnels and chambers—they meet the beast at the bottom, thrusting the palms of their hands upward, catching her as she eases forward. Their hands form her stage. Their feet, her vehicle.

Dozens of her slaves now make up a roving dais.

They hum and sing gibberish as they draw her forward.

Their gibberish dissolves into a single word:

"Niima. *Niiiiiimaaaaa.*"

They haul her forward, this long-tailed worm. It is Niima who will help them. It is Niima who will open the way to find Rax.

On this world, Rax is a ghost.

Nobody knows him. Nobody's heard of him. Sloane

and Brentin went to every ramshackle shantytown they could find, from Cratertown to Blowback to hovels in the desert. They visited with Teedos hiding in their trapdoor tunnel systems. They asked questions of Blarina traders, of kesium gas-miners, of black-market merchants. Rax was a non-entity.

Then someone said something—a bartender back in Cratertown, one of the first people they'd met on this world. He said for them to be careful, that someone had been stealing children.

The Empire needs children. Wasn't that what Rax told her?

She asked the bartender: "Where? Why?"

He said he didn't know, but they'd been taken by thugs belonging to Niima the Hutt. Most taken from small villages and from the makeshift orphanages run by the anchorites. "That's where most of the kids are kept. Nobody wants children running underfoot when you have a heavy-gauge blast-drill blowing chunks of canyon wall apart. So they dump them there, with the anchorites and their nurse-women." The bartender added: "I would've never let my kids go there."

The thought hit her: If Rax had been a child here, what if he was there? An orphan left behind for the anchorites?

That's when she found the trail. And it began with a man named Anchorite Kolob. He was a wretched old monk, carved by wind and sand and worst of all by time. She found him kneeling in a mud-daub hut with a bent metal roof. He was praying. When she demanded he help them, he did so willingly. But he also said the man she seeks is *not* a man named Gallius Rax. Rax is a lie, a false identity, he explained.

"Galli was the boy," Kolob said, his voice shaking.

He said to her that Galli was always a rebellious one, always running off and chasing stories. Then one day something truly changed in him. He became defiant. He led the other children astray. They began disappearing. And one day, Galli disappeared, too.

"Now the child has returned, and he is a child no longer." The anchorite tried then to sermonize to them, some nonsense parable about seeds growing in dead ground, but she cut him off and asked:

"Where did he go when he used to disappear?"

"The Valley of the Eremite. Near a rock formation called the Plaintive Hand. That was where he could be found, the stories say. He wouldn't let anyone get close. He had . . . traps, he had children protecting it, he had trained beasts to guard it. It wasn't far from the orphanage . . ."

"It's not far from here?" Brentin asked.

"It's quite far from here. This orphanage is not that one." The old man's eyes fell into a dead, faraway gaze. "That one burned down."

Brentin said, "Let me guess. That was the last you saw of Galli."

"It was, it was."

"Do you know what's there now?" Sloane asked.

"Nothing, as far as I know. Just the valley, the Hand, and the desolation that this world knows so well. But I know this: Now that Galli is back, he has returned to the Plaintive Hand. We've seen ships, and none may go that way. For that way is protected."

"Protected by whom?" she asked.

"By Niima the Hutt."

They needed more information. At first she assumed, who better to ask than the troopers and officers who now occupied this world? Together she and Brentin watched them and waited—but it soon became apparent that this was not the Empire she knew and loved.

These men and women were undisciplined. Their armor was filthy and in disrepair. Their weapons were crusted with the grit of this planet. Many troopers failed to wear their helmets. The officers looked ragged and run-down. And yet they were paranoid. They were brutal—abusing villagers, stealing food and water, lording over the small towns like emboldened bullies. Worst and most important: They were believers in what Rax had done here. They carried his banners. They gathered around and told stories of the man. "They have to buy all the way in," Brentin said. "This isn't a military anymore. It's a militia. Any sign of doubt will be beaten out of them, I wager. And such bold bravado is the only way to justify following the Empire to this place."

"Easier to lie to yourself that this is what's best than admit you've become part of something terrible?" she asked.

"Maybe."

"Then we need an unbeliever." She described the unbeliever simply: Someone who did not want to be here on Jakku. Someone who was swept along and was now caught in the machine and unable to climb out. Someone who was a loyal soldier, but not a sycophant.

Brentin, with his technical skills, helped Sloane rig up a crude listening device. With it, they were able to capture bits of radio transmissions and conversations between Imperials.

Then one day, they heard a trooper (ID# RK-242) telling his superior officer—a sergeant named Rylon—that he wasn't sure what they were doing here anymore and he wondered if there was *any other work* anywhere in the galaxy he could be doing.

"I just don't want to be here anymore," RK-242 told Rylon.

For that transgression, his fellow troopers—led by

Rylon—dragged him out into the desert, stripped off his armor, and beat him bloody. Pieces of his armor littered the ground around him like the fragments of a broken shell, and RK-242 curled up among them in a fetal ball.

That is not Imperial justice, she thought. No honor in that. Just brute-force behavior. *How swiftly order begins to disintegrate.*

They did not kill RK-242. He remained alive, if broken.

Days later, he was back on duty. Limping around. His armor clicking and clattering as he trembled inside it.

Sloane went to him. Had a little talk at the end of a blaster. RK-242 was thankful to see her—the moment she introduced herself, he began blubbering gratitude, snot bubbling at his nose, saliva stringing together his blistered, split lips. Sloane explained to him that this was all a plot against her—whether that was true or not, it mattered little. She said that Rax had committed a coup and had stolen the Empire from her grip.

"He's going to destroy us all," she said.

RK-242, through gulps and sobs, agreed.

And then she pumped him for information. Everything she could. *What is in the valley? What is by the Plaintive Hand? What is Rax up to?*

The trooper told her everything he knew: Rax called this world "a place of purification." The unforgiving planet of Jakku would test them, train them, and harden them to stone. The only way to defeat the New Republic, Rax said, was to be transformed into a greater force, a cruel army, an Empire that could survive the unsurvivable.

(That, and RK-242 referred to the man now as

"Counselor Rax." Seems her target had taken a new title for himself. How coy.)

She explained to RK-242 that the only recourse was to remove Rax from power. Violently, if need be. The trooper nodded, gamely. Sloane said she needed to know everything about Rax, about his habits, his role here, *anything*. But RK-242 couldn't tell her much: He said the Empire had established a base beyond the Goazon, beyond the Sinking Fields, and it was there that Rax was consolidating his power. Every day, the builder droids added more to the fortress, he said. And daily, too, came deliveries of TIE fighters, AT-ATs, AT-STs, troop carriers, new troopers. New ships arrived in the sky. The Empire gathered its assets, its resources, and its people.

All here. On the planet or just above it.

But that still told her nothing she didn't already know.

She asked him again about the Plaintive Hand—

He said that what *he* heard is that some old weapons facility lies hidden in the sand, something built by Palpatine—or put here even earlier by, well, who knows? He heard Rax takes trips there. Alone. And that's all RK-242 knew. He swore. He didn't even know if it was true, but he'd heard it, so, can she help him? Can she rescue RK-242 from this purgatory?

She ignored him and asked Brentin: "A weapons facility? Could *that* be why they're here on Jakku?" Even still, that didn't add up. The Empire needed no new weapons. It built the greatest weapon in the history of the galaxy. *Twice*. It did not need new battle stations. It *needed* new leadership.

But, the Empire *did* love its war machine. And maybe what's out there is something far greater than the Death Star ever was. A desire to find it—and to kill

Rax—arose in her like hot magma churning up through the volcanic channel of her heart.

Sloane thanked the trooper. She said she'd have an important role for him, and when the time came, she'd call on him. "Get back into your armor," she said. "Say nothing of this meeting to anyone."

When he turned around to pick up his helmet, she shot him in the back of the head before he could put it on. Brentin cried out. He said, "We could have helped him." She answered: "There was no help for him."

Then she said they had to go there. To whatever this facility was at the end of the Valley of the Eremite.

One problem: They couldn't take a ship, because they'd be shot down. And going on land meant going through the Yiulong Canyons—and beyond, into the mazelike Caverns of Bagirlak Garu. And *that* meant one thing:

Dealing with Niima the Hutt.

Niima the Hutt owns this part of Jakku. And her slime trail stretches much farther than this territory. Like Jabba on Tatooine or Durga on Ulmatra, her influence (and her corruption) has a long tail. She runs the black market: slaves, scavenge, kesium, bezorite.

She isn't just some fat slug ruler, though. She isn't Jabba with his palace or Durga with his yacht. It's not just gangster business as usual. Most Hutts love their parties and ceremonies. They make sure everyone kicks up a portion of their credits to the big boss that rules the region—whether as protection money or as tithe. No, Niima demands something bigger.

Niima demands eternal service. It is not enough merely to work for her, no. One enters her stable of servants and never leaves.

Though she treats herself as if she is a divine worm

born of sand and stone, those who serve her do so because she has set herself up in the middle of everything—a fat spider in the center of a web, a tumor drawing bloodflow. She has the resources. She has the access. She controls who may move through the narrow canyons and deep caverns. Niima's power comes from what she controls—she controls resources, and so she controls people. Even still, Sloane wonders if over time those who follow her do so out of some kind of misguided worship. Because the rewards Jakku offers are so few and so meager, you either believe in something greater or die hopeless in the dust. Those who give their lives to her see nothing else for themselves. Serving Niima is literally the best option they have in a world of refuse and ruin.

As Niima's long wormbody writhes atop the hands of her servants, she speaks a command: *"Kuba, kay-aba dee anko!"*

Her voice is hard to take: It's as if someone swallowed broken glass and is trying to shriek through the subsequent throatful of blood. The way her gargled cry echoes through this chamber brings it back to Sloane's ears again and again. The sound of it forces a wave of nausea through her.

Sloane knows some Huttese, but this phrase is in a more ancient dialect. It's more ragged, more primitive.

Her statement means, what? "Come to me"?

It must. Because from underneath, one of her very literal supporters emerges—this one, different from the others. A man, similarly shirtless and painted with red streaks of rock dust. His lips are the only part of him that *aren't* stuck with hooks. Everything else—his wrists, the pads of his palms, the flesh of his arms and of his legs—is pierced with metal.

He carries something over his shoulder. From a leather strap hangs a black box and a dented, rusted speaker.

A translator device. This servant climbs atop her, draping the translator over the meaty lump that passes for her shoulder. When placed, the box hangs down below her mouth. Then, the slave waits, crouching upon the top of her head like a pet waiting the next command.

He looks like a hat, Sloane thinks, absurdly.

Niima speaks again: *"Man-tah."*

The speaker crackles with static, and then a word emits from it in mechanical, monotone Basic: "SPEAK."

Sloane clears her throat and remembers: *Be deferential.* Hutts prefer to be spoken to as if they are not merely sentient, intelligent creatures. They like to be served. They want worship. This one more than others, it seems.

Only problem is, Sloane doesn't do the *deferential* thing very well. Still, she clears her throat and makes a go of it:

"Glorious serpent, mistress of sand and stone, Niima the Hutt, I am Grand Admiral Rae Sloane of the Empire. I come today to beseech your help. I and my traveling companion wish to pass through your cavernous territory and on toward the plateau called the Plaintive Hand—"

The Hutt interrupts her with a gabble of laughter. *"Sty-uka! Kuba nobata Granya Ad-mee-rall."* The box translates: "LOOK AT YOU. YOU ARE NO GRAND ADMIRAL."

"I assure you, I am, and I *will* retake my Empire. If you allow me to pass through, I will have much to offer you once I regain control . . ."

But she already hears it in her own voice: She's bargaining from a place of weakness. Niima wants to be served, yes, and she wants to be the Queen Worm, but alternatively, if Sloane has to bow and scrape and act like a wriggling fly trapped on the fat beast's tongue, then she seems weak, *too* weak to be taken seriously. She has to be humble while still seeming powerful. This is not something she knows how to do—how to perform as such a living contradiction. How does that even work?

Answer: It doesn't. Again the Hutt bellows with laughter. She roars in her gargle-shriek tongue and the speaker returns a translation: "YOU WILL RETAKE NOTHING. YOU HAVE NOTHING TO OFFER ME." To her servants, the Hutt screams: "TAKE THEM. STRIP THEM. SHEAR THEM. HAVE THEIR MINDS BROKEN."

No, no, no. It wasn't supposed to go like this. The slaves underneath Niima gently ease her to the stone, and one by one they come for Sloane and Brentin. He flashes her a frightened look, his hands forming into fists.

But Sloane gives him a gentle headshake and mouths four words: *I can fix this.*

"Wait," she says, holding up both hands. The Hutt-slaves do not stop coming, but they slow down, creeping toward her on the balls of their feet. Teeth bared, air hissing between them. "Gallius Rax is a pretender to the throne and he is weak. I *will* be Emperor."

Niima squawks, and the translator box barks: "HOLD."

The slaves stop. They freeze in place, as if automatons. They don't even *blink*. Niima's voice lowers, almost as if she's confiding in Sloane, though the translator box knows no such inflection; when it decodes the response in Basic, it does so in the same mechanized monotone: "I ALREADY HAVE A DEAL WITH COUNSELOR RAX. YOU ARE TOO LATE, GRAND ADMIRAL."

A deal with Rax.

Of course she has a deal.

He has to get through her territory somehow. He's given her something. Or *offered* something.

Sloane just has to find out what.

Once more the slaves surge toward her, grabbing at her wrists, her jaw, her throat. There's the flash of a blade, and she thinks, *Don't fight, wait it out, keep talking, keep digging.*

Then something turns inside her. She's been on this forsaken planet for months now. She's tired, raw-boned, and in pain. She is an admiral in the Imperial Navy and the only one deserving of ruling the Empire.

I will not be abused anymore. Forget bargaining from weakness.

It's time to try the other way. It is time to remember the strength of a grand admiral.

Sloane roars, and throws a punch. Her knuckles connect with the trachea of one of Niima's Hutt-slaves, and he staggers back, clutching at his throat and keening in a high-pitched whine. All her NCB pugilistic training comes back to her, and she adopts a strong stance with one foot behind her and starts *swinging* as if each punch has to save her life—and she fears that each punch has to do exactly that. Her fists connect. A jaw snaps. A tooth scatters. A slave grabs a hank of her hair and she traps his arm, twisting it so hard she *feels* the bone break—the freak screams and drops, writhing like a spider set aflame.

They keep coming. She keeps ducking, moving, punching.

But she's getting fatigued. Pain throbs in her middle, radiating out like the ripples after a heavy rock hits calm water.

The Hutt screams and the box translates: "STOP."

Sloane sees Brentin—he is against the ground, his arms bent painfully behind him. Blood pools beneath his busted nose. Sloane thinks: *Forget him. Let him go. He has served his purpose.* And yet a part of her doesn't want to. Loyalty has to count for something. And Sloane doesn't want to be alone. Not yet. Not here.

So she waits. She holds up her hands.

And it's good that she does.

Because more of the Hutt's servants are crawling down out of the tunnels. Dozens of them now. A few of them with blasters, many with knives and clubs, all their weapons bound with tendon and bone.

I can't fight them all. I just can't.

"What has Rax offered you?" she asks the Hutt.

The Hutt gargles a reply. The box translates: "WE PERFORM . . . WORK FOR HIM. HE PROVIDES US WITH WEAPONS, EQUIPMENT, SUPPLIES. WHATEVER I ASK."

Work? What work is the Hutt doing for Rax? That means her role goes beyond merely allowing him passage. Suddenly it dawns on her: What Anchorite Kolob said, about children being stolen? What if the Hutt's people are doing the abducting? *The Empire needs children . . .*

The slave-boys advance upon her. Slowly. Step by step. Their blades swish at the air. Their blasters thrust and point.

"Children," she says. "You bring him children."

The Hutt says nothing. But that silence is telling.

"Did Rax tell you where he's going?" Sloane asks. "Did he tell you what he's doing out there beyond your canyons?"

One-word response: "NO."

The Hutt's face betrays the monotone of the translator box—the slug's eye, the one ringed by glittering metal embedded in the flesh, opens wider.

A sign of curiosity, Sloane thinks. Good. She presses the advantage: "Don't you *want* to know?"

"TELL ME."

And yet, Sloane hesitates to say more.

If she gives this up, she's giving up more than information. What waits out there in the sand is perhaps useful not just to her, but to the whole Empire. The trooper said it was a weapons facility. Sloane dismissed that idea at first, but maybe there really *is* something there. Rax is no fool. If he wants it, *she* wants it, too.

The slaves continue creeping toward her.

They're going to kill me. Or turn me into one of them. She flashes on that: her and Brentin, bleached white, painted with blood-red dust, kissing the rotten flesh of this wretched slime-snake. Their "mistress."

She tries to imagine the Empire that she will one day rule: And the image of it, once strong in her head, is now a fading picture, like a painting under floodwater, its colors running, bleaching to the point of oblivion.

It's ruined. It's over. There is no Empire.

I'll never be the Emperor of anything.

The Hutt is right. I'm no grand admiral.

I have my revenge and only that.

That decides it. She hurriedly tells the Hutt:

"What's out there is a weapon. You let me go—you let me get *Rax*—and you can have it." The Hutt dismisses it with a wave of her long-fingered hand, and the slaves advance. Brentin cries out as they smash his face harder into the stone. Sloane feels her blood pulsing in her neck like a bird trapped in a tightening grip. She keeps talking: "The weapon out there is bigger than any Death Star we've ever built. Imagine it. Imagine it being not in our hands, and not in the hands of the New Republic, but in the hands of the Hutts. *Your* hands. It is a weapon built for a *god*. Or . . . a *goddess*."

It's a deception. She has no idea what the weapon is.

Or if it's a weapon at all. But if the lie gets her passage, lets her survive . . .

Niima's hand goes up, quivering fingers splayed out. The Hutt-slaves cease their advance.

"Mendee-ya jah-jee bargon. Achuta kuna payuska Granee Ad-mee-rall."

The words echo louder when the box translates them:

"WE HAVE A DEAL, GRAND ADMIRAL. YOU MAY PASS. YOU WILL TAKE ME TO THE WEAPONS FACILITY."

"Take you? No, I must go—"

Alone.

But the Hutt is already turning around, slithering back toward the tunnels. Her slaves are again struggling to get underneath her, and when they do, they lift her up back toward the nearest chamber.

As she slithers forward, the Hutt says, translated:

"COME, GRAND ADMIRAL. MY TEMPLE AWAITS. FIRST WE FEAST. THEN AT DAWN WE LEAVE."

INTERLUDE

THEED, NABOO

THEY CALL HIM the old veteran, which is funny because he's only ten years old. But he's been here longer than all the other kids. Refugees come and refugees go, all from worlds either damaged in war or where the Empire was run off, leaving only chaos in the absence. Some of the children stay for one wave, two, even three—but eventually someone comes, someone fancy, and adopts them.

But not Mapo.

Mapo, with one ear gone, half his face looking like the business end of a woodworking rasp. The scar tissue, like bad ground, runs up from his jaw, over the hole that used to be his ear, and to his scalp. The hair doesn't grow there. For a while he tried growing the rest of his hair out and letting it fall over that side like a river going over a waterfall, but the maven said it just made him look even less approachable.

(As if such a thing were possible.)

His arm on that side, too, isn't so good anymore. It's bent and hanging half useless like the arm of some clumsy blurrg. It works. But not well.

Now he stands in the Plaza of the Catalan, on the far side of the Silver Fountain. Theed is a city of plazas and fountains, but Mapo likes this one the best. The kids call it the mountain fountain, what with the way

the jets of arcing water make the shape of a mountain-
ous peak, a peak that towers easily over those gathered here in the plaza to watch the tik-tak birds or
paint the Gallo Mountains far beyond the capital's
margins.

Through the spray, he sees a shape sitting on the far
side. Just a silhouette blurred by the rush of water.

"You can go talk to him," Kayana says. The young
woman is one of the Naboo here. She's a minder, one
of those who watch the children.

"No, it's okay," Mapo says. "It's fine. He's busy."

"I'm sure he'd love to meet you."

She gives him a little shove. He grunts and thinks,
Nobody wants to meet me. Maybe that's why Kayana
is shoving him, because she's shuttling him off to
someone else. He heard the minders talking a couple
of weeks back and they said he was a real downer.

Still, maybe she's right. And it's not like he has anything else going on. Mapo won't be adopted today. Or
tomorrow. Or never ever ever.

Mapo walks the circumference of the fountain. The
wind carries the mist over him, cooling him down. He
lets his finger trail along the stone top of the fountain's
border, drawing lines in the water that fast disappear.

And then there he is:

The Gungan stoops down, sucking a small red fish
into his mouth with a slurp. A tongue snakes out and
licks the long, beaklike mouth, and the funny-looking
figure hums a little and sucks on his fingers.

Mapo clears his throat to announce his presence.

The Gungan startles. "Oh! Heyo-dalee."

"Hi," Mapo says.

The two of them stare quietly at each other. The silence stretches.

The Gungan has been here as long as Mapo has.
Longer, probably. Since children started coming in by

the shipload as refugees, the Gungan has served them, performing for the kids once or twice a day. He does tricks. He juggles. He falls over and shakes his head as his eyes roll around inside their fleshy stalks. He makes goofy sounds and does strange little dances. Sometimes it's the same performance, repeated. Sometimes the Gungan does different things, things you've never seen, things you'll never see again. Just a few days ago, he splashed into the fountain's center, then pretended to have the streams shoot him way up in the air. He leapt straight up, then back down with a splash. And he leapt from compass point to compass point, back and forth, before finally conking his head on the edge and plopping down on his butt. Shaking his head. Tongue wagging. All the kids laughed. Then the Gungan laughed, too.

The clown, they call him. *Bring the clown. We want to see the clown. We like it how he juggles glombo shells, or spits fish up in the air and catches them, or how he dances around and falls on his butt.*

That's what the kids say.

The adults, though. They don't say much about him. Or *to* him. And no other Gungans come to see him, either. Nobody even says his name.

"My name's Mapo," the boy says.

"Mesa Jar Jar."

"Hi, Jar Jar."

"Yousa wantin' some bites?" The Gungan holds up a little red fish and waggles it in the air. "Desa pik-pok fish bera good."

"No."

"Oh. Okee-day."

And again, silence yawns between them like a widening chasm.

The boy can see that the Gungan is older than some of the others he's seen here in Theed. Already Jar Jar's got wiggling chin whiskers dangling—not hair, but little fish-skin protuberances. They dance when he moves, like when he gently brings a fish to his lips, his movement slow and hesitant as if he's not sure he should. The Gungan is watching Mapo more than he's watching his fish, though—and suddenly it slips out of his hand. He tries catching it with his other hand, and the fish slips from his grip there, too. He makes an alarmed squawk, and suddenly his tongue shoots from his puckered lips, capturing the fish midair and launching it into his mouth. Jar Jar winces as a little sound (*grrrkgulp*) comes from him.

Mapo laughs.

Jar Jar offers a big smile. Like he's not even embarrassed by it.

It just makes Mapo laugh harder. Jar Jar seems pleased by the sound. As if it's music to him.

"Where yousa comin' from?"

"Golus Station." The blank look in the Gungan's eyes tells Mapo that he doesn't know where that is. So Mapo tells him: "It's above Golus. Gas planet in the Mid Rim. The Empire was there. They used us as a refueling depot? But when they left, they decided to . . . blow the fuel tanks. I guess so nobody else could have them. Take my toys and go home, that sorta thing. My mom and dad . . ." Mapo is angry with himself that he can't say it even after all this time. The words lodge in his chest and he just looks away.

"Oie, mooie." Jar Jar shakes his head, looking down in his lap. "That bera sad-makin." Then his eyestalks perk up. "Yousa wantin to see a trick?"

Mapo arches his one remaining eyebrow. "Okay, sure."

The Gungan chuckles and dips his head in the fountain, filling his face with water. His beak and cheeks bulge. Mapo expects him to spit it out, but he doesn't.

Instead he seems to tighten his body, his neck thickening with tension and his eyes popping wide.

Then: Water *sprays* from the Gungan's flappy ears. *Fsssht!* As his cheeks shrink, the water comes gushing from each side of Jar Jar's head.

Mapo can't help it. He laughs so hard his ribs hurt. Jar Jar doesn't laugh, but he sits back down, looking as satisfied as anybody can get.

When the boy is finally done, he wipes the tears from his eyes.

Mapo grins. "That was gross."

Jar Jar gives a thumbs-up.

"Nobody really talks to me," the boy blurts out.

"Mesa talkin to you!"

"Yeah. I know. For now. And nobody else does. Nobody even wants to look at me." Mapo doesn't even feel real, sometimes. Like maybe he's just a ghost. *I don't even want to look at me.*

Jar Jar shrugs. "All-n nobodies talkin to mesa, too."

"I noticed that. Why don't they talk to you?"

"My no so sure." The Gungan makes a *hmm* sound. "Mesa thinkin it cause-o Jar Jar makin some uh-oh mistakens. *Big* mistakens. Der Gunga bosses banished me longo ago. Mesa no been to home in for-*ebbers*. And desa hisen Naboo tink I help the uh-oh Empire." For a moment, the Gungan looks sad. Staring off at an unfixed point. He shrugs. "My no know." Though Mapo wonders if he knows more than he's saying.

"I don't think you helped the Empire." Mapo says that without being sure of anything, but he doesn't get the feeling this strange fellow would've done anything like that. Not on purpose. He's just a sweet old clown. "Maybe you just don't belong anywhere, like me."

"Mabee dat okee-day."

"Maybe it is, uhh, okee-day." Mapo sighs. "I don't think I'm going anywhere, Jar Jar."

"My no go somewhere, either."

"Maybe we can go nowhere together?"

"Dat bombad idea!"

"Oh." Mapo dips his chin to his chest. "Sorry."

But Jar Jar laughs. "No. *Bombad*. My smilin! Wesa be pallos, pallo." The Gungan pats the boy on the head.

Mapo doesn't know what's going on, but *bombad* must mean "good," somehow, so he goes with it. "Can you teach me to be a clown, too?"

"Bein clownin is bombad, too. My teachin yousa, pallo. Wesa maken the whole galaxy smilin, huh?"

"Sounds good to me, Jar Jar. And thanks."

Jar Jar gives him a thumbs-up and a big grin. Pallos, indeed.

CHAPTER TEN

NIGHT ON CHANDRILA. Wind eases in through the windows, the curtains blowing, the breeze bringing the smell of sea brine and late-summer mist.

"Look," Solo says, the holographic star map floating in the space amid him, Temmin, and Sinjir. "Jakku's a dirtworld, so that's good. You won't need to find a spaceport. The trick is getting past the blockade and landing somewhere they can't see you." He swipes the air and the hologram goes away. "I don't have any good maps of Jakku, but I can tell you most of that place is just dunes and rocks. But the buttes and plateaus lead into canyons, and canyons are a fine place to lose the Empire." He smirks. "Trust me, I know. Any bolt-hole you can find: Take it."

Sinjir watches the smuggler. A smuggler, or a hero of the Rebellion? Does it even matter anymore? He's about to be a father. That's his role, now.

And it's driving him nuts, by the look of it. Sinjir's seen something similar: Back in the Empire, you'd have officers stationed in faraway places, remote locations, distant bases. Some of them had that *glint* in their eyes, the wild stare of a tooka-cat someone tried to domesticate—it's the spark of dissatisfaction with your own captivity. Like you're trapped. Always imagining a different life.

It's important to see that spark, and to know it can turn into a full-on steel-melting fire if you aren't careful. Sinjir always knew to look for those around him with that flash in their eye. It was always they who would betray the Empire. Their wildness made them dangerous.

Solo's like that. That wildness—some combination of foolhardiness and happy lawlessness—is there behind his stare. He *longs* for adventure. Craves it like some poor souls crave a smear of spice on the tongue. (*Or a drink on the lips,* he thinks.)

And in this way, it makes sense suddenly that Solo fit so well inside the Rebellion. The Rebel Alliance was just a formalized coalition of criminals seeking to undermine their government, rebels angry at their captivity—caged, as they were, by a lack of choices. (Though maybe that's Sinjir's lingering *Imperial* side talking.)

All this is why Sinjir could never be a father. Solo will eventually find comfort in his captivity, but Sinjir would never find such peace. Settling down just isn't one of his skills. It's why he had to be rid of Conder.

(*Conder . . .*)

His mind suddenly wanders, his heart flutters, and he curses himself.

Solo confirms what Sinjir already suspects when the pirate says: "Now, I told you, you can take the *Falcon . . . but* you'd be a good sight better if you let me captain it. You don't know her like I do. She's . . . finicky."

"I flew it back from Kashyyyk, y'know," Temmin says.

"Not it. *Her.* Give the *Falcon* some respect, kid."

"Fine, yeah, okay. I just mean: I can fly it. *Her.*"

Right now, it's just the three of them in Leia's apartment overlooking the coast. Ten steps to their right and they'd be out on the balcony, gazing out over the Silver Sea, the stars scattered across the night sky like a million eyes gazing back. *I'd kill to be out there right now with a jorum of skee in my hand, a little ice in the glass, and nobody to bother me.*

(*Conder . . .*)

Foul, traitorous brain! Quit your meandering.

He has to bring himself back to the task at hand. Jakku. Norra. Jas. Fine, yes, *the droid,* too. And Solo's helping them.

He's helping them without Leia knowing, too.

She's gone. Probably all night. The princess is with the chancellor and a spare few others, trying to determine the best course of action for the Empire and Jakku. That path, however, is a political one. Temmin and Sinjir have no time for politics. By the time the political machine growls to life and churns out a solution to their problem, Norra and Jas will be dead. So will Sinjir and Temmin. All of life in the galaxy will be dead because politics is slower than a mud-stuck AT-AT.

The plan is simple: Fly in with the *Falcon,* fast and furious.

The plan is also very stupid.

Sinjir says, "Might I offer a contrary suggestion: How about we *don't* immediately fly a recognizable rebel ship into a starfield filled with the vessels of an enemy fleet. Instead, let me suggest sweet, sweet subterfuge. Those ships are being supplied somehow. We discover their supply line, we sneak aboard a cargo ship or shuttle—costumed in the guise of *freight*—and we let them deliver us to the surface like a *present* for a *king.*"

"You want us to hide in a box," Temmin says, scowling.

"Well. When you put it that way, it sounds rather

dreadful. But yes, we could hide in a box." He's about
to ask Solo again if maybe, *just maybe* the smuggler
has a bottle of Corellian rum hidden somewhere in
this domicile—

The front door opens. The droid, T-2LC, steps inside with a servo-whine. And following after is Princess Leia.

She stops when she sees them. With a sigh, she says,
"I should've known a conspiracy would bloom in my
wake."

"Hey," Han says, laughing. "Don't blame me."

"I always blame you."

He says to Sinjir and Temmin, sotto voce: "She really
does."

The princess comes and sits down next to her husband. It's fascinating to watch, because usually, Leia
was all about the formality: Dealing with her sometimes felt icily mechanical, like you were meeting an
assassin droid who, quite frankly, had precisely *zero*
increments of time for your foolish human nonsense.
Now, though, they're seeing her in the midst of her
humanity—at home, tired and pregnant, the airs of
her royalty put aside for a time. Either that, or they're
really becoming friends.

Leia sits and her hands move to encircle her belly,
settling on the underside. It must be quite a weight.
She's getting . . . full, Sinjir thinks. He decides that it
must be a horrid thing, to carry a child. It's a parasite,
basically. Amazing that humans are willing to procre-
ate when *this* is the burden that results.

He's glad he doesn't have to worry about any of
that.

"You're back early," Han says to her.

"I have the kind of heartburn that would drop a
tauntaun faster than a Hoth winter," she explains. "Mon
is with Auxi, now. And Ackbar, too. They'll be fine."

"Here," Solo says, hurrying to his feet. "Lemme get you a glass of ioxin powder, that'll settle your chest."

"No," she says, waving him off. "Let me just sit. Besides, that stuff tastes like I'm sucking on an Imperial credit." Her dubious, laserlike glare suddenly turns to Temmin and Sinjir. The both of them look to each other, like vermin fixed by the stare of a nearby raptor. "I assume you're all cooking up a plan to go to Jakku and rescue Norra and Jas."

"Uhh," Temmin says, obviously unsure how to answer.

Sinjir shrugs. "Well, we're not forming a boys' choir."

"*You're* not thinking of going along." That, directed at Solo with a thrusting, accusatory finger. It's not a question; it's a command.

"Me?" Solo says, smirking nervously and offering up both palms in a kind of *ha-ha* surrender. "I'd never! You can't get rid of me that easily. I'm here with you and the little bandit."

To Sinjir and Temmin, Leia says: "You could wait, you know. In fact, I'm *advising* you to wait. The chancellor will try to move quickly with this, I suspect. Let it play out."

"No," Temmin says—the word is sharp and abrupt. He's upset by the idea, that much is clear. "That battle could go on forever. It'll be like a siege! And what if the New Republic doesn't win?"

"Thanks for your confidence," Leia says, eyebrows arched.

Solo sits back down. "Kid's right."

"And just the same, flying through a blockade will be a lot easier when you're not the only ship trying to do it."

"She's got a point, too," Solo says.

The boy's face tightens into a stubborn mask. He wants this and he wants it now. Sinjir can't blame him.

The boy—really, a young man at this point—has been through considerable trauma. The events on Akiva, on Kashyyyk, and here on Chandrila with his own father? Sinjir considers himself a bulwark of unsentimentality (*Conder . . .*), but even that would rattle his cage. Temmin wants this. Temmin *needs* this.

And Sinjir needs it, too.

He misses Jas.

Sinjir fits with her. Like a painting ripped in half, then taped back together again. When he first saw her on the Endor moon, her about to retreat, him covered in Endor dirt and the blood of his fellow Imperials, he saw something in her eyes that *just made sense.* Absurd, beautiful sense. It's not romantic, of course. It's something far deeper. Something in their bones. It's not that they're all that alike, either. Maybe it's better *because* they're not all that alike.

He'd do anything for her.

Including run an Imperial blockade in a rickety, rag-dog freighter.

He tells them as much: "I fear you won't dissuade us, Princess. Our destiny is a fixed point. We are going to Jakku. Will you stop us?"

Leia sighs. "Officially, I have to try."

Blast it.

"*But,*" she adds, "if you have not noticed, I am very, very pregnant. I don't think I realized you could *be* this pregnant. As such, I consider it entirely possible— likely, even!—that tomorrow morning I won't be up early because tonight will be characteristically sleepless. Which means if you try to escape in the *Falcon* before dawn, I might miss the chance to stand in your way. Which would be a shame. So please, do me the favor and leave later in the day?"

Sinjir grins at her. *Message received, Your Highness.* But the bigger smile comes from Solo. His face is damn near cut in half by the grin that spreads. It's like he's proud of her.

He leans in and kisses her cheek.

And *that,* Sinjir decides, is that. In the morning: Jakku calls.

Temmin pushes along a couple of crates on a grav-lift. Up over the landing platform he spies the edge of the sea and the searing laser line of morning sunlight burning along it. From the other side of the platform comes a familiar face: Sinjir. The ex-Imperial crosses the platform, walking in long, sleepy strides and yawning as he does.

They join up and walk side by side toward Hangar 34.

Sinjir yawns again. "It's disgustingly early."

"Did you sleep?"

"Of course."

"Really?"

"If by *sleep* you mean sat up in bed, reading a book and sipping tea? Then yes, I slept."

Temmin gives him a look. "And by *tea* you mean rum."

"Pssh. No. I'm out of rum. This was proper Chandrilan raava."

"You always find something new to drink, don't you?"

"Variety is a vital component of a happy life."

"Are you drunk right now?"

"I am a professional. I do not get 'drunk.' I get 'pickled.' "

Temmin gives him *another* look—this one so fierce he likes to imagine blaster bolts coming from his eyes and knocking that smug look off Sinjir's face.

The onetime loyalty officer rolls his eyes. "Come

now, I stopped partaking around midnight. Then I gathered supplies and . . ." His words drift.

"And what?"

"And we have company."

Ahead, the hangar bay awaits. In it, a ship hides under a massive blue tarp, a ship shaped a good bit like the *Millennium Falcon*. Crossing in *front* of that ship are two Senate Guards. Red helmets. White plumage.

Batons at their side, hands waiting—as if ready to draw them.

More footsteps reach Temmin's ears. He looks left and right—

More guards. Two coming up on each side.

"What is going on?" Temmin asks in a low voice.

"Just keep walking," Sinjir says.

"Leia send these guys?"

"I hope not. Or we miscalculated in trusting her. Hand on your hip."

He means: hand on your blaster. Temmin has a small pistol hanging there under the hem of his shirt. His fingers feel along the holster, drifting to the grip. These are Senate Guards and he hopes this is all aboveboard, but everything seemed okay on Liberation Day, too. Until it wasn't.

"Stop there, sir," one of the guards ahead says, one hand out peacefully—but the other idly fingering that baton at his hip.

It's a threat. Subtle. But a threat just the same.

"Do you know who we are?" Sinjir asks, chin up, nose down. He has engaged full-bore haughty-prig mode. "Well. *Do you?*"

"You are Sinjir Rath Velus and that is Temmin Wexley."

"Oh." The ex-Imperial looks like someone popped his bubble. "Yes, that's us, then. What is this all about?"

The lead guard stares out over a smashed-flat nose with steely eyes. "You're to turn around and return to your quarters."

"We have business with our ship," Temmin says. "So move."

The guard's hand tightens around the baton. "The ship in that hangar belongs to General Solo."

"He's not a general anymore. And he's letting us borrow it. *Her.*"

"Be that as it may, we have strict orders, and those orders are to ask you to turn around and go on your way."

"You asked," Sinjir says. "And we decline. Like the boy said: Move."

"Sir, I don't want this to get ugly."

"Have you seen your face, guardsman? Too late to wish for pretty."

Temmin feels the other guards—all four of them—encroach tighter behind them even as those in front grab their batons.

"Sir, we have *orders*—"

"Whose orders?" Temmin asks. "Who's keeping us here?"

"The chancellor herself."

Sinjir and Temmin look to each other. Both of their faces war with the question, *Is this real?* They're both suspicious.

Temmin steps up, shirt pulled up, blaster revealed. "Guard, you better move now or me and my friend here—"

"Will leave peacefully," Sinjir says, pulling Temmin back sharply. He protests, but Sinjir shushes him and continues: "We didn't mean to step out of line, and please assure the chancellor we are returning to our quarters."

Temmin tries to pull out of Sinjir's grip, but the man's

eyes meet his. There's an intensity there—and a message. That message is, *Let it go.*

The boy grits his teeth. He wants to charge past them . . .

But he doesn't. He lets it go.

As they hurry away, Temmin hisses: "What was that?"

"I don't know," Sinjir says. "But we're going to find out."

"Where are we going?"

"Where else? We have no other friends here. We have to see Leia."

"Leia."

Her name, spoken in the dark.

Luke. She reaches for him but doesn't find him.

The dark, now lit with stars. One by one, like eyes opening. Comforting at first, then sinister as she worries, *Who is out there, who is watching us?* Hands reach for her, hands of shadow, lifting her up, reaching for her throat, her wrists, her stomach—

Inside, the child kicks. She feels her baby turning inside, right-side up and upside down, struggling to find his bearings, trying so hard to find his way free of her. *It's not time,* she thinks. *Just a little longer.*

"Leia."

Luke, she wants to cry out. But her words won't come. Her mouth is sealed, a hand pressed over it. One by one, stars go dark again, winking out of existence as if by a hand slowly closing over them—

"Leia!"

She gasps and wakes. Han. It's just Han. He's by the side of the bed, rousing her, gently shaking her shoulder.

The dream recedes like a wave going back to sea.

"Hi," she says, her mouth tacky, her eyes full of sleep. Her middle twists, too—it's not the baby. It's some unseen fear uncoiling. The remnants of the dream haunt her—but they break apart like a sand castle as she sits up and clears her head, doing as Luke taught her to do.

Breathe in, breathe out. Be mindful of the world, the galaxy, and your place within it. Everything will be okay. The Force will be your guide.

"You sleep like the dead these days," he says.

"And probably snore like a Gamorrean." She blinks and regards him. He's fully dressed. That means he's been up for a while. She senses something coming off him: a restlessness, a fear of settling down that only leaves him more unsettled. An image forms clear in her mind: Chewbacca. Han misses his copilot. And why wouldn't he? Those two have been together for so long, he should probably be married to that lovable hair-suit instead of her. "It's early. You're awake." He's always slept like a scoundrel: one eye open, ready for whatever may come. He said he used to sleep in fits and starts whenever he could grab a little shut-eye. And he has a hard time calling this place home. Home for him has always been the *Falcon*.

Even still, he's not a morning person. But since Kashyyyk, since saying goodbye to Chewie, this is how he's been. He goes to bed after her. Wakes up before her. Like an animal in a cage, pacing, pacing.

But today, a new feeling: He's worried.

"You need to see something," Han says.

"Can it wait?"

"I don't think it can, sweetheart."

HoloNet News.

It's been a long night, and Mon Mothma thought they

had gotten somewhere. If the Empire was on Jakku, she had to take careful, measured steps to see the shape of the threat that awaited them. That meant sending probe droids to scout. Maybe a ship built for stealth flown by one of their best pilots. It meant trying to see if they had anybody at all on Jakku who could report in—seeing what was going on in orbit didn't give a sense of what was happening on the ground. Was it an occupation? Were they even on the surface? Could they be looking for something? Or someone?

Now all the careful planning, all their consideration—

Gone. *Shattered.*

There, on the holoprojector, stands Tolwar Wartol. He, like other Orishen, has smooth skin peppered with uneven, asymmetrical, disconnected plates—the plates are smooth and catch the light like black mirrors. The HoloNet is presently replaying a speech he just gave here on Chandrila, down in the Eleutherian Plaza. His supporters gathered to hear him. He spoke with passion, his nose-slits flaring, his bisected lower jaw giving his mouth the look of a blooming flower whenever he hit the speech's talking points.

And oh, what a speech it was.

Mon, Auxi, and Ackbar had all settled their plan and were—just before sunset—ready to break for the day and attempt to catch a few scant hours of sleep before putting actions in motion to study the Empire more. Then a call came in from Sondiv Sella: *You need to turn on HoloNet News.*

The first thing Wartol said to the crowd—and to the civilized galaxy, thanks to the reach of the network—was this:

"The Empire has been found."

With those words spoken, Mon's heart froze in her chest.

What? How? How could he know . . . ?

Presently, HoloNet News is repeating his speech. This is the third go-round. His name is trending. His popularity, surging.

On the screen, Senator Wartol is saying:

"Chancellor Mon Mothma has discovered where the bulk of the Imperial forces are hiding, and it is on a distant world near the Unknown Regions. A world called Jakku." Then comes the accusation: "You did not know this information, and I did not know it, either. Because the chancellor has been sitting on that information—nesting upon it like a serpent hoarding precious treasure. Why didn't she say anything? What did she plan to do with this knowledge? If the New Republic is to be free of corruption, offering a government that belongs to the galactic citizens, should there not be total transparency and accountability? Secrets separate us. I would seek to demolish that wall of secrets, my friends. We must be partners in this!"

The crowd cheers. Joyous rhetoric from a man painting himself as the savior—everyone likes to be sold easy promises, don't they?

He goes on to outline his plans for the chancellorship: transparency, a strong central military, and policies that will ensure "everyone's voice will be heard." He continues on: "We see the Empire now and we must act. The chancellor wishes for us to sit on our hands. And every moment she waits, the Empire grows stronger, like an infection we thought had been beaten back—if we do not intensify the cure, the disease will return. It will attack once more, just as it attacked on Chandrila. Can we afford to pursue peace before the war is done? Can we afford such soft hands steering our nascent democracy? I think not, my friends . . ."

"Turn it off," the chancellor says.

Auxi does.

"Preposterous," Ackbar announces, gruffer and

louder than usual. It was only recently that the chancellor resumed even *speaking* to Ackbar—he and Leia both are still somewhat political pariahs for their actions on Kashyyyk. Though that effort secured the New Republic a much-needed win, it still painted them as iconoclasts—rebels, ironically. Now, though, she's thankful to have Ackbar here. He remains a voice of stability and sanity. He goes on: "You had this information for less than a standard day. It would be impossible, not to mention unethical, to immediately tell the galaxy what has been discovered. Chaos would ensue."

"Chaos *will* ensue," Auxi says. "Thanks to the senator from Orish."

"And none of this explains how he even *knows*," Mon points out. She fears the worst: Someone close to her is the leak. But who? Auxi has been here nearly the whole time, taking only a few breaks to pick up food or check on her children or her tooka-cat. Could she be the leak? Certainly it wouldn't be Ackbar. Though he *did* go against her with Kashyyyk. Could he slyly be supporting Senator Wartol's bid for chancellor? That seems unlikely. The Mon Cala admiral is a warrior, yes, but a warrior committed to peace in their time. War is a means to an end, but the way Wartol talks, it is the persistent and never-ending means—he sees peace being maintained by a strong military and a willingness to deploy it freely, even *after* the Empire is gone. Mon wants a coalition of militaries, an alliance-driven pact of peace that systems could join to support one another when danger encroaches. Ackbar supports that dream.

That leaves who?

Leia? Han? No. The boy, Temmin, and the ex-Imperial?

Could be. They certainly wanted to take swift action. The boy in particular may be suffering from the impetuousness and naïveté of youth. His mother is gone. His father, the foe who almost killed her. Certainly a young man like that could be drawn in by a figure like Wartol. She reminds herself to keep a wary eye there. Perhaps that boy should not be trusted.

She tries to flex her fist again. Mon's connection to her own fingers is soft and distant. As if they belong to someone else.

She erupts suddenly, a fit of forced optimism: "This is all normal. These are the necessary bumps and scratches of a growing democracy. We should not expect politics to be neat and tidy and we are reminded of that today. Enough looking back. Now we look forward."

"We have to respond," Auxi says.

"And soon, I fear," Ackbar adds.

"It seems that even a few hours of sleep are no longer in our equation," Mon says with a beleaguered sigh. "I shall begin working on my response immediately. Auxi, contact HoloNet News, have them ready for my statement. And Admiral—"

"I will initiate the probe droid and scout immediately," he says with a brusque nod.

"Good. Let's remain vigilant. We have a long day ahead of us, and I fear that traitors are afoot."

CHAPTER ELEVEN

EVERYTHING MOVES FAST as lightspeed.

Fast until it stops, like a ship plowing into the side of an asteroid.

"It wasn't the chancellor," Leia tells them, taking a cup of tea from her protocol droid. "Thank you, Elsie."

Sinjir cocks an eye at her. He's angry. Irrationally so, perhaps. He likes to keep things cool—he imagines his heart is less an organ beating blood into his body and more a collection of icicles hanging from the chin of some malevolent snow-beast—but he can keep that veneer no longer. He knows full well that running off like a soggy drunk adventurer into the crushing maw of the Empire's fleet was not a wise decision, and a little part of him is thankful they're not right now being blasted to bits by a Super Star Destroyer in the space above Jakku. But the rest of him seethes over the fact that Norra and Jas are still down there somewhere. Hopefully alive. And nobody coming for them the way *they* have come for *others*.

Lucky perhaps that Temmin isn't here. Sinjir sent the boy to see the pilot Wedge Antilles. Wedge might know how to get them to Jakku.

"Then it was you," Sinjir accuses. "*You* blocked us."

Leia gives him an incredulous look. "Do you truly believe me so duplicitous, Sinjir?"

"Yes." He frowns and shakes his head. "*No*. I don't know! Someone sent those guards. They didn't send themselves."

Han passes behind Sinjir with a cup of caf in his hand. "Mon can be a slippery one," he says. "But this isn't like her. Here, drink this." He thrusts the cup into Sinjir's hand. "You're gonna need it."

"I'm going to need something considerably stronger."

"That comes later. If we win. Or if it goes the other way."

Sinjir runs long fingers through his dark muss of hair with one hand while sipping the bitter caf with the other. It's got a hard afterburner kick to it, like drinking a mug of vaporator sludge. "We need to get to Jakku."

"That just became a whole lot harder," Leia says.

"Explain to me again—what exactly happened?"

"Mon's opponent in the upcoming election, he knew. Wartol knew about the Empire, and worse, he knew that *we* knew. Our window to get you to Jakku was very small already. And him making that public just closed it."

"Why?"

"Because," Han interjects, "this just became officially political. You go zipping off to that dirtworld, it'll look like an act of war on behalf of the New Republic before the Senate had time to do squat about it."

"You mean like, oh, say, Kashyyyk?" It's a barb, Sinjir knows, but he means for it to sting. He grows weary of double standards. As weary as he grows of politics. And of nearly everything at this point.

"Don't look at me. I say you still go."

"*Han,*" Leia cautions.

"I know, I know. But it's what I'd do. And what you'd do, too."

Sinjir groans and takes a long, stiff sniff of the caf underneath his nose. "None of this explains who sent those guards to meet us at the platform, does it? And who told the Orishen senator about all this?"

"It wasn't you, was it?" Leia asks. She's serious.

He retorts the same way she did: "Do you truly believe me so duplicitous, Princess?" Before she can answer, he cuts in: "Never mind. Don't answer that. No. Of course not. It was not me, nor was it Temmin." He declines to remind everyone here that once upon a time, Temmin *did* betray them at the Akivan palace, and he is young and a bit of a firebrand . . . but no! That's impossible. "We had an answer. We had a way to Jakku. There was no need to complicate the solution we already had for our problem."

Then it hits him.

It wasn't just that Senator Wartol knew something he shouldn't. It was that someone knew everything that went on here.

Which means—

Oh, drat.

Sinjir says with a vicious scowl, "The walls have ears."

"Huh?" Han asks.

But Leia understands. Her eyes go as big as battle stations and she thrusts a finger to her lips before offering a gentle nod to Sinjir.

"I'll be back," Sinjir says. "Time to pay our mutual slicer friend a visit." His heart races as he exits the apartment, one name waiting on the back of his tongue, unwilling to be spoken but present just the same.

Conder . . .

* * *

Chancellor Mon Mothma is bone-weary already, and the day is young. With her one good hand, she smooths the fabric of her white gown.

"Are we good?" she asks the woman nearby.

That woman—Tracene Kane from HoloNet News—stands at the fore of the platform. She looks to a chubby Sullustan nearby who clucks in Sullustese as he crouches down, connecting cables from the hovering cam to the holoprojector platform. Mon has elected not to speak in front of a crowd—stars forbid that someone out there boo her or harangue her from the audience, only furthering the assured descent in her approval numbers. Better here, where she can control the environment. And HNN likes the exclusive, especially in an age when they will no longer be the only player. Other networks have begun springing up to compete. Which is the earmark of a healthy democracy, Mon believes.

Many voices competing, not one voice dominating.

Though, she wonders, if Wartol wins the chancellorship, then what? Will it be his voice that dominates? Or is she demonizing her opponent too much? Surely he wants the best for the galaxy, even as they disagree on how best to accomplish that uneasy feat.

"Thank you for coming on such short notice," Mon says.

"My pleasure," Tracene answers. "I was . . . out in the field for a while. Covering the war."

"Why did you return to cover politics?"

The journalist hesitates. "I couldn't look at war any longer."

"You and me both." Mon sighs. "It feels like we've always been at war. I aim to stop that, but to do so . . . well, not to put too fine a point on it, but that means

the only way out is through. We must end the Empire
to bring peace. And to end the Empire, first we must
endure *politics*." Suddenly, she smirks. "Be cautious,
Miss Kane: War may seem like a pleasant dream when
you look too long into the abyssal eye of the political
machine."

"Noted," Kane says, returning her own small smile.
"Birt, are we ready?"

The Sullustan cam operator grunts as he stands,
then gives a thumbs-up. His face flaps lift to show a
gummy grin.

With that, Mon Mothma steps into the circle.

Moments pass. She steadies herself, and tries very
hard to stop her left hand from shaking. The platform
glows blue around the edges.

Tracene gives her a gentle nod.

Words spring up in front of her, the words of her
speech in a slow-moving crawl—it is a speech too
hastily written, she knows. Usually, she would take as
much time as she could on any speech that goes out
this far and this wide. But time is a luxury now, and
she has to get ahead of this thing before it becomes a
scandal hung around her neck like a heavy weight.

"Yesterday, I became aware of the possibility that
the Galactic Empire had retreated to a planet in the
Inner Rim, near the Unknown Regions: a planet of
relative insignificance known as Jakku." Already she
curses herself; should she be saying that about any system in the galaxy? *'Insignificant'*? A bloom of embarrassment rises to her cheeks, and it only confirms that
she is off her game and *has* been off her game since
coming out of critical care here on Chandrila. She pushes
past her doubts, because what choice does she have?
Keep talking, Mon.

"Our military has already begun efforts to confirm
this information. We have launched a ship, the *Ocu-*

lus, under the command of Ensign Ardin Deltura, an expert who similarly helped us discover the threat on Akiva. We believe his efforts will confirm what our initial scouting showed: that much of the Imperial fleet is now in space above the planet Jakku. It remains to be seen, however, if this also includes a ground occupation of the planet or is something else that is not wholly understood."

Uncertainty plagues her. She hates using the military as a lever. And yet at the same time she now fears that she was too hasty in relieving herself of certain powers. Certainly this would be much easier if the allocation of military resources did not rely on politics. Ah, but isn't that exactly how Palpatine felt? The Senate stood in the way of progress. So he manipulated the Senate, overwhelmed it, and inevitably abolished it. No. She is doing the right thing. Politics is meant to be turbulent. It is meant to be slow and steady—elastic, too, so that the system bends but does not break.

"I would not normally divulge such information publicly, but my hand has been forced—further, it is safe to assume the Empire is aware of our probes testing the margins of their occupation. Which means we must act quickly to seize what advantage we have. As such, I am calling the Senate to an emergency session tonight, where I will resolve that we must mobilize our armed services to war against the Galactic Empire in the skies above Jakku—and perhaps even upon its surface. It is with a heavy heart that I call us to war once more, but I am vigilant that the threat of the Empire must not stand in the way of our safety and our sanity. I know that the Senate will stand with me. And when they do, I am confident that this will be the end of the Empire."

The chancellor gives a curt nod and steps out of the circle.

Tracene gives Birt, the cam operator, the signal. He cuts the feed.

The circle goes dark.

"You did fine," Tracene says.

"You must have sensed my apprehension."

"No."

She's lying, Mon thinks. But so it goes. It is rare that she receives the straight truth from anybody anymore.

"It's just—it must be hard, being you. Under siege from every direction."

"Yes," Mon says. "It is hard. But we persevere. Like the Rebel Alliance before us, like the New Republic now. We persevere."

The man with bronze skin and a scruffy, sand-colored beard seems taken aback by the guest at his door.

"Oh" is all he says.

"Hello, Conder," Sinjir says as greeting. He chills his voice, putting some ice into it. Just to ensure that it is clear he is not here on a mission of mercy. Also to make it clear that he has no feelings here at all, lest anyone believe him somehow sentimental.

"Sinjir."

"May I come in?"

"And if I said no?"

"Then I would pout so powerfully, my mopishness would take corporeal form and kick the door down."

Conder's warm eyes light up as his face softens. "Same old Sinjir. Sure. Come on in."

Inside, the man's apartment is the epitome of austerity. Sinjir's fingerprints are long gone—he, too, prefers spartan living, but still likes a little splash of color now and again: the bloody blush of a hai-ka flower bouquet or the rich cerulean of a saltwater octo-fish tank. Conder has gone back to décor that is black, white, and gray. The only flash the domicile offers is a punctuation of brushed-chrome cabinet handles or silvra-stone tile. *He would have done well as an interior decorator in the halls of the Empire.*

"I don't feel like the same old," Sinjir says. "Maybe just old."

"You are *not* old. Neither of us is."

"Fine. Old*er*, then. And definitely not the same."

"You seem the same to me."

"Well, I *feel* different," Sinjir snaps. *Oh, my, this isn't going as expected.* Not that he should've expected anything else, he supposes. "I need you. Your *help,* I mean." *By all the bloody, stupid stars, untangle your tongue, Rath Velus.* "It's not even *me* that needs your help, so don't get any damn ideas. It's the princess. She needs you."

"She could've called me herself."

"Yes. But this is sensitive."

Conder leans up against the counter. "You want to sit? Have a drink?"

I would like that very much.

"No!" Sinjir answers sharply, *too* sharply, despite the contrary thought doing loops in his heart. "No, I would *not* like a drink."

"Then maybe you really are a different Sinjir. Not one here to kill me, I hope? Chip stuck in the back of your head?" Conder was one of the ones who helped decipher that little riddle for the New Republic. It's why Sinjir is here, now, to see him.

"I believe we have a bug. In Leia's domicile."

Conder *hrm*s and scuffs a heel against the ground. "This about what's going on? The Empire at Jakku?" Suddenly he stands up straight. "Oh, Sin. Tell me you're not somehow involved in all that."

"Two of my people are there. Norra and Jas. On the

ground. Under the Empire's boot. This may be related to all that. I . . . don't know, yet."

"They're my people, too." Conder reaches out to touch Sinjir's arm—

But Sinjir pulls away.

"Will you help?" he asks Conder.

"On one condition."

"There are no conditions. You'll not hold me hostage with emotional blackmail. Either you will help or you won't."

Conder sighs. "I just want to know why you left me."

"Because we were done."

"You could've fooled me."

"Obviously, I *did* fool you."

The slicer chews on that. "Yes. Indeed you did, at that." He's angry, now. Good. *Be mad, you fool. Don't be so daft as to fall for a villain such as me.* "I'll help you. I assume you mean now?"

"I mean yesterday, but it's too late for that, so now will have to do."

"You're mad," Wedge says.

"And you're doing busywork," Temmin snaps.

Captain Antilles looks down at the datapad in his hand. It's true. He *is* doing busywork. But what else is he supposed to do at this point? Behind the two of them, the hangar bustles with activity. Though they have not yet gotten the call to battle, they were told to be ready when it came. That means fueling up. That means loading munitions. Cross-checks abound. Some of these starfighters—X-wings, Y-wings, A-wings, and even that prototype T-70 in the back—will end up on various capital ships before the New Republic fleet flings itself through hyperspace into the theater of war, where the Empire's own malevolent forces gather.

Of course, Wedge thinks, *I won't be going along.* None of Phantom Squadron will. The pilots in his nascent squadron are washouts and weirdos to the last: his favorite kind of crew. Reminds him of the days— not that long ago!—in the Rebel Alliance when you took whatever bush pilots and womp rat hunters you could find, and you stuck them in battle-scarred fighters. You went to war with the pilots you had. Now things are more formalized—more training, more boxes to check, more *politics.*

And he fizzled on that last part.

Going out to Kashyyyk with Leia and Ackbar was the first outing of Phantom Squadron—

And the *last.*

But what was the choice? Abandon Han and Leia? Let Kashyyyk fall to the bombs dropped by those Star Destroyers? Sometimes doing the right thing didn't mean following orders. Following orders would've meant never betraying the Empire in the first place. Never joining the Rebel Alliance. But that's tricky, isn't it? That transition from a ragtag bunch of dissidents and mutineers to a proper government is a hard one. Many of them still have rebel hearts beating in their chests—it's in them to question orders, to fight back when something doesn't seem right. Even if it's coming from someone you trust. People trusted Palpatine, once.

Doesn't matter now. In public, Wedge got a medal. In private, he got reamed out. And Phantom Squadron was shut down.

His crewmates have gone on. None of them are pilots now. They're all support crew. Koko runs fueling lines. Jethpur is an engine mechanic. Last he heard, Yarra gave it all up and she's out somewhere on a fishing rig—one of the organic-led ones that cleave to the old Chandrilan ways of hauling fish up one at a time on lines of braided dyan-thread.

And here he is. Doing busywork. Managing a hangar.

"It's necessary work, Snap," he tells the young man.

"Don't call me that."

"Oh. Sorry. I . . . I thought you liked the nickname."

"I did but now I don't." Temmin steps in front of him, arms crossed. "You like her."

"What?"

"My mother. You like her."

"I . . ." Wedge feels nervous, suddenly, thinking about her. His mouth dry as a new shirt, but the back of his neck goes suddenly slick with sweat. *Norra.* "Snap—sorry, Temmin—I was close with your mother, we were friends—"

"You were *more* than friends." With every word, Temmin thrusts an accusing finger. Then he throws up his hands, exasperated. "And fine. I don't care about that. But *you* care about *her.* So, she's out there, Wedge. She needs our help. She's trapped on a planet and we can go, *right now,* to save her. You have clearances. I know you do."

Wedge barks an uneasy laugh. "I don't have those clearances anymore, not after Kashyyyk. And your mother . . ." He sighs and sets the datapad down. "I do care about her. A lot. And part of why I care about her is that I know she's tough as a handful of hexabolts. That planet won't break her. The Empire won't break her. And we'll get her out."

"So you're just abandoning her."

"I'm not. I swear. But I'm just one guy without a whole lot to say about any of it. What I *can* do is what I have to do. This isn't just busywork. It's making sure our ships and our pilots are ready to fly, because they need to hit that fleet like a fist. That's how we get your mother back. We don't just send you or me or the *Falcon*. We send the whole New Republic."

Temmin sneers. "Glad to hear you've made yourself feel better about not doing a damn thing. I'll see you, Wedge."

"Snap—" *Damnit*. "Temmin! Wait."

But the boy is already hard-charging away in long, angry strides.

Sinjir watches Conder through the window. The slicer asked them all to stay outside while he does his scan of Leia's domicile. From the center of Conder's palm rises a small, hand-machined probe droid—like a little wobbly ball with a nest of needled antennas coming off it at all angles. It hums and thrums and bobbles around the room, a green beam of light sweeping across every corner, every counter, every bit of bric-a-brac.

It's not the probe droid that Sinjir is watching, though.

It's Conder.

Conder is comfortable in his skin, and even more comfortable in his role. There's just something *enticing* about seeing someone so capable, so confident. The hinge of Sinjir's jaw tightens, like a trap eager to spring.

Look away, you daft clod.

He's suddenly self-conscious about it. Sinjir isn't exactly *alone* out here, is he? Leia, Han, and their insufferable protocol droid are with him.

"Mum," T-2LC is saying as he hands over a digestive biscuit to the princess. "A small bite of bland food to calm your nerves—"

"I don't need that, Elsie, but thank you." Leia waves

it away. Then, to Han: "I can't *believe* I was so foolish. A listening device? In our home?"

"Relax." Solo shrugs it off. "We don't even know if
that's what happened yet. Maybe this is some kind of
fluke."

"No," Sinjir says. "This is no fluke. Someone is listening in. It's the only explanation." *Except for Temmin having betrayed us all.*

"I confirmed with Mon," Leia says. "Those guards
that turned you away from the *Falcon*—she didn't
send them."

Han nods. "That means Wartol did it."

"Does he have that kind of power?" Sinjir asks.
"He's just a senator."

"A senator running for the chancellorship. And,"
Leia adds with a sigh, "currently pulling ahead with a
rather robust lead."

Solo throws up his hands. "Politics is mean business. I'd rather fall into a nest of starving gundarks
than get caught up in those gears. Wartol has power in
places we can't see. He's close with the Senate Guard,
too."

"As a candidate, he has access to them. They protect him."

This Orishen—Sinjir would very much like to pay
him a visit. He would then like a heavy stick to pay a
visit to the man's knees.

"Be assured," Sinjir says, "Conder will find something."

Minutes later, the slicer emerges.

"I didn't find anything."

Well, thanks for that, Sinjir thinks. "How? How is
that possible?"

"How? There's nothing to find. No listening devices. No cams. Unless Wartol has someone building
devices who's more sophisticated than I am." The

slicer smirks. "And no one is more sophisticated than I am."

That damn smirk. That big-eyed confidence. Those cherub cheeks puffing out underneath his scratchy beard. *You adorable, incorrigible demon.*

Still. Can't let Conder have his day. "You failed us. Someone out there *is* more sophisticated, it seems, because—" *Because it's easier to insult your abilities than admit I'm wrong.* "Because I'm right. Plain and simple."

"I'm sorry, Sin, but I mean it—I didn't find a damn—"

The small probe droid, held fast in Conder's hand, begins to beep in fast staccato. It shudders in his grip. The slicer utters a grunt of surprise as the droid suddenly leaps out of his hand and takes flight.

It doesn't go far, though. It whirls around in a circle and stops in front of the protocol droid's gleaming face.

"Oh, my," T-2LC says, alarmed.

The probe scans the protocol droid's face—

And then it lights up like a detonator about to pop. Flashing lights! Klaxons! A vibrating buzz! Conder swipes it out of the air and powers it down, clipping it to his belt as it falls silent.

All eyes turn toward the protocol droid.

"It's not me, mum!" the droid objects.

Han Solo scowls and reaches for the protocol droid. "Elsie, you oughta hold still. This is going to sting a little."

Mon Mothma comes into her office. Tired. Feeling gutted. She has just given her speech to the Senate— her last plea, an easy one that asked for their vote to send the brunt of the New Republic's military to Jakku in order to end the Empire's oppression once and for all. She was uncharacteristically jingoistic, but they need this vote. The chancellor told the hundreds of senators present in the last Chandrilan session that this will be the defining battle of the war. It is likely to be the *final* battle of the war. She presented to them all the facts as they had them: data from probe droids and the *Oculus* that demonstrated *plainly* that the bulk of Imperial forces are present and accounted for. The numbers, she reminded them, are on their side. They are no ragtag junkyard fleet going up against a monolithic battle station, not this time. Their own military forces have more than tripled since the destruction of the second Death Star at the Sanctuary Moon. Meanwhile, the Empire's own fleet has been whittled away—

A tree, to a branch, to a bundle of splinters.

And then dust that becomes nothing as the wind takes it away.

Or so she hopes.

We can win this, she told the Senate. She meant it.

Then her time on stage was over. Applause came up behind her like a rising wave, urging her forward out of the Senate house and pushing her all the way back to her office. Now she feels stripped down, hollowed out, weary, bleary, and done.

I can't be done yet. Soon. But not yet. Yes, the day has nearly eaten her alive. But it did not. She has persevered.

And soon, Mon Mothma shall be triumphant. At every turn, some new snarl presented itself and she (or Auxi, or Ackbar) had to spend additional time unraveling each knot. Never mind the overwhelming number of administrative duties that threatened to draw her down like a slurry of sucking silt-sand. Everything is prepared. The moment the Senate gives their easy approval, the mechanism of war will wind up quickly, triggering events as needed. It calls to mind a match of rivers-and-roads, the old Chandrilan game of toppling over tiles—one falls into another and into the next thereafter, and they speed along. If you place them correctly, they all fall down, and they fall more swiftly than those of your opponent. If you fail . . . they fall too slowly, or never fall at all.

Once the vote is in, the ships launch.

The ground forces mobilize.

Everything begins.

And hopefully, her tiles fall faster than the Empire's, and this is truly the end of that oppressive regime's rivers-and-roads.

She collapses into her chair.

Auxi sweeps over, a bulbous long-necked bottle of *very good* brandy held in the same hand with which she precariously grasps two glasses by their rims. "I think this calls for a nip."

"What's the old saying? *You can never count the stars, for some may already be dark.* The vote isn't in yet, Auxi."

"But it will be. Momentarily." She sets the glasses down and begins to pour. Rich amber liquid sloshes around the bell of each. "And we'll win. But what does it matter? After the day we've had, I think we deserve a bit of the good stuff. Oh! And your numbers are already improving nicely. They were up before you even stepped on stage."

Mon sighs and takes the glass in her good hand. "People *do* like war."

"No, shh, stop that. People like to know that they are *safe.* And in this case, if that safety is earned by grinding the last Imperial stormtrooper into the dirt— then count me among them."

Their brandy glasses *tink* as they tap together.

Mon takes a sip. The liquor is warm in her mouth,

and as she swallows, it spreads its heat to her throat and her belly. As it goes down, it's like a zipper opening her up—all this *tightly packed* material inside her heart suddenly unspooling. She feels like she is *almost* ready to breathe a sigh of relief and sleep a very long sleep.

Don't get too comfortable, she cautions herself. *You won't be able to rest long on your laurels. Ackbar will lead this battle, but it is you who oversees the war, Chancellor.*

As if on cue, her office door chimes. Ackbar enters.

She is poised to ask him if it is time. Time to launch. Time to complete the dread task they set out to complete many years before with the first stirred embers of the Rebel Alliance. But she sees now the stark look on his face. Mon Cala are hard to read for most humans, but she knows Ackbar well—and she spies the reluctance in his stiff-backed posture, in his curling chin tendrils, in his half-lidded eyes.

"Tell me," she says.

"The vote did not pass," he says. "We are grounded, Chancellor. The fleet will not go to Jakku, and there the Empire shall remain."

PART TWO

CHAPTER TWELVE

COLD, RANK WATER hits Norra in the face. It pours over the top of her head, a sour bile-spit smell filling her nose. She coughs and sputters, standing up inside her cage. Two stormtroopers stand on the grated metal ceiling of the prison in which she sits. Above them, the Imperial fleet hangs, veiled behind bands of gauzy clouds.

One of the troopers holds a bucket. The other has his blaster rifle pointed down. From her vantage point below them, with the sun above, the Imperials look like little more than shadows—scavenger birds ready to pick her bones as soon as her flesh gives up.

"Wake up," the one with the bucket says. He lets it hang loose, and it knocks against the side of his armor—armor that's no longer the pristine white of most stormtroopers. This armor has been marked and gouged, painted and carved into. The one with the blaster rifle has blood-red dye spattering the face of his helmet, shaped into the crude icon of a skull—taking what was always metaphorical about the stormtroopers and literalizing it. *We are the agents of death,* it says. *We are killers.*

"I could just shoot her," the rifle-holding trooper says. He gestures down through the bars of the wrought-metal cage, the tip of his rifle poking through. "She's just another mouth to feed. I could close that mouth. Permanently."

"Do it," she whispers.

He does.

No!

The blaster goes off, and everything around her lights up red—

The bolt digs a furrow out of the hard sand-pack beneath her feet. She dances away from it, panic throttling her.

"She's awake now," the bucket-holder says.

The two troopers laugh and keep walking, boots clanging.

Norra kneels down and weeps.

Hours later, she's up and working a kesium gas rig— it's a big cylinder-bore screwed into the sand, and it needs people all around it to turn valves and tug levers to balance the rush of gas coming up from beneath the mantle. Let too much up at one time and the whole thing pops its top, maybe blowing them all to vapor. Let too little up, and the shaft-line seals shut as the sand collapses back into the channel. She's here, chained along the edge with half a dozen other prisoners, all shackled around the circumference of the well. If any one of them fails, they either get punished or get dead.

Worse, she still smells like bile and spit. That, courtesy of the bucket dumped over her. It wasn't water. Oh, no. Nobody would waste water on this planet just to wake up a prisoner. It was backwash from a happabore trough: rancid water sloshed in and out of their leathery maws.

Norra, at this moment, has never felt so alone.

When the troopers brought them here, they scanned and ran their faces, said that there was a bounty out for

Jas. Before Norra knew what was happening, they were throwing her friend aboard a sand-scoured shuttle— and just like that Jas was gone.

That was a week ago. Or longer. Norra can't even tell anymore.

After they took Jas, some pock-cheeked officer asked Norra point-blank if she wanted to die, or if she wanted to work. The answer was easy. If Norra gets dead, then that means Sloane escapes. Death was not an option. Not until revenge had its day.

I'll work, she told him.

So they brought her here. Where *here* is, though, she barely knows. Kilometers from someplace called Cratertown, apparently.

And so she works. Every day she works this same black valve, the metal on the wheel so hot it first blistered her fingers—by now, though, those blisters have turned to calluses, and the skin around them is dry and splitting. It doesn't even bleed. *I don't think I* have *blood anymore.* Just dry Jakku dust whispering through her veins.

To her right, a hollow-eyed alien hunches over a set of levers. The bone-white creature doesn't talk much. Occasionally it moans into the backs of its hands. It weeps tears that glitter like silica.

To Norra's left is a dirt-cheeked man, his face round and thick even though the rest of his body looks like a skeleton draped in the rags of his own skin. He sometimes grins over at her—the broken-toothed smile of a bona fide madman—and he sings little songs.

Gomm is his name. *Gomm, Gomm, the biddle-bomb, the womble-balm, speaking on the intercom, doozy woozy holocron* . . . His words, not hers. One of his bizarre songs. He reminds her in a way of Mister Bones, if Mister Bones were a lunatic prisoner stuck on a dead dirtworld.

"Fancy a mancy," he says to her.

"Fancy a mancy," she answers back, not having any idea what it means. It matters little.

Norra needs to get out of here.

An obvious sentiment, but true just the same. She's been thinking on escape plans, and none of them are sensible.

The chains that bind them are literally just that: chains threaded through metal manacles. Breaking them doesn't seem to be an option. Not by herself, at least.

She thought about sabotaging the rig and letting it explode. But what good would that do her? It's a fantasy to think that somehow it would bulge and detonate in *just the right way*, shearing her chain and letting her free. Far likelier to turn her into a scattering of charred bone across the sand. Plus, this kesium rig is not the only one. Front to back, another dozen rigs topping another dozen wells sit all around. If this one goes, they all might.

Which means she might not kill just herself.

So that's not an option. What, then?

She has no answer. She keeps working. She tries to cry but no tears come. Norra has no more tears just as she has no more blood. It seems that on this planet she'll just dry up and flake away when the night winds come.

At the end of the day, they throw her back in the cage. A portion of food lands in with her: a rubbery plastic packet of protein mush. Sometimes it's a powder, and they give her a little water with it, and the powder sizzles and turns into something: a ballooning piece of bread, a cup of gruel, a biscuit so hard it's like biting into a fresh-baked brick. Today, though, it's just this packet of goop. She tears the top off with her teeth and greedily slurps it down. It tastes like the happabore spit smells.

But it will sustain her.

"Ah, nothing better than eating one's own sick."

That voice. She knows it.

She wheels around on the one who spoke.

And there stands Sinjir outside her cage. A cocky tilt to his hips and a smug, self-satisfied sneer on his face. He nips from a flask. "Norra, dear."

"How . . . ?" she asks.

"Who can say? I am called and conjured. I'm here to rescue you. My, my, we do find ourselves in cages, don't we? And I don't mean that as a *thematic conceit*, either, I mean—well. Look around you. Metal cage. Imprisoned once again. Naughty business, this Empire."

"Well, get me *out* of here!" she says.

A hand falls on her shoulder. She startles, crying out, raising a fist to whoever would grab her—

"Whoa," Temmin says, holding up both hands. "Hey, relax. It's okay. It's me. It's your son. We're getting you out of here. Me and Wedge. Just sit tight."

Her son. He's *here*. He came back for her. And there behind him is Wedge Antilles, and he's got that boyish smile and those dark, warm eyes, for a moment the pulse in her neck quickens . . .

And yet how are they here in the cage with her? That doesn't make any sense at all. Suddenly she's doubling over, her middle clenching up as waves of heat and cold take turns crashing into her. Sweat slicks her brow even as her lips go dry. She tries to say her son's name, but all she can manage is a sad mewling, like a rodent caught in the teeth of a trap.

She looks up to him, but he's gone.

So, too, is Sinjir.

They were never here at all, were they?

No. Just illusions pressed upon her by the heat. Suddenly she understands Gomm—the sun and dust have blasted his sanity away, like a coat of paint scoured free. And she wonders if sanity is really just that—something to be worn off, a veneer that with enough pressure and effort can be stripped away. Civilization, too, can fail the same way, can't it? Scraped down to nothing, leaving only the raw metal of anarchy and oppression behind. And madness. *That* is the Empire. *That* is what it has done to her and to the galaxy. A corrosive force, eating away at everyone and everything.

A new illusion seizes her. *This* hallucination reaches her ears before her eyes, and she hears the mechanized voice of her son's droid, Mister Bones. Trails of sand slither along on a sudden wind like snakes, and they carry those familiar words of his, "ROGER-ROGER," distorted and broken by static. And sure enough, the hallucination completes itself as it reaches her eyes, too. Norra lifts her head (no small effort) and glances over her shoulder to see Bones trotting along through the camp, pushed along by a stormtrooper whose mask shows the carvings of endless jagged spirals.

The trooper says to a nearby officer, "Found this out by the steppe. It was poking around another escape pod."

"Look at this old thing," the officer says, sitting under a small tent pitched in the dirt. It's the same pock-cheeked prig who brought her here. Effney, she thinks his name is. *How kind of him to participate in my hallucination,* she thinks, and laughs out loud at the absurdity of it. He lifts the saw-toothed beak of the old droid with one hand while using the other to dab his brow with a wet sponge. "This old clanker has seen some modifications since the Clone Wars. Probably belongs to some nomad or spacer."

"I fitted it with a restraining bolt," the trooper says. "What do you want me to do with it?"

Effney pulverizes the sponge in his fist, and a stream of water spatters his outstretched tongue. Norra knows the droid is just a vision, but that water isn't. It's real. So real she can almost taste it. *Water . . .*

The officer, done drinking, wipes his mouth with the back of his hand and answers: "I don't care one way or the other. Destroy it. Wait. No. Send it on the next transport ship heading back to the *Ravager*. The Old Man is up there, and I'm sure Borrum would find it a fascinating piece of antiquity—maybe he'll pull for us to get some more portions down here."

"Yes, sir." To the droid, the trooper says: "Move along, B1."

"ROGER-ROGER."

Norra pushes her forehead against the scabby metal of her prison. She watches Bones march away, his servos whining, his joints crunching as this world's grit grinds between them.

This hallucination is quite the persistent one. Unless . . .

Poking around another escape pod . . .

What if . . . ? Could it be?

What if Temmin sent Bones? Before the *Moth* hit hyperspace, what if he ejected the droid? Or himself? The heat once more is pushed away from her, this time not from feverish chills but from the cold realization that this is no phantasm. That mirage is no mirage: It's Mister Bones. It's really him.

I fitted it with a restraining bolt . . .

Send it up on the next transport ship . . .

No. She needs that droid. Bones can save her.

Norra has no plan. Not that there's any time for one. Suddenly she calls out: "That's my droid!"

The trooper halts. So does the officer.

Bones keeps walking, until the trooper grabs him with a rough glove and yanks him back. The officer and the trooper share a look, and with the hook of a finger Effney gestures them forward.

The officer stands in front of her.

"You," he says. "What did you say?"

"I said that's my droid." Her voice is raw, as if her vocal cords have been dragged behind a speeder over volcanic stone. She bares her teeth. "I want him back. Now."

The trooper stands there, looking from her to the droid. The officer just laughs. Bones, for his part, seems to pay no attention to any of this. In the center of his narrow, rib-cage-like chest sits a black restraining bolt.

"You're telling me *you* own this droid?" the officer asks.

"I am. You let him go. And me, too. Or you're in deep spit."

"Hm." The officer grabs the stormtrooper's blaster rifle. "*This* droid?"

He points the blaster and fires. The droid's arm spins away, detached from the body. The shoulder socket sparks as the arm hits the ground.

"No!" she cries out. "Wait. Please—"

"Are you sure you mean *this* droid?" Effney says through a venomous scowl and slams the droid up against the cage. *Clang.* She reaches for Bones through the metal, but suddenly the air lights up with blaster-fire. She can't see the officer, not at first, because Bones's frame blocks her view—but as laserfire tears bits of the droid off, piece by piece, so does her view of that officer become more complete. His face is a mask of rage, and again she has that image of sanity being scrubbed away, revealing something altogether more monstrous underneath.

Bones stands there. And takes it. Parts of him, shot off by the blaster rifle, limbs and bits banging against the cage before hitting the ground.

Until he has been broken apart into a pile of constituent pieces.

Until Effney is standing there, sweating, panting, leering.

Until she, too, is broken, collapsing backward. She sobs, though again no tears come out. She turns and throws up, but it's just dry-heaving. Norra curls up on her side and gazes into the eyes of her son's droid— eyes that flicker before finally going dead and dark.

Effney offers a dismissive sniff. He tosses the blaster rifle back to the trooper, who barely manages to catch it. "Sorry, scum. It seems *this* droid is malfunctioning." To the trooper, he says: "I suppose Borrum won't get to see this curious antiquity after all."

"Should I clean it up?" the trooper asks.

"No. Let her look upon the wreckage of this mutant machine." He gasps, suddenly. "Gods, it's hot. I need water, let's go."

They walk away. Bones remains in pieces. Norra curls up into herself.

CHAPTER THIRTEEN

A PATCH OF blood decorates the stone wall of her cell.

It's dry now. Dry for days, maybe. And once Mercurial catches sight of her, it's easy enough to see what happened: She fought back, and Niima's blank-eyed slave-boys roughed her up. The side of the Zabrak's head is scuffed raw and scabbed over. Her hair—normally thrust up like the feathers of a proud bird—flops over that side of her head, matted there with blood. The blood's dried in purple streaks down the deep-sea blue of her skin, forming new tattoos all the way to her jawline, framing that famously vicious grimace of hers.

Jas Emari. You are mine.

He doesn't bother greeting her. No words. Just a smile, big and beaming. It's enough to show her: *I'm the one who caught you, little fish.* She thought she outsmarted him back on Taris. And, he admits, she did. But it was only a temporary embarrassment—a failed move in a bigger game.

A game he just won.

He nods to Niima's freaks. They murmur and mumble as three of them storm into her cell, looping rope—*rope*! Of all the primitive things—around her wrists and dragging her out.

Mercurial is glad to have Niima's hospitality—and

he's just as glad the Hutt isn't here. He doesn't know Niima, but he knows Hutts. They're given over equally to brutality and formality, and he has no time for either of those things. (Plus, they're disgusting. Giant, slime-lubed parasites drinking from the blood flow of the universe. Mercurial has little issue with parasites, given that he is one himself. But the slime? That, he can do without.)

Haughtily, Mercurial leads the way. The Hutt-slaves drag Jas behind them, and she struggles to keep up. The bounty hunter is buoyant with triumph. He feels a spring in his step. *This is going to be a good day.* Her capture was easy. He thought he'd have a long hunt ahead of him, so he hired a whole crew to help. And then the girl just drops into his lap?

An easy win. One that still required him to be in the right place at the right time, of course. He deserves it. He deserves the payment, too.

But does his crew?

Maybe he won't pay the crew, after all. A few credits to get them on their way. Or maybe no credits at all . . . after all, what work did they do? It darkens his feeling of victory, a little. Having to share the cut with those old knobs? It would be much better to keep it all—*especially* since they did literally nothing except come along for the ride.

He ponders this as they walk down the smooth stone passageways of Niima's cavernous temple. In this, she's quite unlike the other Hutts he's known. They favor opulence and amusement. Jabba's palace on Tatooine was positively baroque. This, though, is about as spare as they come: It's just boreholes and tunnels sculpted out of the fire-red stone. The tunnels are smooth in some places, scalloped in others, and he doesn't know if they're natural to the landscape or if the Hutt chewed or somehow *secreted* her way through the rock. Stranger still, there's almost nothing powered here. Minimal electricity. No droids that he's seen. Even Emari is bound with rope—not chain, not shackles, not cuffs. Common *rope*.

They pass by more cells. In one of them, the Hutt-slaves hold a man down, carving off hanks of the old spacer's hair. The man screams as they shear him down to the skin. The freaks stuff something in his mouth—a dirty rag. One of them sticks a needle in the corner of his eye. His screams dissolve into mushy murmurs behind the gag. A puff of coppery dust and they begin to paint the man's face red . . .

They're making more of themselves, Swift thinks. Niima enslaves her acolytes, and in turn they make more acolytes. Like a spreading disease.

He keeps moving, putting forth a brisker pace. The sooner he can be done with this, the better. His ship, a Corellian shuttle, awaits.

Still. Something nags at him. His good feeling is erod-ing, fast.

He also doesn't like that Emari hasn't said a word. She's keeping her mouth shut, and while that should please him, it doesn't. Because it means she's not giv-ing him any satisfaction at all.

And Mercurial demands satisfaction.

The bounty hunter tells himself he's not going to say a word, either, and next thing he knows he just can't help himself. He keeps walking, facing forward as the words tumble out of him: "I don't think you appreci-ate the trouble you're in, Emari. And I don't think you *get* that I'm the one thing standing between you and Boss Gyuti taking your head as a trophy. So now's the time." He grins, flippant. He makes a lasso gesture with his finger above his head. "You want to beg, beg. Plead if you can. Cut me a deal. C'mon, Emari. You're a bounty hunter. You know the art of the swindle. Unless you just want me and my crew to bring you in . . ."

And yet, nothing.

So disappointing.

He stops suddenly and rounds on her. "The bounty is for you alive *or* dead, Emari, and I'm happy to take your head—wait, what are you doing?"

Her hands, bound in front of her, hang in front of her mouth. Her cheeks bulge until they don't. A slick string of saliva connects her lower lip to her knuckles. Her eyes flash with mischief.

Mercurial only realizes what's happening when it's far too late.

Jas tilts her head—and the hair upon her scalp flips from one side to the other. When it does, it reveals the topography of her skull, and gone from that side of her head are her spikes.

Three of them. Broken off. The nubs puckered with dry blood.

Where the . . . ?

Oh. Oh, no.

The spikes are in her hand.

Swift staggers backward, heels scuffing stone as he reaches for the batons that hang at his side—

Emari's hand forms a fist around the spikes as she moves forward fast, *too* fast, and already those bony thorns are thrust up through the gaps in that fist, sandwiched between squeezed fingers—

His fingers find one of his batons—

Slow, too slow, the Hutt-slaves don't even know what's happening—

Her fist flashes in front of his face. Three spikes slash—drawing sharp lines from his chin all the way up to his brow. Pain throbs. All he sees is red. He whips out the baton but his fingers fumble, and it drops.

Swift trips over his own foot. His shoulder slams

hard into the wall as he falls. Above him, he sees the blurry image of Jas Emari vaulting over him—with a pivot-twist of her wrist, she uses the rope to yank two of the Hutt-slaves with her, and both of those freaks collapse into Swift just as he tries once more to stand. Her knee connects with one of their heads—and *that* head slams into the bridge of Mercurial's nose with a dull *pop*. Behind his eyes he sees hyperspace streaks. He roars with rage.

When next he opens his eyes, he sees Jas stab out with a high kick—taking out the last Hutt-slave. The neck snaps. The slave drops.

Jas Emari backpedals. Sawing at the rope with her own horns.

"Emari," he growls, trying to stand.

She cuts through the rope. *"Please don't hurt me, Mercurial. Please don't take me to Boss Gyuti."* She makes a gesture at him with her free hands—the backs of each finger swiped along her cheeks as her upper lip twists into a sneer. He assumes it's a rude gesture.

Then she finds one of the bolt-holes leading up through the Hutt's temple—she clambers her way up through the space and is gone.

Her head hurts. Bad. The horns on her head are *bone*. Breaking them off meant breaking her bones. Slamming the side of her skull against the unforgiving stone wall of her cell and snapping them off one by one was no easy feat. After each attempt, she had to sit. She tried not to throw up. Once, she passed out. And then it was back up at it again—wham, wham, wham. Blood slicking the wall. Her brain doing dizzy loops. Until she had three of her thornlike horns in the flat of her palm.

Three keys.

She'd had one actual key hidden there—a lock pick concealed in a fake horn—but the Hutt-slaves found it and took it away.

Which left her with one choice: break off the horns.

They were her way out. And she needs it, too, quick as anything, because this vicious diversion paid an unexpected bounty: *She knows where Rae Sloane is.* She *saw* her. Here in the temple, working with Niima the Hutt. Going together on some kind of *expedition*.

She has to get back to Norra. And fast.

She had no idea who was coming for her, but it being Mercurial both pleases her greatly and worries her deeply. Swift is no fool, and he said something about bringing a crew. Him? Working with a team? Mercurial doesn't play well with others. *These are strange days, indeed*.

Whoever they are, they're now a part of her plan.

They came here somehow. A ship, she assumes, if he has a crew with him. And if he has a ship? Then that ship has clearance codes. Clearance codes mean they can take to the air and the Empire won't shoot them down on sight. It won't be an advantage they can use forever, but it's something.

First, though, she has to get to that ship.

And then she has to *take* it.

The tunnels here in Niima's temple are a worm-eaten labyrinth—she thinks she's headed in the right direction, but suddenly the tunnel curves back on itself and goes the other way. Most of the tunnels look the same. Every time she believes she's figured it out, the tunnels prove her wrong, and she worries suddenly that she's going over the same area, again and again. Is this mark a scuff mark from her boot?

Fear assails her. *I could die in here. I could get lost and starve to death*. Or they'll come for her. She stops crawling and takes a moment just to listen—turning her ear to the tunnel ahead.

Sounds. Scraping. Murmuring. Coming closer.

Jas hunkers down and lies in wait as the sounds grow louder. It's them. Niima's mind-wiped acolytes. Can they smell her? Do the Hutt-slaves know their way through this maze?

From an intersecting tunnel, one appears. Pale face. Sharpened teeth. The slave's mouth widens in alarm, mad eyes flickering, and he comes at her fast—scurrying like an animal, teeth snapping at the air, *clack, clack, clack.*

She kicks out with a boot, catching him in the mouth. Teeth shatter and her foe gags on them. A little voice inside her says, *He's a slave, he doesn't know what he's doing, don't kill him,* but it's too late for him—there's nothing there, no mind, no rational thought, just pure feral zeal. Jas has to do what she's gotta do.

But even taking that time to worry about it distracts her.

Hands come at her from behind. They close around her throat and drag her backward—the back of her skull slams into the stone. Nausea rises in her, threatening to take her insides and send them outside, nearly overwhelming her as the second Hutt-slave draws her back through the tunnels. She kicks her legs and paws fruitlessly at the stone, trying to get her moorings, working hard as hell not to be wrenched away by this gabbling, mind-wiped mutant—but it's no use.

Instead of resisting, she decides to go with it. Like a swimmer, she pulls herself in the same direction the Hutt-freak is dragging her—it gives her just enough momentum to overtake him and crash into him.

They bowl over. She fights into position. He howls as she crunches an elbow into his trachea. The howl is cut short, stopped by a squeaky gurgle. Jas doesn't stop and wait. It's time to move again—and so she does, finding an adjacent channel and wriggling through. Anytime she finds a new borehole, she takes it. *Just keep going. Don't stop. Don't vomit.* She'll find something. Some way out. Some way *forward*—

Another sound halts her progress.

This time, the sound isn't coming closer.

It's distant. Someone yelling.

It's him. It's Swift.

(She gets a small thrill from hearing the panic in his voice.)

She focuses on that sound, zeroing in on the direction.

That's the way she heads, now—through tunnels that corkscrew, where the Hutt-slaves have carved mad icons of their mistress, Niima. And then, from an adjoining tunnel she feels it—

A faint current of air.

With it, a smell: metal, kesium, ozone. The smell of a starship. That means a hangar bay or landing pad. A new sound arises, too. This sound is musical and discordant in equal measure, and now she *knows* she's close, because as they dragged her through Niima's temple, they pulled her through the Hutt's throne room—a cathedral-like area shot through with holes that hummed and howled like a wind instrument, like a musical organ formed of ancient stone. Whether that was designed intentionally—lunatic music to appease the slug—or is simply a natural effect, Jas doesn't know and doesn't care. It means the way out. It means freedom.

She follows the air and the strange music and starship stink that it brings. Ahead, a smooth borehole dropping down awaits . . .

The bounty hunter drags herself along it on her belly. She peers through the space, and sure enough, there she sees the prize. A shuttle by the looks of it—an older-model Corellian ship. Flat, short wings. Big, tubby engine. At the fore hangs a blunt nose cone. *That's my way out.*

One problem: It's got a guard. The rest of Swift's crew, whoever they are, don't seem to be here—they're probably off looking for her. Jas isn't a gambler but she'd bet credits that's what Swift was yelling about.

One guard, though? She can handle it.

From here, she spies the broad, rimmed hat of a Kyuzo. Familiar. *Too* familiar. It can't be . . .

As he turns, looking around the room, she spies his face and recognizes the bounty hunter who used to run with her aunt's crew: Embo. It's him. Even now, she misses him sometimes. He was quiet, and spoke only in his native tongue. But she took the time as a child to learn his language, and as a result they became close. Like family, in a way. (Jom Barell reminds her a bit of Embo. Silent, deadly, but sweet, too. Hard to get close to, but once you do, you see how good he can be.)

Of course, if this is really him—then what? Does she know he's here to hunt her? Does his loyalty side with the job—or with her? And if he sides with the job . . . mercy. The Kyuzo are capable fighters. Embo is older, now, but if she had to lay credits down, she'd bet he hasn't lost a step.

She must tread carefully.

Jas centers herself. She's still dizzy, but she'll have to push past.

With a fluid, silent movement, she slips through the hole and hangs there, her fingers finding a narrow, smooth groove in the stone to help hold her. Her feet dangle. Below, Embo paces near the shuttle's ramp—he's a good way down, but she can handle the jump as long as she doesn't go straight to the ground. Instead she swings herself forward and—

Jas is in midair. Arms out. Legs crouching as she lands atop the shuttle. *Whump*. She lands as quietly as she can, but still, it makes a noise even as she ducks and rolls. There's no time to waste as she quickly sidles forward, ducking behind one of the shuttle's fins and flattening herself against it.

Footsteps. A grunt. Embo is looking . . .

If I can just sneak past him, this gets a whole lot easier.

Jas whips down along the aft side, jumping from one engine booster to the next, until she's on the ground and creeping up alongside the ship—maybe, just maybe, if she can dart inside, Embo won't even see her. Then she can fire up the ship and—

A tall shape lurches into the space in front of her. Perfectly silent. A bowcaster points at her—a crossbow big enough to take her head clean off her shoulders at this range.

Embo has found her. Orange eyes glow in the dim half dark of the temple hangar. His breastplate is scarred up, the gold long since worn off, and the red Kyuzo battle-shirt is ragged at the hem.

"Embo," she says, startled.

The bowcaster doesn't waver. He tilts his head and in his Kyuzo tongue says: "Old friend. It *is* you."

She licks her lips, looking around. Embo could kill her. He could end it for her right now. He's gone up against bounty hunters, pirates, Jedi, Sith—and he's either triumphed or survived to fight another day. She swallows a hard lump and feels her palms sweat. "It's good to see you again, Embo. It's, ah, been a while. Marrok around?"

"He passed away some years ago." Marrok: Embo's pet anooba. A vicious beast to Embo's enemies, but to her, the long-muzzled hound was ever the diligent cuddle-bug, never failing to roll over and seize a belly-scratching opportunity as the young girl giggled.

"I'm sorry to hear that. He was a good hound."

"He was."

"So you're, ah, you're working with a crew again?" Her two hearts hammer inside her chest, beating so fast it's like cannon fire underneath the mantle of her breastbone. *If I move, he'll end me.*

"I always work with a crew. It is the Kyuzo way to not be alone."

"But Swift, huh? I wouldn't have thought . . ."

To that, Embo says nothing. He only shrugs.

She asks: "You always know you were hunting me?"

"I did."

"How's this going to end, then, Embo?"

From behind the bounty hunter, the faraway cry of another voice she recognizes—the blunt, workman accent of another bounty hunter Sugi worked with once upon a time: Dengar. His presence here is a surprise—Swift is really bringing the history with this crew. Sugi always hated Dengar. Everybody always hated Dengar.

Of course, they hate Swift, too . . .

"Back to the ship! She came this way!" Dengar says.

She can't see that old salt. Not yet. But he'll be here, soon.

C'mon, c'mon, c'mon.

"Embo," she says, "I know you have debts. You and Sugi—you two helped people. You did the right thing and I know that upset the wrong people. It cost you. I have her debts, too." She realizes now, the deal for the Kyuzo is probably simple: Embo's slate will be wiped clean if he brings in Jas. Debt for debt. Credit for credit. She starts to hear Dengar, now. Closing in. "Sugi always did what was right even though she didn't admit it, and you were loyal to her. I'm trying to do something good here, too. The right thing. Even if it's not the easy thing. Even if it makes the wrong people mad. Even if it costs me. So, I need you to not bring me in. And . . . I need that ship."

Embo seems to consider this.

"I am old," he says. "And Marrok always liked you."

He lifts the bowcaster and steps away from the ship. Her path is clear. She lets out a breath.

"I won't forget this, Embo."

"As you say, child."

She wants to do more. Even just stand here and *talk* to him—she regrets suddenly having lost touch with him all these years. But there's no time for that. Already as she runs toward the ramp, she spies that old bastard Dengar trotting up, his long-barreled rifle swung up by his hip.

"Jas! Don't you dare run!"

His cannon rifle goes off—she winces as a bolt shrieks over her shoulder. Nearly falling, she manages to hurry up the ramp, slamming the button closed behind her—it begins to ascend as she dives into the cockpit, opens the gunnery panel, and sets the shuttle's nose-cone turret to drop.

As she warms the engines, the turret begins barking fire through the hangar. Dengar dives behind a rock formation just as the turret blasts a small crater where he was standing only moments before.

Time to get out of here. Time to find Norra.

INTERLUDE

TATOOINE

"BRING HIM OUT!"

Two Red Key raiders—Yimug the Gran, Gweeska the Rodian—drag the man in all-too-familiar Mandalorian armor out into the center of so-called Freetown. The man staggers forward, his hands behind his back. Yimug throws him to the ground. Gweeska kicks him in the tailbone so that his helmeted head pitches forward into the sand.

Lorgan Movellan steps up. All around, the Red Key raiders applaud and hoot and catcall. They line the walls all around Freetown, raising blasters in the air, some firing them. The people of this town are huddled together down here in the center. Some lie dead, serving as lessons to the others. The rest wait with weapons against their heads to remind them to remain docile, lest they, too, find their brains cooking on the sand.

Movellan looks down his long, crooked nose and scowls at Cobb Vanth. He lifts his lip into a sneer and hawks phlegm into his mouth, then spits. It spatters against the Mandalorian helmet.

"You don't deserve that armor," Lorgan says, his voice a hiss like sand against sand. For good measure, he kicks out with a cobble-tread boot, kicking Vanth in the head so hard the so-called mayor of Freetown goes down like a sack of mox-spelt. "Is it even real Mandalorian armor? Looks like something hammered out on a swindler's forge. Besides . . . wearing a strong man's armor doesn't change how *weak* you are. Take his helmet off."

Gweeska and Yimug work in tandem, unscrewing the helmet off Vanth's head with an unceremonious twist. With that done, Lorgan now can look into the eyes of the man who has been giving him so much trouble.

"You've been like a grit of sand in my under-carriage," Lorgan says, baring his teeth. "Cobb Vanth. Noble lawman. Sheriff and mayor and all-around thorn in my hind end." He shrugs. "I'm not impressed."

"Gotta give me some credit," Vanth says, gravel grinding in his voice. "I was enough of a pain in the ass to bring you out here."

"Who are you, anyway?"

"Just a man trying to do right."

"What's your game? What do you want? Not power? Not money? Surely this little . . . *cult* of per-sonality is paying off? Is it women? Maybe the armor has given you delusions of grandeur."

"I want freedom."

Oh. So that's it. He grabs the man's head, pushing it forward hard enough that Vanth's teeth clack as his chin slams into his own chest.

There, on the back of Vanth's neck: a symbol formed out of scar tissue, like a primitive star with a series of dots and hashes. An owner's mark. "You were a slave."

"Sure. That's the story we can tell."

A playful flash glints in Vanth's eye, and it only enrages Movellan further. He was nobody, and now he's very much somebody. A slave turned sheriff. A ghost into a man. With Jabba gone and the Hutts in disarray—and further, with the Empire and its slave tax having disappeared once the second Death Star went kaboom—it makes sense that the slave class here on Tatooine would break apart. Its slaves, once given a measure of freedom, would not go so easily back to the cage. But who owned him? And why risk his neck for the others?

"Lemme ask *you* a question," Cobb says.

"I'll allow it. Ask, though no promises you'll enjoy my answer."

"What do you want with this place anyway? Tatooine is a sandbox. Water's scarce. It's hot and dry as a dead man's mouth. Why not leave it alone? Why not leave its people alone?"

Lorgan takes a long draw of air through his bent nose. The stink of the man—and really, of all these Freetowners—is nearly overpowering. Sweat-slick and oily. "If you must know, the Hutts consider this world vital for reasons I care *not at all* to comprehend. What I do know is that Tatooine has its resources. Dilarium oil. Silicax oxalate. But its so-called people are the most vital resource of them all. Some of the galaxy's legacy breeding stock is here, and we wouldn't want to diminish those slave bloodlines." He says this last bit as a dig against Vanth. "Your failure here today will see all these people back in chains. You, too. Your time in the wilderness is over."

"It's not my time that's ending," Vanth says. "You'll see."

Lorgan considers rebutting the man yet again, but what is the point? It doesn't matter. He's taken the town. He's got the man in the mask. Red Key is ascendant both here and across the galaxy.

Now only one more thing.

"I find it strange you thought your ploy could work," Lorgan says. "I mean, really. Just because you have a Hutt-slug doesn't mean you can install it on the dais and control Tatooine. That's what this really is, isn't it? You don't want freedom for people. You see this place as a resource just as I do. Just as I see *you* as a resource. Now I'm going to take that Hutt-slug and I'm going to sell it back to the Hutts. You will be dead by then."

He thrusts up a finger, and two more of his raiders come forward—the wattle-necked Ithorian Vommb, and that broad-shouldered brute woman, Trayness. They come dragging a ripped red tarp, a tarp that squirms and squeals as the slug inside it tries to escape. Behind them, on a chain, comes a fat-bellied man in a long leather hood, his shirtless skin grimy with some sort of foul grease. *Slug slime*, Movellan thinks.

Another twirl of the finger, and they unroll the tarp. The Hutt spawn slug—young, barely an adolescent— rolls out, small arms flailing, craterous mouth crying in fear and pain. The hooded man hurries to its side, cooing to it, shushing it, stroking its ooze-slick brow.

"Shh, shhh," the Beastmaster says. In a singsongy voice he adds: "Everything will be okay. Everything will be fine, baby Borgo . . ."

Borgo. They've gone and named the thing.

He looks to Vanth one last time and says, "The Hutt is ours. These people will all be slaves. You picked the wrong hill of sand to die on."

"So did you," Cobb says through bloody teeth.

Then a moment passes between Cobb and the Beast-master. Vanth gives a small nod and a wink. The Beastmaster returns the nod and begins stroking under the Hutt's chin, whispering something—

Lorgan barks an order to Trayness, and she moves fast, clubbing the Beastmaster in the head with an open fist. The man bleats and falls, clutching his now bleeding head.

The Hutt spawn lifts its head to the sky. Its slit mouth opens, and its tongue wiggles out, tastes the air. And then it howls. What comes from its whole-bodied throat is a shrieking, ear-bleeding dirge.

There's a stir at the margins. Movellan's own people suddenly turning and pointing beyond the walls of the town—he cannot see what they see, but when they begin firing their blasters, he knows something's gone wrong.

Then comes a sound—a terrible howl followed by a mad battle cry. Red Key raiders begin falling from the walls as blasts from outside take them out. Movellan turns, his finger in a wild lasso gesture—to Vommb and the others he says, "Go! Go find out what that is."

They hurry off, but he doesn't have to wait for their answer.

The front gates of the town bash open—

A massive bantha, bigger than anything Movellan's ever seen, crashes through the opening. It has one eye scarred over, and its fur is matted with filth and wound with bones and rusted gears. Atop it is one of the Tuskens, those feral desert raiders who have given Red Key so many problems over the last year. This Tusken is, like the bantha, bigger than all his cohorts—huge, bristling shoulders hold up a head wrapped with ragged fabric and plastered with massive black goggles gleaming in the sun. Red Key raiders attack the bantha, but the Tusken maneuvers atop the beast like a circus performer—swooping down, breaking one Red Key neck with his crude stick weapon, then scrambling underneath the bantha and up on the other before unslinging a cycler rifle and firing a trio of shots, all of which find a home in the heads and chests of Movellan's men. Then the Tusken is back in the shaggy beast's saddle once again.

Other Tusken brutes begin clambering up over the

walls, swarming the Red Key. And yet the Freetowners are untouched . . .

They knew. This isn't a random attack.

Lorgan wheels on Vanth—

The sheriff is standing there. Behind him, the cuffs lie in the sand. The Beastmaster—looking gleeful, like a pleased baby—stands there with a magna-driver, having clearly helped remove the shackles.

Lorgan is fast, but not fast enough—even as he brings his blaster up, Vanth backhands him hard. He goes down. A boot finds his wrist, pressing down hard enough that his fingers uncoil from the pistol's grip. The shadow of the lawman falls onto him, and he stares up at the suns-edged silhouette. All around him, the bark and gargle of Tusken battle cries.

"Funny thing," Vanth says. "The Tuskens consider this place sacred. And they don't like slavers any more than we do. We cut them a deal. We give them water, they leave us alone. They like that we have a Hutt, too. Earns us a bit of respect. And my friend here, Malakili, he procured for them something real special: a pearl from a krayt dragon's belly. That afforded us the last piece of the puzzle: their protection. Though I think they might've done it for us anyway— they don't like you syndicate types out here."

Lorgan tries to crab-walk backward, but Vanth presses down on his wrist hard enough to hear the bones start to grind. He cries out. "You don't know what you're doing, Vanth. You're an idiot playing a game against gods. You stole that suit thinking you can fill it, you stole a Hutt thinking you can raise it to the dais—you'll never succeed here. My masters will come. They'll kill you. *They'll wipe this place off the map.*"

Vanth kneels down on his chest. "What you think I stole, I say I earned. You think I'm just some slave, and that's one part of the story. But you don't know the rest. What I've seen. Who I was before. And I know my time is short. I've poked the monster, and now it is awake. I'll die in service to this town, and maybe this town will die with me, but we won't be the last, not by a long shot. The next ones who come, they'll know me, they'll know my time, they'll carry the flags of Freetown even if Freetown is gone. And one day, Tatooine is free even if me and my 'swindler's forge' armor and my little town have been claimed once more by the sands. Now hold still. I gotta carve a message into your face before I send you on your way."

Lorgan cries out as Vanth reaches for him.

CHAPTER FOURTEEN

THE SKITTERMOUSE DOES what the skittermouse does: It skitters.

Across the desert, its little paws tickle the deadland as it runs—tiny claws make tiny sounds, *ticka ticka ticka ticka.*

This skittermouse is like the other skittermice here on Jakku: small enough to never be seen, skinny enough to fit through a bit of pipe or tubing, and curious enough to look for food in the strangest of places.

Currently, though, it is not seeking food.

It wants to build a nest. A burrow. Its last one was taken over by a pole-snake, and the mouse wants no part of that serpent. A skittermouse burrow is a peculiar thing: The critter tends to find a hole in the stone or the sand, and it lines its future home with bits of detritus scavenged from, well, anywhere and everywhere. A dead man in the desert will remain only so long before the skittermice come and take whatever the carrion birds have not: leather from a boot, tufts of hair from the top of the scalp, fingernails. Stories have been told of nomads in the desert seeing a bubbling fountain oasis in the distance only to come upon it and find the fountain is really an undulating pile of skittermice. Scare them and they scatter, revealing a dead man reduced to little more than bone.

Once the mouse has its burrow material, the creature begins to look for a larger object with which to plug its burrow to keep out other animals such as, say, pole-snakes. Presently, this skittermouse has found a bit of *wire*. Wire is good. Wire can be bent with the mouse's tiny scissor teeth, and turned into a little place to curl up and sleep—or a place for babies to do the same.

But these wires are stubborn. They *just won't move*. Tug, tug, tug.

Nothing.

They're stuck. Anchored tight to a bulky hunk of metal—at least, a hunk of metal bulky by the skitter-mouse's standards.

Ah. But what is this? A black metal thing. Cylindrical and already hanging off the side—it hums and sparks. This would make a most excellent burrow plug, would it not? The mouse gives up on the wires and moves now to this other thing, and the skitter-mouse squishes itself between the black object and the metal bulk to which it's attached—the mouse suffers a sharp spark, but for a good burrow plug, it will endure. It *must* endure.

The mouse squeaks as it noses the black piece free.

The mouse gets behind it and with its delicate front paws begins to roll the cylinder into the dark, hoping very hard that ripper-raptors or vworkka do not spy it doing the industrious work of merely surviving on this heartless, desiccated planet.

For a time, all is still after the mouse leaves.

Then—*then*—two lights flicker and go bright as moons.

Slowly, surely, something comes back to life.

* * *

This is Mister Bones.

The B1 battle droid's memory matrix remembers many things:

It remembers darkness.

It remembers marching with its skeletal brethren in perfect lockstep, advancing on a village surrounded by green grasses, innocent people huddling there in the night. Innocent people who would not survive thanks to this battalion of battle droids.

It remembers spears of light, green and blue, cutting through the night and taking those metal men apart, one after the other after the other. Showers of sparks. Searing magma lines of melted metal. It remembers an incongruous memory, too: those beams of light held in its own hands. Not two hands, but four. Spinning about, *vwom-vwom-vwom-vwom*.

It remembers—no, *he* remembers dancing the la-ley. Singing for children. A program to amuse them. A program to please.

It remembers triple sixes. A designation, perhaps. Once.

More darkness.

This matrix is not one thing. It knows that. Bones is many minds and many lives. Some known. Others hidden. Protocol programs. Martial arts. Combat strategies. Puppetry. Child-rearing. They are fitted together by an eager if inelegant hand, the hand of a clever boy who needed a friend.

Bones recalls him, too. Friend. Boy. Temmin.

MASTER.

Though the boy is not his master because of how he is programmed. Temmin is the droid's master because Bones knows the value of gratitude. Bones has lived many lives. All of them except this one are now ended. To be given life again—even as a patchwork quilt of identities—is a special thing. Rare and precious, and Bones knows that Temmin is his Maker.

And so, Temmin is his Master. It is only fair.

Bones, above all else, cares about fairness. About loyalty.

About friendship.

His friend's face swims into his matrix-mind. Embers of data in the darkness bloom like mechanical synapses, and Bones remembers Temmin—panicked—giving him one last set of commands: *Launch and get to Jakku. Find Mom. Protect Mom!*

Mom. Mother. Temmin's mother.

NORRA.

That is her, there in the dark. A newer, fresher image hits the droid's memory banks like a concussive explosion: the image of blaster bolts clumsily dissecting him. Bones struggles to extend his matrix-mind outward to his limbs, but none of them respond. Diagnostic checks cascade through him and all of them report back:

DESTRUCTION. All four limbs are detached and unresponsive. The droid's head, too, is *partly* detached—its socket lies ruptured, but the metal skull remains connected to the torso by a telescoping cable.

Woe darkens the matrix-mind. Despair is not merely a human condition; droids know the doom of existence and the end of things. And Bones worries suddenly—a deep, hungry worry like a slick-walled pit one cannot escape from, a pit where even light is swallowed whole. He worries that he is dead. That he will not be able to fulfill his mission. That the life his Maker and Master gave him has been squandered, ended now on the floor of this desert, near to the Maker's own mother.

The droid wills this to be untrue. Bones struggles

against the fear that all his lives have led to this one worthless moment.

But! The restraining bolt that the trooper put upon him—his diagnostics return and inform him that though his limbs are gone, so too is the lock. And then, in that revelation, a new memory surfaces. Or, rather, *resur-*faces. That memory brings with it three letters: *ARM*.

Three letters that stand for three words:

Autonomic.

Repair.

Mode.

YES.

Bones is often getting into trouble, but the anatomical framework of a battle droid is quite simple. And so begins a self-repair routine: The cable connecting the droid's head to his torso suddenly retracts—*vvvvvvipp*—and the socket, though damaged, telescopes open and once more embraces the stem of the B1's neck. Bones shifts his head down. His serrated beak digs into the dirt and cinches shut, moving him forward.

He does this again and again. Each time, it moves his frame forward by a few centimeters. It is slow and arduous. But it is progress.

When he closes in on the nearest arm, he again digs the front end of his raptor-skull robot head into the ground, but instead of moving it up and down he swoops it from side to side. Servos whine and grind. Again, it is enough to move the body to the right—centimeter by centimeter until the torso taps the disconnected arm waiting there. *Tink.*

ARM, autonomic repair mode. The socket at the side of the torso thrums as it magnetizes. The arm judders on the ground, twitching as if suddenly and independently alive. It slides swiftly toward the body. Ball joins with socket. Metal claw-clips fix it in place.

Bones sends a ping down the length of the limb. Fingers move. The arm bends. I HAVE AN ARM AGAIN. That arm is a vital tool that allows the droid to—like a dead thing reanimating to life—lift himself up off the ground, where he sees his other three limbs. Two legs. One arm.

He begins to reassemble himself.

Piece by piece. Appendage by appendage. Buzz and click. Durasteel talons pin wires inside joints. The droid readjusts a few bent rib bones. His hand functions as a wrench—enough to tighten his spine, but not enough to fix the bowing, bent posture. The left arm is not fully functional. The right leg isn't fully functional, either. External repairs will be needed.

But the droid now stands in the dark by Norra's cage.

This is Mister Bones.

In the blackness of the Jakku night, Norra stirs. Her eyes bolt open. Something's off. Something's *wrong*. No—

Something has changed.

She swallows and it's like choking back broken blast glass. Everything feels dried out, and when she blinks the grit is only ground deeper into her eye. She winces, reaching out, pulling herself to standing.

The shape of the droid's parts in disarray is gone. *Bones . . .*

They must've come for him and taken him away after she fell unconscious. Once more she feels dreadfully alone.

Out there in the darkness, someone screams. That scream is cut in half. Moments later something rolls out from behind the kesium rig wells. Something that tumbles up to her cage with a *clong*.

A helmet. White, mostly, though striated with finger marks of Jakku dust. It belongs—or belonged—to a stormtrooper.

Blood soaks the sand beneath it.

Out there, another piercing scream. Blasterfire fills the air just after, lighting up the dark. Something moves in the shadows, and Norra presses her face against the cage to see two more stormtroopers running toward the shape—they disappear behind the kesium well, and that's the last Norra sees of them. But she hears their cries. Their bleats of pain.

Now, from that direction comes someone else.

Effney, the officer. He staggers forward, falling to one knee, though momentum bounces him back up to running. He's shirtless and sweat-slick, a white cloth swaddled around his brow. In his hand hangs a small blaster.

He fires it behind him as he runs. He screams: "No! Get away! Get away from me, you monster!"

He is prey. And his predator reveals itself.

The battle droid moves in herky-jerky fits and starts—Bones is broken, Norra can see that much. His right leg is slow and wobbles at the joint every time it touches down. His left arm—blade extended—convulses even as the other arm remains steady, pointing its weapon.

Effney's shots go wide, missing the droid by a considerable margin.

He's running toward her cage. He'll be alongside it—

She growls, scooping up a handful of sand and dirt in her open palm, and as he comes past, panicked—his mouth wide, his eyes wider—she flings the debris into his face. He cries out, clawing at himself.

It stops him long enough for Bones to catch up.

Effney swivels, pointing the blaster. It's too late. The droid's blade cuts that arm off, and it thuds against the sand. Then Bones does to him what he did to Bones—one piece after the next, until Effney is just a pile of himself sitting outside her metal cage.

Bones swipes his vibroblade downward, buzzing through the lock on Norra's cage. The door swings open.

"I HAVE PERFORMED VIOLENCE," Bones says.

"Yes, you have," Norra says.

"FOUND YOU."

"You sure did. Thank you." *And thank you, Tem, for building him.* Her strange, cackling, dancing, knife-slicing savior. "We have to go, now, Bones. Or we're both dead."

"ROGER-ROGER."

CHAPTER FIFTEEN

THE DAYS OF Counselor Gallius Rax are busy. Busier than even he anticipated, for the act of running an Empire is a complicated feat, and he can only delegate so much. Some things require his hand. *Many* things do, in fact, and it is vital that he remain the one in control.

In the morning, everything is administrative. He sits at a desk under a tent atop the roof of the main building. This vantage point allows him to gaze out over their base here in the shadow of Carbon Ridge on Jakku. From here, he can see the yield of his efforts laid bare. The data on his screen is brought to life as *his* Empire grows to power: All Terrain Armored Transports march the perimeter, a line of AT-STs wait on the left, ranks of TIE fighters wait on the right. And above, the ghosts of Star Destroyers, ready to drop from the sky and slice the enemy in twain like an executioner's blade.

Day by day, the Empire grows. The weakness from within is cut out—like a soft, overripe part of the fruit sliced free and left on the floor—and the strong are summoned. They come here. They come to his testing ground.

They come to his *home.*

He draws a deep, centering breath as he is wont to

do. In that breath he smells the scents of the planet on which he was raised—the smell of sun-warmed stone, the stink of sand, a heady whiff of something dead. It dries out the inside of his nose. The rest of him is that way, too: the moisture wicked free from his insides. All of the Empire is hardening—a fatty cut of meat cured into a bitter, leathery strip that has no purpose but to *sustain*.

Sometimes he stops and looks in a mirror. Even he, who has kept up a rigorous physical regimen since he left this planet, looks tightened, stripped down, worn away. The transformation is a pleasing one. *I am metal hammered into a blade.* As he does this, he hums to himself: an ancient madrigal called "Treachery and Countenance." A favorite of Palpatine's.

Soon he is done regarding himself and his Empire.

He goes then and meets with his inner council: the general, Old Man Borrum; the architect of the new stormtrooper program, Brendol Hux; the propagandist Ferric Obdur; and by hologram, Grand Moff Randd.

Rax tells them that war is coming. "It's inevitable," he explains almost dismissively. "We've seen now one rebel ship enter our space, barely managing to escape. Not long after, we detected a probe droid and a scout ship haunting us from the next sector. We've all seen Mothma's precious little speech. Though I am told she is bound in the torpid politics of the New Republic, I assure you: the battle is coming."

"Coming slowly," Borrum says. And he's right. Rax wonders why that is. He's been assuring his council that the attack from the New Republic is imminent. And it should have been—but the days pass and no attack has come. At first he worried that the Republic had a different strategy in mind, one he could not foresee—but now he suspects the reality is all the duller: They've gone timid. The New Republic is not a military entity. It is one of *democracy*. And it is painfully naïve to think that democracy can work on a galactic scale. It is a very bad idea to expect a starship piloted by a thousand monkey-lizards to do anything but drive itself straight into the sun.

Borrum harrumphs and crosses his arms. "I grow impatient. We can stand on alert for only so long. It wearies the men. It tests the soul."

My soul is indeed tested, Hodnar Borrum.

Randd, ever the taut pragmatist, says: "Let them arrive to the battle as slow as they would like. It gives us more time to bolster our numbers. With each day we see new ships join us. Just today the veterans of Ryloth joined us in the Star Destroyer *Diligent.*"

"The messaging of our occupation here—" Obdur starts to say, but Rax cuts him off with a hissing shush. Obdur is an admirable lout, and truly, Rax appreciates the power of propaganda. It is a necessary and theatrical component of what they do, and Rax loves nothing more than he loves theater. But Obdur's function dwindles. There is no more "message." The value of propaganda is nearly zero. Unless it could be used to taunt the New Republic into attacking . . .

No. That would be too bold on the face of it. A magic trick is best performed when the audience doesn't know it's a trick at all.

It is decided. He will have Obdur killed. It's no great loss. Obdur was a staunch ally of Sloane, and look how *she* turned out. (So disappointing.) Ending him must be done quietly, though. Rax will not bloody his own hands, not in this. Perhaps this is a test for Hux's new recruits . . .

Speaking of Hux, the man looks worried. As usual. His broad shoulders curl inward—his posture has been wretched of late. This world is having its effect on him. And admittedly, Rax has been making inordinate demands of the man and his talents. Thing is, Gallius *needs* Hux. Not just now, but for what comes later. He must be preserved in sanity and in body. It may be time to confide in the man more completely.

Of course, that went poorly with Sloane.

A conundrum. One that will have to wait. For now, a different matter calls, one that demands he bloody his hands.

Rax leaves them before the meeting is over.

He heads downstairs, past the prefab training facility—where troopers gather and battle, encircled by their mates and cheered on by bloodthirsty officers. Betting is fast and furious. Their training is more brutal now. Survivalist, animalistic—as fits this vicious world. He has no time to watch them maul one another.

Rax heads deeper still.

It's cooler down here in the sublevel. Pipes and conduits line the hallways, circumnavigating the base's necessary mechanisms. He winds through the hallways and finds the door—the room beyond is mostly just storage of unimportant things: uniforms and manuals, mostly, both elements of a more refined Empire, an Empire that cannot endure.

In this room, a very old man waits. His hands are bound behind his back; his knees touch the floor. Like he's praying. How appropriate.

"Anchorite Kolob," Rax says.

The man lifts his head, his eyes narrowing to tired slits as he stares through the half dark of the room. Even from here, Rax can see how old he has become. Everything looks pinched and puckered. Deep lines and liver-dark blotches mark his face, his neck, his hands . . .

"Who is that? Who are you?" The voice is trembling and cracked.

"You don't remember me," Rax says.

"Should I?"

"Is your mind weakening? Or am I merely that forgettable?"

The anchorite sighs. "My mind is flint-sharp. It is capable of seeing all the suffering of the waking world, just as it is sure to remember the Eremite's precepts on torment—"

"Don't. I do not require your spiritual lectures. I require only that you see me. Do you know me?"

"I . . ." But Kolob's eyes widen and focus. His mouth moves to form a smile as the memory forms— and then, appropriately, the smile falls away. "Ah. Yes. The boy who left. The boy at the margins. Galli, is that you?"

"It is, Kolob."

The man's shoulders sag. "It's been you all along."

"Pardon?"

"You've been the one stealing our children."

A small smile grows on Rax's face. "And why would you say that?"

"Because you did it then, too. As a boy you wooed the other children away from the orphanage. Brev. Narawal. Kateena. They became wayward as you were wayward. Wild and rebellious."

"No, not rebellious. I merely found purpose away from your foolish faith. And the children found that purpose, too."

"And what became of them, Galli?"

I killed them to keep a secret. "They fulfilled their purpose."

"And why are you stealing children now? It isn't your Imperials coming for them. It's thugs and hunters and scavs coming for them in the night. But it's your hand I see directing them. Why hide it?"

Why hide it, indeed? "I am taking the children because they, too, will serve a purpose for me. They will be the first."

"The first what?"

But that, Rax will not answer. Behind him, someone emerges from the shadows of the hallway: a man in a red mask, pointed and demonic, cast out of metal and fixed with hell-black rivets. That man is Yupe Tashu, once adviser to Emperor Palpatine and now an adviser to Counselor Rax.

Tashu says, "The anchorite's faith has ties to the Force. To the light side. A thousand years ago, the anchorites of Jakku bound themselves to the Jedi. But now the dark side prevails."

Tashu bows his head and hands Rax a long knife with a black blade.

"Look at you," Kolob says. "A little savage who learned to sing. Knowing what fork to use makes you no less of a feral child. Here you are, come to show me how much you've grown, and yet I see you've grown not a whit. You speak of purpose. What is our purpose today, little Galli? Why bring me here? No. You don't need to answer that. I see the purpose is now in your hand. Though after all this time, why?"

Rax steps into the room. The knife is light, but feels heavy. Its blade is nocked with teeth.

Rax closes in on the bound man, speaking as he does. "You told me that children were best when they were seen and not heard. You said that children were meant to be quiet and to serve. To kneel and to suffer and to not ask for a life of any merit, for service is reward enough."

"I did say those things. I believe them."

Rax leans in. His voice lowers to a whisper. "You

believe lies. It is not our job to suffer. It is not our lot to simply *serve*. My destiny was greater than that. If I had listened to you, I'd still be here on this *rock*. Kneeling for you. Praying for you. Listening to your bone-chimes ring. Doing the chores you demanded I do. But I have only one chore here today."

He thrusts the blade into the man's middle. He works it deeper. His hand grows warm and wet.

"Galli . . ."

"Gallius Rax, you mean. No more children will be swept aside by your hand. No more will be made to serve the anchorites."

The man smiles, a grim, red smile. "I told you all of life was suffering. And for you, the suffering is just . . . beginning. You are hunted, Galli. All your plans will . . . unravel . . ." He slumps backward, the blade freed with a faint sucking sound as he falls away, dead.

It is done.

Rax feels a great weight lifted from him. A hand on his shoulder eases him back. Tashu says quietly in his ear: "A necessary sacrifice. The dark side is stronger. Our mission here is blessed, now."

Yes, it is. The true mission, at least. He nods and goes along with what Tashu says—though the man has knowledge greater than most, even still, he is a madman. An ardent believer in the black-edged side of the Force, and Rax cares nothing for such mysticism. But if it appeases Tashu, then the illusion that he, too, is a believer may commence.

He'll need Tashu, after all.

Now Tashu says: "I do not wish to rush the sacrifice. I want to gift you the time to revel, but time is narrow and you have a visitor."

"A visitor?"

"Yes. *Come.*"

*   *   *

They go deeper into the underground, around a bun-
dling of power cables, past a coupling of ion panels,
into a pitch-black hallway.

The lights come on. There, at the end, is a figure in
a red cloak.

Rax knows who, or what, it is. He steps forward,
suddenly concerned. "What is there to report?" He
knows it must be something, and it must be important. A visit from a sentinel like this does not come
lightly.

The figure in the cloak turns.

The face of Emperor Sheev Palpatine looks back
upon him. That face flickers across the glass bulge of
the droid's mask. It is artifice, but even as a proxy it
is close enough to the real thing to haunt him. Other
sentinels were merely messengers: They appeared, gave
commands, and were gone. But these, the ones reserved
for Rax and their master plan, are smarter. They're
sentient. Though none truly match Palpatine's strate-
gic brilliance and his dark, terrible mind, they approx-
imate it enough.

The voice, too, is close enough to curdle his blood.
The droid sentinel speaks in Palpatine's voice: "The
farthest perimeter has been breached."

"Show me."

From the sleeve of the red cloak, the droid's black
metal hand emerges. In the center of its skeletal palm
is a projector, and now that circle beams a holographic
image into the air, gently turning.

The three-dimensional image shows a caravan traveling across the valley floor: wheel-cars and beast mounts
and wanderers. At the end of it all is a raised platform
held aloft on hover-rails, eased along by men holding
heavy-gauge chains. And on that platform is a Hutt.

Niima.

The droid's thumb flicks reflexively—like a spasm, but one that has a function. With every twitch, the image changes. It shows the caravan from different angles—sometimes at a distance, sometimes close. The valley is littered with cams, long hidden under the sand and dust or embedded in the rock. All part of a network that's been in place for nearly three decades, now. The image suddenly zooms in on the platform, and Rax gasps.

The image shows a woman. Her black hair is pulled back under a winding of ratty ribbon. Her eyes are concealed behind thick goggles. Her skin is dark.

He knows her. He would know Grand Admiral Rae Sloane anywhere.

"She lives," he says.

"And," Tashu says, "she closes in on the Observatory."

"How soon?"

It is the sentinel who answers: "Given rate of movement, three days."

Three days. Good. That is plenty of time to end their journey.

To the droid, Rax says: "Arm the defenses."

Sloane, I admire your tenacity. But I have to finish this.

CHAPTER SIXTEEN

SLOW, SLOW, LIKE a belly-slit-worm-struggling-through-a-rut *slow*. Rae Sloane walks alongside a massive platform—a stage, really, a dais on rusted hover-rails chugging and buzzing. It's drawn forward by Hutt-slaves pulling on fat chains draped over their bony shoulders. On the stage sits Niima the Hutt, coiled in a nest of ratty pillows under a massive leather tent.

The Hutt sleeps. Snorting and snoring, bubbles of mucus burping up through her nose-slits. The occasional wind comes and tousles the filthy red ribbons tied around her many nodules and protuberances.

This is the rear of the caravan, but the stage and its riders are far from the sum of it; ahead walk dozens of Hutt-slaves. Others ride wheel-bikes or old speeders whose grav-lifts have broken and are now mounted atop rolling platforms, their engines converted from clean turbines to growling, smoke-belching loco-motors. Some ride leathery, reptilian beasts whose bodies are fitted with metal plates and crude bionetic enhancements like telescoping eyes or pneumatic jaws. All of it churns and trundles along through a sun-scoured, wind-whipped valley—and on each side of them stand spires of red stone and anvil-shaped plateaus. Like the guardians of a forbidden place.

Those plateaus cast long shadows across this deep valley.

"This is *arduous*," Sloane growls.

Brentin Wexley looks up at her. He's weary. Lines of frustration have been permanently etched into his forehead. His cheeks are reddened by the blowing sands. Her own cheeks must be stung the same way. Her goggles are already caked with dust, too—and, as she does every couple of minutes, she has to wipe them free with the backs of her hands.

The two of them hang back beyond the dragging dais. Though Niima sleeps, they dare not say anything against her within easy earshot.

"Progress is progress," he says. Ever the optimist. Surely by now it's just a show? "Our fates are married to the Hutt's."

"It's been nearly a week."

"I know."

"We need to seize the moment. I've been thinking," she says.

A look of worry crosses his face. "Do I want to know?"

"You do and you will and you'll not dismiss me. I have a plan."

"What is it?"

"The Hutt sleeps during the day. Which means that is the time to strike. Soon, even. Today."

"Are you batty? Killing a Hutt is no easy thing—"

"We're not attacking her."

"Who? Her . . . people?"

She sneers. "Don't call them people. They're barely that anymore. They've been enslaved for so long they've been programmed into something else." But even as she says it, she hears the way it must sound to him. Brentin flinches, as if the words were almost physical—the back of a hand swinging for him. "I don't mean it like that, Wexley. They're not like you."

"It's fine," he says, newly curt. "Let's not debate what makes us human. You want to attack the slaves, then. We don't have weapons."

"They do. And I am a weapon. I'm trained. I can fight."

"We can't fight them all."

"I only need one or two. They have those wheel-bikes. We take out the riders and steal the bikes. Those engines must have some power. We grab one and we *go*. Fast as we can."

"They'll come after us."

"I know. But what choice do we have?"

"We keep going. Same as we've been. Like you said, it's been nearly a week. Why change course now?"

She steps in front of him and blocks his path. "Because I just thought of the plan." It's a lie, and he calls her on it, his voice low as he does.

"The plan isn't even a plan. It's so obvious, we could've done it from the beginning. No, what's changed is you're desperate. Hungry to have vindication and you hate that it's delayed."

"You don't feel the same way? You want your vengeance, too."

His face is suddenly stark with—what is that? Is it sadness? "Sloane, it's not vengeance I want."

"Don't lie. If it's not vengeance, then what? What drives you to be out here in this hell-blasted dead-land?" She leans in close and lifts her goggles so she can stare at him with her cold, dark eyes. Rage flares up in her at the thought he does not share her desire for comeuppance. "You mean to tell me you *don't* want to put a blaster to Gallius Rax's forehead?"

"I do. Stars help me, I do. But that's not why I'm here. I want to make up for what I did."

It's so absurd an idea, Sloane can't help but bark an incredulous laugh. "Make up for what? Chandrila? Someone stuck a chip in your head, Brentin. You were dancing on the end of Rax's puppet strings." *We all were.* "You don't have to own that. You can just cut his strings because it feels good to cut his damn strings."

"I need to stop Rax because it's how I show my wife and my son that I'm not the man on that stage. It's how I fix what I did."

Sloane grabs a fistful of his shirt. "You're a fool. It's vengeance that carries us. Forget everyone else."

He pauses. The sadness on his face deepens. The look he gives her is one of . . . pity. "You don't have anybody, do you? That's why you don't understand. There's nobody out there who you love or who loves you back." Those words are like a blaster shot to her middle—clean through, leaving a hole as big as a fist. He keeps going: "You have to have something or someone to fight for. Not just this. Not just . . . revenge."

"I have what I have."

"You have the Empire. You can save it."

"This is rich. The *rebel* telling *me* how to save my Empire. My Empire? *It's dead.* It died the moment it touched this planet. The only thing I have—and the only thing I *need*—is the look on Rax's face as I take it all away." She looks over her shoulder at the caravan. Already their lagging is being noticed by the bone-faced acolytes. "I'm retaking control of this situation. You can come with me, or you can die a Hutt-slave."

And with that, she turns and marches back to the caravan. Sloane is singularly focused—ahead, the slaves on wheel-bikes do loops in and around the caravan, the kesium fuel burning black out their tailpipes. She storms up alongside the dais, calculating her path of attack.

One Hutt-slave walks in front of her. He's one of the

few with a blaster—a rifle cradled in some creature's rib cage, the barrel framed by a pair of broken tusks. One punch, and she'll have that blaster.

That will draw attention. She'll need to run and gun.

But that'll time out right—the one on the fat-bellied wheel-bike doing loops will be within range. Take him out. Grab the bike. It'll be like that time on Yan Korelda when she was just a recruit in the Empire and barely got away from a gang of rebel thugs after refueling her speeder bike. One of their blaster bolts literally cooked a tuft of her hair—she could smell it burning for hours after.

She charges forward. Past the dais. Past a duo of Hutt-slaves who babble at her as she pushes onward. Sloane has no idea where Brentin is—if he's hot on her heels or burying his head in the sand. She doesn't care. She *can't* care. Her goal is the blaster rifle, then the wheel-bike.

Then Rax.

The Hutt-slave doesn't even know to suspect her. By the time she's upon him and he's turning his head toward her—

Wham. She drives a fist into the back of his skull. His teeth snap together and he doesn't even make a sound. All he does is pitch forward, face-planting into the sand . . . and as he does, she catches his blaster and wrenches it out of his grip. Now she has a weapon. Niima didn't let her or Brentin have blasters—on this journey they've been nothing but spectators, buckled into a ride they didn't ask to take. That changes now.

But the wheel-bike that had been coming her way suddenly kicks up a spray of sand and goes back the other way, its engine growling. *No! Get back here, you Hutt-sucking freak.* She starts to run, but now cries of alarm rise up around her—Niima's slaves howling and calling for their mistress. And the Hutt does not disappoint: Sloane hears the mechanical gargle of the slug's translator box as it transmits her rage to the world:

"STOP HER."

It all happens so fast.

One slave comes up at her and she cracks the butt end of the blaster rifle into his chin. He swallows teeth and goes down, flailing—and two more come charging up in his place. Sloane raises the rifle, aims.

Two spears of laser light end them as she fires the blaster. Each slave goes down with a smoking hole in the center of his chest.

Something clubs her in the side of the head. Her ears ring as she tumbles to the sand, rolling over and reflexively holding up the blaster across her face just as a slave brings his sharpened machete down—*thunk!* The blade sticks into the side of the rifle. The slave struggles to extract it.

Someone tackles the slave from behind, knocking him back.

Brentin.

Wexley kicks at the freak with a boot, then grabs the machete with one hand and helps Sloane up with the other.

As he hauls her to standing, Sloane hears a sound: The hissing of sand, the chanting of the slaves, and it's then she knows that something is coming.

Niima.

If Sloane has maintained one common belief about Hutts, it's that they are indolent, lethargic creatures. They are called slugs for a reason. But Niima defies this handily. This creature is not some torpid glob. Sloane looks back over Brentin's shoulder, and fear fills her empty spaces the way fire gobbles air—the Hutt slams down off her dais, hitting the sand with a cough of dust. Niima slithers toward them fast as a viper. Hutt-slaves cling to her like riders, their mouths open, their teeth bared. They have blasters. They start firing.

Sloane grabs Brentin's arm and they break into a hard run.

Blaster bolts kick up sand around their feet.

Behind them, the hissing sound of Niima's body sliding across the sand grows louder and closer. She has no idea how near the Hutt is to them—but it's close enough that Sloane starts to smell the foul stink of the monster. She thinks to turn behind her and fire into the serpent's face, but the slaves will just swarm her. No. The plan is the plan and she needs to stick with it: *Get to the wheel-bikes*. She takes aim as she runs, tracking one of the riders with the sights of her rifle . . .

But something distracts her. In the distance, far away in the valley, she spies a flash of light—something glinting off the high-day sun.

The Hutt roars behind her. A shadow falls upon her as Niima rises up, lifting her whole corpulent body with the sheer strength and will of her tail—

The air fills with white light. A shrieking pillar of green fire fills the space and before Sloane even knows what's happening, there's a thunderclap and she's thrown to the ground. A column of smoke drifts from somewhere, and her eyes follow it to the source—

Niima's hoverdais is collapsed into the sand, sheared in half.

The Hutt mistress herself is within spitting distance. The slug is dazed, tilting toward her side. Niima shakes her head as her reptilian eyes refocus. Sand streams from her crumpled, rotten skull.

The Hutt bellows something in proto-Huttese, but the translation is lost to another bolt piercing the air, and one of the wheel-cars suddenly flips up, turning once, twice, before slamming back down on top of one of the beasts. The creature screams as its back snaps.

Turbolasers. That's what's firing on them. Sloane knows that sound. That beam. She's never been on the ground when they've been firing—and she's never been the one in their sights—but she knows what they can do, and if they don't move, they're all *dead*.

Change of plans.

The wheel-bike won't save her. But those plateaus? They might. She reaches down to find her one ally in all this—

Sloane looks over and sees that half of Brentin Wexley is missing.

Oh, no.

But then he sits up, sand and dust seeming to melt off him. Somehow a wave of it buried part of him. He coughs and hacks, but there's no time for him to clear his lungs, so Sloane gets behind him and helps him stand.

She points. "The plateaus. *Run.*"

They run.

Just as another turbolaser blast turns one of the wheel-bikes to ash.

INTERLUDE

CHRISTOPHSIS

ON THE FIRST day, five pilgrims depart from their starship and set out across one of the countless deep cave systems of Christophsis. They set out with great purpose, bringing with them a sacred gift that was stolen from this place not that long ago: kyber crystals, gems that grow at only a few precious spots here on this world. (Though much of this world is crystalline, the kyber crystals are considerably more rare.) The kyber crystals were taken from this world by the Empire and used to construct the world-killing laser of the Death Star. Though they were also used by the once peace-keepers of this galaxy, the Jedi, in constructing their lightsabers. Brin Izisca said that these must be returned from whence they came: Christophsis. To their, in his words, "home."

One of the pilgrims is a droid—an MA-B0 cargo lifter droid they call Mabo—and he is the one who carries the crate that holds what was stolen.

On the third day, as they march up a steep rocky embankment studded with crystal spires and slippery with scree, Addar the human confides in his friend Jumon the Iakaru: "I don't know why we are doing this."

Jumon shrugs it off and growls, "Because this is

what must be done." His whiskers twitch when he says it, as if this explains it all.

And yet Addar—who is young, untested, and uncertain—persists: "I just mean, what's the point?"

"Tonight, around the fire, we will watch the holo-vids again to help you understand." And they do. When night falls, they start a fire underneath one of the vents leading out to the open sky (where Addar looks up and sees a spray of stars that gleam and glit-ter like the walls of these caves). Jumon has Madram-magath the Elomin set out the projector disk. From it emits the crackling, staticky holoform of Brin Izisca: the pastor and philanthropist who governs their faith and their community, the Church of the Force. The image of Izisca goes on about the heritage of the Force, about how all things are connected, and about how the Jedi do not control the Force but rather, are merely conduits for it—"antennae attuned to that cosmic fre-quency," the man says, and even in the holoform it's easy to see the wonder dancing in his eyes like torch-light. But Addar isn't feeling it. Addar isn't feeling any of it.

When the vid is done, Jumon must sense his appre-hension and barks: "We do it because we do it. Be-cause these must return home." Jumon rolls over in his pack and goes to sleep.

And that's the end of that.

On the fourth day, they enter the crystal forest. Here the trees are weak and wispy, their bulk more like threads than trunks, their branches like filaments—and yet they stand tall because they are encased in blue crystal. Some even grow up from the ground and marry with the ceiling. When the cave wind moves through them, it keens and moans, a shrill cacophony coupled with dread, groaning lamentations.

As the fourth day ends and the fifth day begins,

Madrammagath consults with Uggorda the Duros.
His cheeks lose their rosy bloom and his horns twitch
as he says: "We are being hunted." Uggorda confirms
it, and she says: "Stay vigilant." Given how rarely she
speaks, the warning carries extra meaning, and fear
scurries through every micrometer of Addar.

We shouldn't have come, he thinks.

On the sixth day, Madrammagath is found dead. He
goes off into the crystal trees to relieve himself, and
he never returns. They discover his body, cut to pieces
as if by saw-blade.

Jumon snarls: "Now we know what hunts us."

"What?" Addar asks.

"Kyaddak."

They do not stop to camp that night. They hurry on.

On the morning of the seventh day, they hear the
Kyaddak: the *tak-tak-tak* of their many limbs, the *click-
click-click* of their chelicerae. By midday, they begin to
see their sign: scratches in the crystalline trees, gleaming silicate scat smeared across bulging rock. By eve-
ning, they see them: just flashes and shadows at the
margins, far away and down branching tunnels, but
closer than anyone cares to discover.

His voice trembling and his breath weak as they
hurry on, Addar says, "I hate those things. Why won't
they leave us alone? We should kill them."

Jumon says, "They are creatures of the Force, too."

"So?"

"So, we do not attack."

"But we know they'll attack us."

"It is their way."

"Maybe *their* way is the dark side."

"Maybe Brin has it right," Jumon says, "maybe
there is no dark side."

"It can't be that simple. I believe in evil. So does
Brin. Besides—" Addar lifts his shirt and shows what

he brought—a small blaster pistol. "I have this. We can use it."

"You *shouldn't* have brought that. A lethal weapon? Here? On this sacred place? You know the—"

Uggorda shushes them both and they continue on.

On the eighth day, Uggorda is dead. Or so they believe. The Kyaddak come out of nowhere, three of them—their saw-blade limbs cutting her down as the massive bugs pounce upon her, pincers holding her fast. Jumon has his telescoping staff out quick as anything, and he bares his teeth as it spins in his hand like a whirring rotor—he and Mabo leap into the fray. The droid lifts one of the Kyaddak high, flinging it into the trees—branches snap and crystal rains to the ground like a hail of singing, tinkling glass. Jumon's staff connects with one of the bug's many-eyed heads, closing it permanently as it erupts in a gush of fluid. The thing shrieks and skitters away. The last one is Addar's—he rushes up to it, fear governing his limbs. He closes his eyes and draws the blaster pistol, firing it wantonly in the air—not to kill, just to scare it off. He knows that when he opens his eyes, the monster will be upon him, cutting open his middle—

But he hears its many limbs going *tak-tak-tak* in the other direction.

Addar opens his eyes and it's gone.

Together they stare at Uggorda's dead body—until she sits up suddenly, slick with her own blood. Addar wonders if she came back from the dead somehow or if she was just not injured as badly as he thought. Uggorda wheezes, "Let us keep moving. Those three will just be the first. They claim this forest as territory—when we are free of the trees, we are free of the Kyaddak."

They do as Uggorda says, helping her along.

On the ninth day, they are out of the forest. Here the

rocky ground gives way to crystal beneath: slippery and smooth, a thousand facets on which to lose one's footing.

That night, they sit around the fire again. Mabo tends to Uggorda's wounds with a surprising tenderness—delicate despite the droid's massive box-lifting limbs.

Around the fire, Addar says to Jumon: "I want to ask you something."

"Ask," Jumon purrs.

"When did you become a believer?"

Jumon shrugs like it's no big thing. "I had an experience. A vision called to me three years ago. It showed me a path through a wilderness not far from my home. I followed it and there I found Brin, injured after having fallen into a crevasse. I helped him, and he told me it was destiny that we met. That what guided me was the Force."

"You're lying. The Force is only for the Jedi."

"No!" Jumon says, not angry so much as he is incredulous. "They wield it, but the Force is in all living things. It is what gives us our intuition, our drive, it's what connects us to one another. We are all one with the Force."

"The Force, the Force, the Force! Everything the Force." Addar is frustrated and afraid. He has no faith in this, or in Izisca. Just because his mother helped found the church doesn't mean he has to be a believer, too. Does it? This is a fool's mission. A death parade. One of the so-called pilgrims is already dead, another has almost perished. He whispers: "How many more of us have to die to carry this burden? We didn't steal these things. The *Empire* did. They should be the ones performing penance."

"We all carry the burden. We all pay the penance. Because—"

"Yes, yes, I know, because we are *all* children of the Force."

"You should watch more of Izisca's holoform."

"I don't want to."

But after the others are asleep, that's exactly what Addar does. He watches a vid of Brin reading from the Journal of the Whills:

"The truth in our soul,
Is that nothing is true.
The question of life
Is what then do we do?
The burden is ours
To penance, we hew.
The Force binds us all
From a certain point of view."

Addar fails to understand what it means, but he admits: He enjoys listening to Brin. He falls asleep wondering who the man really is—no one seems to know much about him. He and many of the patrons and matrons of the Church are mysterious.

On the tenth day, they walk underneath an outcropping of crystal-encrusted rock, and a jagged stalactite of midnight glass breaks off. It spears Uggorda through the top of her head, and with that she is truly gone.

Then they are three.

On the twelfth day, they are hungry. They have food, of course, but all that's left are protein packets and nutro-pills, and though such grim victuals keep them going, it's hardly satisfying.

As night falls on that day, Mabo missteps across weak ground, and the crystalline mantle cracks hard beneath him. There is a moment when everyone realizes what is happening—the droid clings to the shelf, his telescoping eyes glowing white with panic—

Addar leaps for the crate, and catches the handle.

Mabo lets go, because surely the droid understands that Addar cannot hold both the machine and the crate. (And also, as Jumon will soon point out: "Mabo had faith. He was a believer, a pilgrim like us. And a friend." But Addar must ask himself, is he really a pilgrim? Or did the droid have more faith than he?) Addar saves the crate, even as the droid falls through the open gap.

"Brin would be proud," Jumon says, grinning a feral, vulpine grin. "You made a leap of faith. And the Force rewarded you. The Force rewarded us all." He smirks. "I have something to confess."

"So confess."

"The vision I had. I still believe in it but . . ." His voice trails off.

"But what?"

"I *was* drunk at the time."

"Let's just get this done," Addar says, rolling his eyes. "We're almost there." He and his friend both carry the crate—it's heavy, so they share the load.

And on the thirteenth day, the Kyaddak return. They come fast, limbs clicking and clacking as they swarm from above *and* from below, pouring out like liquid shadow. They shriek and stab, and Jumon tells Addar to go, go, keep going. Jumon takes out his staff, spins it, and begins whipping it about. It connects with one Kyaddak, then another, and the bug-fiends are flung against the wall, screeching in pain—

But there are too many. They swarm Jumon.

Addar hugs the heavy crate to his chest and runs.

His calves burn. His knees feel like they're going to pop. Everything hurts but he continues on—

A locator at his wrist beeps. *This is it. This is where the crystals belong.* Smooth boreholes litter the walls— here the crystal isn't faceted but rather sculpted like wind-shaped glass. It's just like in Brin's drawings. He rushes forward, nearly tripping on a berm of argonite poking up through the quartzine mantle, but he manages to stay on his feet as he ducks into the darkness of this new passageway. Deeper, deeper he runs. Grunting in pain. Holding back tears. Ducking spears of crystal. Slipping on smooth ground. *I've lost them. I've lost the Kyaddak.*

And I've lost Jumon, too.

Soon the cave begins to glow.

In the dark crystal walls are other, smaller gems— each glowing bright. Different colors. Like eyes watching. Red, green, blue. A feeling overtakes him. A strange, giddy madness. It rises within him, effervescent like bubbles, and he wonders, *Is this what being drunk feels like?*

Then the *tak-tak-tak* of Kyaddak limbs.

They're coming.

Panic rushes through him. He turns and sees that the way he came in is the only way—there are no other points of entry. Out there, the shadows move and shift, sweeping in with alarming swiftness, and he pulls his blaster and grits his teeth and begins firing wildly into the space.

Plasma bolts cook the darkness. Kyaddak scream.

And crystals shatter. The walls and ceiling begin to fracture. The air is filled suddenly with the roar of the crumbling roof, and Addar falls, crab-walking backward as the cave passageway is swiftly closed off by a wall of ruined, broken crystal.

He can barely catch his breath.

The Kyaddak are gone. The wall is impenetrable. Many of the creatures may be buried beneath it, Addar doesn't know.

When he has his bearings, he sees now that there is nowhere deeper to go. This is the end of this cave. He tries fruitlessly to dig himself out, but it is no use. The crystals cut his hands. The wall will not be moved.

Instead he slumps back against the wall and draws the crate toward him. He pops a series of latches; the lid opens. Inside waits a series of crystals like the ones in the walls and ceiling above. Hundreds of them.

Addar stifles a cry, then withdraws another of the projector disks. He places it in his lap and ignites it—again, the holoform of Brin Izisca appears. The vid of Brin says: "Just as the Jedi are a lens that focuses the Force, so is the kyber crystal a lens that focuses the light inside the Jedi—and the light inside the Jedi's weapon, the lightsaber. But those crystals can be used for greater, more evil powers—the Sith focus the Force, too, but they use it not for light, but only for destruction. These crystals were taken from Christophsis to power two of the most insidious weapons built, the legacy of Galen Erso, the legacy of Orson Krennic, of Tarkin and the Sith, of Palpatine and Vader. The Death Stars are gone. Light has persevered through the necessity of dark. These crystals must go home. That is your task."

With that, Addar begins taking the crystals out one by one, setting them down into the cave from which they had been taken years before. He sets the disk to project the holoform once again. He tries not to think about how this is the place where he is going to die—or, in Brin's words, where he will join soon with the living Force, all hail the light, the dark, and the gray.

CHAPTER SEVENTEEN

AT THE CAMP, the troopers are dead.

Effney has been reduced to spare parts.

Bones frees the prisoners. Gomm gabbles as he's let loose, scrambling on all fours around the sand. The skull-eyed thing warbles with laughter, kneeling and raising its arms to the sky to take in its freedom. The others filter out to gather around the Imperial water supply and drink till their bellies must hurt.

Norra tells them they'd do best to hightail it out of there, because the Empire will soon come. And next time they might put them in graves, not cages.

She finds a speeder bike. She and Bones steal it and go.

Together they travel for hours. Endless sand streaks past in mounding dunes that grow higher and higher, and soon the bike is cresting each hill and leaving her stomach behind with the drop back down on the far side. Bounce and dip, rise and fall. Worse, she has to close her eyes most of the time—she has no goggles, and the streaming sand burns her eyes. And it's not like she even knows where she's going. Right now, the priority is *get away in any direction.* The direction she picks is the one they chose at the outset: In the distance she sees canyons and plateaus. The same ones, she believes, that they saw when they crash-landed here.

So that's where she points the front prongs of the speeder.

The blue sky begins to dim, bleeding at the horizon line. In the distance she sees a pair of goggle-eyed humanoids half her size digging in the sand. They don't even look up as the bike zips past.

She hears something. An engine. A *ship*. That can't be good. The Empire controls the airspace here. Ahead, a small shape in the air grows larger and larger until she can see that it's a shuttle. Imperial, probably.

Norra turns the speeder next to a heaping dune and lurks in its shadow as the ship passes overhead.

It's not Imperial. It's some other make. *Corellian*, she thinks.

It burns sky and keeps going until it's gone.

Norra tells Bones to hold on again, then she throttles the speeder. It leaps forward like a haunch-whipped varactyl—and again they're up and racing across the sands, fat plumes of dust filling the air behind them.

Soon, though, she hears that ship once more, and she hears it too late to hide. The shuttle blasts past. It's not the Empire, so they should be safe, right? Except now the vessel is slowing down. It eases to a stop, hovering above the next dune—slowly its blunt front end starts to rotate back toward her direction. *Oh, no.* Whoever it is, this can't be good. They have to keep on moving.

Go around, she thinks. She turns the speeder so it'll take a far path around the shuttle. Just in case.

But as she whips past, someone is yelling.

At her? To her?

Wait. They're yelling her *name.*

"Norra!"

She tilts her heels back and pops the brakes. The bike skids to a halt in a spray of sand. She was right— the pilot of that ship *is* a bounty hunter.

There, on the far dune next to the shuttle, stands Jas Emari.

Jas takes the shuttle up toward the red-rock canyons, and there, as night falls, they park the ship in the shadows of a rocky overhang.

Without even caring whose ship this is or where Jas got it, Norra greedily feasts on food from a locker. It's not good food—it's a survivalist ration of kukula nuts, dried galcot, and kalpa sea-threads. But just the same, it may be the best thing she's ever eaten. And they have a water recycler, too. That she gulps down. It's cold and hurts her throat and it's amazing. Everything is amazing. She wants to sleep. She wants to dance the way Bones is dancing right now. Dance, then sleep. Sleep, then dance.

I'm alive. I'm with Jas. I'm fed.

Jas stands in the doorway as Norra fills her cheeks with food. The bounty hunter has her arm against one side of the frame, her hip cocked and pressed against the other. "You look hungry."

"They barely fed us."

"Me neither. Trust me, I had my gorge-on-everything moment, too. Sorry I didn't come sooner. I was in a similar predicament."

"How? What happened?"

Jas tells her. About Niima the Hutt, about Mercurial Swift, about stealing this ship. "Your head," Norra says, suddenly seeing the crust of blood and the missing horns. "You need bacta."

"I need nothing. I'll be fine." Jas, always stoic. "My horns are broken but they'll grow back. Over time.

Don't worry about it. What we need to worry about is our next move. We have a ship and I checked the computer—it has Imperial clearance codes. They work for now, though if Swift reports it to the Empire, that may not last forever. But with clearance codes in hand . . . Norra, we could leave Jakku. Right now."

Reflexive fear rises inside Norra's heart at just the thought of once more flying through the Imperial fleet massing here. Like the Death Star run all over again. But no. This would be safe. They have the proper codes.

And yet to what end? Their mission is a failure.

"I . . . suppose we should do that. Get back to Chandrila. Tell them what we've seen here." She sighs. "Though that means none of this was worth it. We found nothing. Sloane gets away and we've made no difference."

Jas arches an eyebrow. "Well, there is one thing."

"What?"

"I found Sloane."

Those three words. Colder and more refreshing than any water. Norra can barely breathe. "Tell me."

"I didn't see much. It was as they were taking me in. The Hutt was getting ready for some kind of . . . expedition. The whole place was like a nest of redjackets knocked out of a tree. Sloane was with them."

"And do you know where they were going?"

"I heard a little. They were going to head past the canyons. There's some valley beyond it. That's where they're headed. Part of some caravan."

"And Sloane? What was she doing there?"

Jas shrugs with her eyes. "No clue. She didn't look like she wanted to be there, but she wasn't a prisoner. And . . . I almost didn't recognize her."

"Why?"

"She wasn't in uniform. No Imperial gear or markings or anything. She looked like any other dust-sucker or scavenger. She was talking to someone, a man—another scavenger, I guess. And that's all I saw. They dragged me back into my cell."

Norra finishes chewing one last kukula nut. She stares off at an unfixed point as she speaks. "We could go home. Or we could go after Sloane."

"Unless you want to set up shop on Jakku as a couple of sand merchants, yes, I figure those are our choices."

"We should go home. That's the smart thing to do."

"It is."

"Though we don't *always* do the smart thing."

"We rarely do, it seems."

Norra sighs. "What about you? What do you think?"

"Norra, I'm a bounty hunter. I'm like an anooba with scent in its nose. I don't like to stop until the target is clamped tight in my jaws. But I'm not the boss here. You are. You brought us here, so I leave it to you."

"I want Sloane."

"Then let's go get Sloane."

Norra stands and thrusts out a hand. Jas takes it and shakes it. They embrace. It feels good. Bones is there suddenly, thrusting his jagged-toothed droid skull in between their hug. Slowly, his metal arms enfold them, patting them both awkwardly on the back.

"HELLO. I AM ENJOYING THIS HUG, TOO. HUG HUG HUG. A HUG IS LIKE VIOLENCE MADE OF LOVE."

Jas asks Norra, "And where did you find him, exactly?"

"I didn't find him. He found me."

PART THREE

PART THREE

CHAPTER EIGHTEEN

Jom Barell is drowning. He cannot get air and he struggles against the sea as it drags him down. His lungs burn. Something coils around his foot—sea-vines or an eel. He can't get traction. His hands flap like the broken wings of a dying bird, a bird who can't lift off, who can't escape what's coming—the salt water fills his nostrils and his one empty eye socket and the other eye bulges like a cork in a bottle about to pop—

"Wake up!"

He gasps and sits up. His clothes, his sheets, everything pickled in sour sweat. But still he can't breathe, and he grabs at his face and finds something there—a wet cloth. He flings it away like it's vermin.

Someone is standing by the bed. Jom grunts and throws a punch—

But the trespasser handily sidesteps it.

He glares through one bleary, sleep-pebbled eye at his intruder. Jom knows the cut of that jib: a shadow long and lean, skin the color of sakai-wood, everything sharp as a pair of snip-shears.

"Sinjir," Jom snarls. "How nice of you to pay me a visit and . . ." He picks up the washcloth. Water drips from its corners. "And drape a wet washrag over my face as I slept."

"A small torment in an attempt to wake you up," the ex-Imperial says.

"You could've tried, oh, *Hey, wake up, Jom.* Or how about a nudge? Maybe a little tickle." His voice sounds like gravel grinding in his lungs.

"I don't go right to simulated drowning, you old gill-goat. Don't you military types sleep light? I *tried* the sweet-talking and the gentle shake-shake-shake, but as it turns out you sleep like you're temporarily dead. I yelled, nothing. I kicked your bed and . . . nothing. *That's* when I turned to torture, when everything else I tried failed." Sinjir *hm*s. "The story of my life, really."

Jom drapes his legs over the bed. He feels around nearby for his eyepatch, which he pops on over his head and missing eye. They offered to do something better for him—a fake one or, even better, some kind of ocular implant—but he told them to shove it. A proper old eyepatch it would be.

"What do you want, Rath Velus?"

"God, you stink. You were drinking, you naughty lad."

"And I'll be drinking again as soon as you leave me alone."

Things have been tough for Jom. (A small voice reminds him: *You made them tougher, though, didn't you?*) After Kashyyyk, he felt lost. Publicly they gave him a medal, but privately he'd abandoned life as a commando. They chastised him for abandoning his role and breaking rank. He didn't know if they'd take him back . . .

He never asked.

He just . . . didn't have it in him. Didn't have *any-thing* in him, it seemed. Like he was a cup tipped over, his contents spilled out.

It had (and *has*) nothing to do with Jas, he reminds

himself daily, nightly, hourly, every-waking-momently. It's *definitely* not that he loves her and misses her and feels lost without her—because no, hell no, that would make him a fool. A starry-eyed, gas-brained fool.

(Fine, *maybe* it's that he misses her.)

But he also misses work. *Proper* work. He's out of SpecForces. That, thanks to Kashyyyk. He went astray there, committing himself to an unsanctioned—meaning, illegal—military action. Of course, it was a military action that went well, and brought success to the New Republic at a time it needed it. Which means his discharge was an honorable one.

But he's still out.

So, he drifts. He takes jobs where he can. Recently, he washed up on the shores of the Senate, working as a bodyguard in the pool of freelancers the Republic is using to provide extra protection for its politicians. (Their first vote after Liberation Day was to give themselves extra security. Which was probably smart, but to Jom reeks of overindulgent self-protection.) He's assigned to whatever senator requests protection. It's dull work. He'd rather be back with his fellow commandos, dropping down out of orbit, into atmo, locked and loaded with his mates at his back.

Those days, he fears, are done.

These days, he works for the Senate when they need him. The rest of the time, he sleeps. He drinks. He showers—occasionally.

Sinjir says, "And here I thought *I* had a problem. At least I don't wake up smelling like I've been brining in my own grief-sweat for three days. I mean, I think we need to face the delicious irony that right now, I am sober as a vicar and you're the one sauced to the gills."

"Go back to where you came from."

"The Empire? I think that job prospect is soon on its way to extinction. In fact, that's why I'm here."

"I'm done fighting the Empire."

"Perhaps you are. But Jas is not."

Jas.

"Jas can do what she wants," Jom grumbles.

"That much is abundantly clear. She did you, after all." That last bit spoken with trademark Sinjir cheek. Jom should punch him. But every time he moves, his head feels like an aquarium whose glass is being rapped by a bratty child. "And yet Jas needs your help."

"Then she should've come here herself."

"Maybe she would have, oh, I don't know, if she wasn't *trapped* on Jakku with *no hope of rescue.*"

Jakku. That name bubbles up out of the septic murk that is presently his memory. He cares little to follow the news, but some news is so big *it* follows *you*—and you couldn't go anywhere nowadays without hearing how the Empire is there on Jakku, could you?

Wait. Jas is on Jakku?

"Why? Why is she there?"

"She and Norra . . . ahem, took an unscheduled escape pod ride down to the surface, and now we have no way to extract them."

Jom lurches to his feet. He kicks around the trash on his floor looking for a shirt, or pants, or something. "Then what are we doing standing around—" He suddenly *urp*s into his hand, choking back vomit. "Standing around here? Find me my blaster. And some clothes. Let's go get her."

"It's not that easy."

Jom turns on him and thrusts a callused finger up into the ex-Imperial's face. "It *is* that easy. It's always that easy."

"Not this time," Sinjir says, his tone dire. "Surrounding that planet is the entire Imperial remnant. One imagines it's like Akiva—a total occupation. Except this is ten times worse than Akiva. A *hundred* times. Jom, we don't even know if Jas and Norra are *alive* down there. What we do know is, if we have any shot here, that means hitting the Empire hard as we can. And to do that, we need a resolution to engage them. We need to finish this war."

"I'm afraid that's above my pay grade, Sinjir."

"But it isn't. I have a plan."

Jom scratches his unshorn face—the mustache and chops he used to keep neatly trimmed have grown into a scraggly shrub on his cheeks and chin. "*You* have a plan. This ought to be rich."

"It is. You work for the Senate now, correct?"

"Nngh. I work the security pool, yeah."

"Good. How do you feel about Nakadia this time of year?"

CHAPTER NINETEEN

SENATOR TOLWAR WARTOL'S yacht is a Ganoidian tri-deck cruiser. Spare in its design, it is far from a luxury craft. Everything is hard angles and flat surfaces. The front end of the ship looks like a set of steps. Most of the vessel is boxy in some parts, knife-like in others. Presently it sits docked at the Senate hangar—it is one of the last ships remaining, the rest already having gone on to Nakadia, where the Senate will now convene. The cruiser's engines are cycling, and harbor crew perform all the proper cross-checks. A droid disconnects a fueling hose from the tail port.

Wartol does not expect her, and so it is the perfect time to strike. Before the ramp can be raised, Mon Mothma marches forward—a diligent woman of purpose flanked by two plume-helmeted guards—and storms right on board the ship. Wartol's own guards, all Orishen, attempt to stand in her way, crossing pikes in front of her. She sneers at them, undaunted.

"Do you think that's wise? One suspects the senator will be disappointed to learn that his guards cost him a measure of popularity because they turned the chancellor of the New Republic away through the threat of violence." Frankly, she suspects that at this point turning her away might *earn* him a bump in popularity.

But the bluff works—their nose-slits twitch and pucker as they pull their pikes away.

She steps aboard.

Wartol stands nearby in a sitting area, and it gives her a bit of joy to find him startled by her presence. He turns quickly away from the viewport, like a naughty child caught spying on a neighbor. He regains his composure a moment later, and the victory is small, but right now Mon Mothma takes whatever edge she can get.

"Chancellor," he says. His voice is a booming drum in the well of his chest. It has a rich vibrato to it, a doomed music. "Apologies, I was lost in thought. And I did not expect you."

"Odd, given that I have been trying to pin you to a meeting for the last week." She smiles stiffly.

"Things, as you know, have been rather busy."

"You're not busy now. I will join you on your trip to Nakadia. We can enjoy the journey together, Senator. Does that sound all right?"

"Do I have a choice?"

Her icy smile is unswerving. "Not an easy one."

With a gesture of his long-fingered hand, his own guards disappear from the room. She dismisses her own protectors accordingly.

The sitting room is spare: Everything is as boxy inside the ship as it is outside. The chairs are hard enamel. The viewports are tall and topped with telescoping steel shutters. The floor is cold. The room contains no fabric, no softness, nothing to endear you to it. It is as unwelcoming as a brick.

Like Wartol, in a way.

Still, she sits when he offers her a chair. It isn't comfortable, exactly, but she admits that the rigidity of it suits her.

Wartol takes his seat across from her. He lifts a bowl

off a nearby table—as he hands it to her, hard, osseous little sockets rattle around inside it. They look like knucklebones. In each is a bit of yellow flesh, dried and dusted. It's food . . . she thinks.

"Nektods," he says. "Little pod-creatures that form on the sides of our ships, filtering in whatever micro-fauna they can eat. They survive the vacuum of space. They are quite tough, but you marinate them and roast them slowly over low heat, and they become a snack."

Mon has politely eaten the food of countless species—decorum demands it, and she does not disappoint here, either. She takes one of the bony bits and turns it over in her hand again and again. He instructs her to place it to her lips and suck the meat out of its center, which she does. She expects it to taste . . . well, bad. Fishy or mealy or fungal. But it is oddly refreshing. A citrus tang and salty wave hit her tongue.

He eats one, too. Wartol does not look at his food as he eats, though. The X-shaped irises of his deep-set eyes stare at Mon, as if dissecting her. The corneas drift and pulse. It's almost hypnotizing. His regal, deep voice and his kaleidoscopic eyes give her a sense of why he's so popular. That, and he carries the invisible mantle of leadership. It fits him well.

He could win this thing, you know . . . What would you do if he did? Where would you go? What role would you serve, Mon?

Outside: The *clang* of the fueling hose decoupled from the ship jars her from her poisonous thoughts.

The engines hum to life and the ship begins to lift.

"I cannot imagine this is a pleasure visit," Wartol says.

"It is not."

"It's certainly unorthodox."

"I don't think so. Is it strange for a chancellor to want to speak to one of her senators?"

"A senator who opposes her in the election, you mean?"

She smiles. "Surely despite the election, we have shared interests. We both want the best for the galaxy, do we not?"

The Orishen's lower jaw splits and his tapered pink tongue licks along the serrated teeth on each side. "There's no audience here, Chancellor. We're not in the Senate house. Jettison this masquerade and speak plainly—what is it you want and why are you here?"

"The resolution to attack the Empire's fleet on Jakku."

"The one that failed, you mean?"

"The vote failed to pass by five votes. Just five."

He discards an empty nektod shell into the bowl. The ship shudders as it enters atmosphere, and soon thereafter all of space and time seem to *slide* out from under them as the ship launches into hyperspace.

Wartol shrugs. "That's how it happens sometimes, as you know. Votes fail, sometimes by one, sometimes by one thousand. Not that the Senate is that big yet to have a thousand votes, but it will be. When I am chancellor, new worlds will return to us."

"As you say, there's no audience here, so you don't need to sell me on your candidacy. I want to talk about those five senators. Senators Ashmin Ek, Rethalow, Dor Wieedo, Grelka Sorka, and Nim Tar. Five senators, all of whom have voted with you in the past. Five senators who have worked with you across various councils and caucuses. And yet, while you voted for intervention with the Empire, they did not."

He frowns. "They're not automatons."

"No. But they do take their cues from you."

"They did not this time, it seems."

"And yet you have not gone out of your way to convince them. The re-vote is tomorrow." She's fortunate—present rules allow for her to plead her case anew, further allowing for a re-vote. That is due to the fact that the margin of failure was particularly narrow: under ten votes separating the outcomes allows for the mechanism of a re-vote to trigger automatically. After this, no such mechanism will save her. No such re-vote will come into play. Which means she needs to nullify those five votes. "Why would you stand in the way of the progress you so desire, exactly? Why not chase it down? You have sway with these senators. Use it."

"As you note, I voted *for* your resolution, Chancellor. I want this over with as much as you do. The Empire must fall."

"So, I ask for your help to convince those senators," Mon says.

"Help you? Liberation Day really did rattle your head, didn't it?"

She leans forward. "And here I thought you said you wanted this over with as much as I do. Apparently not. You're quite the politician. Happy to cast away your principles in favor of a victory."

"If you say so."

"Let me paint a picture," she begins coldly. "You know that my resolution failing to pass is a mark against me. It reflects a failure of leadership on my part. And so you convince five senators to vote against the resolution while you protect yourself by voting in favor of it—that way, I cannot easily call you out, lest I look conspiratorial."

"Conspiratorial, indeed."

"You've laid your principles on an altar and sacrificed them."

Now Wartol brings the heat to his voice. His jaw

bisects and his tongue ripples. "You do not get to speak to me about sacrifice, *Chancellor*. Orish knows sacrifice. Orish knows what it is to poison ourselves so that the Empire may not consume us and our world. What do you know of it? The Empire never quite made its way to Chandrila, did it?"

"Yes, but I made my way to the Empire. I fought them. I lost people."

"But you didn't lose your *world*. You had the privilege of pursuing this fight. My people had no such privilege. The fight came to us. They enslaved us. I watched them shackle us. And beat us. And begin strip-mining our world, pilfering its resources. Our place, our people, all held under the Empire's thumb. Until we found a way to wriggle free."

"And I would never dismiss the perseverance of your people."

"Dismiss it? No. You'd simply *squander* it. You don't know what it takes. I and the other Orishen are masters of sacrifice. We know its value. We know how to wield it."

"Is that what this is, then? Sacrifice?" Mon asks. "You will throw our war efforts away for your own conquest of the New Republic? The sacrifice of one-self can be noble, Senator. But the sacrifice of the safety of a *whole galaxy*? That is an attack on us all and I cannot abide it!"

He stands up, looming over her. She tries not to show that she feels the threat of his presence—he could crush her quite easily. She could be dead, jetti-soned into space, and that would be that.

"You don't get to tell me that. You don't have the right. Perhaps the truth of the thing is that I feel a Republic with *you* at its helm is the greatest concern," he seethes. "You are weak. Your leadership is spineless and indulgent. Liberation Day shows the truth of that."

"You *did* do it. You sabotaged the vote."

Wartol does not sit back down so much as he falls backward against the chair. He looks away from her as he says, almost dismissively: "I admit to nothing. I will not give life to your conspiratorial fancies."

"Then let me try a new conspiracy." She opens her hand and lets a small device clatter across it. The device has a pinhole mike at its top, and from its bottom, a squid-tangle of severed wires.

He barely glances at it. "What is that?"

"You know what it is. It is a listening device. A bug."

"So you say."

"You planted it."

"That is a heady accusation. I assume it comes with proof?" He waves her off, his hand then closing into a fist. "Oh, no, it doesn't. Just another baseless allegation from the besieged Mon Mothma."

"You knew. You knew that the Empire was at Jakku. You knew that two of our own were going to take the *Millennium Falcon* to that world, and you stopped them. Oh, the guards wouldn't admit it was you, and they tried to claim it was me who stopped the *Falcon.* But they listen to you. You have authority. You have your little feelers everywhere, don't you?"

"You can prove none of that."

"That is correct. I cannot. So I'll have to do it the old-fashioned way: by beating you to a bloody pulp." Her eyes flash with mischief. "In the election, I mean."

"Ho, ho, good luck with that, Chancellor. Your precious re-vote is in the morning. Less than twelve hours away. We land soon—I hope you scramble the votes you need. But time is ever-dwindling."

She smiles. "If only there were some way to delay the vote."

"Hnh. You should be so lucky."

The ship jolts as it comes out of hyperspace. Outside the viewport, the blue lines shorten to pinpricks and once more they're in the deep well of space—but from here she can see the crescent edge of the world upon which the new Senate is housed: Nakadia.

"Beautiful world, Nakadia," she says.

Tolwar Wartol grunts in reply.

"Interesting fact about Nakadia," she continues. "We liberated them from the Empire and now they provide a great deal of the food for our troops. Something about the soil composition—it's just right to grow a variety of vital crops. It's a pristine environment with a huge food yield for us. The vote to make it a Class A protected planet—well, *that* was an easy vote. You voted yes. We all did. We came together on that one."

"History lessons are most effective when they are interesting," he says. "And this does not pass that test, Chancellor."

"I'm sorry to bore you. *I* thought it interesting."

The door to the sitting room opens. A narrow-shouldered Orishen stands there—not a guard, but a pilot in gold and red with his helmet on, his visor up. "Senator, we have a problem."

Wartol looks to the pilot, then to the chancellor, then back to the pilot. He is suspicious now. Good. He should be. "What is it?"

"Nakadia isn't allowing us to land, Senator."

"And *why* would that be?"

"They're saying that preliminary scans indicate we are host to a restricted agricultural product. Potentially invasive."

Wartol turns to her. He already suspects that she did

something. And of course, he's right. "Chancellor. *What did you do.*"

A statement, not a question.

She fakes embarrassment as she pulls out a small, palm-sized fruit from within her robes. "Oh, my, my, my. Look at that. A little pta fruit. Already half squished." She pulls her thumb away from the inside of her index finger—the sap leaking from the punctured skin of the dark orange fruit is brown and sticky and nearly glues her thumb to her finger. Seeds glom onto the glop. What's important, however, is not the seeds or the glop, but rather, the off-gassing fragrance: one that the ship's own environmental sensors would have picked up. And Nakadian off-world scanners do a passive reading of every ship's own sensors as they pass through. Which means those sensors would have picked up . . .

"The pta is restricted on Nakadia, isn't it? They'll have to do a full sweep of the ship and scan for other contaminants. Oh, my. I fear this will cause us quite a delay. Don't you, Senator?"

CHAPTER TWENTY

THE MAGIC NUMBER is five.

Five spies for five senators.

The secret hope is this: The five senators voting against intercession against the Empire are corrupt. There exists a tiny glimmer of evidence toward that end: Conder sliced—not *quite* legally—into the electronic ledgers of those senators' accounts, and in two of them he found unusual credit deposits of unidentifiable origin. (Those two senators: Ashmin Ek of Anthan Prime, and Dor Wieedo of Rodia.) That in and of itself is not *much*—in this time of a waning Empire and a rising New Republic, certain investments are paying off well. The markets are volatile as old industries collapse and new corporations come online, and where there is volatility there are people getting surprisingly and suddenly rich.

That, though, coupled with the fact of a listening device found inside Leia's protocol droid . . .

They discuss it onboard the *Falcon,* in orbit above Nakadia. "Where there's smoke, there's usually fire," Solo says before adding quietly, "Usually an electrical fire near the hyperspace drive, which Chewie always warns me about . . ." He stops talking, looking lost in his own head. Conder jumps in and says:

"Solo's right. There might be something here."

"We follow the smoke," Sinjir says. "We find the fire."

Only then will they find something to help them get the votes to send the New Republic to Jakku, he explains.

But they're running out of time.

Nakadia.

It's an agricultural world—broad fields, orchards, pastures. The sky has a violet tinge to it even at the peak of day, and at night the two moons brighten the dark. The air is often warm like bathwater, with just a faint breeze. It's pastoral. Some would even say backward. The cities are small. The towns are villages. There's tech, but it all goes to the function of farming—for aerating soil, for injecting micronutrients, for harvesting.

The capital city is Quarrow, and it's where the Senate will be housed for the next year-cycle, and maybe more if the Senate votes to extend its stay. Quarrow is a city of only a few thousand. No building is taller than three stories. The fibercrete streets are for biologicals only: no speeders, no machines, no droids. (In fact, the planet has something of a bias against droids. It uses them where necessary, but generally it is the Nakadians themselves who work the soil and tend to the crops. Nakadia has a long memory, and it remembers the waves of droids that occupied it during the Clone Wars. It accepts these machines but Nakadians do not treat them as equal, or even as sentient.)

Quarrow is a city with little nightlife. Frankly, it is a city with little *day* life, as well—it has restaurants and taverns, yes. It has one poma-club, where you can go and sit in a deprivation chamber as throbbing pulse-music massages your every molecule—those chambers are filled with bubbling poma, a fluid derived from the seeds of the inedible poma-drupe fruit. It relaxes the muscles. It releases the mind. Some hallucinate a little. The next day they return to the fields—freshly invigorated and freed of what they call psychological baggage.

There's little crime.

There's little drama.

There's little anything, really.

Life on Nakadia is not easy, but it has an easy *lean* to it.

Simplicity is king.

And so the challenge for the five spies is this: How exactly will they capture any of the five senators in wrongdoing when everything is so simple, so untainted by corruption, so boldly out in the open?

Night on Nakadia. Tomorrow morning, the Senate is primed for its first session here on the planet, but right now Quarrow is alive with the kind of life it has not seen . . . probably ever. It's not just that there are now 327 senators encroaching on the quiet city, it's that those senators also come with their own entourages: droids, advisers, attachés, siblings, children, mates, and lovers. Ships clog the docks. Hanna City, on Chandrila, was ready for what was to come. Quarrow on Nakadia is not. It is a logistical logjam. And one by one, senators disgorge from their vessels, tainting this very nice world with the smug and indulgent cloud of *politics* and *government*.

That, at least, is how Sinjir feels about all of it.

Presently, he is assigned to watch Ashmin Ek, of Anthan Prime. They wouldn't be here if it weren't for Jom. Here, the only ones allowed onsite are senators, their staff members, their security, and those who petitioned for the exception list. Those on that list of exceptions might include journos, celebrities, certain business barons who want to press the flesh and try to encourage industry-friendly policies . . .

Thing is, that list is curated months in advance. The slots are limited and have been full since it opened. Yes, Mon Mothma or Leia probably could've pulled the strings to get their names on the list—but doing so would have been an obvious gesture, and one that connects what she's doing on Wartol's cruiser to their efforts down here on Nakadia. The chancellor wisely did not want any threads connecting *her* to *them,* lest this all blow up in their faces.

That's where Jom came in.

Jom, now working as security, was willing to, *erm,* adjust the list—he knocked off a handful of questionable journalists and added *their* names to it, instead. Solo and Sinjir were easy: Both count roughly as "celebrities" among the most narcissistic of politicians. Solo as a bona fide hero of the Rebellion, and Sinjir as a freakish curiosity ("Oh, look at the funny Imperial. Gasp, did he know Darth Vader?"). Conder has worked for senators before, so he, too, was a value-add for the list. Temmin was tougher to get on, but they used his nickname ("Snap") and put him down as a "military veteran," and nobody looked askance.

So now they wait. And they watch.

It is predictably dull work.

Across from the Quarrow Senate house sits a restaurant—Izzik's. It's mostly outdoors, and underlit tables populate a trio of staggered, hovering patios. Senators crowd around them, elbow-to-elbow, shoulder-to-shoulder, tentacle-to-eyestalk, gassily congratulating one another on their debatable achievements. Laughing and lightly applauding, and now the tentacled senator from Torphlus is gurgling something that may be a song or may be a cry for help and there's more laughter and more applause.

Ek, for his part, is a mover and a shaker. Some sit in one place, dropping an anchor at a table and hanging tight in little cliques, but the Anthan Prime senator is a veritable social pollinator, flitting from political flower to political flower and sprinkling a bit of himself on everyone. He's like a droid on a program: He says the same things, makes the same sounds, offers the same congratulations, bellows the same laughs at the same times.

None of it is untoward. It's all entirely aboveboard.

That worries Sinjir. Because right now, they're looking for something that may not be there. The simplest answer is almost always the truest, and here the simplest answer is that the five senators who voted against Mon Mothma's resolution did so because they are politicians. They have agendas and those agendas needn't line up with the safety of the galaxy. Oh, sure, it's lovely to believe everyone has the best interests of the greater good at heart, but to seek power—to want a hand helping steer the galaxy's fate!—is an act of ultimate ego. It is an act of *self* no matter how self*less* one portrays it. Which means there is likely no conspiracy here except the all-too-common conspiracy of *aggressive self-interest*.

As Sinjir slowly orbits Senator Ek, winding his way surreptitiously through the crowd of (shudder) politicians, he spies a familiar face across the uppermost patio: Conder.

Conder smirks. Coy, boyish, playful. That monster.

Sinjir ignores him. Or tries to.

He leans back against the bar and gently speaks into the comlink at his wrist: "No good news to report."

"I got good news," Solo says through Sinjir's earpiece. Han isn't here—he's at the northernmost spaceport just outside Quarrow, where Senator Dor Wieedo from Rodia remains in his ship. Solo's enough of a known quantity in the New Republic that putting him somewhere too public like Izzik's is a good way to gum up the works. Everyone would be stopping the "hero of the Rebellion," fawning over him, asking him about Luke, about Leia, about that damn Kessel Run he likes to go on about. "Mon's plan worked. I just heard it from one of the stevedores on break: Wartol's ship is being held out of queue in quarantine while they wait for an inspection crew to come aboard. It'll be awhile, but I don't know that it buys us much time. Twelve hours at best, and I never like to expect the best."

"We're not going to find anything," Sinjir says.

Jom's turn to talk: "We need to kriffing find something." He's watching Rethalow of Frong at one of the poma-clubs. "I still don't understand why we can't just go up, knock these traitors on the head, and ask them what they're up to. Sinjir, you can do that. Tell them to vote how we like or they'll have to listen to you drone on about whatever it is you like to drone on about. That'd be real torture."

A laugh over the comlink. Conder.

Conder's here at Izzik's watching Nim Tar, the bobble-headed Quermian. That long-necked senator sits off in the far corner, nervously nursing some kind of fruit drink and looking like he doesn't want to be here at all. "Patience," Conder says. "Night's still young."

"I'm still young, too," Temmin says. He's the last of them, and he's across from the Senate house on a balcony, keeping an eye on Grelka Sorka, the senator from Askaj. She's already busy working, running some committee about—well, Sinjir forgets what. Probably a committee designated to give themselves pay raises.

Or a committee designed to design other committees. Temmin groans. "I'm young now but I feel myself getting older by the minute. This sucks vapor. I hate it."

Sinjir wants to chide the boy—*It is necessary, Temmin*—but that's a line he's not sure even he buys. He wants to do what they all want to do: grab the *Falcon*, fly to Jakku, blow up the Empire single-handedly, and save Norra and Jas as an epic, heroic gesture. Except they can't. They'll get killed. Or start a galactic incident and end up getting Wartol elected anyway. So here they wait. Watching senators in the hope that at least one of them is visibly corrupt in a way to provide them with enough leverage to win the vote.

Hours pass.

Nothing happens. At least, nothing *interesting*. At Izzik's, the Torphlusian tentacle-pile is still "singing." Two Verpine advisers got into a loud argument at a table, chittering and rubbing their saw-blade arms together (the resultant sound made Sinjir want to puncture both of his eardrums with a toothpick), and now those *same* two Verpine are leaning over a *different* table, lustily rubbing their mouthparts together. Otherwise, it's the same glad-handing, back-scratching crowd of politicos.

Ashmin Ek is tireless. Other senators have gone, their numbers replenished as the night goes on, but not Ek—the senator from Anthan Prime remains, the same plastic smile on his face, the same half-full drink in his hand, the same time spent whirling about.

The others aren't having any luck, either. Dor Wieedo remains in his ship. Rethalow remains inside its poma-club dep tank. Temmin reports that Grelka Sorka is no longer in committee and is now outside the Senate house, just milling about. Nim Tar has loosened up a little bit and has left the safety of her corner table, moving one table over to talk to the young Ryloth emissary, Yendor. (Sinjir spies Conder hovering about in that direction. Every time he catches that glimpse, his heart rate picks up, his mouth goes wet, his throat gets tight. He tells himself it's because he's bored, or anxious, or not properly drunk enough. Which is to say, not drunk at all—a heinous mistake if ever there was one.)

Night drifts toward the cliff's edge of morning.

And then Solo says:

"I got something here."

A flurry of questions: What? Who? Where?

"Couple of Nikto. Plus a Klatooinian. They're headed toward Wieedo's ship. They're not armed, but they sure don't look like they're from Nakadia, and neither could be senators. I know scum when I see it."

"Be careful," Jom says over the comm.

"Relax, I got this," Han says.

Now Sinjir's blood is up. It's probably nothing, but his skin prickles with the twin sensations of excitement and fear. He roots himself near the bar and keeps an eye out. There's Ek, over by a table of Arconans— and approaching now is someone in the gold, red, and white of Alderaan. Did they finally elect a senator, even though the planet is destroyed? A nail of guilt sticks in Sinjir's heart. He had literally nothing to do with the destruction of that planet, but even still, when he heard that the Empire had destroyed it, he had weeks of nightmares about it. Millions of people dying . . .

A hand grabs his elbow.

He tenses up like an animal about to strike, spinning heel-to-toe—

Only to see a young woman standing there. A young man hurries up behind her. She has golden hair and bronze skin. He's a bit shorter, with a body thin as an antenna but a head round as a moon.

"You're him," she says.

"And you're her," Sinjir answers, irritated. "Glad we got that out of the way, now if you'll excuse me—"

"You're the Imperial," the young man says, beaming.

"*Ex*-Imperial," she corrects with a very temporary scowl before her big smile returns. To Sinjir she says in a low voice: "You'll have to excuse Dann, he is a bit thick. My name is Merra."

"Yes. Good. Fine. Nice to meet you."

In his ear comes Temmin's voice: "Hold on. Senator Sorka is slipping away—she's ducking around the corner. I'm gonna follow her."

"Be careful," Jom chides. "Han, you got anything?" But there's no answer.

Sinjir tries to push past the two wide-eyed wonder children standing there, but the girl reasserts herself in front of him, blocking his path.

"We're Akivans," Merra says excitedly. "Our mother, Pima Drolley, is the newly appointed senator here."

"Lovely," Sinjir says. He lifts his eyes above them, expecting to see Ashmin Ek with the Arcona contingent—but they're there alone with the Alderaanian woman. Ek isn't there. *Blast it all to hell.* He scans the crowd looking for that meringue peak of silver hair—there, is that him? No!

"Akiva," Dann says, laughing nervously. "You know, the planet you . . . helped liberate?"

"Uh-huh, wonderful planet. Hotter than a bantha's belly, but just wonderful." Still no Ek anywhere. He's taller than most here, so he lifts himself up on his toes and glances over toward Nim Tar—

The Quermian is gone.

And so is Conder.

"I have to go," he says suddenly.

The young woman interrupts again: "If you have a moment, our mother would like to meet you and thank you in person—"

"No time."

"You're not a very good senator," Dann says, suddenly bitter.

Sinjir bares his teeth. "That's because I'm not a senator, you bloat-headed buffoon." He pushes between the two of them and heads deeper into the crowd. He's not thinking straight enough to be surreptitious, so he speaks right into the comm: "Hello?" he says. "Conder? Where is he?"

"How should I know?" Jom asks. "Han, Tem, you got anything?"

Neither of them answers.

"Jom, what's at your location?"

The commando answers: "Nothing. Everything's fine here. Rethalow's still in the dep chamber."

"No suspicious characters? No *shenanigans* of note?"

"No. Where is everyone else?"

"I don't know." Sinjir winces. "I lost Ek, too."

"Bloody kriffing *hellstar,* Sinjir."

Don't worry, I'm just as disappointed in myself. He says nothing and gets moving, cleaving a hard line through the crowd of senators, looking for Ashmin Ek or Nim Tar or Conder (*please be all right*) and seeing none of them. He hops down off the farthest patio, onto the fibercrete street—he does a loop around the whole restaurant. He moves past the trash compactors out back, feet splashing in puddles from a recent rain. Then he moves up the other side of the building, down a narrow alley—

There.

Ashmin Ek *and* Nim Tar. The man from Anthan Prime is shorter than the Quermian, and yet somehow seems to lord over Nim Tar—Ek is seething. He's got the long-necked alien by the scruff of his shirt, and with his other hand he thrusts a smug, accusatory index finger up in the alien's face. Sinjir begins to march right toward them.

"Hey! Hey, stop right there," he says before a plan actually forms in his head. *I'm not security bureau, what am I doing?* They turn toward him, looking like children with their hands caught in the sweets drawer.

Ek's eyes flit to him. And then *past* him. As if—

Sinjir hears the scuff of a boot.

There's someone behind me.

Something hard clubs him in the back of the head. A white flash pops behind his eyes, and it's lights-out even before he hits the ground.

INTERLUDE

CORUSCANT

CORUSCANT IS IN chaos, and Mas Amedda is trapped.

He's a prisoner of his own Empire. Those few remaining here in the impenetrable Imperial Palace are keeping him to his quarters. He has not left in months. Those present are loyal not to him, no. They belong to another: to Gallius Rax, the true keeper of the Empire's fate and fortunes.

Rax sent him a handwritten letter—a rare thing to see, something only Palpatine himself was known to do from time to time—when this all began. It said, quite simply:

Glorious leader of the Empire,

I have taken Jakku. I have brought the Empire with me. You are still its leader in name. But you will be confined to your quarters until it's all over. Do not try to leave. The doors are sealed (even the ones to the balcony, in case you entertained the idea of jumping), and any attempt to escape will be met with reciprocal violence meant to hobble you. I assure you, this is to keep you safe so that you may lead us again one day.

With great honor and respect,
Counselor Gallius Rax

What a pompous gas-bladder.

Rax was making no joke when he said he would hobble Amedda given any escape attempt. Just days into his cozy imprisonment, he tried to assault the two guards outside his door. He broke a plate across one's head, threw a clumsy, telegraphed fist at the other. They handily dispatched him. Before he knew what was happening, a boot connected with his knee and he went down on the floor. One grabbed that leg and gave it a twist—the tendons tweaked and he couldn't walk for days. Even now it gives him some trouble, with lightning whips of pain going up from his heel and into his hips. Woe and misery.

They bring him food—good food, not victuals fit for an Emperor, no, but it's not gruel, either. Most days he's alone, the exception being when they bring him those meals. He wondered at first why they didn't just kill him. Why would Rax want him around? Then they showed him. Blaster pressing hard against the back of his head, a band of ISB agents forced him to record a holovid, thanking the troops for their service, thanking Gallius Rax for his military leadership, and assuring the Empire that victory would soon be theirs. They force him to do this from time to time. Once every month or so. It is soul crushing. He'd rather die.

(Though sometimes, that desire to find death is supplanted by something else: a parade of fantasies where he wraps his fingers around the neck of Gallius Rax and crushes the man's windpipe.)

For a time, he hoped that Sloane was his salvation. They had a common enemy. But Rax found a way to end her. Lured her to Chandrila where, as the rumor goes, she fell off a skybridge to her death.

And now Mas Amedda has nothing and no one. He looks around his quarters. It is filthy. He has not washed himself in days. The room's practically a mid-den heap at this point. Even his clothes are dirty. He would send them down the laundry vacu-tube—but that stopped working days ago.

Instead, he sits. He makes tea. He stares at the wall.

Inside this room, all is quiet and serene.

Outside in the city, madness has taken hold. He can see it from his windows when he chooses to look. Once in a while, an explosion will bloom in the distance. Anytime he opens the blinds, he can spy wreckage—usually Imperial, an ISB speeder or ship, sometimes crashed into the ground, sometimes into a rooftop. When they bring him food, he asks questions: What is happening? Who is out there? Are we safe? The only answer he gets is that he can be assured that the Imperial Palace is impenetrable. Then the guard will say something along the lines of, "The city is fine and remains under ISB control." Which is a lie so obvious it's like an ugly nose: Everyone can see it, even the one who wears it.

This is the best that Mas can figure: They have lost Coruscant.

Given that he has not seen New Republic ships, he wonders to whom it has been lost. Is there still an Imperial blockade in space? Or has the criminal underworld finally ruptured like a straining boil? Have the inmates taken over the asylum? He always warned Palpatine that curating such a close connection to the underworld—and keeping them so *near*—was a dangerous gambit. Mas Amedda is a creature of law and order—a man of numbers, a man of rules. Cozying up to scum like that always bristled him.

Though he never said much in objection, did he? The Emperor had his design. He did not brook dissent. He did not brook something so disagreeable as a dubious glance. Palpatine only accepted advice when it was asked for—and never before.

The Empire. What a grand and malignant failure. A

pile of waste, and Mas Amedda is seated precisely at its pinnacle.

He wants to weep. But he has nothing left.

He sleeps for a time.

Then, a noise. It must be mealtime once again for the prisoner.

No. This sound is coming from . . .

The laundry vacu-tube?

It's faint, the sound. A thumping here. The straining of thin metal there: *da-dunk, barrump*. A faint susurrus following.

Ah. Someone is, at last, repairing the damnable vacu-tube. Well, at least he'll be able to get his clothes clean once again. If he cares enough to bother. And maybe he doesn't.

With that mystery solved, Amedda again drifts off to sleep.

That is, until another noise startles him awake. This time, when his eyes pop open, he discovers with bowel-clenching shock that he is not alone.

He is, in fact, surrounded.

Filthy urchin children form a half circle around his chaise, and their presence confirms for him what he has long feared: His mind has been well and truly lost and he is now in thrall to a very vivid hallucinogenic life. At the fore of this vivid delusion is a soot-cheeked redheaded boy, his lip cleft by a fishhook scar, giving him a natural sneer.

Naturally, the child has a blaster. They all do.

"Go on, do it," Amedda says drearily.

The boy seems taken aback by this. He shares looks with the other five children. A girl with dark braids forming a crown on her head makes a sour face. "You *want* to die?" she asks. "Iggs, you hear this bugger?"

The sneering boy—Iggs, apparently—lifts the blaster.

"Well, Nanz, I suppose we oblige this leech and send him on to the next life."

He lifts the blaster, and it's then that Mas Amedda begins to cry. The tears are not tears of fear or hate or rage. They are the blubbering, plaintive cries of a man set on the edge but never allowed to come away from it—nor allowed to leap over its precipice. Here, finally, a release awaits. Even if this release is the dream of a sleeping mind or the vision from a broken one.

The blaster barrel, like a black eye, stares at him.

One of the other children—a bug-eyed Ongree boy—twists the mouth that sits in the center of his bulbous forehead and says to Iggs: "I don't think this is gonna work, Iggsy."

"Bah, kriff it, I think you're right, Urk," the towhead says. He lowers the blaster. Amedda shakes his head.

"No! It'll work. Just do it. *Please.*" He paws at the weapon, but the boy pulls it away in a taunting gesture.

"What am I missing?" Nanz asks. "Let's ax the monster before anybody hears us! We have to get back *out,* you know."

"Look at him," Iggs says. "He's not who we thought. This blue bucket of flab couldn't lead a fly to a stack of dung much less the whole of the Empire. We pop him, we probably do him and the rest of the bucketheads a favor." The children all look to one another and seem to come to the same conclusion with a series of half shrugs and nods.

Amedda presses himself further into the comfort of the chaise. "What will you do, then?"

Nanz says: "I guess we haven't figured that out, yet."

"Who . . . who are the lot of you?"

Iggs lifts his chin with pride. "Anklebiter Brigade. Or part of it."

One by one, they identify themselves.

"I'm Iggs," the redheaded boy says.

The girl with the braids: "Nanz."

Bug-eyed Ongree: "Urk G'lar."

A pair of Bith who may be twins or who might just be Bith who look like each other (Mas Amedda has a difficulty differentiating them) name the other: "He's Hoolie." "She's Jutchins."

"Wenchins," says the last, another human boy.

"How'd you get in here?" Amedda asks them.

The Ongree, Urk, says: "Laundry tube. We broke it. Climbed up. Big enough for a kid to get through."

How foolishly simple, Amedda thinks. And then comes the mad irony that Imperial engineers and architects were very good at creating very narrow—and very vulnerable—spaces in their designs. He begins to wonder if they had rebel collaborators building in such weaknesses . . .

"Help me escape," Amedda says.

"You must be a real dum-dum," Wenchins says.

Iggs waves it off. "Can't fit you down the vacu-tube."

"I can get us executive access to the turbolift. We just have to clear the hallway. We get to the lift, I can get us out of here. The hallway has three guards. I cannot overpower them, as I have no weapons. But you . . . you have *blasters.* Help me escape and I'll help you."

Again the children confer silently. Raised eyebrows all around.

Urk leans in, staring with those big yellow eyes. "What's in it for us?"

"You're rebels?"

"Of a sort. We rebel," Iggs says.

"Get me clear, I can turn myself in. I'll give the Republic the codes to open the doors to the Imperial Palace. I'll tell them everything. I'll surrender the whole Empire." Of course, Mon Mothma did not accept his surrender last time, but these children do not know that. Further, maybe he can offer more this time. Maybe he can do it right. *"Please."*

It's Iggs that finally nods and says, "Deal."

"He could betray us," Urk says.

"Enh. He's done for. I figure he tries that they'll just lock him back in here. Look around—this lump is just a prisoner in his own chambers."

"But we could die," Nanz hisses in his ear.

"That was always on the table," the boy says— a surprisingly stoic thing to say given his age. But Amedda fears this child has seen more than most Imperial bureaucrats ever have. "We die, we die. Least we die with our hands free and not tied behind us. Let's get it done." To Amedda, Iggs says in a low voice: "We're going to get you out of here. But if you try to twist your way out and mess with us, I'll shove you so far down that laundry chute you'll wish you were back here sleeping in your own filth again."

"Deal," Amedda says.

"Deal. Now let's get you to the Republic."

CHAPTER TWENTY-ONE

THE OBSERVATORY'S DEFENSES made short work of the Hutt's caravan, but Gallius Rax can see that, regrettably, they failed to finish the job. Now night has fallen and his quarry is positioned defensively behind pillarlike plateaus down in the valley. He flicks from screen to screen, watching. Sloane and someone else—some man he does not know—are behind the eastern pillar. Niima and some of her Hutt-slaves are hidden in the shadow of the western plateau. The good news is that they're all trapped, pinned there by the turbolasers. They could try to run, but they would end up like the rest of the caravan: smoking wreckage and tangled corpses.

Rax remains down in the bowels of the Imperial base. The sentinel stands in the corner, projecting images from the center of its hand.

In walks Tashu. And with Tashu comes Brendol Hux.

"I have retrieved him," Tashu says with a dramatic bow.

"It's late," Hux says, his lips smacking drily together. "What is all this? Why am I summoned at this hour?"

It takes a moment for Hux to regard the strange scene: a spare room with dark blastocrete walls, a red-robed sentinel with Palpatine's face, and images of the Jakku desert projected into the air.

"I need your help," Rax says to Brendol Hux.

"Wh . . . what kind of help?"

"I need to know: Are your recruits ready?"

"I need more time . . ." Hux flinches. "*They* need more time."

"They have no more time. Prove your worth to me, Brendol."

Hux's eyes search the screens and the sentinel's flickering face, trying to make some sense of all of this. "I . . ."

"Prove yourself and I'll tell you what's really going on."

"I don't understand . . ."

"Fail me and you will spend the rest of your days wandering this graceless desert." It is a bold offering. Rax knows full well that Hux could try to leave here and tell the others in the council what's happening. They could attempt a coup against him, though it would not succeed. Still, Brendol Hux is not a popular man. He isn't army, he isn't navy. He's cold, smug, stubborn. He spends his time alone. Even his own son stays away from him—and that boy has no friends here, either. With the fall of the Empire, Hux and his son have been increasingly alienated.

And this is a way back in. A way out of isolation. A reward, dangling there in front of him.

Will he jump for it? Or will he wilt like a flower in this dead place?

Hux nods, puffing out his chest. "They'll do what you need. Just tell me what it is and I will have them ready to serve."

Rax smiles. "Good."

*   *   *

"What happened down there?"

Norra asks because the fuzzy view through the quadnocs—stolen from the Corellian shuttle, now parked behind them—gives no meaningful answer. Jas flew the ship up here to the effective end of Niima's canyons and caverns, parking it atop a tall, toothy ridge that overlooks a broad valley that opened up in the desert. There the valley extends outward, guarded on both sides by a gauntlet of plateaus and megaliths, striated in the colors of fire and blood. But it's not the valley that puzzles them.

It's what's in it.

Down there, about five klicks out, is a caravan in ruins. Something laid waste to it. A dais sits collapsed, broken in half like a shattered table. All around lie the smoking remains of wheel-bikes and speeders. Pack beasts dot the area, dead. And there are human corpses, too. White as bone. Painted that way, Jas said: Hutt-slaves belonging to the slug boss, Niima.

Niima is there, too. Norra spies the long-tailed slug waiting on this side of one of the plateaus. She's not alone—some of those white-painted slaves crawl all over her like bugs swarming a fallen log.

Norra leans into the crook of where two jutting stones meet, then turns the 'nocs east—

That is where she finds Sloane.

Sloane's hunkered down there between the wall of an anvil-like plateau and a small pile of ancient broken boulders. The admiral, too, is not alone: Someone is with her. A man, hiding behind a spire-like stone.

"My take," Jas says, "is that we're talking turbo-lasers. Look past the broken caravan. Another couple of klicks." Norra refocuses the quadnocs for a more distant view—they're night-vision, but the thermal view still distorts what she sees. Just the same, she sees *something* out there. Something boxy, moored to the

slopes of low mesas. Beyond that, there's a final plateau that closes the valley: This plateau looks like an
outstretched arm with a cupped hand at the end of it,
as if looking to catch whatever might fall from the sky.

"I think I see them."

"They're usually for ground-to-air—"

"But like Akiva, they're being used for ground-to-
ground, too."

"Correct. Which means they could tear us in half if
we get hit."

Norra stands and leans against one of the jagged
stones. The 'nocs hang by their strap. "What do
we do?"

"The more important question is, What's your plan
with Sloane?"

"I don't follow."

Jas crosses her arms. "We have two ways to deal
with her. One involves capture and extraction. That
means taking her back to Chandrila—or Nakadia, or
wherever—to face a tribunal."

"And the other way is to kill her."

"Correct. Assassination. Here and now. A proper
revenge."

Norra knows what she wants to do. And Jas only
makes that choice easier when the bounty hunter explains: "If we want her dead, we head in that direction, our cannons going at full blaze. She gets hit and
dies, or she runs out into the open where a turbolaser
turns her to dust on the wind."

"And the other way?"

"That gets trickier. Because it means we need time
to get her on the shuttle, and that area she's hiding in
doesn't afford us much room. Pretty cozy down there,
so our tail feathers will be hanging out."

"Damnit."

"The question is, Do you want justice, or do you want revenge?"

"I . . ."

Images flash. Sloane having Norra's son thrown off a roof at the satrap's palace on Akiva. Sloane escaping in a TIE fighter. Their fight on Chandrila—brutal, bitter fisticuffs. *I want her dead and gone. I want her to pay. I want my revenge for all that she's done.* But other images cascade: Her son's face. Leia's, too. Everyone she knows makes an appearance—Sinjir, Solo, Jom, even Brentin.

All of them are good people. Even when they're doing bad things. But is she that? Perhaps she is their opposite. Or maybe killing Sloane is a bad thing, but it wouldn't change that she's a good person.

She tells the truth when she says, "I don't know. For now, we . . . do whatever it takes to capture her."

"Fine. How?"

Norra thinks. A plan—clumsy and terrifying—forms. "We can't take out those turbolasers." She remembers rocketing over Myrra on Akiva in a TIE fighter—those ships are insanely maneuverable, and even then it was a struggle not to get fried. "Instead we fly down, but never stop moving for long. Someone drops out, grabs Sloane. We use Bones as backup." Bones is presently on the shuttle, charging his batteries and doing light diagnostics on himself. "Then whoever's flying the ship brings it back around just long enough to drop the ramp so we can all get aboard. And while the clearance codes are still good, we get offplanet and back to the Republic with our prisoner in tow."

"It's dangerous." Jas's face wrinkles up into a frustrated knot. "We'll probably die. Then again, we've survived this long, and your plan might be the only way. I like it. There's one other thing, though."

"Do I want to know?"

"It's time to consider the possibility that Rae Sloane is no longer in charge of anything down here."

"What do you mean?"

"Think about it. The grand admiral of the whole Empire is down there in the company of a Hutt gangster. She's clothed like a common scavenger. Sloane has lost control, Norra. She's not in charge of a hill of sand, much less the Empire. And whatever's out there is important enough to be guarded by a bank of high-test turbolasers, but *secret* enough to have no visible Imperial presence. Something's going on here. Something big."

Norra paces. Jas is right. And yet—what can they do? How can they see the scope of it? Do they even need to?

They don't, she decides.

"The goal is the goal," Norra says. "Get Sloane. The rest is for someone else to uncover. We do our part, and if we bring back the erstwhile grand admiral, maybe she can do *her* part and shine a light on these shadows, show us what's really going on."

"Sounds like a deal. Ready to try to not die once again?"

"It seems to be my calling."

Something is up there.

Sloane is sure of it. She's been staring up at the distant ridgeline for the last hour, certain that something is hiding there behind the rocks. At first she thought, *Maybe it's just an animal.* In her short time here on Jakku she's already seen creatures she hopes to never see again: devouring worms underneath the sand, birds whose beaks can punch through metal, massive lizards that run across the hot desert as fast as lightning. For a time she thought maybe it was some beast watching, waiting to feast upon them should they dare to sleep. But now she's not so sure. It's the way that the shadows move, and the way she sometimes catches the flintiest glint of starlight. It's some*one*, not some*thing*.

She tells Brentin as much. He remains crouched behind a bent and crooked stone, and he asks the natural question: "Who?"

"I don't know. We don't have any friends here. But I don't think it's the Empire, either, or they would've come already." Or so she thinks. The turbolaser turrets out there—they're guarding something spectacular. Something that belongs to Gallius Rax.

But does it belong to the Empire? Or just to Rax?

"Could be scavengers," Brentin says.

"Could be." Just as an animal might look to devour them, scavengers might hope to do the same—looking to plunder not their meat but the debris field scattered out in front of them in the open valley.

"Niima still isn't happy."

It's hard to see the Hutt now, but it's easy to hear her. The distance that separates the two groups from each other is close enough that the slug's snorts and hisses and gurgles of rage are clear across the quiet night. There arises a thumping, too—the Hutt's tail, pounding the desert.

Sloane is sorely tempted to lure the Hutt out of hiding and hope that one of the turbolasers turns the worm to a red mist and a rain of foul blubber. But it would do Sloane no good, of course, beyond affording her a moment of pleasure—and eradicating one of her enemies.

"What do you think Rax is hiding beyond the valley?" Brentin asks.

"I don't know. The rumors said it was some kind of weapons facility."

"Why would he hide that? He seems to be hiding it from his own people."

"I don't know that, either." Certainly the Empire had its secrets. Layers of them, actually. Even she does not know them all.

"I heard a rumor once." Brentin sits up with a groan, his back scraping up the side of the rock. "Working pirate radio for the rebels meant not only getting propaganda out to the galaxy, but also intercepting communications from the Empire. I worked with guys who knew how to slice those frequencies, how to tap into feeds and transmissions—they even figured out how to hack hyperspace drives to snatch those frequencies right out of far space. This one Abednedo I worked with, Awls Ooteek, he said they caught a snippet that came from some far-off system. Adumar, I think. In Wild Space. The transmission said something about a . . . laboratory, a hidden facility. We sent scouts to look for it but nothing ever came of it, and it's not like we could devote a lot of attention to that endeavor. The Alliance had to be careful how it allocated its people. But I wonder if something was out there. And I wonder if what's here is like that."

Something the Emperor himself set up? That could be. Sloane's mind flashes to that image she saw in the Imperial archives: Palpatine, Yularen, Mas Amedda, and the young Gallius Rax. Rax was a hero of the Empire, but his record remains clouded behind layers of classification. How close was he to Palpatine? What was his true role?

What if what's out there was like the secret facilities that helped to develop and design the Death Star? Or what if it's something far stranger?

Whatever it is, Rax cannot be allowed to control it. He's not to be trusted.

In her belly, there's a twinge as that thought repeats

itself: *He's not to be trusted with* my *Empire*. New purpose burns like lava in her marrow. Maybe Brentin Wexley is right. Could be that she requires a purpose beyond merely cutting out Gallius Rax's heart.

Maybe she can reclaim the Empire. Maybe she can save it.

And maybe whatever he's protecting and hiding will help her to do just that. Which means they have to find a way past those turbolasers and—

"Look," Brentin says.

Sloane is jarred loose from her momentary reverie and follows his pointing finger. There, up on the ridge, she spies movement.

A ship. A shuttle.

It lifts up and points toward them.

Sloane's mouth spreads into a wicked grin. "Get ready."

"For what?"

"We're going to take that ship."

Jas says that Norra should pilot the shuttle down to the surface, and Jas will be the one to hit the sand and grab Sloane. That fulfills each of their roles. They are each trained accordingly—Norra is a sly pilot, one of the best the Rebellion had. And Jas is a bounty hunter. She knows how to fight. She knows how to subdue.

But Norra's not having any of that. Her jaw locks tight. Her eyes are open and intense. When she says through trapped teeth that she wants—no, *needs*—to be the one to take in Sloane, Jas agrees. The bounty hunter knows this is a fight she can't win. So she acquiesces.

They're in the shuttle now. The ship rises fast off the ridge, and Jas plots the vector—swoop west and come in from an oblique angle. The plateaus will block any meaningful fire from the turbolasers. Norra waits on the ramp with Bones, ready for what's to come. If she fails to grab Sloane, the droid will be able to do the job, and at the very least he'll defend Norra from the admiral and whoever she's with. Jas will do a looping slalom through the valley plateaus, then return to pick up Norra and Sloane.

Easy. Or so Jas hopes.

But it's never easy, is it?

As Jas swings west, she turns the ship toward Sloane's position.

And that's when her screens light up with incoming ships.

Norra has no intention of "taking in" Sloane. Already her heart is telling her that in the battle between justice and revenge, she knows what has to be done. As they get closer and closer, her urge to see that woman pay for what she's done grows like an infection. If she has a shot, she's going to take it. There will be no need to bring her aboard the shuttle. Jakku will take her body after Norra does what must be done.

The wind whips across Norra as she hangs on to the pneumatic piston that allows the ramp to hang open even as the Corellian shuttle darts and dips back toward the valley. Bones is behind her, hanging from the other piston like it's a streetlight from which he dances—one arm and one leg out as if he just finished a magic trick, ta-da.

With her free hand, Norra brings the quadnocs to her eyes once again. She points them toward Sloane's position. The blurry image grows clearer as they approach—fat pixels resolve into small ones, and she sees Sloane standing up, pointing right at the incoming shuttle. Her heart burns with the need to see this woman defeated.

Good. Know that I'm coming for you, Rae Sloane.

Then the man hiding there stands, too.

The 'nocs focus on him and his face clarifies . . .

No. It can't be.

It's like being dropped into the airless nowhere of space. The void consumes her, sucking all the oxygen out of her lungs as she realizes:

It's Brentin.

It's her husband.

She almost loses her grip on the piston as her head goes swimmy—the quadnocs *do* drop from her hand, but Bones is fast and snatches them with a snapping claw before they fall into the void.

"Brentin," Norra says, but her voice is swallowed by the roar of the shuttle's engines and she can only hear the name spoken inside her own head . . .

Norra grabs the quadnocs from Bones and looks once more.

Sloane and Brentin are no longer looking this way.

They're still looking up. This time, in another direction.

That's when the shuttle suddenly pulls hard to the left—heading back west again *away* from Sloane, *away* from her husband. No! That's not possible! She yells back inside the ship: "What are you doing?" Fury surges inside her like a living thing, and she launches herself back inside the shuttle and makes her way through the main hold and into the cockpit. The ship banks again and she almost loses her footing as she staggers up behind the bounty hunter and reaches for the controls. "We have to go back!"

Jas yells: "We have incoming Imperial ships!"

"It doesn't matter. Brentin is down there! *My hus-*

band." She wrestles for the flight stick. Jas grabs Norra by the chin and pulls her close.

"Listen to me," she says. Her voice is cold, her eyes are deadly serious. "If we go down there, we're dead. We're *all* dead."

"Please," Norra begs.

"The Imperials aren't following us because we have clearance codes. We watch. We wait. We do this right. Okay?"

"It's Brentin, Jas, *it's Brentin*." Even Norra hears the madness in her own voice as she pleads.

"I need you to trust me, Norra. Do you trust me?"

"I do . . ."

"Then buckle up. We need to get out of here. Fast."

"We have nowhere to go," Brentin says. And he's right. They flee the protection of the plateau, and turbolasers will end them. Stay here, and they're a target for whoever it is that's coming for them.

Sloane doesn't understand what just happened. The ship that was coming—a Corellian shuttle by the look of it? It turned away at the last second as a trio of Imperial ships came up over the ridge. Those three ships are *Lambda*-class shuttles and they roar in and swoop low over the desert, dust swirling behind them. The Corellian ship flees. Scavengers, run off by the sight of the Empire? Or saviors? She'll never know, it seems.

Sloane looks at the blaster rifle in her hand and tries to imagine what to do with it. *Put it under your chin,* she thinks.

But no. She'll see this through. There is no escape from this situation, but one way or another she will find a way forward. Sloane will end Rax. Sloane will retake the Empire. She'll do it with her biting teeth and scratching fingernails. She'll claw her way back to the seat of power. Maybe this is how she gets there. *Seize any opportunity,* she thinks.

The shuttles land, far enough apart to block any chance she and Brentin might have of fleeing into the night.

Ramps descend with off-gassing steam.

Stormtroopers come off those ramps in no formation—just a sloppy, chaotic disgorgement of soldiers. More like mercenaries at this point.

Then *he* comes.

Gallius Rax.

He wears the white of a grand admiral, somehow clean despite the filth of this world. A red cape swoops behind him, stirring dust.

Stormtroopers surround her and Brentin. They bark orders for her to drop her weapon, and she does.

They part to let Rax through.

"Sloane," he says, dipping his chin in a small nod.

"Counselor."

"I thought you had been killed on Chandrila." The wind whips his cape. "Or taken prisoner."

Her pulse throbs in her temples. Her fingers tighten reflexively into fists. Sloane's greatest desire is to leap forward right now and drive one punch into his face— a single hit that pistons his nose into his brain. But she'd be cut down by blasterfire before she even got close.

"I am alive. I will retake the Empire, now. Thank you for safeguarding it, but your time is done." She says that with bluff and bluster, knowing full well he won't simply accede.

"Your Empire has moved on without you," he says, his hand going to the air with a frittering gesture. "You understand. After a period of mourning, what else could we do?"

"So you brought it here. To this dead place."

"We have a destiny here. We all do."

My destiny is to see you die, she thinks.

And then, from the other plateau, a roar of fury. Out there, Niima the Hutt bellows and slithers swiftly across the desert floor toward them. The turbolasers don't fire as she crosses the expanse. (That confirms Rax controls them—the turrets didn't autotarget him or his shuttles.)

Niima shrieks in proto-Huttese, the translation box offering its interpretation in loud mechanized monotone: "COUNSELOR. WHAT HAVE YOU BEEN HIDING OUT HERE IN THE—"

But Rax simply holds up his finger and loops it in an almost lazy, dismissive gesture. The troopers turn toward the Hutt, rifles up, and begin firing. Red lasers spear the night, sizzling and pocking as they pelt the Hutt and the slaves who ride her. The slug roars. Slaves fall.

But she doesn't stop.

Niima suddenly changes course, heads toward one of the shuttles. Wailing in pain and rage, the Hutt moves with terrifying speed toward the closest shuttle, and she hits it like a charging beast. Her head gets under the ship and lifts—Sloane audibly gasps as the shuttle flips onto its side, the wing snapping as the troopers continue firing upon her.

Now the Hutt is coming this way. And Sloane thinks, *This is it, this is my way out.* She begins to eye the troopers, assessing which she should take—

Niima slumps, sliding forward. Her last Hutt-slave, the one who originally draped the speaker around the worm's neck (or, rather, *lack* of neck), hits the sand running, ululating—

One shot between his eyes drops him.

And again all is still.

"Nasty business, dealing with traitors," Rax says.

"It is," Sloane says. "As you'll see."

"Is that a threat?"

"It is." She feels her body moving in time with her heartbeat—rocking side-to-side, bobbing up and down in case she has to run, attack, punch, kick, anything. She flits her gaze to Brentin. In it she attempts to convey a clear message: *Be ready for anything.* She looks to the stormtroopers again—no, not to all of them. Just to one. The one closest. That trooper stands there, his helmet crisscrossed with angry carved hashes filled with the accumulated rust-red dirt of Jakku. To this trooper she says: "I am Grand Admiral Rae Sloane. I command you to capture Counselor Gallius Rax on the charge of treason against the throne."

That trooper flinches—but doesn't budge.

"They aren't yours to command," Rax says plainly. "A noble effort. And I'm sad you think that what I've done is treason. Don't you see, Sloane? I've given the Empire a place again. A *purpose.*"

"It's come to this, then? Death on a dead world. You've driven us all to the edge of the galaxy. To the edge of everything."

"As I say: There is a purpose."

She sneers. "But let me guess? I'll never see it."

"To the contrary. I'm taking you back. Alive."

"Why?"

A slow, self-satisfied smile spreads across his face. "A show must have its audience, dear Sloane." He turns to Brentin. "But whoever he is, he can go."

The troopers raise their rifles—

Brentin cries out as fingers curl around triggers—

Sloane steps in front of him. "No. *No.* He comes with me."

Rax laughs. "But why?"

Because if anybody can help me, it's him. He saved

her once. He's helped her countless times already. If they kill him now, any utility he may yet possess will be gone.

Not that she can say that to Rax.

"He's a rebel, if you'll believe that. He had a chip in his head, a chip you helped put there. Don't you want him to see what your seeds have grown? You want an audience? A witness? Then let him see what you've wrought."

"Oh. Hm. A rebel, you say?" Her enemy pauses to think, and she watches him come to some silent conclusion. "I can use him, too." To the troopers, Rax says: "Get them on board. We'll take them back to base."

The troopers gather her arms behind her and shove her forward, past Gallius. As she passes, she spits on his uniform—summoning that much moisture is a nearly heroic effort, but the result is as desired: Her saliva is laced with the filth of this planet and it stains the white accordingly.

He says: "This world has transformed us all, it seems."

"You have no idea," she says as they push her toward the shuttle.

"Welcome to Jakku, Rae Sloane. Welcome to Jakku."

CHAPTER TWENTY-TWO

ALREADY THE MORNING sun is a searing presence, oppressive, like a boot on the back of the neck. Jas watches Norra stalk the wreckage—she moves through the debris of the caravan like a ghost. Her wailing is done. She spent that time last night, howling and raging. Now she's a gutted thing. Probably thought it couldn't get any worse. Then they saw Brentin.

And then they saw Brentin taken away again.

Jas has no idea what any of that means. Mysteries persist. Why is Sloane in scavenger robes? Why did they capture her and Brentin as if they are enemies to the Empire? Why was Brentin here at all? Why did Niima go along with it—and why is the Hutt now dead?

"Nothing here," Norra says. Two words she's said already half a dozen times. Her raw, red eyes search the wreckage, looking for any answer to those questions Jas keeps in the back of her head.

"We should go," Jas says.

"Yes," Norra says, but she continues wandering. She kicks over the smoldering wreckage from a wheelbike. She nudges the elbow of a dust-blown Hutt-slave corpse. Jas tries to summon her back again, warning her that those turbolasers are off, now—but no telling if they'll remain so.

"Norra."

"I know."

"We have to go."

"I *know.*"

"We can get him back. Him and Sloane."

"How?" Norra asks, that one word spoken louder than all the others—the word rough-edged with sorrow, desperation, and anger. "We don't know where they went. Or *why.* We don't have anything, Jas. We were close. We were *so close.* And then just . . ." She holds up her hand and closes it on open air. Fresh tears threaten to leave new tracks down her dirt-stained cheeks.

Jas doesn't know how to answer.

She wants to offer hope, but that's not really her thing. Jas doesn't want to lie. Losing Sloane and Brentin like that means hope is fading fast.

Then—

A gassy belch erupts as the Hutt carcass rolls over. Norra cries out. So does Jas, startled as she staggers backward, hissing an old Iridonian curse. She raises her rifle, pointing it at the slug.

Niima paws at the ground, struggling to get up. Dark blood oozes from holes in her body in gummy runnels and rivulets. She gurgles in some old form of Huttese—"*Uba, Zabrak! Nolaya bayunko.*" The body rights itself, then slithers over the carcasses of her slaves. Every movement draws a grunt of anguish from the slithering worm.

Norra throws Jas a panicked look. In it, the message: *What do we do?*

Jas gives an alarmed shrug. *Let's let this play out.*

Finally, the Hutt seems to find what she's looking for. She scoops up a black box off the ground. It looks to be a translator device. With a leathery mitt, Niima slaps the box against her chest—it sticks to the dry, slimy blood.

Again she bellows in Huttese, but this time the box offers a staticky, grinding translation: "YOU. THE ZABRAK. YOU WERE IN MY DUNGEON."

Jas keeps the rifle pointed. "That's right."

"AND YET NOW YOU ARE HERE."

"That's . . . also true."

"I SHOULD KILL AND EAT YOU."

The Hutt's black tongue slides along her slitted mouth. Her one eye winks reflexively as a little river of fresh blood trickles into it.

"I don't think you're in much of a position for that."

The slug regards herself. Then she looks to the corpses around her. Her wormbody visibly slumps in a noncommittal shrug. "YES. YOU MAY BE RIGHT. YOU HELP ME AND I WILL HELP YOU."

Jas and Norra consult in an unspoken look. Norra gives Jas a small nod. *Okay, then.* Jas injects a little deference into her voice when she says: "What do you need, O great-and-powerful Niima?"

"TAKE ME TO MY TEMPLE."

"And what do we get out of the exchange?"

"I CAN GET YOU CLEARANCE CODES."

"We have codes already."

"NOT TO THE IMPERIAL BASE, YOU DON'T."

Well. That answers that.

Jas nods. "Norra, go get the shuttle. Let's take Niima home."

CHAPTER TWENTY-THREE

"CONDER!" SINJIR CRIES out, gasping as he lifts his face from the hard, cobbled stone of the alleyway. His chin peels away, sticky with blood. He gasps, tasting that wet copper tang. A hand waves in front of him.

His vision resolves and there stands Temmin.

He growls as he takes the hand. The young man helps him stand.

"What . . ." Sinjir coughs. "What happened?"

"I . . . don't know," Temmin says. "Grelka ducked away and I tried to follow. But something was blocking my comm."

"The others," Sinjir says. He looks up, sees that the sky is blushing lavender. It's morning. How long was he out? "Where are they?"

"I don't know that, either. I can't get anybody on the comlink. I came around the side here and found you, facedown in the alley."

Not the first time that's happened, Sinjir thinks.

The memory of last night resolves: waiting around Izzik's, losing sight of Ashmin Ek, seeing Ek and Nim Tar in the alleyway before *someone* clobbered him in the back of the old braincage, forcing him to stop and take a long dirt-nap. That proves something's up. But what?

* * *

They find Solo in a trash bin behind the landing bay where Dor Wieedo's ship was (but is no longer) parked. He is alive. It doesn't take much to bring him back to consciousness—a few light slaps to the cheek does the trick. He clambers out, snarling.

"Why do I always end up in the trash?" he asks. When nobody says anything, he asks: "What? Nobody has anything funny to say about that?"

"I have no witty retort," Sinjir says. His nerves roil like storm clouds. Worry *corrodes* him from the inside as he envisions Conder caught in a panoply of bad situations. "Just . . . tell us what happened."

"Enh," Solo says, brushing some half-rotten leafy greens out of his hair. "I followed the thugs. Was gonna sneak onto the ship. But there was a fourth one and he snuck up on me and—" He claps his hands together. "Stun blast to the back. And then they threw me away with yesterday's garbage."

Temmin picks some kind of noodle off Solo's left shoulder.

Sinjir's about to say something—

When his comlink crackles.

Conder.

But it's Jom. "—ello? I've—" More static. "—gone and done something—" Hiss, crackle. "—aboard the *Falc*—"

"Sounds like we better get to the *Falcon*," Solo says.

Jom awaits them on the *Millennium Falcon*. And he's not alone.

Sitting next to him by the holo-chess board is Senator Rethalow of Frong. The Frong's forearms—long and blue and lined with contracting suckers—are bound up with what looks like some kind of electrical cabling. The Frong's face-tubules tremble and twitch, and its big black glossy eyes contract as they approach. Jom sits, one arm around the senator. The onetime commando's hair is mussed. Everything about him screams that he's on edge—sparking like a frayed wire. Sinjir thinks: *I can relate to that.* And he understands the source of it, too: *We have people we care about caught in bad situations. We'd burn down the world to save them, wouldn't we?*

"Jom," Sinjir says slowly, as if talking to a child. "What did you do?"

"Not a thing," he says, waving it off. "Okay, fine. *Maybe* I caused a minor intergalactic incident. Maybe. Nothing that can't be forgiven and forgotten, I'm sure."

"Jom."

"Fine, fine. I broke open the dep chamber and dragged the esteemed Senator Rethalow here out kicking and screaming. Busted my comlink, too, the fat-bellied little traitor. But after that, the senator told me some *real* interesting things, figured you might all want to hear."

All eyes fall to Rethalow.

The Frong remains quiet. Jom drives an elbow into the senator's side. "Go on, barnacle. Tell them what you told me."

"Our votes were bought," the Frong says in Basic, the words coming out so quickly that at first it barely registers with Sinjir. "Three of us, anyway. Me, Ek, and Wieedo."

"We know Ek and Wieedo got payouts," Solo says. Admittedly, they *didn't* know that, but now the assumption is a safe one. "What did *you* get?"

"A . . . a trade deal," the Frong stammers.

A trade deal?

Sinjir leans in. "And the other two? Nim Tar and Sorka? What did they get for their vote?"

"Threatened. Th-they were threatened. Nim Tar's child was taken. And Senator Sorka's jerba, too."

Sinjir throws a look to the others. "Jerba? Help me out, please."

It's Solo who answers. "Kind of a . . . smooth-haired animal. You can ride 'em, milk 'em, eat 'em. There's a whole subculture of breeders—I once smuggled a mated pair off Tatooine for a private seller. Personally, I think they're uglier than the back end of a shaved bantha, but that's me."

Sorka gave up her vote because her prize animal was taken, Sinjir thinks. *How charming. Democracy is well and truly fragile, isn't it?*

Sinjir asks Rethalow, "Who did this, Senator?"

"I . . . mustn't say."

Jom looks like he's about to drive another elbow into the Frong's ribs, but Sinjir leans in and stops him with a gentle hand and a shake of his head. Then he kneels down in front of Rethalow.

"Senator," Sinjir says, his voice calm and slow even though his mind is a hurricane whipped with fears over Conder. "I need your help here. A friend of mine remains missing and I believe whoever has solicited your vote is responsible. They offered you a trade deal?"

Hesitantly, the Frong nods. Its tubules curl inward with fear. "Th-the New Republic hasn't yet secured the Outer Rim. Frong is v-vulnerable. By giving my vote, I'm earning protection for my planet and my people. You see? Do you see? The New Republic c-can't afford to extend its protection to us, not yet, *not yet,* and until then we have no navy, no fleet . . . !"

It's not a trade deal. It's a protection scheme.

That means—

"Criminals," Sinjir says. "You've given your vote over to criminals."

"Y-yes."

"Who?"

"I . . ."

Still it withholds. And why wouldn't the senator? The Frong knows who has the power here. Sinjir needs power. He needs *leverage*.

So, he lies. A little.

"I'm close with the chancellor. I am an adviser of hers. I can assure you that we will extend New Republic protections to your world immediately. We won't leave you to the darkness. That is, *if* you comply. If you give me what I need to know, we will help you. If you fail, this is the end. You will no longer be a member of the Senate. Your world will be fed to the monsters and we will offer little more than a sad wave goodbye. You will be shamed for how you failed them. Which is not your fault. But this situation cannot go unrectified, and so either you help us, or that's it. The door closes and we have nothing but exile for you."

It's all calculated. Sinjir doesn't know a great deal about the Frong—their world is in a fringe system with a dim star and they have little to offer the galaxy except some fruit, some spice, and clean water. But he *does* know that the Frong are insular and clannish. They are tight-knit, coming from practically incestuous bloodlines. When he says words like *shame* and *exile*—those are concepts the Frong know intimately. And it registers on Rethalow's face, too: Its eyes dilate tighter as Sinjir speaks.

"I'll . . . tell you."

"Who did this, Senator? And where are they?"

"I don't know where. I don't! But I know who. Black Sun and the Red Key Company have formed an alliance. They've . . . partnered."

Two syndicates. Venerable Black Sun and the upstart Red Key. If the two of them are allying, it's a sign of things to come. Sensible, in a way. If the New Republic wins a final victory, then it behooves the syndicates to shore up their assets and form alliances against the looming threat of a government that will not tolerate their illicit activities.

Then it hits him. Sinjir understands. *If* the New Republic wins a final victory at Jakku, the Empire is done. The longer the war rages, the better the chances that the syndicates will survive—they can feed on the chaos and use that time to bolster their efforts. That's what this is. The vote to delay the war isn't about politics at all. It's about the syndicates staying in the game.

He stands up. "Thank you, Senator. Let's get you to safety." He means it, too. If the Black Sun and Red Key guess that one of their senators is compromised, they'll put a laser bolt through one of his eyes. His mind races—the others are talking to him, saying who-knows-what, but he's not listening. He's trying to think of a way to find Conder, to find Nim Tar's child and Sorka's stupid show-jerba. Would their abductors remain here on Nakadia? They would remain close, surely. Both to watch the vote and to ensure that the Senators vote the way they're supposed to. Which means they'd be on the planet's surface *or* out in space—

In a ship.

He blurts it out: "They could be in a ship."

He watches the realization cross Solo's face. "Right. *Right!* Dor Wieedo's ship was gone from the docking bay."

"That's where they are. But they must be close. In orbit."

Solo grins. "Let's take the *Falcon* for a spin."

* * *

Tolwar Wartol spends his time ricocheting between periods of brooding, simmering silence and moments of rage against her. In those latter times he stands and marches about and threatens to destroy her in the media for what he calls her "nasty tricks," playing games as she does with the political process.

Mon simply sits still and quiet, occasionally reminding Wartol that he is free to talk to the media if he so chooses. "I'm sure HoloNet would be very interested in a story where your entire political mechanism was held hostage by one woman and a small fruit."

He rages, then sits, then goes quiet once more.

On the outside, she is a calm façade—an undisturbed Chandrilan lake, placid and unbroken. Inside she is tumult and tumble. She knows time is fast escaping. Her delay will not work forever.

The Nakadian inspectors come aboard, clothed in thick bubble-suits with aerator masks. They do a slow and steady sweep of the ship, both outside and inside. Wartol, to his credit, is polite even if his anger ripples just beneath the surface. He does not berate them; he does not chide them to hurry. The inspectors sweep handheld scanners across all the nooks and crannies of the cruiser—an emerald beam searching for further contaminants. The chief inspector, a woman named Rekya, explains to them in *great detail* how Nakadia is a protected environment that takes great care to balance its ecosystem and keep out invasive species—and she reminds them, if a bit testily, how all the Senate should have received messages in their personal digital folders reminding them of *exactly this*. "Democracy grinds to a halt when protocol is broken," Rekya tells them. "And believe me when I tell you, *protocol has been broken*."

All the while, Mon nods and smiles, listening carefully while hoping the delay is worth it. Leia's agents on the ground *must* find something, and soon. Because when the inspectors leave, the ship begins to move once more toward landing on Nakadia. Wartol says, "There. Your nasty tricks have bought you little time." He informs his guards that he and the chancellor will be heading *directly* to the Senate chambers immediately upon docking. "No more delays," he says. "It is time to face your failure, Chancellor."

The *Falcon* perches in empty space. Most of the ships above Nakadia have gone and landed, now—the Senate vote was scheduled for an hour ago, which means all of the voting body should be present down below for when the delay (caused by the chancellor herself in a plan that was of Leia's design) is finally rectified.

There, through the viewport, hangs Wartol's cruiser.

They watch as a pair of Nakadian ships—each a talon-shaped cruiser, four-person, small and nimble— drifts away from the Ganoidian-made tri-deck vessel. Those ships reenter atmosphere with a hot burn.

And Wartol's ship begins to move toward the surface, as well.

Sinjir curses. "We're nearly out of time." *And we've found nothing*. Dor Wieedo's ship isn't up here. Which means it either leapt into hyperspace and is gone, or is simply somewhere else on the surface of Nakadia. The former doesn't make much sense, though—Wieedo and the others will need to be present to vote. That means they're back on the surface. "Coming up here was a waste of time. It was a mistake. I made a mistake."

He's talking directly to Solo, who sits in the pilot's seat, staring out.

"Solo?" he asks again.

"Yeah, I hear you." The man's voice is quiet, like

he's far away even though he's sitting right there. It takes little effort to see what's happening. Solo thinks he's good at being the tough-talking, rough-skinned scoundrel—he's always got his shields up, ready to defend with swagger and bluster.

But Sinjir sees how the man keeps looking over in this direction. At the console. At the copilot's seat. He really does miss that Wookiee. At first, that made little to no sense to Sinjir. Because, really. It's a *Wookiee*. Chewbacca is lovely and all, but he's a gargantuan pillar of hair who smells not unlike a moist gundark's undercarriage. And all that nonsensical growling? And the *hugging*?

And yet—that was the man's copilot. His friend. His family.

I have copilots, too. It's taken Sinjir some time to see that. Certainly he's come to see these people around him as his *friends,* as his *family.*

And yet there's one more copilot out there.

Conder Kyl.

Damnit, blast, damnit.

I never should've left him.

Conder makes Sinjir a better man. Just as Chewie helped to make Solo one, too. *We both need our copilots, it seems.*

"We need to think," Sinjir says, "because I need to get Conder back. He's important to me, Solo. You understand?"

"I hear you loud and clear."

"Why would they even take him?"

"Bargaining chip, maybe. Or because he's a slicer and they want him to do something for them."

"Bargaining chip. Yes. Because even if we intercept the other senators before the vote, they'll have Conder to play. That's their plot, isn't it? *We have him, so don't disrupt the vote or he gets it.*"

Solo looks disappointed. "Why didn't they take me?" He pouts. "They threw me away like I was trash."

"They didn't take you because you're too high-profile. They take the venerable Han Solo and they risk his old friend Luke cutting them all to bits with his fancy laser blade." Sinjir thinks but does not say: *They didn't take* me *because I'm ex-Imperial and they couldn't risk the lack of sympathy. Oh, well, it's just Sinjir. Nobody will miss him.* "If they want to use him as a slicer, they'd need a building near the Senate house with some digital pipe—some cabling. That might stand out here. Nakadia isn't well connected."

"Still means doing a ground search," Han says. "We don't have the time for those kinds of—"

Their comlinks suddenly crackle to life in unison.

From the static comes Conder's voice:

Kkksssh. "—ere am I?"

Sinjir's heart leaps in his chest like a hare over a puddle. He speaks into the comm: "Conder? Where are you? Are you all right?"

But the slicer doesn't answer. At least, he doesn't answer Sinjir, but he *does* keep talking. "When my friends get here, you'll be sorry."

"He's broadcasting," Solo says. "Somehow."

C'mon, Conder. Tell us something. Anything.

The slicer continues: "Don't think I don't see that Red Key mark on your biceps. I know who owns you. And you there. Black Sun?"

A muffled sound: someone speaking back to Conder. But Sinjir can't make out the other person's words. *We already know it's Red Key, Conder. And Black Sun. Keep going. Keep telling us information.*

"Looks like a—" A burst of static eats the word, but it resurfaces through the crackle: "—rehouse. Red roof. Two story—"

The other person says something. Sounds like *Shut up*.

Then: *bam*. The comlinks blast a dull thud and a loud high-pitched shriek before going dead once more. "Conder? *Conder?*"

Jom and Temmin poke their heads into the cockpit.

"You hear that?" Jom asks.

"I think he said warehouse," Temmin says.

Sinjir grips the back of the copilot's chair so hard he's afraid he's about to rip it out of its mooring. "We need to—"

"On it."

Solo's already leaning on the thrusters. The *Falcon* jumps forward—and in moments the ship is shaking as it burns through the atmosphere, the black void of space giving way to the daytime sky of Nakadia.

We're coming, Conder. We're coming.

The chancellor moves slowly, faking a limp as she steps off the ramp of the Ganoidian cruiser. She waves to those gathered—it seems their time trapped in space caused a bit of a stir, a little drama, and now Nakadians have gathered to watch it end. Cams hover nearby, broadcasting. She spies a familiar face at the margins: Tracene Kane, of HoloNet News.

As she hobbles forward, Wartol steps next to her. He's smiling, waving at the crowd, but his low-spoken words to her betray any mirth he broadcasts on his face. "Quit. Limping."

"I seem to have injured my ankle a touch. I'll get along."

"Another ploy."

"Hardly," she lies. "My good friend Ackbar has had me on a rather strict exercise regimen ever since the attack left me in critical care, and I fear I've overexerted myself just a touch. How does the saying go? Slow and steady wins the race?" She emphasizes those last three words: *wins the race*.

"It shows how pathetic you are that you're resorting to cheap stunts such as this one. It only delays the inevitable, Chancellor." He nods at a nearby cam in an avuncular way before returning to hiss in her ear: "You'll still lose. You'll lose everything. No ruse of yours will stop that."

Over their heads roar the engines of a familiar freighter—

The *Millennium Falcon*.

Hope is a small ember, but with the sight of that, it burns brighter. Mon prays they have found something, anything, to give her an edge.

Two streets over from the Senate house sits an agricultural warehouse with a red roof. Behind it are docking platforms meant for harvesters and agridroids, but one of them is occupied with a different ship: Dor Wieedo's Tyrusian sky-sloop.

That's it. Sinjir knows it. He has to hope they're not too late. They have little time to discuss a plan. What they know is this: Summoning the Senate Guard or the Nakadian peace officers won't work. The common problem: no time.

They think to intercept the four other bribed and blackmailed senators inside the Senate house, but that, too, is an impossible task—security there will be tight, and trying to bust in with guns blazing will only get them shot.

They could attempt to stop the vote. But the vote needs to happen. If any of this comes to light, the result will almost certainly be a vote delayed by an investigation—which could take weeks to resolve.

Weeks when Jas and Norra are left on an Imperial-occupied world.

And those plans also leave Conder on the hook.

That leaves them with one avenue of action and not a lot of time to plan out their assault. Solo finds no safe place to put the *Falcon*—no nearby docking bay, no hangar, no platform.

He grins, then. That scandalous, boomerang grin.

"I have a plan," he says.

"Do it," Sinjir says, without even asking what it is.

They pull him out of the Academy. He is hand-selected by a brutal, brick-faced woman named Officer Sid Uddra. Uddra tells Sinjir Rath Velus that he will be no trooper: He is too angry and he is too smart. Both qualities that make for a poor soldier. "They are just fodder anyway," she says as an aside, dismissing an entire army with a sour sneer.

He ends up in a new training program, this one located in a boxy, duracrete building. This severe structure is the Viper's Nest and it sits on a peak surrounded by the roiling oceans of Virkoi. It is where the Imperial Security Bureau trains its LOs—the loyalty officers.

Uddra tells him that she comes from the same system as he: Velusia. He is from Sevenmoon, she from Six-moon.

"You are like me," she tells him. "You get along with no one. They don't like you and you don't like them. It matters little where it started—over time, you've learned to protect yourself by preemptively hating everyone else. You distrust and despise even me. Good. That hate will save you. More important, that hate will save the Empire." And she explains to him what his role will be in the Empire from now

on—he will train to become Loyalty Officer Rath Velus. He will hide in plain sight. He will use that hatred of others to see in them their weakness—every weak Imperial is a fontanel where the skin goes thin and the Empire becomes vulnerable.

Then she tells him his training begins now.

She beats him. He is young and foolish and thinks he can fight back against this small, hard stump of a woman. He is wrong. Uddra's movements are short and precise. He swings. She ducks. He leaps. She side-steps. Every time he misses, she lands a hit. To his ribs. To the side of his neck. To his kidneys. Soon he is left panting and sobbing on the floor, on his hands and knees. Uddra goes to work on him. Whipping him with a wet towel rolled up. Bending his fingers back— not so they break, but so the pain forces him to con-fess everything about himself. Inserting small slivers of metal under his fingernails. The pain is intense. It is clarifying. It rips him open and everything that he is spills out of his blubbering mouth.

This happens again and again. Sinjir trains during the day. He suffers at night. Uddra never shows emo-tion. She studies him like an eight-legger deciding which part of the fly to eat first. Uddra dissects him.

He is unlike her. He is not cold and calculating. He is angry, vicious, full of rage. Uddra explains: "I will burn that out of you until all that's left is charred and black. A hot coal gone cold." Then she breaks his toes.

Then one day, it is his turn. Not to fight her, no. But to turn what he has learned—what has been visited upon him—against another.

She shows him a door. In this door is a window, and through that window he sees a man in a black officer's uniform—bars on the fellow's chest indicate that this *man with pinched eyes and a pug's nose is a lieutenant serving the Imperial Navy.*

Uddra tells Sinjir: "He will be your first." She explains why the man is here: "We believe he is part of a cabal of conspirators who seek to unseat Palpatine from the throne by committing to an assassination plot against the Emperor's enforcer, Darth Vader. You will root out the names of the other conspirators. Before you do, however, there is one last lesson."

She takes him outside, where a storm rages. On Virkoi, a storm always rages. Uddra takes a blaster rifle from a rack against the wall of the Viper's Nest and she points it off at the black, storm-crushed horizon.

Uddra fires.

The bolt cuts through the rain and the winds. It moves fast—a bright flash lancing the dark until it's a pinprick, then gone.

"You must be like that," she hisses in his ear. "You are that bolt of searing plasma. You will always be unswerving. No matter the rain or the wind. No matter how hot or how cold. Through the air. Through the void. You must be the brightest beam of light. Only then will the truth be out."

Sinjir understands. He pushes his anger away. He tortures Lieutenant Alster Grove for two nights straight until the man yields the names of his fellow conspirators. Uddra dumps Grove screaming into the churning sea. The other conspirators are hunted down by Vader and beheaded.

I am the brightest beam of light.

All else is chaos. It is like the wind-whipped sea of Virkoi. He will not be fazed by it. He *must not* be fazed by it.

Solo uses the *Falcon*'s belly turret to blow a hole in the top of the warehouse roof. Then he sets the *Falcon* right down upon it. *Whump.* Temmin stays behind to watch Rethalow. The rest of them are off.

Sinjir is first through the breach.

The warehouse is dim. The noise has already drawn foes. They come up on him in what seems like slow motion.

I am the brightest beam of light.

A thick-skulled Nikto swings a saw-toothed ax at his head. He deftly dips away from the blade, then twists the thug's arm back, back, back—until there's the dull vegetal crunch of tendons ripping. Sinjir pitches the Nikto behind him just as a plasma bolt snaps through the air, taking the thug out. That, from Jom, coming up behind—he's yelling something to Sinjir, something about keep going, keep moving, *I'll cover you,* but the ex-Imperial barely registers it at all.

I am the brightest beam of light.

Two more Nikto thugs come up between shelf-stacks of motor-vator parts—two more bolts of light through dark space. One from Han, the other from Jom. Both foes find their heels skidding out from under them as they are taken down, one after the other.

Sinjir stalks the half dark. He draws his own blaster. Some bent-necked Ithorian comes charging up—but Sinjir's arm is already up, his finger is already tightening. The Ithorian goes from two eyes to three as a searing hole opens in the center of his head.

I am the brightest beam of light.

The storm of violence roils. A shelf crashes down against another. Jom is on the floor, tackled by a smash-faced Iotran—the two wrestle against his rifle, thrashing about. Ahead, Solo runs and guns, ducking and darting, his blaster spitting plasma.

Bright spears of red crisscross in front of Sinjir, carv-

ing scorching lines in his vision. Motion comes from
his right—Sinjir does not even pause to regard it.
His movement is automatic, driving the butt end of his
rifle hard to that side—it crashes into the throat of
some one-eyed pirate with a little head and a big gut.
The man yowls and gargles past his own crushed trachea. Sinjir shoots him in the chest, then kicks him
away before continuing through the warehouse space.

I am the brightest beam of light.

And that light now shines on Conder Kyl. Everything focuses on that point: Conder at the far end of
the warehouse, kneeling on the floor, his head down,
hands bound behind him. Beyond him, another figure:
a child in a metal cage, a child with a bobbling wob-
bling head atop a white stalk neck. Nim Tar's child,
abducted and kept close. No sign of the jerba, but Sinjir can't give one hot damn about that. Truth be told,
he cares nothing for the child, either. The only one he
cares about is Conder.

A massive Herglic stands by the slicer, rubbery mitt
grabbing the back of Conder's head—the monster
wrenches his head backward, and now Sinjir can see
Conder's bruised, nose-broken face. The Herglic's
massive maw opens and roars a threat—*Come closer
and I'll break his neck*—and Sinjir knows the beast
can do it. *Will* do it. But only if Sinjir is slow.

And Sinjir is very fast.

I am the brightest beam of light.

Even as the brute finishes his threat, Sinjir is already
firing his blaster.

The blaster was never his specialty. Uddra told him,
*You are the weapon; no blaster will ever do the dam-
age you can do when you're up close.* But he isn't
close, not now, and this is the only tool he has. He has
to shoot true. He has to come correct.

The plasma bolt spears the air.

The Herglic tightens his grip—

Don't you hurt him, don't you dare hurt him—

Conder cries out, his eyes going wide—

No, no, no—

The plasma bolt punches through the Herglic's roaring mouth and out the back of his head. The Herglic moans, the bleating cry of a dying aiwha, and drops backward like a stack of crates.

Conder topples over to the side. Unmoving.

I am the brightest beam of light.

Brightest, yes. But was he the fastest?

The blaster rifle clatters—

Sinjir's footsteps echo in time with his own pounding heart. He drops to his knees, sliding forward to scoop Conder up, cradling him. The slicer's head flops lifelessly to the side and Sinjir feels his eyes burning hot tears—

I wasn't the fastest. I was too slow.

Then Conder's one eye wrenches open. He gasps. Sinjir gasps with him. "Conder. You're okay? Tell me you're okay. *Tell me you're okay.*" He's used to pulling information out of people one fingernail at a time; now he just wants the most basic data: *Are you okay, Conder, are you okay?*

"Took you long enough," Conder says, woozily smiling.

Sinjir stoops and kisses him. His long-fingered hands pull the other man's scruffy face into his own. The moment lasts forever.

And it still doesn't last long enough. Because now here's Han, and he's got a hand on Sinjir's shoulder—

"We're not done yet, remember."

Sinjir remembers. He stares deep into Conder's eyes. "I'm going to get you free. I know you're hurt. But we need your help. Can you slice?"

"With you by my side, I can do anything."

CHAPTER TWENTY-FOUR

THE NAKADIAN CHAMBER house isn't like the one on Chandrila—the Chandrilan chamber had an epic sweep to it, with endless scalloped balconies atop endless balconies, as far as the eyes could see. The one here on Nakadia is smaller, more humble. It's wood, not stone. Simple chairs in wooden boxes. Nothing is sculpted, nothing ornate. The seats are not merely before her, but all around her in what feels like a whirling cyclone of faces looking down upon her. Judging her, she suspects.

The speech Mon Mothma gives ahead of the vote is essentially the same as she gave back on Chandrila a week before, but it is shorter, and it is angrier. The anger is real because she fears that no matter what she says, it won't matter. She fears she is screaming into a void.

We have to vote yes.

We have to end the Empire.

We mustn't be hesitant. Not now. Not so close to its conclusion.

And she adds in one last barb, a line she knows she will one day regret because it does not sound like her—the threat, the bluster, the venom—but she says it anyway: "Those who vote no: Recognize that you are marked. You will be marked as cowards at best and traitors at worst."

She does not like the way she sounds, even though she knows the words are sincere. *I sound like a dictator.* She sounds like Palpatine.

The chancellor leaves the circular stage by going down a set of spiraling steps. At the bottom, she nearly collapses against the railing, she's so tired, so bone-weary. After righting herself, she ends up in the small office afforded to her, an office underground whose window is literally pressed up against the soil: In the rich tilth she sees the lightning shape of forked roots and the turning tunnels of crawling worms.

Auxi enters after. "That was a great speech," she says.

"I pushed too hard at the end. I went too far."

"Maybe they'll respect someone who goes that far."

She tells Auxi that she needs to be alone for a while.

After Auxi leaves, Mon spends time trying to flex the hand at the end of her injured arm. The fingers have the strength of moth wings. She spies a stain at the end of her sleeve: a bit of pta juice, from the fruit. Mon sits like that for a while. Staring down. Flexing her weak fingers. Hunching over farther and farther until she feels like a monk so reverent and so worshipful that she'll fold in on herself and become one with the living Force.

The air changes. Someone is here.

She looks up, embarrassed, a blushing bloom rising to her normally pale cheeks. There stands Auxi. Her face stark.

The vote failed again. She can see it.

"Now what?" Mon says weakly, desperately.

"We finish the war," Auxi answers.

"What?"

"The vote passed, Mon. *The vote passed.*"

PART FOUR

INTERLUDE

DEVARON

IN THE DEEP shadows of a moonless night, deeper shadows gather. Beyond them wait the low slopes of the Karatokai Mountains. Ahead of them is a narrow valley, in which there sits an outpost that has changed hands many times over the centuries: Once a Republic outpost, it fell to the Empire when Imperial reign ruled over Devaron, and now yet again it has returned to the hands of the revivified Republic.

Here the jungle is noisy. Flocks of gold-feathered taka-tey roost in the vine-tangle above, chirruping and *cack-cack-cack*ing. A thousand different insects hum and chatter in a cacophonous choir. Something kilometers away bellows, calling to another of its kind in the opposite direction.

But the shadows remain silent and still.

They are patient. They are waiting.

Down in the valley, the outpost is lit by bold beams from spotlights, beams that capture the slippery, sliding night mists. A flurry of activity sees ships landing and unloading supplies. The New Republic is establishing outposts new and old across the planet's surface. They bring people. They bring food and potable water. They have diplomats, liaisons, scientists, and of course soldiers.

They are invaders.

This is a sacred place. A hundred klicks from here is an old Jedi temple. It is not the only place on this planet strong in the Force. The shadows cannot feel this themselves, for they are not conduits for the Force, but merely slaves to it. (As are all living things. All are caught in the river of power that is the Force, trapped by its currents. Only those who wield the dark side of the Force are capable of changing those currents; they are riverbreakers. They do not surrender to fate. They are its foes.)

The shadows are Acolytes of the Beyond. Here wait two dozen of them, though they are only one cell among many across the galaxy. Though they grow restive, they know to wait. They mustn't disappoint their masters.

Kiza, a young Pantoran woman from Coronet City on Corellia, faces a wave of sudden doubt. She stands among people who are not her friends, not exactly, but who are her cohorts: Yiz, Lalu, Korbus, and her fellow Corellian, a friend and sometimes lover, Remi. She's not at all like Remi, though she pretends to be. He, like her, like *all* of them, has had the dreams. He's received the visions of the darkness: dreams of Sith, both ancient and recently living, plaguing his nights. And he loves it. He loves being a part of something. The darkness hasn't taken him—he has given himself to it.

Kiza pretends to be the same. But she's not so sure. She's angry, that much she knows. As a street rat in the worst parts of Coronet City, she has a lot of rage divvied up among an unholy host of those who have made her life harder: the peace officers that hassled her, the chits-and-debits office that chased her for every last debt against her family's accounts, the highborn Corellians who would stare down their noses at a lowborn gutter girl like her. When the dreams started, and when the man came to recruit her, the

Acolytes seemed an easy fit. She had anger to spare, and she was told that her anger was purifying—it was a virtue, the man told her, a necessary vice. It was anger that shaped the galaxy. It was rage that fueled the engines of change. It made sense. It felt like home.

She started low in the order, as they all did. She tagged walls with the Vader mask sigil and the warning: VADER LIVES. She stole credits and tithed them to the cause. While others were slicing into the HoloNet or attacking security forces, she was still scouting locations for dead-drops or safe meets. Then came Remi. He had this perfect mix of *confidence* and *injury*—like a monster who had been tamed, a fire whose flame was both brutal and beautiful. He was young. He was angry. He was gorgeous.

That's when he told her what they needed her to do next. She would get a job inside the P&S station. Kiza would work with the peace officers. They had rigged up new papers for her, new thumbprint scans, a new digital history. Gone was Kiza the street rat. Here was Kiza the doll with good breeding, the dame from the secretary pool.

Then came the night when the Acolytes attacked the city. A distraction so she and Remi could steal something from the archives underneath the station: a relic from a fallen Sith.

A lightsaber.

That lightsaber now hangs at Remi's belt. Since that night, Remi has grown more egotistical. He ignites the blade sometimes and stares into it, his mouth moving as if he's whispering to it. Other lightsabers, they've sacrificed to the Sith beyond—those who have died and who wait beyond the veil and whose orders the Acolytes follow. (Those ancient specters are the ones who give them the dreams, after all.) But now they've begun to keep the lightsabers. They have those and other artifacts, and only the most esteemed of the Acolytes are allowed to hold, use, and keep them.

Tonight they move beyond the collection of relics. Tonight they attack. Not just here. The strikes will take place across the galaxy. This is the first attack, and as such it is a small one: In various systems, the Acolytes have gathered on different worlds to slaughter enclaves and outposts of the New Republic. They do not have the number or the power to achieve bigger, not yet. But they will. This is just the start.

And Kiza is afraid.

She doesn't know if this is who she is.

She doesn't know if she's as strong as Remi.

She doesn't know if the visions she's experienced were even real.

Kiza thinks, *If I go ahead with it, if I go on this attack, I'll just stay in the background. I'll make it look like I'm doing something. Like I'm participating. Maybe I'll hit somebody. Or throw a detonator and blow up a shuttle.* The anger she's felt for so long curdles and goes sour. It turns to fear. Puzzlingly, it is that fear of which she is afraid. If she runs—if she seizes the fear and lets it guide her—they'll come for her. Remi won't let her escape. He'll find her tonight. Or in a week. Or in a year. Remi does not tolerate things that disappoint him.

As she works diligently to still her heart—a new shadow joins them. This shadow, blacker than all the others.

It is their master. It is Yupe Tashu.

The Acolytes bow to him. They gabble their glee at seeing him again after so long. He is not their only master. He is one of many (though their living masters number far fewer than their dead ones), but he is the closest they have to the Sith Empire created around

Sidious and Vader. They paw at him, and he adores it, his crevasse-lined face tilting back with pleasure.

Kiza does not join them. She's too afraid to do anything, even to move. It's as if she's a stack of little rocks and if she moves, all of who she is will crumble apart and collapse.

Tashu begins giving them their weapons. They were to wait for him here. He says they are special. They receive artifacts and relics from the ancient departed Sith. To some, he hands dark robes. To others, he gives glowing red crystals around gut-leather cords.

Then he turns to Kiza.

He hands her a mask.

The mask is burnished bronze. The smooth metal is peppered with tiny, hammered divots. The eyes are black glass. There is no nose or mouth—though where the mouth should be is a line of black rivets.

"The mask of Viceroy Exim Panshard," he says, giggling. "A mask made of meteoric metal and containing the screams of a hundred innocents slaughtered for the viceroy's pleasure. Masks have power. Some are worn in the grave. Others worn in life. This, like the others in my collection, has gathered the darkness of the living Force! Wear it. You are anointed, Kiza of Corellia."

"I . . ."

The others stare at her. Some, in awe. Others balefully.

Remi's gaze is poisonous. He says, suddenly: "I should have that." And he reaches for the mask—

Tashu snaps at him. Literally. His mouth opens and closes on open air, the half-broken teeth clacking together as Remi's hand recoils. "You do not deny the wishes of the venerable specters," Tashu hisses.

"I . . ."

"Also, the lady needs a weapon. Does she not?"

Tashu's eyes twinkle with a special kind of madness as he reaches down and snatches the lightsaber hilt from Remi's belt. He places it gingerly in her hand.

It throbs with power. She knows not to turn it on—not yet. Its red glow could give them away. But its *potential* thrums against her palm. And as she lifts her chin and lets the mask rest upon her face, she feels a wonderful darkness sweep over her. It is a consumptive void and with great hunger it chews into her fear and swallows it in great, greedy gobbets. With the fear gone, her anger emerges anew. It springs forth like a living thing inside her. A vicious creature hatches within her heart.

Time moves strangely. She blinks and it has begun. She's there, now, at the outpost. *I'm not alone,* she thinks. The others are here. They have their mundane weapons: clubs and machine shop blades and ugly chop-axes, all painted the red of blood, the red of Sith. Republic fools scream and flee. One comes toward her and the red blade extends from its hilt in her hand—she can feel its vibration up through her elbow, all the way across the bridge of her shoulders and into her very *teeth*. A swipe of the blade cuts one scream short. Another takes the legs out from under a fleeing woman. Hate pulses in her. Her heart beats so hard, it feels as if it'll shatter her breastbone in twain.

Kiza moves with little precision. She swings and swipes with the blade. The Force does not move through her, but the weapon is still unlike anything else she's ever seen—it cuts through flesh, bone, metal. The light leaves streaks of itself burning across her vision. It thrills her.

Then she's down. Something slams into her. Her head snaps against the ground. *New Republic scum!* Anger not entirely her own threads up through her like braiding vines, and as she rolls over she sees it's not a Republic soldier at all.

It's Remi.

His face is pale and struck with fury. As he yells at her, spit flecks from his mouth. "You aren't worthy. That's *mine*. Everything you have been given, *I gave you!* You weak stripling! You coward! You *thief*."

Her hand is empty. The lightsaber hilt is gone. She paws at the ground, kicking at him with clumsy feet as he descends upon her. Remi's long-fingered hands find her neck and close around it. He's weeping and laughing as his grip tightens. She gags trying to get air. Her own hand bats at the wet grass, finding no lightsaber. Above them is the darkness of the outpost landing platform, and she hears the screams and yells of the Acolytes and their victims. Someone falls off the edge and lands nearby—*thud*.

Everything starts to go black.

Her eyelids flutter.

Then she finds it. Her fingers close around cold metal.

It happens fast, but feels slow. She jams the unignited blade against Remi's temple. His eyes are round and suddenly afraid.

The red blade spears through his skull. His eyelids strain open. The eyes themselves cook and go red before burning to cinder.

He drops.

Kiza stands, adjusting her mask.

Then she lets the anger take her anew, and she resumes her assault. Soon, the outpost falls. Soon, the Acolytes claim triumph.

CHAPTER TWENTY-FIVE

WAR IS COMING.

Leia sits and tries not to think about it. She doesn't turn on the HoloNet. She doesn't go to her balcony on Chandrila and look up in the sky to see the fleet gathering in orbit. Instead, she sits on a chair in the room that will very soon serve as the nursery to her son. The cradle sits nearby. Next to it is the sanctuary tree, the one given to her by the little Ewok, Wicket. She's never been able to feel the tree—the so-called serpent's puzzle—with the Force, but she can see with her eyes that the burnished golden bark shines with health, and every day the twining branches sport new scarlet leaves.

But her baby boy? Him she can effortlessly feel inside her. Not just the way that all mothers can feel the living creature within, but she can feel him with the invisible hands of the Force: With it she senses the margins of his burgeoning mind, she knows his mood, she can tell that he's healthy. He is less a human-shaped thing and more a pulsing, living band of light. Light that sometimes dims, that sometimes is thrust through with a vein of darkness. She tells herself that it's normal—Luke said to her, *Leia, we all have that.* He explained that the brighter the light, the darker the shadow.

Right now her son is upset, tumbling inside her as if he can't get comfortable. His light, flickering with the dark. She centers herself and concentrates. The walls of the room fall away. Everything is white and then it's black. Then she's in the calm, airless void. As Leia finds her peace, so does her son. He stops turning . . .

Then he gets the hiccups.

Hic. Hic. Hic.

She sighs and it brings her out of it. But she laughs, too. Because the hiccups tickle her. They're like little bubbles inside—a curious effervescence like nothing Leia has ever felt before.

My son is alive. The future is bright.

That bright future casts dark shadows, though, and now war is again on the horizon. Not a new war—no, the same war they've been fighting all this time. A war that began as a rebellion and soon transformed into a proper struggle between the Empire and the Republic. Now, she hopes, this will finish it. The future is bright, yes, but only if this goes well. Only if the Empire burns out in a searing flash, gone to ash.

Han comes home not long after, and he finds her there in the room. He tells her only a little about what happened on Nakadia, but it's enough for her to know that he had a hand in making things right.

"That's what you're good at," she tells him, reaching up to meet him as he stoops down. "Making things right."

She kisses his cheek. He looks aw-shucks embarrassed.

"It's happening," he says. "Jakku."

"I know."

"It's gonna be one helluva battle. It might get bad."

"I know that, too."

He chews his lip. "It feels weird, doesn't it?"

"Not being there, you mean."

"Yeah. You, me, Luke. *Chewie*. The *Falcon*. Those two walking talking garbage cans. It feels weird we're not part of it."

"We've got our own adventure." She pats her belly.

"End of an era," he says.

"And the start of a new one."

The baby turns inside her again, troubled by something she cannot feel and cannot yet understand.

War is coming.

And hopefully soon after, it ends. Sinjir cares little for the vagaries of war—he tells himself he has no investment in whether the New Republic wins or loses even as he feels himself looking forward to the demise of the Empire he once served. Rather, he needs the war because that is the only way he fears he'll ever get to see Jas and Norra again.

"Ow," Conder says, wincing. "You're not paying attention to what you're doing again."

"I'm paying attention perfectly," Sinjir says, screwing a small plug of absorbent fiber-cloth into Conder's nose. The slicer winces and pulls away.

"Your mind is wandering like a child at a toy market."

Sinjir shrugs. "Fine, yes, perhaps. Sorry. I'm more used to causing pain than soothing it." He winds another bit of cloth into the other nostril.

The two of them are back on Chandrila. Solo brought them home. They toyed with staying on Nakadia for a time, but Conder frowned at the notion, saying that the pastoral planet made Chandrila look like Coruscant. *It's all just . . . crops,* he said at the time, and Sinjir was inclined to agree.

Now Sinjir works to mend the slicer's abused face. Bacta, gauze, fiber-cloth, and a good old-fashioned needle-and-thread. The worst hit was the last one Conder took—the one they heard over the comlink.

"I must commend you again," Sinjir says. "A transceiver tooth? Genius. And I never knew." That's how Conder broadcast to them—using his tongue to slowly, arduously flip to their comlink channel. The broadcast ended when that Herglic thug whapped him in the face.

"A man must keep his secrets."

"Not me. I have none. I am done with secrets."

"Somehow, I doubt that, Sin."

Conder's gentle eyes twinkle. Sinjir admires the man. His drive. His capability. After rescuing the slicer from the warehouse, they had to move fast—the good news was, as suspected, that the Black Sun and Red Key thugs had hacked a line to the datapads of their five senators. The line was encrypted, though, which is where Conder came in. The slicer did as the name suggested, slicing through algorithms like a man with a blade cutting ribbons. In only a few minutes, Conder—beaten, woozy, caked in his own blood—stole access to the senators' datapads.

And from there, they delivered the messages.

Sinjir's initial idea was to threaten them. But Sinjir also knew that threats created fear and fear made people act a certain way. It's one thing to have someone bound to a chair; there, you control the fear. You wield it like a weapon. But those senators were in the wind. A fight-or-flight response could've had them doing any number of unpredictable things—turning themselves in, running for the exits, or even voting as the syndicates demanded they vote in the hope it would save them.

No, instead Sinjir said to make them an offer—an offer braided into the threat. He had Conder send a missive telling them they would be given pardons if they voted with the chancellor. And further, they told Nim Tar that his child was safe and Sorka that her prize jerba was rescued. (That latter bit was a necessary lie. Sorka will soon learn that the syndicates already sold her prize animal on the butchers' black market.)

And with that, they did it.

They solved the plot. They got the votes. The final battle is coming.

Conder says: "You're worried."

"Am I that obvious?"

"Usually not. This time, you are." Conder clasps his hand. "Jas and Norra will be fine."

"I could go. I should go. Demand to be put in a ship. Like Jom. Like Temmin. I should *be there*."

"You're not a soldier."

"I trained to be, once," Sinjir says. "I know how to fight."

"If you want to go, I'll go, too. Maybe they can use a slicer."

Sinjir nods. "I suppose it's not impossible." He hates that he wants to be there. He knows himself and he should be balking at this. Loyalty only goes so far, and despite once being the man who tested the loyalty of others, he himself is not particularly *fond* of the concept. And yet here he is. Wanting to rush into danger *again* for his friends. He supposes he should stop being surprised. *I've become a different person than I expected.* Or maybe he was a different person all along, led to a myth *about* himself created *by* himself. Is that how people are? Do they all have two sides? Who they really are, and who they believe themselves to be?

"Who do we ask?"

"Considering the size of the favor we just performed in service to the chancellor, I think we might ask her."

Conder draws a deep breath. "Are we going to Jakku? Are we really doing this?"

"We might be, dearest Conder, we might be."

"I had hoped for a nicer vacation."

Sinjir *hrm*s. "You and me both."

War is coming.

It's what Jom Barell is built for. He never really felt like he trained for war but rather that he was just plain made that way. All his life it's been about the fight. He fought against the Empire on Onderon. He fought against his own bloodline *brothers* there. He fought as a rebel. He fought as a commando for the New Republic. He fought with Norra and her crew.

And now he wants to fight again.

Sergeant Dellalo Dayson is, with her SpecForce team, loading munitions onto a low-atmo U-Wing. It's a fat-bellied starfighter used as a troop transport, meant for fast, dangerous insertion into enemy territory. It's an old class of fighter, but this is an old class of soldier. Jom feels that way, too.

He whistles to Dayson as he skirts past one of the ship's four engines. "Sergeant," he calls.

She turns and stares down her long nose at him. "You cleaned up," she says. And he has. He shaved everything down—though he left the handlebar mustache and the meatchop sideburns. He combed his hair. Best he can do to look like a proper commando again. "Whaddya need, Barell?"

"I need to go with you."

"No can do. Not my call. You want back in, there's a whole chain of command you gotta climb." She sees his face and offers both hands up in a peaceable gesture. "Don't get mad at me, Jom. You broke ranks and did your own thing. You go and talk to General Tyben, maybe he gives you a stamp and gets you back on your way. But it won't be with my crew."

"Damnit, Dayson—"

"Sergeant Dayson, if you'll recall."

His nostrils flare. "*Sergeant*. This fight? It matters. Maybe more than all the others." She probably thinks he means it because this could be the Empire's last hurrah. And that's true. But for Jom, it's personal. For Jom, it's about Jas. He drops his bag. He cranes his neck so that the vertebrae pop. "I'll fight you for it. I'll fight the whole platoon for it. I take even *one* of you out, I want to take that commando's place."

Dayson laughs. "We'd kill you."

"Maybe. But that's better than having to go through the bureaucracy."

Coming off the ramp, pushing an empty grav-lifter, is another SpecForce commando: a goat-snouted, three-eyed Gran by the name of Margle. Jom knows him a little. He's like Jom: good with heavy ordnance. "I hear something about a fight?" the Gran growls. "I'm in!"

"*Cool it,*" Dayson says. "Nobody's throwing fists today. And you're right about the bureaucracy. You start making noise here I might have reports to do— and damn the stars, I *hate* filling out reports"

"Dayson. *Sergeant*—"

"Stow it, Jom. You want in on this mission? Fine. I got an extra jump seat. You want to do your part, I'll say you came aboard and hid in the head until we were pushing hyperspace. But after that, I won't stand for you. You come home, they might have a court-martial or a dishonor badge for you. That weight's on your shoulders and I won't carry it."

"Thanks, Sarge."

"We leave in five. Step to it, commando. The war won't wait."

* * *

War is coming.

And Temmin wants to be there. He steps in front of Wedge and drops his hastily packed rucksack on the ground with a *thud*. Wedge looks at it and arches an eyebrow. "What's this?" he asks the young man.

"I'm enlisting."

"It doesn't work like that, Tem."

"I don't care. I want to go to Jakku."

"You're a boy."

"Not anymore. You were training me to be with Phantom Squadron. I can fly an X-wing."

Wedge sets down his datapad. All around him, the hangar buzzes with activity—already, most of the star-fighters and their pilots have gone on to join the fleet massing above Chandrila, soon to fly on to Jakku. But all the same, that's just the first wave. They have to prep more fighters, more pilots. Prime torpedoes, test weapons systems, get the next set of pilots ready. There's a lot to do and he tells Temmin as much:

"You can fly a training simulator. Kid, I've got work to do—"

"I've piloted the *Halo*. I've piloted the *Falcon*. You even let me do a few rounds in an X-wing. I can fight. And I will. I'll steal a ship if I have to. I'll steal a flying brick cargo loader and crash it into the front deck of a Star Destroyer. I'm *going* to Jakku. And I'd rather you be there with me."

"Phantom Squadron is shut down."

Temmin steps over his sack and looks up at Wedge. The young man's eyes flare with eager fury. "Then bring it back from the dead! Nobody has to know we're doing it. Nobody has to see us coming. We can be like real phantoms, Wedge. Not heroes in the books, but who cares about being in the books?" Now tears shine in Temmin's eyes. "My *mom* is there. My droid, too. I want them back. You don't want to help me get them? *Fine.* But then I'll know who you really are, and it isn't the guy who flew against two Death Stars and all the Empire. I'll know you're not a pilot anymore. You're just some hangar-monkey, some tired old *sir-yes-sir* game-leg who cares more about docking ledgers than he does about *actual people.*"

Now it's Wedge's turn: Anger and grief rise up inside him, the anger like fire, the grief like smoke. He wants to tell Temmin how wrong he is, but he can't. Because the kid *isn't* wrong, is he?

Again Wedge is reminded of the Rebel Alliance. And Kashyyyk. And all the sacrifices made on behalf of the New Republic.

Sometimes doing the right thing wasn't the same as following orders.

"Ah, forget it," Temmin says, wiping his eyes with the back of his hands. His lip trembles. "I should've known you were out of the game."

"*Wait.*"

Temmin pauses in picking up his bag. "Why should I?"

"Meet me in Hangar Forty-Seven on the north side in two hours."

"What's in Hangar Forty-Seven?"

"Phantom Squadron."

War is coming.

It waits out there in the black. Commodore Kyrsta Agate stands on the bridge of the *Concord,* the first Nadiri Mark One Starhawk commissioned for the New Republic, and not the last—two more Starhawks hang out there in the space above Chandrila. They wait with dozens of other capital ships: the Alderaanian *Sun-*

spire; the Corellian *Redeemer,* an assault frigate; and of course, their flagship, the Mon Calamari's *Home One.*

Her hands are shaking. As they do.

In the glass of the viewport, though, is a ghost hovering amid the fleet, a ghost with a ruined face. Half the face is smooth and plasticky, fitting poorly against the other, more natural half. That plastic has none of the blemishes associated with flesh: no moles, no marks, no crow's-feet by the eyes, no curving lines carved around the side of the mouth. It is an imperfect fit, as well—around the eye, the skin ends prematurely, yielding the dark, turning mechanics that support the mechanical eye.

That eye glows red. It telescopes as the aperture opens and it focuses on its own reflection, for the face of the wraith is just Agate's own mask.

On Liberation Day, one of the Rodian ex-captives turned on her, driven to the act by a control chip in the meat of his brain. He fired, and she took the hit on the side of her face. They reconstructed the bone, but the flesh was gone. What's there now is nu-skin, grown in a lab and applied with a brush. Over time, it is meant to look more natural, but it'll never be her own. Agate will always know.

The eye had to go. She asked for a mechanical replacement: The oculus-lens that they installed at least has function, if not form. It is ugly and protrusive and makes her feel less than human. But with it, she can see heat signatures and other data as long as she closes her other (human) eye.

"Commodore."

Behind her, Admiral Ackbar steps out of the turbolift. It shushes closed behind him. Ackbar has been a friend through all of this—a comforting presence at her bedside and through all the surgeries.

"I never thought I'd be back," she says. Her voice is different since the attack. The blast took out some of her teeth. Messed up her jaw. It's all been reconstructed, but now she *sounds* different. She hates it.

"I'm glad you accepted the invitation."

She turns. The Mon Calamari approaches, his hands clasped behind his back. As he walks, she tells him, "It means a great deal to me, Admiral. But I still have reservations. I don't know that I'm ready."

"You are. You must be. Commodore, you are among our best and our brightest—"

"Some of the light has gone out of me, Admiral."

"And *despite* what happened, you remain one of our most vital commanders because you recognize the burden of war. You do not go to it lightly. You do not arrive with anger, not even after the Empire struck us at home and stole your eye from you."

"I gave up command of this ship."

"And I have returned it to you. Lieutenant Commander Spohn is glad to serve at your behest."

"I'm not ready."

Ackbar's voice softens. He reaches out and places one of his webbed hands on her shoulder. "None of us are ready. No one can ever be truly ready for what war brings. The best we can do is meet it with our face forward and our hearts clear. You will do that. I know you will."

"They know we're coming. They must. With an open government and a free media, that means the HoloNet will have reported on the vote. And surely the Empire knows about the *Oculus* spying on them from afar."

"Almost surely. Ensign Deltura reports that their fleet has grown and is consolidating in a defensive arrangement. This will not be a surprise for them or for us. It is the purest form of battle. Both sides, ready to fight."

"It may be a ruse. They may be luring us in—"

"If they are, we will be ready."

She feels a single tear threaten to slip free of her one good eye and hastily blinks it away. "Tell me we're going to win this. Tell me this will be the end of it. The end of the Empire and the start of a new galaxy."

"I'm no prophet, Kyrsta. I do not know who will win this day or who will even survive it to see the outcome. I only know it will be an honor to fight alongside you once again, whether this is our last battle or the first of many more to come." His long fingers give her shoulder a squeeze.

Agate struggles not to cry out. She wants to run off this bridge and go home. Get in her bed, hide under the covers, turn out the lights, and wait for HoloNet to tell her who won, who lost, who lived, who died. *When did I become this coward? Why am I quaking like a gun-shy child?*

"May the Force be with you" is all she says.

Ackbar nods. "And with you, Commodore. I must go. It is almost time."

War is coming. And soon, she prays, it is ending.

CHAPTER TWENTY-SIX

THE IMPERIAL SHUTTLE circles the base. From up here, Sloane can see everything: the command HQ, the landing platforms, the lines of walkers and starfighters. Everything looks prefab, as if it was hastily constructed.

As if it's all temporary, she thinks.

The shuttle lands around the far side of the base, easing into a hangar bay whose mouth is eclipsed by the shadow of a tall ridge.

Rax is not on this shuttle with her. Brentin is. He sits silently across from her. He's frightened. She can see it in his eyes—the eyes of prey looking up into the jaws of a predator.

Sloane will not be scared. She refuses. *I am the predator,* she thinks. *I'm close, now. So close.* Rax may have taken her captive. But that also puts her hands very close to his neck.

The ramp opens. Sloane sees that the other two ships sit to their right. One of the troopers shoves her and Brentin down the ramp. Wexley loses his footing, falling hard without his balance, and the trooper ushering him forward stops to kick Brentin in the side, hard. The others laugh. *This is not my Empire,* she thinks. It is sloppy and cruel.

They pick Brentin up and push him down next to

her. Behind her back, the magnacuffs are uncomfortably tight.

Rax awaits her, already off the shuttle. Troopers have lined up on either side of him. And Brendol Hux is here, too: the man behind Arkanis. Hux was helping to train the next generation of stormtroopers. She, with the aid of the bounty hunter Mercurial Swift, helped to extract Brendol and his son from Arkanis before it fell to the Republic. He's now on Rax's own Shadow Council. The man's a blustering ass, and she sees that he's let himself go: A gut strains at his belt. His hair is a mess. His eyes look tired.

Those eyes look to the margins of the hangar, from left to right, and it's then that Sloane sees that others have joined them, too—

Along each wall of the hangar are children. Two dozen of them, roughly. They are young—some early in their teenage years, others not yet that age. They all wear plain white uniforms. Like nightclothes.

Rax smiles. "Troopers, weapons down, please. We're all friends."

The stormtroopers lower their blasters.

But Rax says, "No, no, all the way down. To the floor."

The troopers give one another brief looks of confusion, but do as asked: They stoop, laying the weapons upon the ground.

Rax walks up to her. Looking her over. "Do you see how the troopers have marked their armor? Painted it. Carved it up. Burned it with hot metal. They have transcended mere service. They are not just soldiers. They are something altogether more tribal, more ferocious, less human, all animal." He sighs. "But I still don't know that it's enough."

"What have you done with my Empire?" she asks, desperate.

He grins. "Ah. Let me show you."

Gallius Rax's hand rises in the air, forming a fist. He snaps his fingers once—

The lights in the hangar go out. Sloane's heart jumps into her throat.

Her eyes are slow to adjust, but her ears hear the sounds of the fracas. She thinks to run, to duck, to flinch, to flee, but she can't imagine where she would even go or what she would do. All she does instead is tighten her body and lower herself to the smallest profile she can—hunkering down so that her chin is tucked between her knees.

Blasterfire lances the dark, now. But that doesn't last long. After which there are thumps, thuds, crunches— and grunts of pain.

Silence, now, stretches out for one beat, two, three—

Until it is ended by another snap of the fingers.

The lights come on. Again her eyes have to adjust. Everything goes from bleeding black to overwhelming white, and as her vision reconstitutes she sees the floor is littered with bodies.

The bodies belong to stormtroopers. All dead, by the look of it.

Standing over them are the children. Many hold sharp, crude knives with handles swaddled in dark tape, the blades made of black, dull steel. Some knives are buried in the backs of trooper necks—shoved elegantly, perfectly up under the helmet into the brain stem. Some are under the troopers' arms, where another gap in armor waits and makes them vulnerable. A few of the children hold blasters, too. Rifles venting smoke.

One of those children is a tall girl with her hair shorn to the scalp. Her face is a dead, emotionless mask. Brendol Hux, in contrast, is smiling. It is the smile of a child—giddy, broad, as if he's just seeing outer space for the first time, or just had his first taste of sweet-taff. Has she ever seen him smile before? It is a terror to behold.

What was it Rax said to her back on the *Ravager*? Back when he commanded her to rescue Brendol from Arkanis? *The Empire must be fertile and young. Children are crucial to our success. Many of our officers are old. We need that kind of vitality. That brand of energy you get with the young. The Empire* needs *children.*

Sloane fails to repress a shudder. She dearly wants to vomit, but she dare not give Gallius Rax the satisfaction.

The counselor, for his part, offers slow, measured applause. "Behold, Sloane," he says. "The future of my Empire. I hope you enjoyed the show. You'll soon see that this is only just the beginning."

She has no words. Brentin is speechless, as well, having fallen back on his tailbone, slumping against the still body of the trooper that was guarding him. His mouth is open and slack. His eyes are wrenched wide with horror. And that's when Brendol, finally composing himself, steps forward and whispers something in Rax's ear.

Now it is the counselor's turn to smirk.

"The final battle is coming," he says. "I'd like you to see it. The both of you. You are witnesses from both the old Empire and the conquering rebels. I have a seat for you reserved. Brendol, you and the children escort these two to their seats, will you? Seems I have a speech to give."

Finally, it has come to pass.

Finally, the New Republic has smelled the blood

he's been casting into the water and *finally*, they are arriving to take a bite.

It's all coming together. Hux's child-soldiers have proven themselves—yes, those troopers were unarmed, but the sheer *speed* with which the children dispatched trained soldiers was thrilling to behold. They did it eagerly, but without joy *and* without fear.

Further, he has Sloane in hand. The Observatory is protected and he can finally show her now what he has been doing—and how her failure to have faith in him has cost her a role in the grand finale to come.

It is time now to give his speech.

He thinks to not give a speech at all. Time is of the essence—the New Republic fleet will be here in a matter of hours. Maybe *minutes*. He and the others have to make their way back to the Observatory . . .

But no. The speech will be essential. He must fill the Empire with fire! It is his job to stir them, to enrage them, to prime the detonator before he throws it. Besides, this will be his final mark. It will be captured and saved. It will be broadcast for generations. This is a moment for history.

I am making history. Rax has to remember that. His footprint will be indelible, forever pressed into the mantle of the galaxy's memory.

He meets with Tashu and Brendol. Both of them seem overly pleased with themselves. (Rax sees no reason right now to remind them that they owe it all to him. Let them bloat on the gas of their own satisfaction.) Together they move outside the base to meet with the rest of his council before his Empire gathers to hear him speak this last time.

Hodnar Borrum walks up, hands behind his back, chin up. He suddenly looks ten years younger, as if the prospect of war is the food that feeds him the same way water wakes a wilting flower. Borrum says as they walk, "We will win the ground battle handily, Counselor."

Randd is in hologram form (for he is currently aboard the Star Destroyer *Inflictor*), beamed by a projector held in the hand of Yupe Tashu. The grand moff says as his projection bounces: "Their fleet will be larger than ours, but we have the *Ravager*. Theirs is still a ragtag force—strategically ill fed and cobbled together of incompatible ships and squadrons. We are unified. And in that unification we will win this battle."

"Excellent," Rax says as he strides boldly toward the stage. And he means it. It *is* excellent. All of it. Even the part where they are wrong.

The general asks: "Where is Obdur? We should be considering our messaging during all of this."

"Ferric has taken sick," Rax answers curtly. It's not a lie. Not really. Being stabbed to death in your bed *is* quite sickening. That moment serves as another success of Hux's program. A few of the children have proven particularly effective, it seems.

His "advisers" want to keep on nattering at him. But what they have to say matters little, after all, and only serves themselves.

It is time to speak.

Rax shushes the others with a hand and strides past them, up a set of metal steps, onto the dais. The stage is small, erected at the fore of the base and looking out over the tens of thousands of troopers gathered.

Above, the fleet hangs like specters. Around him and the troops are TIE fighters, bombers, troop carriers, shuttles, transports, walkers.

The engine of war has thrummed to life.

The Empire awaits his talk, though truly, right now, he has one audience of note: Behind him and above him, on the roof of the command headquarters, he knows that Sloane and her rebel scum cohort sit.

Rax steps out in front of the podium and speaks. His image is projected large behind him, a massive flickering holostatue. His voice is beamed loudly over all of them so it is less like a man speaking and more like a god whose divine command comes as a crashing, crushing wave.

The speech that he gives is one he has been rehearsing for months. It is designed as a mechanism—the best speeches are performances meant not to give information or to convey truth but rather, to leave an effect. It is vital not to make his people *think*, but only to force them to *feel*. He does not want to leave them with uncertainty. They need only answers.

The best speech is not a question mark. It is an exclamation.

His voice booms as he speaks:

Loyal soldiers of the Galactic Empire, madness is at our door. Ruffians and barbarians of the Rebel Alliance have claimed for themselves a government of no legitimacy, a government given over to corrosion, chaos, and the corruption born of alien minds and radical terroristic teachings. It was our own Emperor Palpatine who showed us the weakness that presents itself when a Republic becomes sick with the disease of craven politics and the illness of elite oligarchs who force their agendas upon us.

With the death of our beloved Emperor, our own Empire was cast into disorder. It gave strength to the illegitimate, and emboldened them with a fraudulent claim of bringing peace and justice to the galaxy—and yet, for so long, who have been the champions of peace? The only war visited upon the galaxy has been the one brought by the criminal Rebel Alliance.

Scattered and lost, we could have perished. After attacking Chandrila and injuring the fraudulent politicians who seek to steal the sanctity of our galaxy, I brought us here to Jakku, unifying our people and our powers in this faraway world—a hard world that has tested our mettle and forged us and sharpened us into a stronger blade. A blade with which we will slit the throats of the traitors that crawl on their bellies toward our door. Soon they come! Soon they try to finish what they started. They want to end the Empire. They want to set up as a tumor on a healthy body, leeching the blood while growing fatter like a parasite. They deny our legitimacy. They lie about the stability and sanity we created for the galaxy. For those are their truest weapons: deception and delusion. We must not give in. We must not believe that they are right. We must see them as they are:

Brutes and barbarians! They are subhuman. They are alien to us in the truest sense of the word and are deserving of no mercy from us. This is our zero hour, and I call you now to do your duty by the light of the glorious Galactic Empire. The battle to come is not a fight for Jakku or even a fight for the Empire. It is a fight for all the galaxy. If we fail here, we fail everywhere. We fail our loved ones. We fail our children. We fail all who crave constancy and light in these dark times.

We pursue no other aim than freedom from oppression, liberty from lies, emancipation from depravity.

Today is the day we fight back and reclaim our galaxy.

Today is the day the New Republic dies at the Empire's hand.

Today we take our future!

(If only they knew what that future meant.)

And then it's as if the galaxy is listening, as if the Force is truly on his side, for what occurs is an event of *such theatrical synchronicity* that Gallius Rax nearly drops to his knees and weeps like a baby—

The attack begins.

Thunder ripples as the New Republic fleet spears the sky, already launching a fusillade—and the Imperial fleet above fires its own in response. Far above their heads, turbolasers slash the sky. Torpedoes corkscrew. Javelins of heavy plasma fire slices open the blue.

Rax bellows one last entreaty:

The battle is upon us. Go! Go and drag them down to the ground and break their necks with your boots! Take their heads! End their tyranny!

And now he must go collect the others and board a ship before it's too late. The Observatory beckons, and it is time for his egress.

No, no, no . . .

Sloane is on her knees. Her hands are bound. So are her ankles. Brentin has fallen over, letting himself topple to the side and curl in on himself. The two of them are up on the roof of the Empire's command building, underneath the flap of a tent. They are alone. No one watches them. At first, Sloane thought, *How strange,* but now she sees: She has nowhere to go even if she could get free. As she and Brentin are forced to sit

there and stomach Rax's speech, she tries to understand what's even happening here. Why let her witness
this? What is she even meant to see?

The man's speech is base and dull and full of the
pompous rhetorical milk on which Gallius Rax is fed,
and yet—it works, doesn't it? Sloane feels it in her
own belly. The trumpeting, triumphant roar of an Empire spurned. The fear of a New Republic ascendant.
The certainty of being in the right and committing violence against those in the wrong . . .

And with that, a tiny mote of doubt plants inside
her belly. The seed grows fast tendrils, and she wonders: *Am I the product of confidently championed
lies? Was this my Empire all along? Will it die here on
Jakku?*

As Rax's rhetoric finishes, the sky opens up and—as
if perfectly timed to the conclusion of his speech—the
battle begins.

Capital ships rage in the planet's orbit. Weapons
fire drums like thunder. Specks appear in the sky and
turn from translucent ghosts to buzzing black flies—
starfighters spilling out of the New Republic ships.
Already they enter atmosphere, scoring the ground
with plasma.

And the Empire roars to meet it. TIE fighters lift off
and in moments are launching forth like rocks from a
slingshot. Soon the sky is chaos. Fighters erupt in
flame. Laserfire rends the air. X-wings and TIE fighters
dance in and around banded clouds while Imperial
walkers turn to march out into the desert, ready to
protect the base at any cost.

The battle in the skies has begun and soon, the
ground war will rise.

The numbers of the New Republic fleet are superior.
She can see that from here. Perhaps Rax stoked the
proper ferocity in his troopers, and maybe, just maybe,

his people can coordinate a proper pushback. Hodnar Borrum is one of the smartest ground war strategists, and the troops trust him. But if she's correct, Randd is the man in charge of the skies—and though the grand moff is a capable leader, he does not have the courage or the inventiveness to win a fight of this magnitude.

Sloane wishes suddenly to be up there. That is her place: commanding those ships, ruling the heavens, destroying any who dare defile them. The *Ravager* casts a massive shadow, and she knows that whoever is in command of that ship is wrong for the job. It should be her. She could save the Empire with the *Ravager*. If she had a chance to get to it . . .

Such ego, she thinks. Perhaps the firepower of that SSD will afford them the chance to save the day. The Empire *may* win this battle.

But even if it does—at what cost?

And what else does Rax have up his sleeve?

What is the show? Who is the audience?

CHAPTER TWENTY-SEVEN

THE STONE TREMBLES. Dust streams from the cavern ceiling, and scree streams from the smooth boreholes that populate Niima's temple. Norra looks to Jas, worried. "Do I want to know?"

It's Bones that answers. The droid tilts his skullish head toward the ceiling and he *hm*s. "I AM INTIMATELY FAMILIAR WITH THE SOUND OF VIOLENCE AND THAT IS THE SOUND OF VIOLENCE."

"War," Jas says. "Now we're really in the thick of it."

Could it be that the New Republic has finally brought its fleet here? Norra isn't sure what to think about that. She wondered if it was going to be like Kashyyyk—an Empire-controlled planet left to suffer due to the hesitant whims of a nervous voting body. "It'll complicate things," she says.

Jas shrugs. "At this point, I'm not sure it can get any more complicated, Norra."

With that said, the two of them finish putting on their Imperial officer uniforms. Norra in noncom black, Jas in the standard gray. Norra's outfit indicates her role as a prison administrator, whereas the bounty hunter's bars serve to show her ranking as an army staff sergeant.

Bones asks: "DO I GET A UNIFORM?"

"I don't think they have anything in your size," Norra answers.

"Maybe if we collapse you down, you can be a mouse droid."

Norra laughs. It feels good to laugh—even if it's short-lived. Even that small moment of mirth makes her feel better. Like they can do anything. A little part of her thinks that they can pull this off. Yes, it's dangerous. And completely foolish. Probably a suicide mission. And yet what choice do they have? She still wants Sloane, but Brentin is now the priority. It's no longer a mission of vengeance but rather one of rescue.

Niima, to their great surprise, has chosen to help them. (Though, really, *her* aid is not driven by kindness, but rather revenge. Turns out, the Hutt overlord cares little for being perforated by blasterfire.) She's furnished them with an (old-make) Imperial shuttle, a couple of (dusty, moth-nibbled) uniforms, and (hopefully solid) high-ranking codes.

"Are we ready?" Jas asks.

"I don't know that there is such a thing as ready."

"Hey," Jas says, offering a steadying hand. The worry on Norra's face must be broadcasting loud and clear. "We're doing the right thing. We're paying our debts. We're finishing the job. There's no greater honor."

"Jas, I know you've given up a lot to be here. This isn't what you do, and you put your life on hold to do it. I don't think I've ever said thank you. You've taken up a cause that isn't yours and—"

"Stop. It is my cause because I've made it my cause. My aunt was a bounty hunter and she used to help people. She'd abandon jobs to save some group of farmers or help free a bunch of Wookiees—and when I was young, I heard all those stories and I thought she was naïve. I said I'd *never* be like her. But here I am. And you know what I realized? She had it right. The job isn't anything. The job is just a job. And those debts don't mean as much as *these* debts—the ones between you and me, the ones between . . ." She seems almost flustered now, like she's exposing too much of herself and can't find the words. "The ones between regular people and the whole damn galaxy. Crewing with you has changed me, Norra Wexley. And I owe *you* for that."

She offers a hand. Norra takes it. They pull each other into an embrace. Norra says over the bounty hunter's shoulder: "This sounds suspiciously like one of those talks you give before you die."

"I don't know that we're going to die, but we're about to head into the dragon's den *and* we're doing it on a world now smashed between two warring forces. I think it's best to assume we may not make it."

"Good pep talk."

"Could be worse. I could be Sinjir."

"Gods, I miss him. And I miss my son."

"I miss them, too. So let's stop chatting and do the work."

Together they leave this small grotto and head back toward where the shuttle awaits. As they get closer, Jas spins around suddenly, clamping a hand over Norra's mouth and hissing for her to shush.

What the—?

Emari touches a finger to Norra's ear. A sign to listen.

So she listens.

Voices. They float through the passageways—and instantly she recognizes one of them: Mercurial Swift.

Jas waves them forward, whispering for Bones to be quiet. The droid's legs bend inward and he eases forth on the tips of his skeletal toes. Together they gather around the bend just before the passageway empties out into the smooth, sculpted cavern mouth where the shuttle is parked. And it's there they see Swift.

He's not alone. With him are three others: a broad-shouldered Kyuzo, a round-bellied human with a filthy head swaddling, and a tall Rodian with antennae so long they almost droop over her bulbous blue-black eyes.

They stand before Niima. The shuttle waits just beyond them.

Which means the path is blocked.

Mercurial is saying to Niima: "I know she's here, Hutt. We *saw* our ship land. Point us to the Zabrak and we go in peace."

"AND IF NOT?" the Hutt asks.

It's the man in the head-swaddle who answers: He points a long-barreled rifle and growls, "Then you go in pieces."

"IT IS UNWISE TO THREATEN A HUTT."

"That's Dengar," Jas whispers in a hushed voice.

Mercurial leans in, his chin up and out. "And it's unwise to disappoint me. I'm on Black Sun's payroll, slug. I matter. *You're* just some backwater worm with no power in the galaxy. It looks like somebody already shot you up good and I'm happy to finish the—"

Niima's hand darts out, catching him by the throat. She lifts him up high. His legs dangle as his cheeks bloom red, then purple.

"*Grrk!*" is the sound he makes.

"YOU INSIGNIFICANT SPECK OF INSECT WASTE—"

Dengar thrusts his rifle up into Niima's face. The barrel presses hard against her nose-slits. "Careful, love. I don't much like Swift, either, but I'm going to have to ask you to set him gently down. I'd hate to spray your head-slime all over the pretty rock, hm?"

Norra's heart sinks. She hoped that Niima would be able to handle this. But the Hutt does as commanded—she drops Mercurial.

"I have a plan," Jas whispers.

"I'm all ears."

"I'll distract them. You and Bones take the ship and go."

"*What?* You must've given yourself a concussion when you broke those spikes off your head, Jas. I'm not leaving you behind."

Jas eases Norra back and gets in close, nose-to-nose. "Listen, Norra. Those bounty hunters are skilled. If we leave them alive, they'll alert the Empire that we're coming and our cover will be blown."

"Bones can handle them."

The rattletrap B1 nods furiously at that.

"You'll need him," Jas says. "We can't risk it. They want me. So they'll get me. I'll catch up later."

"Jas, wait—"

But it's too late. She goes back the way she came. *Damnit, Emari.*

Next thing she knows, it's happening. Jas yells from somewhere deeper in the passageways, and with that, the bounty hunters turn toward the noise—and true to the plan, they bolt in her direction. The sound of blasterfire fills the temple, echoing through the chambers.

Norra wants to wait and help. She wants to use Bones and take out the hunters. But Jas is right. She can't risk it.

Brentin. Sloane. The Imperial base. That's the goal. The stakes are huge and she can't risk them on this.

Gritting her teeth, Norra tells Bones to hurry, and together they run for the shuttle.

CHAPTER TWENTY-EIGHT

AT A DISTANCE, the tactics of combat are about the battlespace, or the arena one is given in which to fight. The battlespace above Jakku is nearly limitless—its moons orbit far enough away not to enter the fray, there exists no debris fields as yet, and the only object forming a boundary to the assault is the planet itself.

That gives the New Republic the advantage of coming at the arena from all angles except below.

But the advantage of the Empire is that the fleet is neatly compressed—it has created a nearly perfect defensive perimeter formed of its own Destroyers, with the *Ravager* at the heart of it. That dreadnought has the chance to fire its considerable armament from relative safety, but its angle of attack is limited by the ships that form a sphere of perimeter. It cannot fire wantonly and without regard for its own ships.

That is war. It is the placement of ships. It is the advantages and disadvantages of those placements. It's about how you move, how you fire, what weapons you bring. Every piece fits into the larger whole: ammunition in a blaster, blaster in a pilot's hand, pilot inside a starfighter or frigate. Everything is a resource. How do you expend them? In what direction? At a distance, war is a game, however deadly—usher this ship there, that ship here, converge, fire, dominate, defend.

But when you're in it, there exists no distance at all.

When you're in it, the decisions you make feel less tactical and more *elemental*—for you are part of two forces crashing together like waves, like two mountains toppling into each other, like two planets colliding and breaking apart. There exists no distance, no separation. Not for Commodore Kyrsta Agate, at least, who cannot separate herself out from the orchestrated chaos beyond the viewport of her Starhawk—no, she and her crew and her ship are part of the fabric of the battlespace. She is not a divine hand engineering the movement of pieces on a game board.

Rather, she is one of the pieces.

The bridge is swarming with tension. Comm officers keep her in touch with Ackbar and the other Starhawks. Weapons officers, led by Ensign Sirai, a Pantoran, coordinate all systems to ensure the most effective targeting. A trio of white-helmeted navigators sit nearby, guiding the ship's movement through the battlespace—cutting through the chaos like an ax.

And Agate stands in the center of it all. She gets commands from Ackbar. She relays her commands to the bridge via the senior officer, Lieutenant Commander Spohn. All the while, she feels like she is the star around which everything else orbits. She's not, of course, but she suspects every officer commanding a capital ship feels this way—out there, in the broad viewports that rise above her like the arches of a cathedral, TIE fighters slash past, chased by or chasing New Republic ships. Corvettes lead the charge, pushing on toward the Destroyers, launching their full armament ahead of them—torpedoes that leave indigo streaks in the black. The other two Starhawks slide in on each side of the *Concord*—to starboard side is the *Unity*, to port is the *Amity*.

Agate feels it all. As if her skin, her veins, her nerves,

are all connected to the battle by puppet strings. Her flesh prickles. The hairs on her neck stand tall. It's the strangest feeling, and it never fails to find her: the suspicion that if she *blinks* or *twitches* a finger in the wrong way or dares to *cough* or *sneeze,* somehow that movement will ripple out across the battle—her ship will crash, her friends will fall, the enemy will conquer them all. Absurd, but that is how Agate feels about war. No distance to be found at all. It is intimate. It is anxious. She is part of it and it is part of her, the same way a heart is not separate from the body in which it beats.

One of the corvettes goes up in a bright ball of coruscating energy.

An X-wing spirals, sparking, through space.

One of their Nebulon frigates breaks in half—its front end still firing the full detachment of weapons, peppering the side of a Star Destroyer.

Agate feels it all. Every death feels like her own.

But that is the trick, isn't it? She can't let it overwhelm her. That will come when it's all over (should she survive): At night, it'll feel again like she's dropped over the edge of an abyss. Like she'll want to die. She'll bite a belt or the side of her bed to stop all the thoughts and the endless loop of violence replaying in her head over and over.

All she allows now is that slight shaking that always comes, the one she cannot deny, the one that has become part of who she is. Everything else, all the other tremors, will wait until nighttime. Again, if she survives.

For now, she and the other two Starhawks have one job:

Bring down that dreadnought. Destroy the *Ravager,* end the fight.

Let's get to it, then.

* * *

Temmin is lost.

He told himself he'd be fine. He thought, *I've piloted ships before*. And weeks before he was right here, in the same space, above Jakku—he survived that, and he told himself he could survive this.

But now he's not so sure.

Wedge said the plan was simple: They weren't meant to be here at the battle, so their role was to provide support. Stay out of the way of the big ships, and pick off the TIEs swarming around.

Phantom Squadron leapt out of lightspeed late to the battle, and like a massive beast it swallowed him whole.

TIEs roar past. He's separated from the others. Ahead, Star Destroyers loom in space that turns with a kaleidoscopic twist. A Corellian corvette plunges through open space in front of him, its back end breaking apart in plumes of fire that go from red to green to gold as different gases and fuels vent into the black. Temmin screams, pulling back on the flight stick and trying to right the old X-wing he pilots—but he doesn't know which way is up, down, left, right. *Use the screens. Use the console.* He looks, finds the stabilizer display, then looks up again and—

Alarms go off.

I'm about to crash into the side of a New Republic frigate. The side of that ship looms large, coming up fast like a wall crashing down—

Another scream as Temmin turns the X-wing starboard, spiraling through the battle zone so fast he feels like he's about to puke in his helmet.

The ship rocks with laserfire coming from behind. His astromech—a hexagonal-domed droid with designation R3-W5—whistles, and his screen fills with

warnings. His scopes show he's not alone—a pair of
TIEs are on him like a set of blackflies on a nerf's
haunches, except he doesn't have a tail with which to
swish them away. And he just can't shake them. They
sense the stink of sickness on him—he's like the weak
one in the pack, the one a predator knows instinc-
tively to hunt. *Blast it all to hell, c'mon, Temmin, get
your head out of your hind end and stay alive—*

Boom. One of the TIE fighters explodes, turning
into a fiery cannonball alongside him. It tumbles away,
destroyed. Koko's voice fills his comms with a whoop
and a holler. The Narquois cackles and says: "One
down, the whole damn Empire to go!" The fuzzy blue
pilot whistles and belches into the mike just before his
X-wing whips past.

Next it's Jethpur, the Quarren: He says something in
Quarrenese, but Temmin has no idea what it is. Yarra
fills in the details: "Jeth is right. Snap, you're like a
sparking wire out there." The Twi'lek comes out alongside him as her Y-wing blasts through the second of
the TIEs sticking to him like a burr.

Wedge's X-wing pulls out in front. "Everyone form
up on me. Snap, you good? You want to set coordinates home, nobody would blame you."

"I'd blame you!" Koko barks, then belches again.

"No," Temmin says, even though he wants to say
*Yes, yes, yeah, I totally made a mistake, I need to go
home, I didn't think this through.* But then he thinks
of his mother. She's here. So is he. "I'm good. I'll stick
with you. But I gotta be honest, it's crazy up here."

And it is. Even forming up behind Wedge and having
someone to follow—the sheer amount of visual information is about to give him a nosebleed. Streaking
lines of plasma. Torpedoes corkscrewing in the distance between capital ships. Fighters *everywhere,* and
fire, and debris, not to mention that ring of Star De-

stroyers protecting the dreadnought from the encroaching New Republic capital ships . . .

"Kid's right," Yarra says. "It's a little too hot here. Could use some room to breathe." Above them, an A-wing shears through the vacuum. "Got ideas?"

It's Temmin who has one: "Maybe we head down below. We can punch a hole in their air-to-space defenses, get some clearance for our ground forces." It's a dumb idea, he knows it is. And a selfish one—he just wants to get the hell out of here. And he wants to be as close to Jakku as possible. That's where his mother, his droid, and his friend Jas are.

So it surprises him when Wedge agrees. "Snap, that's a fine idea. All right, Phantom Squadron. Let's get a closer look at Jakku. Take out as many of the bad guys as you can on the way."

Koko whoops.

Temmin takes a deep breath and pushes down on the flight stick, following Wedge and the others through the chaos. *I'm coming, Mom.*

Black pillars of smoke rise above the horizon as Norra pulls the Imperial shuttle over the last canyon ridge and back down over the dunes. Above, she sees the two fleets in orbit. The skies flash and pulse with the lightning of ship-to-ship artillery. Down here, fighters already swarm. The New Republic is establishing landing zones a hundred klicks east, toward Cratertown—she sees the U-wings swooping in like fat birds, disgorging commandos. Already she's starting to see the sands littered with debris: skeletal husks and bent beams smoldering in the hellish Jakku sun. Her eyes follow movement and she sees a larger ship—a corvette, by the looks of it—streaking down toward the surface of faraway mountains. The way it moves, it's like slow motion—fire and smoke trailing as bits fall away, catching the light. Like a firework falling back to ground. It would be beautiful if she didn't know there were lives at stake. Those inside may already be dead. If not now, then soon, when it hits. (A sad reality of every downed ship: Not everyone makes it to an escape pod.)

"I got a bad feeling about this," she tells Bones, who sits dutifully next to her. Servos whine as the droid turns his head toward her.

"PREPARE TO FIRE ALL CANNONS," Bones says—his voice warping so that it has a strange, hard-angle accent to it. "COMMENTARY: I SAY WE BLAST THE MEATBAG AND SAVE YOU THE TROUBLE, MASTER."

"Bones, are you all right?"

The droid seizes up for a moment, then relaxes once more. "SORRY, MASTER TEMMIN'S MOM." The droid shrugs. "GLITCH."

Great. Flying into a war zone with a malfunctioning battle droid. In a stolen Imperial command shuttle, no less.

Ahead, the raging battle is like a storm. It has margins. It contains darkness. And she flies right into the heart of it.

Soldiers march below. Blasterfire pocks the underside of the shuttle—because those are Republic soldiers and she's in an enemy shuttle. *Of course* they'll take their shots. She eases back on the stick, lifting her ship higher in the air, away from the ground forces.

It's about five hundred klicks yet to the base—

Her screens flash red. Two ships drop down from below and form up fast on her tail. Two Republic starfighters. The galaxy apparently thinks she enjoys irony, because the two ships it serves up are Y-wings, just like the one she used to pilot.

The shuttle shakes as they fire on her.

Her options are few, and none of them are good. She could try to signal them, but at best they won't believe her, and at worst she risks the Empire picking up her transmission and realizing she's stolen their ship. She could try to take them on, but the last thing she wants on her conscience is a pair of downed allies who had to die just so she could keep her cover. The one option she has is just to outfly them, which isn't easy in this bucket-belly shuttle. A shuttle is an easy target.

But maybe they don't want an easy target.

What if she gives them a *better* target?

There, ahead: just over those mounding dunes, one massive AT-AT walker marching over the surface of Jakku. It's not alone: A pair of two-legged AT-ST chicken walkers strut on either side of it, firing cannons at a wave of advancing Republic soldiers.

There. That'll give the Y-wings something to deal with. The Y-wing is a better bomber than it is a dogfighter— and that AT-AT will make a tantalizing target. Norra grits her teeth and brings the shuttle in low, aiming right for the stooping cockpit head of that big walker. The Y-wings just need to see that they have a better bull's-eye and—

As she closes in—*close! too close!*—Norra pulls up on the shuttle hard. It shudders as it hits a patch of turbulence—she cuts the engines so the shuttle moves into a stall.

Beneath her, the Y-wings blast past. On toward the walker.

Did it. Now to get this ship out of its stall—

The engines rev but don't fire.

No, no, no, c'mon, you old piece of Imperial scrap, c'mon—

The shuttle crests atop a pillow of air . . . and starts

to fall back toward Jakku. Back toward the walkers,
the soldiers, toward the unforgiving sand and stone.
The ship spirals. Norra roars in frustration as she
struggles with the controls, trying to get the engines to
fire . . .

Down here it feels like he can breathe. Space is dizzy-
ing, but the planet's surface as an entity separate from
the blue sky gives Temmin his bearings. And with his
bearings comes his confidence.

He snaps his fingers, cracks his knuckles, and grips
the flight stick. He brings his fighter in and follows the
rest of Phantom Squadron—Wedge calls for them to
break formation over the battlefield and take out any
TIEs or troop carriers they see. Temmin moves the
X-wing down over the rolling hills of sand, and now,
now he's starting to feel it. The ship feels less like a
machine in which he sits and more like a part of him—
like a limb, like a set of wings, like an extension of his
mind. *Don't think about it. Just do it.* Ahead, a transport catches air over a dune, and he scissors his wings
open and opens fire with all four laser cannons—the
wings spit burning light, and he doesn't even need to
scan his scopes. Every blast hits the transport, and the
front end of it craters in, dipping down into the sand
and flipping its back end over its front. *Whoom.*

Koko's mad hoot fills his ears as he pulls up on the
stick. "You're like a surgeon with that thing, Snap!"

Damn yeah I am.

Not far to port, a TIE striker pinwheels through the
air, smashing into the sand thanks to Wedge, who
crosses his T-65 in front of Temmin's. In the distance,
Temmin can see a walker stomping across the sand,
firing at a pair of Y-wings that circle it like starving
vultures.

Over the comm, Wedge says, "Let's give the Yellow Aces some love, help them out with that walker."

Phantom Squadron whips toward the walkers. Temmin thinks to engage the AT-STs—

But a better target presents itself—an Imperial command shuttle spiraling down toward the ground. He thinks to let it be, because that ship is about to be scrap and vapor. And yet, suddenly, the engines glow blue as they refire, and the shuttle pulls out of its tailspin just moments before impact. It catches air, the one wing nearly drawing a line in the sand before righting itself and heading in the other direction.

It's a command shuttle. That means officers are on board.

Officers are high value targets. That he knows from his days hunting Imperials with Mom and the others. Officers are their ones with faces on the pazaak cards—when you're fighting a monster, you cut off the head and the hands. And that's what he's going to do here. He radios to Wedge: "See that Imperial shuttle, Phantom Leader? It's fleeing, but I'm going after it."

"All right. Good hunting, Snap. Don't range too far."

"You bet, Phantom Leader."

Temmin grins, and guns the starfighter toward his new target.

Just as Norra rights the shuttle and points its nose toward the locational reticule of the distant Imperial base, a new blip appears on her scopes, blinking a warning.

An X-wing. Older model—a T-65C-A2.

She moves to evade. Lasers bolt past. Just as she thought she was safe, the chase begins anew. Her heart hammers against the inside of her breastbone—and the ship shudders, too, as the wing takes a hit, peppered by fire from whoever it is that's pursuing her.

Norra brings the shuttle low over the dunes, then high over an arched rock formation that looks like a man on his hands and knees—she whips left, right, but the X-wing isn't persuaded to pull away. It stays on her like it's got a tractor beam lock, perfectly lined and ready for the kill.

More laserfire. One of the shuttle's engines goes out. The ship lists left. The inside of the cabin fills with the stink of ozone and burning electric.

What a thing, she thinks. *To be taken out at the end by my own side.*

The cabin flashes. Missile lock! That X-wing will be loaded for bear with proton torpedoes—that is no surprise. What's a surprise is that whoever is piloting that thing would expend one to take out a command shuttle. It's overkill. The pilot flying that fighter is naïve—there are far better targets out here for that ordnance.

Bones, to her surprise, suddenly stands up. The little antenna at the top of his skull (which is itself bolstered and fixed to a small and narrow pinbone) begins to blink green.

"Where are you going?" she says through gritted teeth, trying to maintain control of the shuttle.

Bones does not answer. Instead he hits a button on the console.

The ramp. He's lowering the ramp. *He's getting off the ship.*

"Bones! Get back here! *Bones!*"

A thrill rises inside Temmin's belly; his blood is up, his nerves are buzzing like vibroblades. He's stayed on the shuttle's tail like he's been glued to it—and it's enough to earn him an easy missile lock. Ahead, the shuttle squares out in front of him, and his thumb finds the top of the flight stick. He has no conscience in this moment. He doesn't think about who is in that ship. He knows it'll kill them but he doesn't think of it that way. Temmin feels something altogether more vicious and aloof—he just wants to *win*, he just wants to *score a victory* for the Republic, and the Empire here is less a shuttle carrying officers and more a symbol.

A symbol he can shoot down right here, right now.

His thumb hovers over the button.

Then the shuttle's ramp begins to descend. In midair. *What the*—? Maybe whoever's in there is trying to jump out. But why? The front end of that thing is its escape pod—just detach and go.

A droid makes its way down the ramp. It holds on to the pneumatic piston from which the ramp descends.

His droid waves at him.

Oh gods, is that—

"Bones?"

Over the comm comes the droid's mechanized voice: "I THOUGHT THAT MIGHT BE YOU, MASTER TEMMIN. PLEASE HOLD."

"Please hold? What are you—? Bones? *Bones?*"

Moments later, a crackle as his mother's voice comes from his wrist comlink: "Temmin? *Temmin?*"

At first, she doesn't even understand it. It all seems so absurd. The droid drops back down into his chair with a rattle and tilts his head toward her, then says: "YOU SHOULD SPEAK TO MASTER TEMMIN NOW."

She does not say her son's name so much as it spills out of her.

And broadcast from the droid's own speaker comes her son's voice—how? Bones has a proximity sensor, doesn't he? He must've turned it on when he landed on Jakku. Soon as Temmin was close, the comms connected automatically. It fills her with light and life when her son says: "Mom?"

Mom. That one word. She's missed hearing it so bad.

"Kiddo," she says, her eyes burning hot with the threat of tears. "I've missed you, kiddo. Where are you? Are you—are *you* in that X-wing?"

"I'm so sorry, Mom, I didn't know—I almost shot you down, please forgive me. Wait. What are *you* doing in an Imperial shuttle?"

"I . . ." But what does she tell him? Does she say that she found his father? The family reunion she longs to have is so close. They could rescue him together. And yet this is dangerous territory. She's heading right into the heart of the Empire's occupation. She knows it seems awfully headstrong, but if she does this alone, maybe Temmin won't follow and won't get hurt. At least in that X-wing he's got control plus other pilots covering his tail. "Is Wedge with you?"

"He is." *Thank the lucky stars.* "I can patch us over—"

"*No.* I can't be on radio chatter. If the Empire picks up what I'm doing, Tem—"

"What *are* you doing?"

"I've got a lead on Sloane. And . . ." In that moment, she decides not to tell him about his father. She knows she may regret it later, but once he hears about Brentin, Temmin will start acting with his heart and *not* his head. "I've . . . stolen a shuttle. I've got clearance codes. I'm headed to the Imperial base past something called the Sinking Fields."

"We'll escort you in."

"No can do, kiddo. They see you on the scopes, they'll cut you to pieces. And maybe me, too." It pains her to say this, but she does: "You stay out here. Stay with Wedge. He'll keep you safe! Let him know I'm okay."

"Are you okay? Mom?"

"I am. I promise. I've got Bones with me. You did good with him. He already saved my life out here once."

"Land the shuttle, Mom. We can figure this out."

"It's a war zone, Tem. I can't land here. Neither can you." Ahead, she sees that the defensive line of the Empire's forces awaits. "You need to turn around. They have turrets. Turbolasers. Mortars. Walkers, TIEs, everything. Who-knows-what else. You don't wanna get close to the base defenses. They see you, they might figure out who I am, too. Then we're both dead." She blinks back tears and pleads with him. "Please. Turn around."

"Mom, wait—"

"Temmin, *please*. Go!"

"Promise I'll see you again."

"You'll see me again." It's a promise she doesn't know how she'll keep. She's not even sure she believes it herself. "We'll be a family again soon. Okay? I love you, kiddo. Stay safe."

"Bones! You take good care of her!"

"ROGER-ROGER, MASTER TEMMIN."

"I love you, Mom. Get Sloane. See you on the other side."

And with that, the blip disappears from her screen as her son pulls away from his pursuit of her shuttle.

CHAPTER TWENTY-NINE

"No."

"I'm sorry, what?" Sinjir asks.

"I said no, Sinjir," the chancellor says.

"Ah. I see. We must be having a *communication* problem. I'm not Chandrilan and though I believe we share the same *crispness of wit,* there must be some crucial language barrier I'm coming up against. I have to assume that because of my *very good deeds* rendered in service to the New Republic that surely, *surely* when I ask if I can go to Jakku to help my friends your only answer would be an unqualified *Yes, Sinjir, absolutely, Sinjir, please take this medal and also this bag of money, Sinjir.*"

Mon Mothma sits across from him. Her hands are steepled, though clearly the one is not functioning as well. It looks palsied the way it droops next to the other. She smiles over the bridge of her fingers, though, as if unfazed by it. Also as if unfazed by *him.*

"Mister Rath Velus," she says, "I appreciate your consternation—"

"Do you? Truly?"

"—but I cannot approve your journey to Jakku. You are not a soldier. Or a pilot. Or an officer. You want your friends back, that I recognize. It is a noble desire. But one I cannot help you fulfill, I'm afraid."

Politics, he thinks. *The only thing worse than politics is politicians.*

He leans over, knowing full well he's not only crossing a boundary here but frankly leaping over it like a punted gizka. "You listen here, Chancellor. I risked my neck and every other part of me for *you*. It took me a day just to *get* this meeting and—"

"If you want to go to Jakku, just go to Jakku."

"What?"

"I can't stop you. Find a ship. Get on it. Fly it to that miserable war-torn desert world. You will drop right into madness and probably be swatted like a pesty fly, but that's your trouble, not mine."

"Fine. Yes. *Good.* I will do exactly this."

She nods her head gently. "May the stars speed your journey." He starts to get up, and she holds a finger in the air. "One more thing, though."

"Hm?"

"If you perish above Jakku—or on it, or anywhere near it—then you won't be able to take the job I'm offering you."

What heinous caper is this? He narrows his gaze to suspicious, reptilian slits. "Job? I don't know anything about that."

"Yes, because you haven't heard me offer it, yet."

"I'm sorry? Am I short-circuiting like a wet droid? What are we talking about here, exactly?"

With her weaker hand, she gently gestures toward the chair. The message is clear: *Sit and hear the offer, or go and do not.*

"Bloody hell, fine." He sits down in the chair like an insolent schoolboy, slumping back, feigning disdain. "What's this job, then?"

"I need an adviser."

"And you want me to find you one?"

"I want you to *be* one."

He brays with laughter. "What? Seriously?" But he sees on her face she *is* serious. Deadly so. He sits up straight, oddly embarrassed. "Oh. You actually mean it. For the galaxy's sake, why?"

"Because you're very good at getting people to do what you want."

"Frequently by bending their fingers back so far they break. That's not a good look for a pacifist of your stature."

Her gaze matches his own. It's only now he realizes how properly *intense* she can be. He doesn't really know what the Force is or how it even works, except that she must possess it given the way her gaze feels like a pair of tweezers picking him apart, atom by atom.

She flexes her palsied hand as if to exercise it. "Yes, your reputation in that regard precedes you, Sinjir. But another reputation is beginning to form and grow: You are even more incisive with your tongue than you are with your violence. You can be alarmingly convincing, as evidenced by what you said to Senator Rethalow. And further how you manipulated those senators into giving me their vote. I need someone like that. Auxi is a most excellent adviser in matters political, but I need a cynic. Someone who distrusts the system—who maybe even despises it. And I also need someone who can play the game and get me what I want. That someone is you."

"This is a joke, right? A bit of a poke-and-tickle? I say yes and then from that potted plant and under this chair, a chorus of onlookers leap out and laugh? Because surely you aren't considering hiring an ex-Imperial torture agent to advise you on *running the entire civilized galaxy.*"

"No joke. I don't have a very good sense of humor anyway."

He sneers. "I hate politics."

"So do I."

"I hate *politicians*."

"Good. So you can manipulate them to do your bidding."

He leans back, crossing his arms. One eyebrow up so far it's damn near in orbit, he says, "I get paid?"

"Handsomely."

"I'll be on Nakadia or here, on Chandrila?"

"My primary office will remain on Chandrila for now, though I will have a proper desk on Nakadia, too."

A job offer. From the chancellor. He has to chew that one a good bit. Of course he doesn't want it. Bah. Pfft. The political realm is a grotesque circus, an erratic carousel drunkenly turning like a blindfolded child wielding a stick at his nativity party. Sinjir's opinion of the whole charade: Tear it all down. Burn it up. Dance among the ashes while swilling a bottle of something good. That's his take. But then again . . .

Maybe he ought to give another go at this stability thing.

If he and Conder are trying again . . .

If the war is truly almost over and the crew is finally done . . .

What place does he have in the galaxy? He confesses, his only option right now is to sashay his narrow hind over to some distant cantina and see if he can't find himself a quiet corner in which to plant himself as the resident barfly. But he admires Conder. There's a man who wants to work. Who wants to do the *right* thing, and do it with skill and aplomb and a smile bridging those fuzzy adorable cheeks. *He deserves to be as impressed by me as I am by him. Maybe this is how I accomplish that.*

"I need time to think about it," he says.

"You have thirty seconds."

"I—what?"

"Decide now. I have to move quickly on this. Having a vacancy among my advisory duo has already hampered my ability to perform as chancellor, and I do not want to wait. So the clock is ticking."

"Chancellor—"

"Twenty seconds, now."

"Well—"

"Let's call it ten."

"It's not ten. You're speeding up the clock. That's cheating!"

"It is, but I'm allowed. Tell you what, Sinjir. I'll offer a bonus. I have two tasks at hand, and if you say yes right now, you get to choose which one *you* do and which one goes to my other adviser, Auxi."

"What are these tasks?"

She waggles a metronome finger. "Ah-ah-ah. Not until you say yes."

"Mm. Fine. *Yes.*"

Her small smile grows by one, maybe two microns and Mon Mothma says, "Splendid. The first task is: shopping."

"Shopping? Did I hear you right?"

"Yes. Do you know what to buy for a newborn baby? After all, our dear friend Leia is expecting."

Sinjir makes a face like he just sniffed a diaper. "Whiskey?"

"That would be better for the mother and father, I suspect. No, not *whiskey*. Perhaps you shouldn't be buying baby gifts."

He puckers his lips. "And maybe you should not relegate this personal, intimate task to a mere adviser."

"Yes, well. Let's try the second task. I need someone to deliver a gift to the senator from Orish, Tolwar Wartol. An apology of sorts."

"An apology? Stars forfend, why?"

The chancellor sighs. "He apparently wasn't malevolently opposing my vote and manipulating senators *directly* . . ."

"Yes, he just failed to help the gears of democracy turn. And he's running against you. He's your *opponent,* Chancellor!"

"One does not blame a tooka for toying with the mouse. He is who he is, and so I thought it necessary to deliver a *small* gift to apologize for my little ploy on his ship."

"Gift delivery does not sound advisory to me, Chancellor."

"Don't you even want to see the gift?"

He says nothing, offering instead a dubious countenance. Mon clears her throat and lifts a small basket covered with a soft, lavender cloth. She tells him to go on, have a look, and he does.

It is a fruit basket. Full of one kind of fruit: the pta fruit.

He cannot deny the smug smirk that tugs at his lips. "Oh, Chancellor. And here I thought you said you had no sense of humor."

"Perhaps there's a glimmer of one, there. As you say: We share a crispness of wit, do we not?"

"I think we do."

"So you'll deliver it?"

"I will."

"Enjoy. And welcome to politics, Sinjir Rath Velus."

CHAPTER THIRTY

JAS EMARI'S WORLD lights up. Her teeth clamp against each other. Her jaw muscles are so tight she fears they'll strain and snap. Then it's over again, the wave of pain and light receding once more. She's left panting and wheezing on the floor of the Corellian shuttle as Mercurial Swift once again pulls the sparking baton away. He gives it a twirl.

"You skag," he hisses. His face, scratched from her attack in Niima's temple by her head spurs, looms over her own. Behind him, Dengar lazes. Embo is at the other end of the shuttle's hold, sitting up straight and regarding the proceedings with all the interest and emotion of a coatrack.

From the cockpit, the Rodian yells: "Swift. It's too dangerous. It's everywhere. Empire. The Republic. Nowhere to go."

The disappointment on Swift's face is palpable. "Fine. Set us down somewhere in the canyon."

Jas rolls over. Every part of her feels like it's been stretched out so far it won't go back to its original shape. Being electrocuted a handful of times is good at making you feel that way, as it turns out. She gasps and manages to squeak out the words, "So, what's . . . your plan, Swift?"

"Shut. Up."

"No, really." She groans. "What's the score? Clearance codes won't keep you safe in the middle of a war zone. Somebody will take a shot at us."

"I don't have to explain myself to you."

"No," Dengar interjects, "but you might wanna explain it to *us*. You know, your crew? You got a plan here, *boss*?"

The way the barrel-chested Corellian says that last word, *boss*, she can tell it's not a term of great endearment. *Interesting*.

Swift heels on the old bounty hunter, like he's about to lay into him. But he seems to cool down a little. "We'll park it for a while. Look for an opportunity to hit orbit and take our quarry back to Boss Gyuti on Nar Shaddaa. We just need to be patient."

"He'll screw you all over," Jas says.

Swift turns fast and drops a fist into her gut. She curls up into herself like a bug. "Be quiet. Nothing's stopping me from taking you to Gyuti in five different sacks."

"He's just mad 'cuz you ruined his pretty looks," Dengar says.

"Shut it, Dengar."

"Don't you . . ." Jas winces as she sits up, her voice a keening wheeze. "Want to know what I'm doing here on Jakku? I could cut you in—"

Bzzt. Another jam of the shock baton, this time against the side of her neck. Her skull is a nest of stinging insects. She tries not to scream but the scream comes anyway, a living thing that will not be contained. Then it's gone. Jas topples over, whimpering.

"I wanna hear what she has to say," Dengar notes.

"I said, *shut it,* Dengar."

Jas blinks, and in the time it takes to do that, she hears the *clatter-clack* of a blaster being cocked. When her vision returns, she sees Dengar has his rifle up over his knee and pointed right at Swift's middle.

"I don't feel like shuttin' it, you smug git. I got a right to talk to the girl. Me and her auntie knew each other. I owe her a convo. Go on, Jazzy."

"I—nggh. I'm hunting someone here."

"Whozat, now?"

"Rae Sloane."

"She's nobody," Swift says. "Sloane was the top of the food chain but that day is over. Now she's nothing."

Jas offers a halfhearted shrug. "Not to the . . . New Republic. They want her bad, and they're willing to pay for her served up to them on a plate. She knows things. She's the key. Or so they believe. I don't even care if they're right—what I care is what they're paying me, and it's a lot."

All that is a lie. But despite the glib saying, the truth will most certainly not set her free.

"How much are they paying?"

That question, asked by Embo. Spoken in the Kyuzo tongue.

She hates to lie to him. Really, she does.

But she does it anyway. "A million."

Eyes go big as battle stations. Dengar whistles. "Lot of money for one girl. Still, working for the New Republic ain't exactly cozy-making, izzit?"

"It is when they offer you full pardons."

And *that* is the statement that vacuums the air from the cabin. They're all left in shock by that offer. A pardon has meaning. They each have a list of criminal sins longer than a Hutt-slug's tail. And with the galaxy shifting as it is toward the New Republic—the day will come sooner than later when bounty hunters are forced to flee to the fringes if they don't want to get swept up and locked away. The tension in the ship rises. Jas seizes it.

She goes on: "You work with me, I cut you in. You all get full pardons. Embo, Dengar. You both worked with Sugi. Maybe there's something to be said for a little tradition, isn't there?"

"They won't leave me," Swift protests with a vulpine stare. "They know their place. Won't do them any good to betray Gyuti and make enemies of Black Sun. They'll stay with me."

"You forgot one part," Dengar says.

Mercurial raises an eyebrow. "What?"

"We don't really like you."

The old bounty hunter clubs Swift in the side of the head with his blaster. The pretty boy collapses next to her, but he's not content to go down quietly, oh, no— Swift moves fast, getting behind her and pulling his forearm against her windpipe. With the back of his heel, he kicks out and opens the side of the shuttle— the wall lifts, the ramp descends, and the brightness of the Jakku sun fills the cabin, nearly blinding them all.

He backs Jas toward the door, using her as cover.

"You could've all been rich," he seethes.

Dengar has his rifle pointed but can't get a shot. Embo stands but seems casually disinterested in the events. She knows that look. It's not disinterest she sees. Rather, it's a look that says he trusts her to handle this.

"You . . . forgot . . . one thing . . ." she says as Swift's arm tightens.

"I forgot nothing," he snarls in her ear.

You forgot that I didn't remove all my horns, idiot.

With a hard grunt, she slams her head backward into his face. Her thorn-shaped horns dig into the meat of his other cheek and Swift howls—and for the hair's breadth of a moment he relaxes his grip on her throat.

Jas moves fast. She slides free like a man slipping a noose, then ducks quickly and kicks out with a hard foot—

It catches Swift right in the middle.

And the bounty hunter sails out the now open door of the shuttle.

Panting, Jas slams her heel against the button, and again the ramp ascends as the door closes. She rubs her eyes and collapses against the wall, weary. Dengar is looking at her with both surprise and satisfaction on his face. He gives her a curt nod. "Nicely done, Jazzy."

Embo nods, too. In Kyuzo: "I am glad it turned out this way."

The Rodian—whose name she doesn't even yet know—calls back: "What's going on back there?"

Jas winces. "She loyal?"

"Who, Jeeta? Pssh. Not to Swift, she isn't."

"Then I guess I have a new crew," Jas says.

Dengar offers a sloppy smile and a wink. "Guess you do, love."

INTERLUDE

CLOUD CITY, BESPIN

"LOBOT, WE'RE HOME." Lando lifts a dubious eyebrow as he looks around, exasperated. "Guess the Empire didn't keep up with housekeeping."

This is the Casino level. Game machines line the smooth blue alactite floors far as the eye can see. Sabacc tables, too. And pazaak. And jubilee wheels. Along the far wall are banks of holoprojectors meant to show the latest swoop race down on the track-tubes piped through Bespin's toxic Red Zone atmosphere. Once, this was a shining pillar of gambling excess: classy and bright with light coming in through windows looking out over the sun-kissed clouds. Now it's wrecked. Trash drifts and tumbles. Machines have been turned over, their credits cut from inside like food from a beast's belly. The windows are covered over with metal. The holoprojectors are dark.

Lobot steps up alongside Lando. The computer forming a half-moon around the back of the man's bald head blinks and pulses, and at Lando's wrist is a communication from his friend and cohort:

I'll look into rehiring staff immediately.

"Do that," Lando says. Then he thrusts up a finger. "Ah. But make sure we're hiring some refugees, will you?" The galaxy's like a cup that's been knocked over, and now everything's spilling out. Whole worlds

have been displaced by the war. Lando can't let Cloud
City turn from being a city of luxury to being a tent
city of expats and evacuees, but he can damn sure give
those people jobs. That's his favorite kind of arrangement: the kind where everybody gets something for
their trouble. They win. He wins. The ideal for how
everything should work.

Cloud City was always that, for Calrissian. It was
a respite—a refuge from the Empire while at the same
time not existing to *spite* the Empire, either. He
thought, *Hey, everybody can be happy, baby.* The Empire didn't have to care. The rebels didn't need to care.
Cloud City could hang in the air above Bespin, separate from all the chaos, from all the strife. Come here,
taste a little luxury. Meanwhile, he could mine the
Tibanna gas, sell it to whatever starship manufacturer
wanted it (the stuff was perfect for making hyper-
drives, because with Tibanna, a little went a long way).
Meanwhile, Lando could sit back, have a drink, roll
some dice, find a lady or three.

Yeah. It didn't work out that way.

He knows now: In a war like this one, you don't get
to be in the middle. You can't play both sides. He'd
lived his whole life shooting right down the middle,
never taking up a cause except the one meant to support his own empty pockets. Those days are over and
so is his love of sweet neutrality. When Vader came
here, everything changed. He lost Han, for a time. He
lost Lobot and Cloud City. He lost nearly *everything*.

But he gained a little perspective.

And he picked a damn side. Because sometimes, you
want to win, you gotta bet big. You gotta put your
stack of chits in one place.

It paid off. The Empire is gone. And now he's a hero
of the Rebellion (and oh, you can be sure he used that
to con more than his fair share of free drinks, not to

mention the attention of beautiful admirers). But all he wants is his city back. After Endor, he thought he would just be able to sweep in here like a handsome king retaking his throne in the sky—but then that son-of-a-slug Governor Adelhard formed the Iron Blockade. He kept the people here trapped not only by a well-organized Imperial remnant, but also by a grand lie: that Palpatine was not dead. And Lando knows that old shriveled cenobite is dead—because he's the one who took out the Death Star's reactor core. And because Luke *said* the monster was dead. *Can you believe it? Palpatine* and *Vader. Both gone. Two scourges, scoured from the galaxy.*

Suddenly he had a *second* war to fight. Here he thought the Empire was done for and Cloud City was once again his. *What an eager fool.* Nothing's ever that simple, is it? It took months and months. He had to stage an uprising. Had to interface with Lobot on the inside. Had to cash in favors with a handful of scoundrels—like Kars Tal-Korla, that pirate. All because the New Republic wouldn't commit a military action to retaking the city. He respects it, he understands it, and Leia put it best when she said, "The Rebellion was easy, Lando. Governing's harder." The chancellor was just trying to hold on to whatever advantage she had—and then with the Liberation Day attack on Chandrila . . .

Well. All that is over and done. No need to dwell.

Cloud City is his once again. Lando starved out Adelhard. Most of the Imperials surrendered. It's over. Thank the lucky stars.

He steps forward into the Casino level, and he and Lobot aren't alone. He's got a ragtag force with him: some of his Wing Guard security forces, but some New Republic soldiers, too. It's just enough to perform cleanup on those who linger behind, clinging to the illusion they can still win this thing.

Together they march forward through the wreckage of the Casino level. He asks Lobot: "The holdouts are ahead?"

Yes. In the Bolo Tanga room.

"Fine, fine, let's get this over with and evict our final tenants."

As they walk, Lobot looks over at him as a new communication flashes across his wrist: *I am told to remind you that the princess will soon give birth and you have not yet procured for them the standard natal gift.*

"What? That's impossible. She was just—I swear they just got married—didn't I just get them a nuptial gift?"

It has been the proper biological time. You just do not realize how much time has passed. We have been busy.

"So have they, I guess."

Also, you never got them a nuptial gift.

He sighs. "Okay, okay. Buying gifts for a kid. Can we get him a cute little cape and a mustache so he looks like old Uncle Lando?"

Lobot doesn't respond, offering only a humorless stare.

"Fine, fine, I'll think about it." His mind drifts briefly to Han and Leia. Han, one of his oldest and greatest friends. And *sure,* one of his greatest rivals, too. He misses that old reprobate. The crazy times they had!

Good times even when they were bad. And now, Han is with Leia. Hoo, boy. Those two are a pair of rocket boosters firing full-bore. Lando just hopes those two engines are both firing in the same direction—because if they're ever pointed at each other, they'll burn each other up.

We're here.

That, from Lobot. Ahead waits the door to the Bolo Tanga room. Lando can see it's been sealed with mag-alloy. He turns to Captain Gladstone of the Wing Guard. "We got imaging?"

Gladstone nods. "They're holed up in there. They've broken through to the beam outtake shaft, which in theory would lead them to the engineering sublayer—"

"But the fumes coming up through the shaft will kill them if they try."

"That's exactly it, Baron Administrator."

"So they're trapped."

"Like crete-bugs in a beetle-bag."

"All right, let's open it up—no, you know, wait. Can they hear me through that door?"

"They can, if you get close."

Lando nods, pulling his blaster—it's a fancy-looking piece of work from back when they put a little *art* into their design. It's a Rossmoyne Vitiator pistol, a bolt-thrower from a more elegant age. (Lando won it recently in a game of Six-Card Gizka Limit from a spice-drunk Aybarian diplomat.) Every Rossmoyne that came off the line was engraved by hand with scroll-work by artisans from the original family. The grip in particular shows these wonderful whorls and curves—like a spiraling maze you could follow with a blind fingertip. Maybe with the Empire gone, craftsbeings will return to the galaxy. And with it, their beauty.

That's later. For now—

He taps on the door with the Vitiator.

"Hello, this is Lando Calrissian," he says loudly so they can hear him. "I'm baron administrator of Cloud City, not to mention hero of the Rebellion. I suspect you've heard of me. Can you hear me all right? Tap on the door if you can."

Nothing. But then—

Three taps. Good enough. He keeps talking, putting a little extra *smooth* in his voice to keep them calm, to keep them listening—

"Here's how this is going to go. I'm a gambling man, and so I'm gonna *bet* that you're in there, hungry and scared and feeling like people without a country—and you are, because by now I'm sure you heard, Adelhard's story about Palpatine being alive was a big old nasty lie. I'm gonna take that bet and I'm gonna say you'd be fine, *just fine,* with dropping your weapons so we can open up this door, escort you out, and get you a hot meal and a warm bed. I'm not interested in prosecuting you. Not gonna throw you into some New Republic dungeon. I'll even put my blaster away so when I walk inside, you know how serious I am about this. Tap if you hear me."

Tap, tap, tap.

"Good." He steps away, tucking his blaster into the holster at his hip. Lando signals to Gladstone. "Unseal it."

The Wing Guard engineers get to work, crouching on each side of it, blast masks over their eyes as they ignite plasma lances to burn through the line of puffy metal alloy sealing the door. Sparks sear lines in the air.

And then it's done. Two engineers stand by the door, one on each side. They use the lever ends of their lances to jack the door.

It falls hard in Lando's direction, and he gently steps aside as it hits the floor. *Wham.* A puff of smoke and a whirl of embers follow. Lando knows that a hail of lasers might come sizzling out of that doorway and cut him to pieces—but he also knows that whoever is in there realizes they'll get cut to pieces in return.

No hot meal. No warm bed. Just body bags for each of them.

As the smoke clears, he sees the Imperial men and women in there, hands on their heads, blasters at their feet. Lando laughs and urges them out of the Bolo Tanga room. They look scared. And tired. Each of them thin-cheeked with dry lips and bloodshot eyes. "C'mon, let's go. It's okay. It's over. You made the right choice."

A few dozen of them come out, taken into custody by the Wing Guard. The New Republic soldiers stand back. Then Gladstone says: "Baron Administrator, sir." A note of worry in his voice. He gestures into the room.

Lando steps in, blaster still at his hip.

One holdout remains inside the Bolo Tanga room, all the way on the other side of the card table, where the dealer would normally stand. It's a broad-chested fellow with only two pieces of armor on: a black chest plate, and a white trooper helmet. He's standing up against the back wall. A rifle is in his hand. The barrel of the rifle is pointed at the ground.

Which either means he's not sure what to do yet—

Or he's been waiting for this moment.

"Let me guess," Lando says. "You're the commander."

A pause before the man says, "Sergeant."

"The last sergeant, Sergeant. Everyone else has surrendered or died. Adelhard's out. And the Empire isn't looking good as an option anywhere, big fella. So that's the deal. You surrender. Or it goes the other way."

The rifle hangs. The man doesn't put it down.

And his hand isn't shaking.

It's gonna go the other way.

It happens fast.

"Long live the Empire—!"

The Imperial swings the rifle up—

It never fires.

The sergeant drops as a single shot from Lando's Vitiator punctures his armor and pierces his heart. The rifle never leaves the soldier's hand—his body just slumps atop it.

Lando tucks the blaster back in its holster. His heart pulses in his chest. A mad thrill goes through him as he thinks, *I still got it*. And that fool was betting that Lando was too slow, and his weapon wouldn't clear the holster—and couldn't punch through that armor if it did.

Wrong on both counts.

"Win some, lose some," Lando says, clucking his tongue. He saunters over to the dead man, grabs the black-lensed helmet from underneath, and pries it off. The sergeant is a square-jawed man with a brow like a rocky outcropping. Tough mug.

But not tough enough.

"Hey now," Lando says, spinning the helmet in his hand. He looks to Lobot. "I got an idea. Every kid needs a lamp, right? Like a nightlight? Can we get the engineers to turn this into a lamp? It'd be something special, don't you think?"

Lobot signals across the communicator: *No*.

"Yeah, okay, that's a compelling argument," Lando says, chuckling. He stands up, tossing the helmet from hand to hand before dropping it to the ground. "Still, kid's gotta see what his parents fought for. And I suspect given his parents, he's gonna do some fighting himself."

That's when Lando gets an idea.

He again draws the blaster, gives it a spin in his hand.

"Kid's gonna get into trouble one day." Every kid does, but with the blood of a scoundrel and a princess in his veins, his defiance will shake the stars. "He's gonna need some help. And that's where Uncle Lando comes in." Lando holds up the weapon, admiring it.

At his wrist, Lobot protests: *We are not giving a blaster to the boy. Children should not play with blasters.* Lobot's face is stern.

"No, not for *now*. For later. When the time is right. Tell you what. I'll write a note, kind of a . . . *Hey, kid, it's me, Uncle Lando, you ever need help and don't wanna call your father, come find me, we'll sort it out.* Put that in with the blaster, then secure it on a locker here on Cloud City, and give Han the key. *Don't* tell him what's in it—he'll pitch a fit if he sees it. It'll be for the boy when he's older."

That fails to provide them with a gift now, Lando.

He tosses the blaster to Lobot, who catches it awkwardly then returns a dour look. Lando rolls his eyes. "*Fine,* fine, send them something else, too. What do we have? Oh, I know. We got that Vantillian catamaran in the western skipdock—give them that ship, they can take it out on, hey, I dunno, family cruises or something."

Lobot nods. One word across the communicator: *Acceptable.*

"Can you believe it?" Lando asks. "Han and Leia. A *family.* Times are changing. You think I should start a family?"

One more word: *No.*

He laughs. "Once again, my friend, we agree. Let's go get a drink."

I don't drink.

Lando puts his arm around Lobot's stiff shoulders. "I know. It's all right. I'll have two to make it *equitable.* That way, we both win."

CHAPTER THIRTY-ONE

RAE SLOANE HAS given up and given in. Gallius Rax has left her here with a front-row seat for what may very well be the last battle of this war—because even if the Empire wins Jakku, then what? The Empire that this world has borne is not her Empire at all. It is a warped and twisted thing, sand-scoured and gone to scrap.

So, she kneels. The burning in her legs has dimmed to a dull, numb ache. Her shoulders feel it, too. Her hips. Her neck. Everything hurts. Her lips are dry. Her eyes feel like fruits left out too long in the sun. Worse, her side aches—right where that damn woman, the pilot, popped her one back on Chandrila. Every time she bothers to take a breath it's like someone is slowly sawing a knife in and out of her ribs.

She can't go anywhere. She and Brentin are on the roof—she pondered crawling to the edge of it and rolling off, if only to fall far enough to break her neck and end the misery. Meanwhile, Brentin is curled in upon himself, moaning and rolling around. Clearly he's lost to madness.

All the while she watches the battle creep ever closer to the base. The Empire's line isn't breaking, but it's falling back. In the distance she spies a mushroom plume of fire erupt from the top of a walker before it tortuously topples over. Not far from that, an X-wing—so far away it looks almost like a child's toy whipping about—clips its wing on a spire of rock and crashes into a DF.9 turret placement. Trooper bodies fly.

In the sky, the two fleets rage against each other. It's hard to tell much of what's happening—the sun is so bright it feels like it's about to set her corneas on fire. Best she can see is that the Imperial fleet is holding firm. The Republic ships aren't making a dent. Not yet. But she fears they will.

It's inevitable.

Soon it'll come here, to the base. That's what Rax wants. Not only does she get to sit here and watch it all collapse, she'll be underneath it when it does. When the base goes, she'll go, too. Maybe captured. Probably dead.

And Rax will get away.

But to where? And why? It's his endgame she can't figure out. All of this is a *show*. It's in service to something. And that place he was protecting out in the valley near the Plaintive Hand—it means something.

Not that it matters. He's gone. She remains.

Sloane laughs, then weeps, then bows her head like a penitent monk.

"Gah!" Brentin cries out, suddenly. He rolls over, arching his back and baring his teeth to the sky. Pain seems to cross his face. Suddenly a wave of energy pulses the air, causing all the hairs on her arms and neck to stiffen. Brentin stands up, shaking his hands— the two cuffs around his wrists drop away.

She looks at him, astonished.

"You're free."

"Uh-huh. And you're next." He bends down, scooping something into his open hands, talking as he does. "You ever notice how dirty this planet is? I don't just mean it like every planet is dirty—I mean, it's so dry, so desiccated, everything erodes to dust. Dust picked up on the wind and blown everywhere. Like here."

He shows her his hands, which are now piled with little puffs of brown and rust-colored dust. Then he gets behind her and begins massaging the dust right into the cuffs.

"What are you doing?"

"Rebels like me, we get trained on how to escape all kinds of situations. Magnacuffs are hard to beat, but not impossible, long as you can get something in between the magnetic couplings. In this case—"

Bzzt! Another pulse of energy as the cuffs fall from her wrists.

"The dust of Jakku."

I'm free, she thinks.

"You're something, Brentin Wexley." She knows now that her instincts to preserve his life were right.

"We rebels had to stay ahead of you Imperials somehow."

"We need to move fast," she says. "Find a ship. Intercept Rax."

"You think he's going back to the valley."

"It's our only shot. Something's going on here. Something big that I don't understand." *Even if he's not there, whatever he's hiding will be the key to understanding it all.* "Come on."

Sloane moves with long strides, ignoring the pain in her side, in her legs, in her throat. She pushes away her dehydration, pretending it just doesn't exist. As she finds the turbolift down, she already begins to formulate a plan in her head—they're going to need a ship. Going overland won't do. Too slow, and the battle raging here will make traversing the surface of Jakku an untenable prospect. That means they need to be airborne in something *fast.* A TIE could work because it's fast, nimble, versatile.

Good news is: They've got plenty of the Imperial starfighters here—an automatic belt-fed line of them set up for fueling, launch, landing, and refueling. Churn and burn. Fighters. Interceptors. Bombers. Strikers. Move them up and out, get them flying.

The lift hums downward. It dings open. They step out and see a dust-swept hallway—it's empty. The base is like a tomb. Dirt-caked and filthy, and quiet as the grave, too. *Abandoned already?* Sloane wonders. Or is it just that the entire breadth and depth of the Imperial forces are already out there, fighting tooth and nail against the New Republic incursion? She suspects the latter. All the pieces have been pushed out onto the game board. None are in reserve. Rax is betting the Empire all or nothing.

A mouse droid wheels past, blurping and squeaking as it rounds the corner. It's the only sign of life they see.

That is, until they round the same corner.

The mouse droid comes squealing back, zipping through Sloane's legs—there's a moment of distraction as she dances out of its way—

And when she turns back around, she's face-to-face with an Imperial officer. Noncom black. Small hat askew. The bars on the woman's chest indicate she's a prison warden, which doesn't make any sense because—

"Norra," Brentin says.

"*You,*" Sloane says to the woman.

A blaster thrusts up into Sloane's face. "Yes. *Me.*"

Norra came out of a docking bay along the side finding a base mostly empty: no troopers, only droids and a few officers pecking about. At the time she thought, *This is it, this is the end of the Empire, they just don't know it yet,* and strange as it is, a sense of hopelessness settled over her, and with it, a feeling of lost purpose. The Empire had been her enemy for so long—what happens when it's gone? It's like putting out a fire by sucking all the oxygen out of the room. The fire's gone, but now how do you breathe?

She had to put that aside, though, because as she reminded herself: She still had a purpose. Find her husband. Find Sloane. And one minute she's wandering the labyrinthine base, stepping past an abandoned, gutted supply room—and the next she's rounding the corner and meeting her quarry face-to-face.

It takes her a second to recognize Sloane.

It takes her even longer to register her husband saying her name.

Next thing she knows, she's got her blaster pistol up and pointed right in Sloane's face. Instantly she wants to pull the trigger and vacate the woman's brains from her skull—a surge of anger geysers up inside her like a spout of corrosive acid. *No justice. Only revenge.* But Brentin steadies her hand. "Norra. No."

"Brentin," she says, the name spoken not happily, but with trepidation and grief. "Get your hand off me. Why are you here? Why are you with *her*?" Paranoia unspools inside Norra's mind. She fears suddenly that he's still programmed, still enslaved to the chip embedded in his brain stem—

Bones takes the cue and grabs his wrist, twisting it so hard he cries out in pain. The droid smashes her husband against the wall.

"YOU HURT TEMMIN."

The heavily modified B1 droid begins to bend the arm back farther, farther, farther, until Norra can hear the bones creaking and straining—

"Bones," she says with a reluctant admonition. "Stop. Just hold him."

"Norra," Brentin pleads, "I'm not with the Empire, I didn't mean to do those things, is our son okay—"

Sloane, with her hands up, says: "He's right. He was made to do it."

"*Shut your mouth,*" Norra hisses at her. "Both of you. Be quiet. We don't have time for a conversation. What's going to happen is, we're going back to my ship. We are getting out of here. And soon as we have a window, I'm taking you both back to Chandrila."

"It's not me you want," Sloane says.

"Norra, she's right—"

"Quiet, *Grand Admiral.*"

"Look at me. Do I look like an admiral anymore? I'm sneaking around an Imperial base with a rebel. Norra, don't be an idiot." At that word, Bones extends his other arm—the one *not* poised to break Brentin's limb—and extends his concealed vibroblade. It thrusts up under Sloane's chin. It nicks the skin; a bead of blood swells up like a little balloon. "I'm . . . *sorry* for calling you an idiot. But there's more going on here."

"Norra, please listen to her."

Sloane continues: "A man named Rax—he's in charge of the Empire. He's the one who put a chip in your husband's head. He's the one who set up the attack on Liberation Day. I was just a . . ." Sloane cringes, as if this is hard for her to admit. "I was just a distraction. He's the puppeteer. There's something out beyond Niima's canyons and caverns—a valley. Rax is protecting something there. Take me there. We can finish this."

Indecision wars inside Norra's heart.

She wants to shoot Sloane right in the chest. Or club her in the head. Or drag her by the hair back to the shuttle. She wants to kiss her husband. And kill him. And throttle him to ask him why, and apologize for leaving him behind, and pretend like none of this ever happened and that she and her son and her man are still back on Akiva, living their best life.

Norra tells herself: *Sloane is lying.* The woman is a practiced deceiver. And Brentin is on the leash of whatever control chip she hammered into his head. And yet she's clearly right. Sloane is no grand admiral anymore. She was brought here as a prisoner. The Empire no longer calls Rae Sloane its leader or even its daughter.

What if she's right?

What if that man, Rax, is the answer to everything?

Norra tells herself, *I don't have to care about that. I can do the job I was brought here to do.* Capture Sloane, save her husband, and *go home.*

But what if that doesn't fix anything? What if Norra has a chance, *one chance,* to stop the real monster behind the scenes? What if this Rax is really the puppet master Sloane claims he is? Can Norra just . . . let him go?

"Let's go," she says.

"Norra, wait—"

"You better be right about this Rax," Norra says. "Because if I find out you're wrong or that you're playing me? I'll have my droid here break every centimeter of every bone in your bodies. Are we clear?"

Sloane grins. "Clear as the blue sky, Norra Wexley."

PART FIVE

INTERLUDE

THE *IMPERIALIS,* TWENTY-FIVE YEARS AGO

IT IS THE first time Galli has been off Jakku in ten years, and only the second time ever—at least, as far as he can remember. He does not know who his parents are or where they came from. Sometimes he imagines that they came from some faraway place, a place of rivers and forests. A place with a sea. Other times, he is angry at them—and he thinks, *Who my parents are does not matter. They aren't my everything. They aren't my any*thing. He envisions in these times of anger that they are dirt merchants or sand farmers from Jakku and it will be his great pleasure to transcend them.

(It is far more likely that they are dead.)

Now he sits in a plush room, more opulent than anything he's ever seen before. This is the same ship as the last time he left Jakku, but *this* time he is no stowaway. This is not some cargo space in which he hides.

He sits on a chair.

It is the most comfortable chair he has ever sat in.

He wants to live in this chair. He may be fine *dying* in this chair.

And dying on this chair may in fact be what awaits him. The man to whom this ship belongs, a man named Sheev Palpatine, is a cipher. Galli has only met him once ever, but the man has haunted his dreams since. Those dark robes, that craggy moon face. They are just dreams, surely, and yet—they seem real. As if the man is truly visiting Galli in some way during those meager hours he could carve out for sleep.

He's met the man's droids, too—some are cold protocol droids, others assassins, astromechs, and excavators who helped clear the ground at Jakku. And he's spoken time and again to an adviser: someone named Tashu.

But Galli has only met the man himself once.

And now he is about to have his second meeting.

He fears that death will be the result. He has been used for one purpose, and that purpose is now finished. The Observatory is built. Galli did what he had to do to keep everyone away. None discovered it, and now it is buried beneath the sands near the Plaintive Hand. *My usefulness is over,* he thinks. The man will kill him. Part of Galli finds strange comfort in that. Another part of him thinks: *No, I will kill the man first.* Even though the man has magic, *real* magic and not the parlor tricks of the anchorites. The way he summoned sand to his hand like a flying serpent . . .

Wait.

He's here.

Standing in the doorway. Hands clasped underneath the draping sleeves of his night-black robes. Only half of his face can be seen underneath the hood. In that glimpse, the boy can see the awfulness there: as if dark magic has distorted his visage. It is a good reminder that this man has true power unlike anything Galli has ever seen, and with that, the boy quickly stifles any threat in his mind lest the old sorcerer have the ability to pluck stray thoughts from inside his skull.

Palpatine enters the room and with a gentle swipe of his hand, a chair moves toward him—it eases and whirls, settling in front of Galli's own chair. The man sits, and his hand begins another gesture: The palm rises, as if asking a worshipper to get off his knees. Galli isn't sure if the gesture is meant for him, but he soon sees it isn't—just as the chair moved, a table moves, too, rising out of a telescoping portal in the floor. This table is like no table Galli knows: It is circular in shape but with a square board carved into its top. That larger square is hand-etched with a field of smaller black and white squares, and in those squares are circles of opposite color.

As the table rises, so, too, do pieces from within those circles. Each idol is a carving, crudely sculpted. They are symmetrical on each side of the board: Each side gets the same contingent of pieces. He sees pieces that look like beasts, like men with large hats, like warriors, like something that may in fact be a starship. He also sees pieces at the far end of each side that look not unlike Palpatine himself—tall but bent, and similarly robed. The one piece in front of Palpatine is in black robes with a white face. The piece in front of Galli is clad in white, with a dark countenance.

"Hello, Galli," Palpatine says.

"Hello."

"It has been some time."

He swallows a knot. *Be strong. You are not some boy. You are almost a man, now. You are vworkka, not mouse. You have killed for him.* With that, he lifts his trembling chin to appear fearless and proud. "It has."

"The artifacts are in place. The core has been drilled. The sentinels and my adviser, Tashu, report you have been very loyal to us indeed." He draws a deep breath and shows his yellow teeth in a smile. "The Observatory is done and so is your time on that wretched planet."

"Yes." *Here it is,* he thinks. His death awaits. The

ten years since he's seen this man were just a delay of the inevitable. "I don't want to die." He says it not to plead, but just to say it. The man must know.

"Of course you don't. You have a destiny. Those with destinies are bound to fight for life because life and destiny are irrevocably intertwined."

"And those without destinies?"

The man waves his bone-white hand dismissively. "They do not know that they crave death, but they do."

"Are you going to kill me?"

"It is not my intention."

"Then why am I here?"

"As I say, your time on Jakku is over. You are done. You did as I asked and so I am rewarding you with a new life away from that place."

His heart leaps. *Away from Jakku . . .*

"Am I to go back there?"

"Not today. Perhaps one day."

"I don't ever want to go back."

A slow smile spreads. The man's lips are empurpled. Like a bruise sliced in half so that a tongue and teeth may emerge through the slit. "And yet it may be your destiny. That part is unclear." Palpatine leans forward, his pointed finger drawing invisible lines over the strange game board there. "Do you know this game, Galli?"

"I don't."

"No, I suppose you wouldn't. It's a very old game. Shah-tezh, in this iteration, though over the eons I have seen it spawn many variants. Dejarik. Moebius. Chess. In most of the iterations the core mechanism remains."

"Are we going to play?"

"We will. But first I need you to understand not just how the pieces move, but *why* they move. Not just how to play, but *why* we play." Palpatine smiles. "Listen closely."

And then Palpatine explains the game.

"In the game of Shah-tezh," Palpatine tells the young man, Galli, "the board is called the demesne, and each piece upon the demesne has its own special role and its own special maneuvers. Each player is afforded one of each kind." With an arthritic claw, the Emperor twists a piece that looks like a too-thin man in a strange, pillarlike hat. "The Vizier can only move along the diagonal, but has no limit to how far he may travel." With the side of a yellowed nail he taps another piece: a hulking, hooded figure with something that might be a long rifle or a long blade—the abstraction of the carving makes it hard to tell. As the nail goes *click click click* against it, Palpatine says: "This is the Knight. He is versatile and can move two steps in any direction at all. Limited distance, but freedom of movement."

He goes on like that for a while, describing piece after piece: the Outcast, the Dowager, the Disciple, the Counselor, the Beast, the Craft. He describes how they move, what role they serve, even a little bit of the history (later iterations of the game, he said, removed the Outcast, for the Outcast was "too anarchic a piece" and the players sought a "more stable game").

Galli follows along, unsure of what he's supposed to be learning. But he pays great attention, never blinking, never turning his gaze away lest it all disappear the moment he does.

"Each piece exists in service to one other piece—" And here the teacher grabs the final figure off the board, the robed piece that looks not unlike Palpatine himself. "The Imperator. *All* the pieces of the demesne are here to protect the Imperator. If the Imperator falls,

the game is over. That is true no matter how many
pieces remain on the board. Do you see?"

"I see."

"Tell me then what that means."

Galli swallows. He concentrates very hard to suss
out the message—the *lesson* that the Emperor is trying
to teach him. He clears his throat and says, "It means
that without the Imperator, the demesne cannot survive."

A smile creeps across the Emperor's face like a cen-
tipede crawling on a cracked wall. "Good. *Good.*
That is true. That is insightful." The smile suddenly
falls away. The man's face twists up in a scowl of disappointment. With venom, the old man asserts: "But
it is not *quite right.* It is not merely that the demesne
cannot survive. It is that those remaining behind do
not *deserve* to survive." His voice is laced with anger,
the volume rising and the words coming faster as he
continues: "They have *one* role. That role is to protect
the Imperator. If an Empire cannot protect its Emperor then that Empire must be deemed a *failure.* It
collapses not only because its central figure is gone,
but because it *must not be allowed to remain*!"

By the end of the old man's tirade, Galli tries to
speak—and cannot. He tries to breathe—*and cannot.*
He reaches for his neck and paws at his throat, a high-
pitched keen the only sound escaping his mouth. His
face pulses and throbs. His vision begins to go dark.

This is it. This is me dying. I have failed the lesson.

Palpatine waves his hand, and the pressure closing
Galli's throat is gone as fast as it came. The young
man gasps and tries not to cry.

Palpatine reaches out and takes Galli's hand with a
grasp that is alarmingly gentle. The man's skin is pa-
pery and thin. It's almost *sharp,* too, as if running your

hands along his flesh in the wrong direction will slice your own like a razor.

"It angers me," Palpatine says sadly, "to think of an Empire that fails its Emperor. But one must admit that it is possible. And in that possibility, it is wise to play the very long game. It is time I look to the unforgivable outcome and plan for that. You are part of that plan."

"How?"

"You, my son, are the Contingency."

"What is that?"

"There are unforeseen costs that must be paid. You may have to be the one who pays those costs, Galli. Which means it is time now to join the Empire. You will serve me in whatever way I require, and if all goes well you will remain the Contingency. If you fail me, then I will find another, for this role is one of great purpose and destiny. Will you be what I require?"

"I will."

That smile returns. "Most excellent."

"But I do not know how."

"Ah. That will come in time. For now: Do you like opera?"

CHAPTER THIRTY-TWO

THE REDHEADED BOY sits on a ship without viewports so he cannot see the endless dunes or the raging war going on above them. All he can see right now is the other children: two dozen of them lining benches on each side of the transport ship, all of them in white, all of them staring at the young child as if he's a gobbet of meat and they're a pack of slavering yenavores.

They are hungry and feral and he tries not to tremble.

But the boy trembles harder, instead.

The door to the transport bay opens, and a man steps in—the boy knows this man: Counselor Rax.

The man comes and stands before the boy, looking down.

"Hello, Armitage."

"Sir," the redheaded boy says in a small voice. "Hello."

"Has your father explained to you what's happening?"

"No, sir."

"Hm. Brendol does not much like you, I suspect."

Tears line the boy's eyelids as he nods in agreement. "I suspect that is correct, sir."

"Listen to you. The pinnacle of a private education. Such a crisp evocation of words for such a young lad. Even in fear you speak clearly and plainly. Well done, Armitage." The man sighs and kneels down. "I was not initially so fortunate as you. I was born here on Jakku. This horrible world. Those born here are already dead, or so I once thought. But I was reborn. I was brought into the Empire by our late Emperor and made anew. I was turned from the little sand-scoured Jakku savage into something considerably more civilized. I was like you in one way, though: I, too, was scared."

"I am scared, sir."

"Yes. That is wise. Fear is useful when it guides us— but it becomes dangerous when it governs us. I am here to tell you what is going to happen. We are taking this ship to a location where a second ship awaits. You and these other children will be taken far away. Your father will come, as will I. We will meet others at our destination. Together we will begin something new. We will leave all of this behind. Do you understand?"

The boy does not, and he says as much. "No, sir. Not truly."

The man laughs softly. "That's fine, Armitage. It will all become clear one day. For now, I leave you with a gift."

"What's that, sir?"

"These other children? They stare at you, don't they?"

"Y . . . yes, sir."

"They want to kill you, I fear. They want to slash you with their fingernails. They want to bite you until you are just unrecognizable pieces. They would, if given half a chance, beat you with common rocks until all your limbs were broken sticks. Just as I was once a savage of Jakku, so too are these children savage in the same way. Your father's work has only heightened that impulse. He has sharpened them the way you do a knife."

The boy is truly afraid. The urge to go to the bathroom rises, and he is suddenly sure that he is going to wet himself. And he knows, too, that when he does, the other children will pounce upon him at this man's command. They will smell his weakness and they will slaughter him.

"I . . ."

"The gift. You want to know about the gift. Here it is, Armitage: You will lead these children. They will serve you. And one day soon your father will pass down his teachings to you, and you will learn to do what he did. It will be your life's work to take children like these savages and hammer their malleable minds into whatever shape you so require. They will be tools built for the work at hand. That is my gift to you, boy. One day your father will die. One day soon, I fear. And you will take his place."

He stands then and speaks to the other children. "Listen to me closely. This boy, Armitage Hux, commands you. You will do as he decides. You will give your lives for him if you must. Nod if you understand."

They all nod in a simultaneity that both disturbs and thrills Armitage.

"Thank you," Armitage says to Counselor Rax.

"It is my pleasure. The future of the Empire needs you. Now sit tight. We're almost at the Observatory. Our destiny isn't long now."

With that, Rax turns on his heel and walks back through the rows of children and back out of the transport hold. The door seals shut behind him.

The children all turn once more toward Armitage to stare. He fears that this has all been some trickster's ruse, some game played upon him—they won't listen to him. He doesn't command anything or anyone. They'll laugh at him and, as the man said, they'll beat him, claw him, bite him.

He draws in a quick intake of breath and points to one of the children with a wavering finger—the child is a boy like him, but with tar-dark hair and sun-marked skin. "You," Armitage says to him.

The boy says nothing.

"Do you agree to do as I say?" Armitage asks.

The dark-haired boy nods.

Armitage balls his fingers into fists as he steadies himself. "I want you to hit the boy to the right of you. Hard."

The dark-haired boy turns to a sandy-haired, sallow-cheeked lad. Then he raises a fist and clubs that other boy in the side of the head. The boy cries out. A line of blood crawls from a small gash in the victim's cheek.

Armitage feels a strange and sinister buzz of excitement.

CHAPTER THIRTY-THREE

ONCE AGAIN THE light of Jakku presses hard against Sloane's eyes as she and Brentin are ushered forth by Norra Wexley and that mad droid. When her eyes adjust anew, the first thing she sees in the sky is her ship.

The *Ravager*.

Sloane has a pang deep inside, like a string being plucked, the resultant vibration humming in her marrow. Regret courses through her like a poison. A choice presents itself, now: She could run, or overpower Norra, in order to steal a ship. She could take that ship up to the *Ravager*. She could land and regain control. Not an easy task, no, but she is confident in her ability to get it done. Then she could take her ship and just . . . *go*.

It would not be an act of cowardice. It would be one of survival. The *Ravager* is a Super Star Destroyer—a dreadnought of mighty proportions. It is by itself a massive flying city. It has enough room to contain a powerful remnant of the Empire. It has the weapons to hold off a whole fleet—as it is doing right now by pushing back the New Republic armada. She could take the *Ravager*. She could spare some portion of the Empire and flee into the stars with that massive vessel. With it she could start over again.

The *Empire* could start over again.

But that would mean setting her vengeance aside.

And that is something she just cannot do. The urge for revenge is like a hook in her cheek, and it's drawing her miserably toward it, tug, tug, tug.

Rax has ruined it all. He has touched the Empire with a filthy hand, and foul streaks of his treachery are everywhere, corroding all that she loves. The Empire to Sloane was an entity of *order* and *discipline*. It was about upholding stability in a chaotic galaxy. It was about vanquishing uncertainty and providing a way of things: a schematic, a backbone, a path for all to follow if they wanted to be safe.

And now it's *this*. A wild, brutal remnant, like a broken spear stuck in the sand. The troopers have turned to common thugs. The officers are haunted and overwhelmed. This is a primitive place, and it has made them primitive in return. The Empire that she loved is gone. That revelation reaches her again, and this time for the last time.

In her heart, she lets the *Ravager* go.

Just as she let Adea Rite go.

And just as she is letting all the hopes for the Empire's future go.

Norra's blaster prods her in the back. "You want to keep moving? We don't have time for sightseeing, Admiral."

"Just Sloane," she says. "I'm an admiral no more." *Just a rebel like you.* She keeps moving toward the shuttle.

And toward her vengeance.

Ackbar's chair swivels from station to station as he examines the battle map—his massive gelatinous eyes flick their gaze among screens, assessing the situation. And the assessment is not ideal.

This should have been easier. The New Republic fleet is larger. The Empire has been waning. On paper, it's an easy victory—

And yet, so far, it has been anything but. They've already lost a contingent of corvettes. Two frigates are down. Countless starfighters have been lost to the swarm of TIEs that fill the void.

Of course, Admiral Ackbar is a student of history, and in many cases smaller, lesser forces have out-matched and outfoxed their betters. The Ghostfinder fleet versus the Sith armada. The Mandalorians versus the Grand Army of the Republic. And, of course, the Rebel Alliance versus the Empire.

History is rife with examples of weaker forces rout-ing the stronger. And that may happen here, too, if they're not smart and cautious.

The Empire has changed their tactics—they are fighting with a brutality and a chaos that has never been seen in their repertoire. One frigate broke in half when a single TIE bomber crashed head-on into the bridge connecting the two halves of the ship. They ex-pend their weapons in every direction. Their attacks offer no rhyme or reason—the old Imperial maneu-vers, always so neatly predictable and textbook, either are being willfully ignored or have simply been forgot-ten. That lends their defense a desperate, dangerous edge. It is, quite honestly, hard to combat. (It's also, Ackbar supposes, exactly what made his own fleet so difficult to fight as rebels.)

The other component is that damnable dread-nought. It has ten times the weapons loadouts of a single Star Destroyer—its shadow is deeper and wider than the dark of space beyond it. The other smaller Destroyers circle it, parting long enough to allow tor-pedoes and turbolasers to lance out in the divide, in-juring the New Republic fleet while protecting it. It's like a hive protecting its queen. *But if we kill the queen, the hive will die.*

Right now three of the best and brightest ships in their fleet are surging against the Imperial fleet in order to take down that dreadnought—the *Unity,* the *Amity,* and the *Concord.* Those three Starhawks, with their blunt hatchet-fronts, are meant to drive a wedge in the Empire's cordon of Star Destroyers—but they're simply not breaking through. They're tangling with the Destroyers while taking fire from the *Ravager.* Taking all of the brunt while earning little of the advantage.

He thinks to engage with Agate to discuss a new strategy—

But that will have to wait, as the hologram of General Tyben appears. Tyben is a narrow-shouldered man, his head as square and bald as a cube of ice (and he's near as pale, too). His features are knotted with worry.

"Status report?" Ackbar asks.

"Ground forces are finding some success, Admiral," Tyben answers. The hologram flickers—not uncommon given the chaos of battle. So many frequencies and energy sources to interrupt the transmission. "We have pushed their line back, klick by klick. We may be advancing on their base by nightfall—that is, *if* we can stem our casualties. We're hemorrhaging lives. The Empire is fighting less like the Empire and more like an insurgent force, Admiral. They take risks. They sacrifice their soldiers. It's pandemonium but they seem to be using it to their advantage and not their detriment."

"We are experiencing similar up here," Ackbar growls. "But we are not so fortunate as you—we have gained little ground. Keep pushing forward. If you find success on the ground it may earn us an edge here."

Tyben nods, and hesitates before saying: "I should *be* there."

"You are best on Chandrila, kept at a distance." And he is. Ackbar told the chancellor to keep one of their best military strategists in reserve, safe with her. He warned her to be wary that Jakku could be a ruse: The Empire tempts them to attack, thus leaving both Chandrila and Nakadia vulnerable to predation once more. That meant dividing their forces and keeping security high in the New Republic worlds. Still, that seems to have been a false concern. There has been no sign of any threat as yet. "You have your men on the ground led by Lieutenant General Brockway."

"But with me present—"

"We have no time for this, General Tyben. I thank you for your concern and your update." Ackbar ends the holographic transmission, then turns to open a channel to Agate. But his webbed hand pauses, held fixed over the console as he gazes out the viewport of the *Home One* bridge—

His blood goes cold as saline as he watches the tragedy unfold.

One of the Star Destroyers—the *Punishment*—turns its nose drastically starboard. It turns right toward the Starhawk *Amity*. And the *Amity* has little room to maneuver given its proximity both to Agate's *Concord* and to the battle raging all around it.

It's suicide, Ackbar thinks. He believes it must be an accident, but it seems to be deliberate. The *Punishment*'s nose is like a sweeping blade, and it crashes into the blunt fore of the *Amity,* shearing through it. Fire blooms in space. Bodies drift. *And the* Punishment *keeps going.* Thrusters burn at the back and repulsors fire along the side—the Destroyer becomes a weapon as it cuts the Starhawk in half, debris from both ships cascading outward as lightning coruscates between the two obliterated vessels.

Agate's own ship is right in the middle of it all.

He hurriedly opens the channel.

Everything focuses to a sharp point. Agate hears Ackbar in her ear, is faintly aware of his presence cast in holographic blue to her right. He's warning her about the debris field coming her way, but he doesn't need to tell her about it. She sees it on her screens: A hundred red motes blink like furious eyes winking in the dark. Each is a piece of debris, and each piece rockets toward her like a weapon—the wreckage of not one ship but two.

That wave of destruction will be here in less than three minutes.

She yells for Spohn to strengthen the port-side shields. But she knows they'll only hold up so long. That many fragments? It's too much.

"Abandon ship, Commodore!" Ackbar roars. "That is an *order*."

"Yes, sir," she says, her voice sounding a thousand light-years away.

This is what it comes down to, she thinks. Her return to war is over as quickly as it began. Their brute-force strategy to break the blockade of Star Destroyers has ended. The *Amity* is down. The *Concord* won't last. She barks for the communications officer to warn the *Unity*—they have room to maneuver, to get out of range. Not only will the *Concord* create its own debris field, but with that Star Destroyer gone and the two Starhawks vacating the field, that will leave the *Unity* vulnerable to attacks from that massive dreadnought waiting in the center of it all.

Abandon ship.

She makes the call. It's the right thing to do. And they're going to have to move fast—worst thing is, they can only use the pods on the starboard side. Otherwise, they'd launch right into the wave of wreckage.

Red lights pulse. Klaxons blare. A flurry of activity rises around her as the people of the bridge do as they have been trained to do, streaming efficiently and effectively toward the exits—the capital command crew have escape pods all their own and within spitting distance of the bridge.

Her artificial eye focuses on the screens. She sweeps her finger ahead, fast-forwarding the expected consequences of what's coming—the computer is predictive and models the likeliest outcome. The debris will damage, but not destroy, the *Concord*. It will, however, leave them open to attack from the dreadnought. And they're close enough to the top of Jakku's atmosphere that the ship will likely drop toward the surface. Crashing into sand and stone. They will lose the *Concord* one way or another.

Spohn grabs her elbow. "Commodore, it's time."

"I'm coming," she says. "I'll be right there."

But it's a lie.

"Commodore—"

"I said *go*. I'll be along."

Ackbar starts to ask her what she's doing. She ends communication with him. *I am sorry, Admiral.* But she realizes something:

If the destruction of the *Punishment* and the *Amity* open up her ship to attack by the dreadnought—

Then it also opens up the dreadnought to attack by the *Concord*.

She has her chance.

It's one she likely cannot survive. *But the costs of war are heavy, even in victory.* That has been one of her guiding, governing principles. It is a grudging reality that informs all that she does in battle.

Her hand is no longer trembling. It has been stayed, perhaps by the first moment of certainty she's felt in a very long time. *How about that.*

She uses her newly steady hand to urge forward the *Concord*'s throttle so that it seizes the gap in the Star Destroyer barricade, thrusting hard toward the dreadnought. Above her head, lights flick from red to green: pod bays launching one after the other as her people abandon ship.

Good. Go. Get safe.

She takes a moment to look around her. She's alone. Like a little island in the center of a calm, quiet lake.

Her screens light up. As expected, the dreadnought is unleashing hell—right as debris from the two eradicated ships begins slamming into the *Concord*. Lights go dark, then bright, then dark again. The ship shakes and bangs as if it's a toy held in the hand of a careless child.

From Agate's bridge console, she flicks over to the weapons consoles. She prepares everything they have, every bit of ordnance this ship has to bear.

Bring hell to my door, I'll bring it to yours.

She fires *everything*. Banks of turbolasers. Ion torpedoes. Concussion missiles. Bright lines of death streaking through the black. Lines of the same—fire, castigation, heat—launching from the *Ravager* toward her. Like threads of light seeking each other. But they will pass each other, instead, each heading onward to an act of destruction, not creation.

The *Concord* roars toward it, even as its deflector shields begin to fail on the side. The ship tilts starboard. Debris punches through the hull. The engines gutter. She wills the ship to keep going.

Hope is a fire fast extinguished inside her. She sees

the fury unleashed from the dreadnought—predictive analysis shows the *Concord* losing this fight. Her volley cannot match that from the *Ravager*. The *Ravager* is a beast and will not be sated. She will damage it. To what extent she cannot say, but if she opens it up to attack—even still, her mind attempts the calculations. If she opens up a hole in the side of that thing, it's something, but it's still not *enough*. And if the other Star Destroyers close the gap and protect the injury made against the *Ravager,* then what?

Out there, through the cathedral-like arches of glass, she sees the weapons streaming toward her.

This is it.

But then: Agate has a new idea.

War brings with it moments of inevitability. A sinking ship. An onrushing horde. A mortal wound. The worst kind, Ackbar thinks, are the moments when you watch friends die. Especially those times when it happens slowly, too slowly, as if all the moments leading up to it are drawn out and given time like images flash-pulsed into your mind's eye.

This is one of those times. Agate cuts communication with him, and he sees the *Concord* burn hard and move toward the dreadnought as both it and the monstrous *Ravager* launch everything at each other.

The problem is, the *Ravager*'s weapons are far greater than those of a single Starhawk. The Starhawk's weapons are prodigious and better than even he has on the *Home One*. It is the uttermost of their tech: bleeding-edge armament. But by itself it can only hope to wound the dreadnought.

And it will die in service of that act.

Agate is still on board. He knows this. She is going down with her ship—a dramatic gesture that he hopes has purpose behind it. He suspects she feels that she must command every moment between now and her end, that it should be *her* hand directing the ship and its fusillade of fire.

But the Starhawk makes an unexpected turn.

The *Concord* banks sharply to the starboard, maneuvering quickly to turn that side of itself toward the incoming attack. The port is already damaged by the debris field. The starboard side taking the hit— with the shields already gone, Ackbar sees—may not destroy the Starhawk outright, but it'll sink it. Already its engines are damaged on the far side. Atmosphere will grab that vessel like mud sucking on a soldier's boot.

A hologram flashes over his console.

It's Agate.

"Agate! Get off that ship—"

"Admiral, listen. Get everyone you can to hit that dreadnought from aft. Take out its engines. Send every starfighter, every CR90, anyone—"

"Commodore, I command you to abandon that vessel."

"Admiral, it literally pains me to deny your order. But please, trust me. Listen to me. The engines!"

Out the viewport and on his screen, he watches the fusillade from the *Ravager* close in on the *Concord*.

"What are you doing? Hitting those engines—the *Ravager* is not moving. The engines aren't where we need to be concentrating our fire—"

"Just *trust* me."

"Commodore—"

"Thank you, Admiral. It has been the highest honor."

"Kyrsta!"

And then she's gone again.

Just trust me.

War brings with it moments of inevitability, yes. But it also carries with it the opposite: moments of grave uncertainty bridged only by acts of blind faith. When they say to one another, *May the Force be with you*, it is precisely this that they mean: It is a wish that when the time comes to leap into the void and to make a decision based on instinct and trust, you are rewarded for that act and not punished. The hope is that if you meet the galaxy halfway, it meets you in the middle and carries you the rest of the distance. Ackbar decides to trust and to leap . . .

And to pray that the Force is with them all.

The exchange of destruction is a mighty one. The *Concord*'s barrage slams into the *Ravager*, ripping a hole in the side of the gargantuan ship with the ferocity of a biting, rending rancor. The injury is black and deep, but not fatal. And the dreadnought's own weapons strike the *Concord*, slipping past what little is left of the deflector shields and punching clean through it. Oxygen whistles out into the void. Fire plumes as chemicals off-gas into space. The ship groans. Somewhere in the belly of the ship, explosions start going off—fuel cells and magna-batteries chain-reacting, boom, boom, boom. It won't detonate the whole ship. But it has gutted it.

The ship is dead in the water.

And without the repulsors from underneath keeping it aloft, the atmosphere of Jakku is like a reaching, claiming hand. She feels the ship drift downward, drifting as it goes.

But the Starhawks were designed with one thing in mind: *upgrade*. So long did the rebels endure an aging, piecemeal fleet that when the time came to finally design something *new* to serve the nascent Republic, they went all-in. Every internal system, every external design feature, every weapon—all of it was upgraded beyond the watermark set by the Mon Cala ships prior and beyond the known capabilities of the Empire's extant ships.

One of the features that saw the largest boost in ability?

The tractor beam.

The role of the tractor beam is simple: to grab an object in space, usually a spacecraft, in order to usher it safely into a docking bay or to seize the vessel and pull it closer. The tractor beams on a Star Destroyer were notoriously vicious, with the strength to draw a Corellian corvette into its bay—or to stop a Nebulon frigate from making the escape to lightspeed.

The tractor beam on the Starhawk is ten times that. Magnite crystals amplify both the range and the strength of the beam. A Starhawk could capture and move a ship many times its own size.

Agate dials up the tractor beam, points it at the *Ravager*—

She fires.

If I'm going down to the ground, she thinks, *you're coming with me.*

Grand Moff Randd sits in a chair on the bridge of the *Ravager*. Up until now, he has felt supremely in control of this battle. The *Ravager* is a vessel whose might is presently unparalleled in the Imperial fleet, and to have been given command of it by Rax himself is an honor he will not squander. His forces have stopped the rebel-born False Republic fleet at every turn—though he is no true tactician, he has many great minds working for him, and their plan of forming a perimeter of vessels around the dreadnought was a sound one.

Until now.

The three ships pressing at the barrier—Starhawks, he believes they are called, manufactured for the False Republic—were held fast at the margins, even though the Star Destroyers were taking heavy fire as a result. And then something happened with the *Punishment*. The officer in charge of that ship, Captain Groff, appeared in a panic: He said that the Destroyer was suffering a coolant leak from the shield generators that was cascading through the upper levels. Some areas were experiencing fires. He seemed positively deranged—that was a factor Randd had long been worried about. Coming to this desolate world, this far-flung system, brought with it the chance to wear on a man's soul. It could erode a weaker mind. When he explained that fear to Counselor Rax, the man said, *Do not worry about that. The Imperials that have come to Jakku are the greatest of our kind. We will not break. The unkindness of this world will only bolster us. We will harden like calluses, Randd.*

And that was the end of that.

In Rax, they trusted.

Randd still trusts him. They have survived this long. And there's no doubt that Rax is admirable, capable, a true hero of the Empire. Randd is a fan of belt-tightening, and using Jakku to harden their hearts against the fight to come was, to his mind, genius.

But now . . . what he feared most has come true.

Groff lost it. He said that he would not abandon his ship. The New Republic would torture him and execute him. His own people would turn on him. He was frothing with distemper, screaming suddenly about how the New Republic were traitors and they all deserved death like dogs and how they must give no quarter, no quarter at all. The last thing he said was, "I must be a stronger blade! A . . . a blade with which to slit the throats of the traitors that crawl on their bellies toward our door!"

Randd recognized it as a line from Counselor Rax's speech.

Groff's comms went dark after that.

And then he crashed the *Punishment* into the nearest Starhawk.

That led to a chain of events even now Randd does not completely understand—debris from the two ships hit a second Starhawk, and that one he felt sure would be out of the picture. But no. That ship accelerated in the gap right toward the *Ravager*. Firing all its weapons, and so Randd demanded they return fire, all the way—reserving every weapons system they had launching ordnance in the direction of the onrushing Starhawk, a ship that now identifies itself as the *Concord*.

The *Concord* turned broadside and took the hits just as the *Ravager* took its own. That ship was scuttled. He did not need his systems to confirm it. His eyes told him all he needed to know. Meanwhile, the *Ravager* was fine—damaged, yes, and now more vulnerable, but he rerouted power to the deflectors to magnify protection over that chasm and—

Then the strangest thing.

The *Concord* snared the dreadnought with a *tractor beam*.

Randd is not a man given to humor—his wife, Danassic, says that she believes he laughs once, perhaps twice a year. But here he almost laughed. Why in all of space and time would the captain of that Starhawk see fit to lash him with a paltry tractor beam? Perhaps to save herself the fall into atmosphere? The *Ravager* serving as an anchor? He hates to tell her, but gravity is a cruel mistress. It takes what it wants and will not be denied.

The *Ravager* moves, suddenly.

It moves, but he does not *command* it to move.

"Status report," he barks, his calm voice suffering a sudden break to it, like that of a boy just getting hair on his chest. *"Status report!"*

Nearby, Vice Admiral Pierson appears, sweat beading on his brow. "The Starhawk has affixed us with its tractor beam—"

"Yes. I know that. How are we—" The ship drifts again. *"How is it moving us?"*

"I—I have no idea, it must be powerful—"

"Strengthen our engines. Reverse course! Fire repulsors—"

Alarms go off. The ship shakes again—this time, the sensation is different. Like something is hitting it.

Pierson's eyes go wide. "They're concentrating fire on our aft."

The screens show a sudden flurry of starfighters—every variety brought to bear against their *engines*. If they lose those . . .

"Engine five just went dark!" an ensign yells.

"Now sub-engines three through six!" an engineering officer cries.

The Concord *is trying to drag us down to Jakku.* The nerve. "Fire all weapons at that Starhawk—"

"Sir," Pierson responds, "the weapon systems will cycle in two minutes. We already hit them with everything we had on your orders."

"Then send TIEs after it!"

"But they're protecting our flank. The engines!"

Again the ship shakes. Worse this time. And when it does, it's like trying to move something heavy and failing until it suddenly gives way—the *Ravager* slides and dips downward so hard, Randd's jaw snaps tight, teeth closing hard on his tongue. He tastes blood and curses.

"The atmosphere," Pierson says. "We're entering atmo, sir."

"Bolster the engines! Bolster the repulsors! Bolster everything!"

But in his head, Randd knows the score: It is too late. The *Ravager* is done for. He has squandered his chance and now, hope is lost. The greatest weapon in the Empire's arsenal is lost because of him. A flagging fear nags him: *It should be Rae Sloane in this chair, not me.*

The one thing about Randd is that he is not a sycophant. He is no zealot. He admires Rax. He trusted him. But he will not be crucified for this.

In the chaos of the moment—the flickering lights, the shaking ship, the flurry of movement going on across the bridge—Randd sneaks quietly away, boards an escape pod, and jettisons himself into space.

The *Concord* has leashed the larger ship with its powerful tractor beam and draws it down toward atmosphere. New Republic starfighters hit the engines of the *Ravager,* one after the other, again and again, a returning loop of fire while a pair of CR90s keep the TIEs off their backs. The *Unity,* the last remaining Starhawk, has pulled back to a safe distance and is using its considerable weapons load to provide the *Concord* with cover, peppering the nearby Star Destroyers with as much fire as it can muster.

And then the Starhawk dips considerably as the atmosphere kisses it, the underside of the ship glowing with the sudden heat of reentry.

Blade Squadron reports that the last of the *Ravager*'s

main engines are out. Only the sub-engines remain, and they won't save it.

The dreadnought's front end is the first to follow the Starhawk, carving a line across the top of the sky where the black goes to blue like a fading bruise—an aura of fire begins to glow around the *Ravager*'s fore.

Ackbar watches the two titans fall.

The *Concord* goes first. Agate likely remains on board. She won't answer his comms, but a scan of the Starhawk shows that not a single pod remains undamaged, and the fighter bays are empty or destroyed. She has no way off that ship, and it is too late and too risky for a rescue.

As the Starhawk drops, it drags the *Ravager* with it. Like a rider pulling its beast mount toward the edge of a waterfall, closer, closer—

Until both plunge through space and into sky. Until the gravity throttles each and draws them ineluctably downward.

Ackbar grabs the comm and warns those below: "Soldiers and pilots of the New Republic! The dreadnought *Ravager* is down—it falls to Jakku! Beware debris and take cover!"

All around him are the cheers of those on the bridge of the *Home One* as they watch the titanic vessel go faster and faster toward Jakku. But Ackbar does not cheer. He nods quietly and mutters a small entreaty to the Force, asking it to protect those down below, underneath these falling giants, and further, to accept Kyrsta Agate as one of its own.

I'm really getting the hang of this.

On Akiva, they have these bugs that fly over still water—polywings, they're called—and they flit over the surface, changing course like the snap of one's fingers. They move this way and that, snagging smaller flies out of the air and eating them on the go, chomp.

Temmin wants to be like those polywings. That's how he sees his X-wing. He pivots the starfighter fast as lightning, moving erratically so that the TIEs don't see him coming. His heart is going so fast in his chest he fears it's going to punch its way out. His blood roars like a river in his ears. An effervescent thrill elevates him to almost giddy heights. He's buoyed, too, by knowing that his mother is still alive. And that Bones is protecting her.

This is a good day, he thinks. *The New Republic is going to win this war. My mother is alive. My best friend is here. And I'm in an X-wing! And I'm not dead!* He cackles like Koko with his radio mike on. Koko cackles right back as the two of them cross in front of the other, slaloming around each other, spitting lasers at escaping TIEs.

One forms up on Wedge's tail, and Temmin bites his lip to repress the grin that threatens to split his whole face. "Phantom Leader, you've got a bug on your back. Lemme swat him for you." Wedge brings the X-wing low over a dry red ravine, past a squadron of New Republic soldiers taking cover there in the shadows afforded by the gulley. The TIE whips through the space behind Phantom Leader's X-wing, and Temmin thinks to come in at an odd angle—otherwise, he risks accidentally hitting Wedge with laserfire. He swoops left then turns the nose of his ship right again—

The TIE lines up in his sights. But Temmin doesn't need screens. He fires, and the four cannons on his open-foil wings throw spears of plasma—

But they never find their target.

Temmin cries out as a piece of black metal crashes down right in front of him, separating him from his oblique pursuit of the TIE. It crashes into the ground, sending up a cloud of red dust. Temmin peels the ship away from its destined course, turning the X-wing sharply to avoid other debris.

Blast it, that looked like a piece from a starship. A turbine, by the look of it. His comms growl with Admiral Ackbar's voice:

"Soldiers and pilots of the New Republic! The dreadnought *Ravager* is down—it falls to Jakku! Beware debris and take cover!"

The *Ravager*? It's down?

He whoops as his giddy feeling surges higher. With the *Ravager* gone, that'll open up a *huge* hole in the Imperial fleet. That big monster was everything the Empire had. If it's gone . . .

That means the New Republic just won this battle.

And maybe, the whole war.

Now it's all just cleanup.

Wedge still has that bug on him, so Temmin flicks the X-wing back to the right again, looking for Phantom Leader in his scopes—ah, there he is, dead ahead, zipping over a flat plane where the sand looks like waves frozen in space and time. He spies Yarra coming in from the other side, and he thinks, *Okay, Yarra, let's see who blasts this bogey first.*

He lines up his shot—

Wham! Something hits his ship hard, and next thing he knows he's spinning like a corkscrew. His brain forces itself to catch up to his head as he spirals out of control, and past ropes of crackling electricity he sees on his screens that the wings have been sheared off on the one side—they're *gone*!

I'm going down.

I'm hit.

Mom—

He pulls up on the stick and levels out, just as the X-wing belly-flops into the dust, kissing the surface of

Jakku and sending up a tidal spray of sand behind him. The ship slides along on its belly, grinding and hissing as it does—Temmin's head snaps hard left and right, cracking into the blast glass of the cockpit viewports, each time rocking his dome dizzy.

The cockpit pops and he paws at the edges of his seat, pulling himself out. Temmin rolls over the edge of the X-wing, landing in the space where the wings should be. His shoulder hits stone. He turns over and dry-heaves.

When he finally looks up again, he sees what took him out.

Two dunes away, pinning a pair of S-foils, is a fist of metal from what looks like a Starhawk. *A Starhawk? I thought the* Ravager *was hit . . .*

And it all starts coming down.

Meteors made of broken starships start plowing into the ground. Each time they hit, Jakku coughs up another geyser of sand. Temmin cries out at the cacophony of sound—the booming drum of the planet being struck, the susurrus of sand rising and falling back to itself, the distant explosions. His ears ring and he clamps his hands over them.

Temmin risks looking up. To see if he can spot the rest of Phantom Squadron. But as he does, the light is blotted out. Day turns to night in the matter of moments.

It's the *Ravager*.

The Imperial colossus drifts in front of the light, eclipsing the sun. Another ship precedes it—that's the Starhawk. Fire comes off the New Republic ship, tornadoes of flame crackling from holes in its side.

He thinks: *It's coming down right on top of me. There's nowhere to run. Nowhere I can go to get safe.* But the panic subsides when he realizes his perspective is off. Yes, the ship is massive, but no, it's not coming down here. It'll hit dozens of klicks away. But what will it hit? Who will it destroy? Their own people are that way. So is the enemy. That's the Imperial line— the fighting is going on *right there*. Temmin pulls up his wrist comm and starts babbling into it, telling everyone to go, to move, to get out of the way, but the device suddenly fritzes out and spits sparks before going dead.

A sound comes out of him: a small, fearful moan. He's never seen anything like it before. He wonders if this is how his mother felt flying inside the Death Star—and then escaping, watching it detonate behind her.

The *Ravager* struggles to stay aloft—he can see, even in the half dark of eclipsed day, how underneath its positioning thrusters fire intermittently, desperately working to keep it from pointing straight at the ground, but failing to stop its fall.

It moves inescapably toward the ground. Leaning hard to the side . . .

The Starhawk hits first. *Whoom*. Temmin runs up to the nearest dune and watches as the New Republic capital ship crashes into the sand, crumpling up as if some giant just stepped on it—he sees an AT-AT walker moving away from the impact site as fast as it can, which from here looks dreadfully, painfully slow. And it won't matter anyway.

With the Starhawk gone, the tractor beam shears and the Ravager's thrusters must cause it to overcompensate—it begins to invert, turning belly up as it drops.

The *Ravager* hits next. It hits broadly, not spearing the ground but crashing flat against it, upside down—the AT-AT never has a chance. Nor do the starfighters trapped in the shadow of the dreadnought before it crashes. Nobody does. It's like watching the ceiling fall down on a child's playroom of toys. The *Ravager* plows into the sand, and the impact rocks the whole world—the vibration moves outward in a monstrous ripple, sending sand up along the shock wave, and when it hits where Temmin is standing, it knocks him off his feet. Again his ears ring. Everything vibrates: his teeth, his toes, all his bones. He struggles to stand anew—

And already he can't see the *Ravager* anymore.

A dust cloud of titanic proportions has been thrown into the sky. An anvil of black smoke goes up. Rolling outward is a cloud of dark dust.

It's coming this way. The blood-red dust cloud bulges and roils, tumbling forward like a wave of death and despair. Temmin scrambles back to his downed X-wing, sliding into the cockpit and slamming it shut just as the dust and the sand wash over him. It brings the white sound of a thousand angry whispers all around him, against the glass, against his ship.

And it goes on for what seems like forever.

"Move over!" Norra barks. "Let me fly it."

"*I know how to fly,*" Sloane snarls from the pilot's seat, her fingers gone bloodless from holding the shuttle's flight stick. She weaves the ship in and out of a rain of falling debris as each piece plunges to the ground like a comet. "I'm a damn good pilot. I got away from *you,* remember."

Norra remembers. She grits her teeth and holds on to a handle above her head as Sloane whips the craft through the raining debris. Brentin sits in the copilot's seat, his face gone white, his eyes closed. *He never was much of a flier.* Part of her wants to comfort him; another part wants to take the blaster and knock some sense into his head with the butt of it.

Bones stands behind her, stabilized without holding on to anything.

She's about to say something else—

The day goes to night. Sloane's gaze drifts upward. She gasps: a ragged, despairing sound. "No. My ship." Those three words transmit such grief, Norra can't help but feel drawn in by them. It's absurd, maybe, to be so enamored with and connected to a ship, but Norra understands it. She didn't have a long career in that Y-wing, but in the short time that she did, she came to love it like Temmin loves that droid.

Norra's eyes drift away from the *Ravager* to what precedes it—it's one of the Starhawks. She can't tell which one, but fear eats at her like an acid. *It's the* Concord, *isn't it?* Norra doesn't know Kyrsta Agate very well, but the woman was kind to her when she didn't need to be. Her reputation was that she was hard, but had empathy—not just for her own people, but for the enemy, too. Norra hopes she'll see Agate again.

The Starhawk hits the surface of Jakku, and moments later the *Ravager* follows. It drops hard. A concussive wave kicks up, rocks the ship. Norra has a distant, disconnected thought that she cannot dwell on for long lest it destroy her: *How many died? How many died on that ship? Or underneath it as it fell?* That, coupled with the feeling of victory in her heart, the one that tells her the New Republic may just have finished this war. It is a crass dichotomy, that feeling; she's felt it before and she'll feel it again. The triumphant heart warring with the grief born of war.

Norra composes herself. Her fight isn't over. None of this is. Sloane seems to pull herself together, too. The ex-admiral sets her jaw and her flight course, pulling away from the direction of the *Ravager*. "Dust cloud coming in," she warns. It's out there, a fast-moving storm spilling toward them. The cloud lights up in places with bilious lightning. Thunder tumbles.

Sloane pulls the shuttle away from it, but still it encompasses them. When it does, the shuttle rocks back and forth, hitting tides of air turbulence that nearly have Norra losing her footing. Through the dust storm she sees black clouds rising up above as pillars of fire and lightning brighten the air. And then it's gone again, washing over them and thinning out. The air is still gauzy with particulate matter, but once more the horizon can be seen.

Bones suddenly stiffens. His antenna glows green, beeping.

"MASTER TEMMIN IS NEAR."

"What? Where?"

"BELOW. MAY I GO?"

Norra knows that him leaving makes her vulnerable. If her husband is still in thrall to the control chip and sides with Sloane against her, she's not sure she can survive. But if Temmin really is near . . . and maybe in danger . . .

Then the choice is no choice at all.

"Go."

Bones flees, his claw-feet clanking as he opens the ramp in the belly of the shuttle. She watches him collapse downward, tucking his narrow beaked head to his chest and wrapping his many-jointed arms around his knees before rolling out of the ship and down to Jakku.

When the storm has passed, Temmin once again reopens the cockpit and emerges—though the wave has dissipated, dust still hangs gauzy in the air, and he coughs and blinks it away as he drops to the ground and staggers through the sand. What passes next are a few moments of almost eerie silence: the world gone still in the aftermath of the impact.

Then, somewhere far away, an explosion goes off— from the *Ravager*'s wreckage, no less. Above the dreadnought, black specters of smoke rise, and those dark clouds pulse with a flickering fire glow. A stink of burning metal and spent fuel stings his nose. After that, the sounds of war return: Blaster shrieks and fighter engines roaring overhead, concussive pulses and grenade detonations. Soldiers screaming. The silence is over. Again he coughs, wincing. In the distance, he spies a contingent of New Republic commandos dug in behind the sand furrow kicked up by a wrecked transport. Troopers advance on them. Temmin thinks, *I should do something. I should help.*

From close by come the pneumatic piston sound and pounding footsteps of something all too familiar: an AT-ST walker. He sees its brutal cockpit crest the nearest dune, the cannons tracking in his direction—Temmin knows he can't take that thing down, so he draws his blaster and runs in the other direction, feet carrying him over one dune and down the other, even as the thing's cannons surely track his movement—

And then, he's running full-throttle into a trio of desert troopers, their armor scarred, the grooves and joints caked with dust.

They raise their blasters and he skids to a halt, holding his in the air.

The troopers don't say anything at first. Already that makes his hackles rise—Imperial soldiers are about protocol. They have a pattern. They warn you. Tell you to drop it. Like they're on a program.

But this time, they follow no protocol. They remain silent.

Behind him, the AT-ST tromps up the dune toward them. Its shadow falls across Temmin, a shadow so damning it's as if it has its own weight. Temmin swallows hard, feeling sweat run down his jaw, his neck, his collarbone. "I . . ."

"Shut your mouth," the middle trooper says. That one's helmet has a hard dent in the plastoid surface. He's got a pauldron over the right shoulder, red and dark as a hot coal. He's the leader. "Rebel scum."

"Let's have some fun with this one," says the trooper on the right—the face of the helmet painted with finger-streaks of gray ash.

The one on the left takes off his helmet. A jowly, scruff-cheeked man's face is underneath, lit up with rage. He points the blaster. "We shoot bits off him. One by one. Hands. Ears. Each knee. See how long we keep him alive. Then the AT-ST can finish him off. Scatter his atoms."

The one in the pauldrons says: "We should do it quickly. Get back to the battle."

"Battle's over," Ash-Streak says. "Might as well have fun."

Nobody's listening to the leader.

Nobody's listening to anybody.

I'm going to die.

Scruff-Cheek looks up. "Hey, what the—"

Whong.

Temmin whirls around to see something land, crablike, on top of the AT-ST's cockpit skull. That something lifts its head, feral and red, showing off a set of hand-cut sawteeth.

Bones!

The troopers open fire, but Bones is fast. Too fast for them. The droid grabs the rail at the edge of the AT-ST, swinging down like a monkey-lizard before flinging himself to the sand, landing in a crouch. Blasterfire riddles the space where he just was as he pivots, pirouettes, and begins handspringing across the sand— plasma cooking the air as he dances around each lance of searing light. Arms snap back. Blades stick out.

Bones goes to work. He gets under the pauldroned leader, sticking a vibroblade up underneath the chin of the helmet with a dull crunch. The man's body twitches as his blaster drops. The modified B1 droid whirls around the still-standing corpse like it's a pole, kicking out with one clawed foot and knocking Ash-Streak back. As that trooper falls to the ground, Bones pounces on his chest and—*wham, wham, wham*—perforates the armor again and again with the blades. The man's heels kick the ground.

Scruff-Cheek bellows for the AT-ST to fire, and fire it does—loud blasts from its cannons biff through the sand, just missing Bones but knocking the droid back, limbs akimbo. The scruffy trooper raises his own rifle to fire on Bones, and Temmin launches himself at the man. His attack is clumsy and broadcast a kilometer away, but the helmetless stormtrooper isn't paying attention—Temmin clubs the soldier in the temple with his own blaster and the man topples like a tree. *Unnff*.

Bones is up again, cartwheeling away from the AT-ST's cannons—it tracks him, but its head is too slow, and the droid too fast. Temmin's mechanical bodyguard returns to the place it landed, scurrying up the side of the walker's leg, metal clicking on metal, until it reaches the top once more.

The droid struggles, his servos grinding and his pneumos whining as he *wrenches* the top off the AT-ST, flinging the hatch behind him. Feetfirst, Bones silently slips into the cockpit of the chicken walker.

Thus commences a bang and a rattle. The walker rocks back and forth just slightly. It takes ten seconds, no more, before Bones pops back out wearing one of the drivers' open-face helmets, a pair of black-lens goggles hanging off in front of the B1's own ocular lenses.

"HELLO, MASTER TEMMIN."

Temmin falls to his knees, relieved. "Bones. I missed you, buddy."

"I MISSED YOU. I PERFORMED VIO—"

Suddenly the top of the walker erupts in fire and shrapnel, exploding. Temmin is knocked backward, the breath knocked from his lungs in a thunderclap of air. He waves smoke out of his face and wipes sand from his eyes, and when it clears he sees the walker standing there—

It's just two legs, now. The cockpit is peeled back like a blooming metal flower, its durasteel petals burned and charred.

Bones is nowhere to be found.

Bones. No, Bones, no . . .

He cries out, wondering what happened—did it detonate all on its own? Was there something the droid did to cause it to explode?

But then a pair of A-wings appear overhead, roaring past.

It was them. They shot the walker.

And Bones along with it.

Temmin crawls on his hands and knees, looking for parts of his droid—he finds seared, melted limbs. He finds rivets and scrap. But he sees nothing else. No skull. No program motherboard. He draws sand into his hands, but it slips through his fingers with nothing to show for it. Bones saved his life and now is gone. His best friend is slag.

Temmin presses his forehead to the hot sand and weeps.

CHAPTER THIRTY-FOUR

"YOU DON'T HAVE to do this," Conder says.

Sinjir huffs a lamentable sigh. "Apparently I do. Job's a job and—oh, gods, I just started a new job. What is wrong with me?"

The two of them stand before Senator Tolwar Wartol's Ganoidian cruiser. Thankfully, it's here on Chandrila again and didn't require them to take a quick hop to Blah Blah Boring Farmworld, Nakadia—or, worse, to the asteroid archipelago above Orish that Wartol and his like call home. Sinjir cares little why he's back on Chandrila; the convenience of it suits him, and he is nothing if not a man who appreciates *ease*.

Conder makes that face—a little pouty, a lot dubious. One eyebrow up, a twist to his lips, a cockiness to his hips. "I don't mean this *specifically*. I mean the whole package. The job, Chandrila, *me*."

"You? I don't follow."

"You don't have to be with me. Fate put us together again and—it's just, we don't have to do this."

"Oh, but we do." Sinjir cups the man's beardy cheek first with a gentle caress and then with a sharp *tap-tap-slap*. "Dearest foolheart, all my time away was spent thinking about how much I hated you, and I hated you because I liked you so much. *Too* much, really. It's gross the way I feel about you. It's like—"

Sinjir makes a face as if he just sucked on a dirty thumb. "It's really not natural to me. But I learned that I don't know what the precious hell I'm talking about. My mind is an idiot. My heart knows all. I want what I want. What I want is a beach view, a cold glass of something very drunk-making, and you. You, you, you, you noble, fuzzy-faced fool. So, if that means becoming just a *hair* respectable and entering into the service of our most estimable chancellor, then that is what will be done."

"You aren't the 'settling down' type."

Sinjir rolls his eyes so hard he fears they might tumble out of his head. "Bah. Who says I'm 'settling'? Settling is such a *passive* affair. Settling is how a Hutt-slug sits down. I've been settling since Endor. Settling for whatever comes my way. Usually a barstool, if we're being honest. You, this job, this life—it's all a mountain. And I intend quite fully to climb it."

Conder smirks. Sinjir destroys that smirk with a hard kiss—hands behind the head, drawing the man's face to his.

"Well, then," Conder says.

"Well, then." Sinjir turns back toward the cruiser. "I suppose I should do this." At his feet sits the basket of pta fruit; looking at it again reminds him how much he admires the chancellor. Not for all her leadership and governance, which is fine, whatever, but for the potent *venom* she quite plainly conceals inside that boring, white-robed façade. She's a vicious twig, a veritable whipping branch of a human being, and he thinks they could have a long and fascinating professional relationship.

"I still think Tolwar is dirty."

"I cannot speak to his cleanliness."

"No, I mean—I think he's corrupt."

Sinjir shrugs. "Of course he's corrupt. He's a politician."

"The bug. The one in Leia's droid? He planted it. I couldn't manage to track it back to him, but he was the one who gained from the information. It had to be him, Sinjir. I know it."

"One suspects that's true. He was using it to gain a political advantage, not a criminal one. The Orishen are almost overly noble, driven mad by an aggressive sense of honor. Something-something sacrifice, something-something stern father telling his son how *hard* it is out there." He sneers. "I do despise how they name themselves, though. Tolwar Wartol. Vendar Darven. TimTam TamTim. You'd think they could be more original."

"It's cultural."

"Well, that's no excuse."

"Go," Conder says. "Deliver your fruit. Be as polite as you can manage. Do not start an intergalactic incident."

"Those I leave to Jom."

"Have fun at work, honey."

"Thank you, doll. And if you call me 'honey' again, I'll rip that beard off your face swatch by swatch with miserable pinching *tugs*." He mimes the gesture with his hand, just in case Conder doesn't get it.

"You're such a romantic."

"My heart is a dry nest of dead birds." He stoops down to kiss the man's scrubby cheek. "Bye, Con."

"Bye, Sin."

Wartol sits. Still as the steeple of an old temple. In front of him is a cup of something bitter smelling: probably some kind of old *root juice* the Orishen people consume. Steam rises off it.

Around, the Ganoidian cruiser is decked out in the Orishen way: severe, spare, blocky, unpleasant. Sinjir likes it. It's quiet, too. No security to be found. No pilot. No anyone except for the senator himself.

He sets the basket on the floor. "A gift from the chancellor."

"You're the ex-Imperial." Wartol's voice is a deep, thrumming timbre.

"And you're the chancellor candidate who has been outplayed at every turn, including by a ginger woman with a single, sour fruit. Oops."

The senator's slitted nostrils pucker with irritation even as his jaw gently eases apart before stitching back together again. "You work for her, now? You're a symptom. You see that, don't you? A symptom of a larger, nastier disease."

"Do tell."

"An Imperial, working for the chancellor? So cozy with her? Oh, my, how *cosmopolitan*. Your presence has infected the process. Whispering in her ear, surely. Ah, but I give you too much credit. You won't lead her. She'll lead you. She'll lead us all. Mon doesn't need you to thin her moral code, because it's already thinner than a slurry made of *spit*. Mon Mothma is weak. She will destroy this Republic if we let her. People like you at her side will only hasten its demise. We'll blink and one day, the Republic will have fallen and the Empire will step out of her shadow and gently take its place."

Sinjir thinks at first to hold his tongue, but really, what's the point? The chancellor knew what she was getting when she sent *him* along. You ask a hound to find a bone, you can expect some holes dug in the yard. And it's not like the pta fruits are a *subtle* message, are they? No, she wants him to scrap a little. Sinjir will do it so she doesn't have to.

He says, "It's ironic, you know? You go on about fearing another Empire, and yet you're the one who reminds me of every Imperial autocrat, every bully-fed officer who thinks that the best way to lead is through acts of severity, through a parade of cruelty just to remind the men *Mmm, life is hard and so you must be harder.* They go on about sacrifice but never really sacrifice squat themselves, oh no, because they're the ones above the heavy boot on the back of the neck, not the ones beneath it. You want war. You want defense. You're a raptor who sees all his people as defenseless little flit-wrens—and you'll save them, if only they give up the fanciful notion that they can lead themselves, that they can protect themselves."

"You understand nothing."

"*Meanwhile,*" Sinjir says, really leaning into it now, "your opponent is a woman who wants to give democracy to the entirety of the galaxy. Freedom for all. Oppression for none."

"It's naïve."

"It may be. But at this point, I'm going to side with her precious naïveté over your authoritarian bluster. Enjoy your *fruit,* Senator. We'll send you a lifetime supply as a consolation when you lose the election."

Sinjir sets the basket down on the table.

And when he does, he notices three things.

First, Wartol never stood up. That's odd. It's standard to get up and greet guests no matter how much you despise them, especially among the Orishen, who have a rather firm grip on protocol.

Second, Wartol's left hand holds the cup of steaming dark juice—but his *right* hand has never gone above the table. It rests beneath it.

Third, on the surface of the table, across from where the Orishen sits, waits a faint ring of moisture. As if from a cup resting there, a cup sweating its condensation or steam onto the tabletop.

Sinjir's gaze turns to it, then to Wartol. The senator is watching him. Wartol saw him look. It is necessary, perhaps, to acknowledge it.

"Had a guest, did we?" Sinjir says.

"Not your business, Imperial."

"No. It's not. You're right." He's acting cagey, the senator. Sinjir knows body language, and a lot of that transcends species, sex, age. It's not just that Wartol is *hiding* something, it's that what he's hiding is up under his skin plates—it's nesting there like worm hatchlings. He's bothered by it. He doesn't want it discovered. So Sinjir decides he's going to pick this scab, see what bleeds. "Still, though. Why don't you tell me anyway? We're friends, aren't we? I won't tell anyone."

Wartol says nothing. He barely even twitches. Sinjir remains where he is, half leaning over the basket of fruit. The silence is a wall between them.

Then the wall shatters. Wartol kicks back, his hand up and out—a blaster is in his clawlike fingers. Sinjir stares down the mouth of that pistol, a fat-barreled snub-chambered Kanji-made blaster—

Like the kind criminals use.

—and the weapon goes off, but Sinjir turns to the side, flattening his profile as the blast pocks the far wall of the cruiser's sitting room. He has no blaster of his own in kind (*Curse you, Sinjir; you should always bring a weapon when tangling with a politician*), so he grabs what's close at hand.

The basket.

He gets his long fingers under the basket's seat and flips it hard toward the Orishen. Wartol bats it away. Fruit goes everywhere. Through a spray of pta juice, Sinjir rushes the man—the air lights up again and something catches Sinjir hard, and his head snaps back and he smells singed blood and burning hair. Everything goes sideways as the world wheels out from under him. His eyes cross. *I've been shot.* An absurd thought, because he's fairly certain he has been shot in the *head,* which is not a good way to live and is in fact a *very* good way to die.

Wartol lurches over him, a blurry shape as Sinjir's vision struggles to find clarity. The blaster is up again—

Sinjir's spidery fingers scrabble over the ground, finding something there, something wet, slimy, seedy—

"It's too late," Wartol says. Cryptic. What's too late?

The blaster goes off. Sinjir rolls aside as a flash of hot energy digs a furrow into the floor right by his head. His ear goes shrill as it rings, and the side of his cheek feels hot, and the *other* side of his head feels slick—

He whips his hand up, flinging whatever was in it.

A pta fruit spatters uselessly against Wartol's face. It hits. It drips. It plops back down to the ground. His jaw extends outward and curls into an underbite, and the senator blasts a puff of air upward, unmooring dribbling pta juice from his nose-slits and brow.

"The fruit won't save you now."

Sinjir says, "No. But it distracted you, didn't it?"

Wartol makes a bewildered, animal sound—*nngh?*—just as a blaster goes off and clips him in the shoulder. He spins like a child's top and crashes against his own chair. His cup of whatever-it-was splashes down against him and shatters. The snub-barreled blaster drops. Conder steps forward, his own blaster in hand, and steps down on it.

With a quick slide of his foot, he sends the blaster spinning to Sinjir, who snatches it and wearily stands.

"Have I been shot in the head?" he asks Conder.

Conder's eyes open in shock, and his mouth forms an alarmed O-shape. *Well, I suppose that answers that.* Sinjir's hand flies to the side of his head—it comes away wet with his own blood. Some of it has already been cauterized, making it tacky against his fingers. The shot glanced along the side of his head, carving a furrow that starts at his temple.

"Sin, I think you'll be all right—"

"I'll be fine. My rather luxurious hair, not so much." He strides forward and stands atop Wartol. "You. Answer for yourself."

"Die, Imperial slime."

Sinjir points the blaster and shoots the man in the knee. He howls.

"Now, I'm of a mind not to actually *kill* you, because I'm one of the good ones these days and I have *appearances* to keep up. But I will whittle you down until you're naught but a talking, jabbering *head*. Why pull a blaster? What are you hiding?"

"I told you, it's too late."

"*What* is too late?"

"I can't call him off now."

Sinjir shoots the other knee. Wartol bellows, sitting suddenly upright like a book slammed shut. He clutches at his knee as purple blood bubbles between his fingers. "Call *who* off? What are you—"

At first, he thinks it's thunder, the faraway sound. But thunder is a low rumble, like a sallow belly expressing its hunger. This is duller, deeper, one and done. A hard, shuddering boom. An explosion.

"What did you do, Wartol? *What did you do?*"

Wartol's laugh dissolves into a blubbering confession: "Sacrifices are necessary, Imperial. Sometimes a disease is so rampant you must cut off limbs to save the body. Like on Orish. The Empire was a cancer on the galaxy. Just as Mon Mothma was a cancer on the Republic."

Was a cancer.

Was.

"You didn't," Sinjir seethes.

But Wartol simply weeps—not from grief, no, but what Sinjir sees is clearly relief.

Conder steps back and unrolls his sleeve—underneath is nothing so small as a comlink but rather, a whole tech gauntlet. With it, he can slice into doorways or program droids or any number of things, but he can *also* tap into various feeds: HoloNet, orbit control, NRN news, and of course local security bureau transmissions. He dials into the frequency—

The air fills with static, then resolves into a voice. *"—code four-two-four, repeat, code four-two-four, reports of an explosion at the north tower of the Senate Building. Code four-two-four—"*

Sinjir thinks, *No, no, no,* it's not possible. He marches straight to the door, to the ramp, down to the landing bay. All of the landing bays here are up high, over the coast, and at this vantage point it's easy to see to the center of Hanna City where the Senate Building sits.

Looming above that building is the tower where Mon Mothma's office sits. Where Sinjir was only hours before.

A hole has been blown in the side of it. Even from here he can see how ash and debris are vacated out into open air, how the white permacrete side is charred with soot and tongues of flame. Smoke billows out like an escaping fiend.

The chancellor. She was in there—

He left her *alone* in there . . .

Sinjir turns, marches back inside. Pistol up. He storms through to the sitting area, past Conder, then

drops to Wartol's chest. He screws the barrel of the
Kanji blaster so hard against the man's forehead it
nearly breaks the hard plating that covers the man's
head.

"You killed her."

"I had it done," Wartol croaks.

"You will pay for this."

"Do it. End me. I have no career. But I have sacrificed myself to make a better galaxy. Chancellor Mon
Mothma will no longer be able to spread her corrosive
stain across the burgeoning New Republic." Wartol
lifts his head into the blaster. "Pull the trigger! Coward!"

Sinjir roars and draws the blaster back. His chest
heaves as rage runs so hot inside him, it's like a star
burning itself up. But he resists. "You'll not die today.
You'll go to trial. You'll go to prison. You'll see your
name and your people dragged out in front of us all as
craven traitors."

He looks to Conder. The man gives him a small nod.
It's a small concession: a mote of light in a suddenly
dark day. But it's all he has, so he holds on to it as
tightly as he can manage.

INTERLUDE

LIBERTY'S MISRULE

THE DREADNOUGHT IS no longer the *Annihilator*. It is no longer called that because that is no longer its function. Now it serves as the capital ship in a new galactic nation forming at the fringes of the galaxy, in Wild Space and beyond. The ship's new name: *Liberty's Misrule*. That name means whatever it means to whoever hears it, but Eleodie Marcavanya—pirate captain of this ship and leader of this new, unnamed nation of deviants and miscreants—chose the name first because, quite frankly, zhe likes the damn sound of it. But also because it means the ship is no longer used to destroy. Now it is used to create: a new government, a new nation, an armada of pirates who take equal spoils in an effort to make something *lasting*.

Most pirates, they take what they take to live and fight another day. They take the spoils to survive or to squirrel away.

But Eleodie wants something bigger. Better. Something forever. The Empire is dead and the New Republic can't handle its business. That leaves room—air whistling between the bricks where Eleodie can slip in and out like a breath, hiding in the interstitial spaces, *growing* like an army of ghosts.

Right now, zhe stands at one of the many thousands of viewports here on the *Liberty's Misrule*, looking out over zher ragtag nation of ships, a nation without a planet, but one that may never need one. *The stars are our nation,* zhe thinks. *We glitter like a thousand suns, our hearts as black as the void in which we travel.* Next to Eleodie stands the girl, Kartessa. The girl's hair is shorn down to the scalp, her cheeks dirty from working in the engine room (her choice, for she claimed correctly to be good with machines).

Kartessa says, "Fleet is getting bigger."

"Every day," Eleodie says with no small pride. The nation fleet is now two dozen ships strong—that's not figuring in the contingent of old starfighters they've brought on board and retrofitted, which are now flying the colors of their new Wild Space nation: red, yellow, and black. The fleet comprises half ships they've stolen, half those brought here out of the chaos of a galaxy gone awry. Pirates and refugees who have nowhere to turn, who have seen the protections of the Empire turn to vapor, and who fear the coming of the New Republic and its laws sweeping across the systems.

Eleodie fears that, too. The New Republic is growing. The Empire will soon be gone. Even now, zhe is reliably informed that on a world called Jakku, the Empire is losing its fight—maybe its *last* fight—against the Republic. What then? What will become of the rest of the galaxy?

Eleodie turns from regarding zher nation outside the Star Destroyer to those within it. Many come seeking asylum but having no ships.

Those who do now serve as crew.

Down below were once a series of connected hangar bays—gray, sterile, with a singular function. That has changed. Now the hangar bays are homes: tents, shipping pods, ramshackle crate-shacks. Thousands dwell here. They live. They operate markets. They cook food using jury-rigged thermal vents carved out of the under-floor ducts. And color is cast far and wide. Motley hues from red tents, spray-tagged containers, the raiment of many cultures and many species and many worlds. Everything is art and chaos and noise. It is just as Eleodie wants it.

"Your mother around somewhere?" Eleodie says to the girl.

"No. I ditched her on the engineering sublevel." Kartessa pouts. "She won't leave me alone."

"She is your mother. It is her job not to leave you alone. You should be nicer to her. Poor fool woman followed you here into this glorious madhouse, this wondrous nation of derangement. Do not shut her out."

Kartessa sighs. "Fine."

"Good."

After a few minutes of scuffing her heels, the girl pipes up: "Can I ask you something?"

"You may."

"How's this all going to work?"

"This all *what* now?"

"This . . . pirate nation. Pirates don't make nations."

"These pirates do. *I* do."

"Why? How?"

"Girl, it's like this: The sea is changing, and the tides are shifting. It's about to get real nasty for us nasty types. Either we're gonna be running from the new sheriff in town, or we're gonna be trying to kill each other in the farthest-flung dung-heap systems, stabbing each other over a few scraps of what was once ours by right. I'm proposing we get together and we stay together. Scoundrels like us, we always worked together—it just wasn't official. So I'm making it official."

Frustration darkens Kartessa's brow. "But that doesn't answer my question. Pirates are selfish. You're in it for yourselves."

"That's true enough," zhe answers. "But we can all be in it for our mutual benefit. Some predators are lonely things, big and scary and all by themselves. Others know when they need each other. They know when to form a pack. Used to be I had a pirate crew of a few hundred. Now I got a crew of ten thousand— and that number is going up, up, up. We will ransack, pillage, and steal. We will kill less, because it is the threat of our numbers, not the threat of our weapons, that will precede us. We will share the spoils equally, not so that we may be rich, but so that we may be fed and fat and happy together. Swilling and singing and whatever other *salaciousness* comes to the fore of our nasty little minds."

The girl appears to chew on this. Like it's a piece of gristle she can't quite get out of her teeth. Seems she's about to say more, but an interruption from her Omwati first mate, Shi Shu, prevents that.

Shi's beak clacks together. "We have visitors."

"Come to revel in my elegance?" Eleodie asks.

The Omwati seems guarded. "We need you on the bridge now."

Eleodie asks the girl: "Want to come?"

"I do."

"Then let's go."

Together they walk the length of the balcony overlooking the hangar deck (presently named Hangartown, though that is its third name and other names may yet come) before turning in toward the turbolifts. They take the lift up to the bridge, riding in silence, Eleodie with zher chromatophoral cape tucked around zher like a cocoon.

Once on the bridge, zhe sees what just dropped out of hyperspace.

Three Star Destroyers. "*Imperial Two*–class," says Gunner Carklin Ryoon, a bug-eyed Ssori with a tiny mouth and sharp teeth. Many Ssori choose to wear mechanical suits to compensate for their diminutive size, but Ryoon has always preferred to remain, as he puts it, "pure organic." The Ssori says: "They're trying to hail us now." One of his bulbous eyes winces. "They might think we're actually Imperials. They haven't seen the rest of the fleet yet. Could be a good ruse."

The Omwati concedes. Shi Shu says, "Yes, yes, that could work. We encourage them to think we're a lingering remnant, we offer them safety and succor, then we press-gang them—"

"We destroy them," Eleodie declares.

"What? But those are good ships."

"We destroy them and we send their pieces to the New Republic. Along with any escape pods we can catch in our pretty little net." Noticing the stares coming zher way, Eleodie clarifies: "These ships are running. Look at the battle damage—they've taken fire, and recently. And behold those hyperspeed vectors—they're coming from near to the Unknown. They're coming from *Jakku*. We do a little cleanup here for the New Republic, then we send them the bill."

"But the New Republic is no friend of ours," Kartessa says.

"No. And they never will be. But maybe this will convince them to look the other way for a while. Maybe this'll give us an *air* of legitimacy," Eleodie says with a sweep of the hand, as if zhe is trying to run zher fingers through a rain of stardust. "Set the whole fleet to attack."

"They have considerable firepower—"

"Do it."

"The other fleet captains will want to confer—"

"If they take damage, I will personally repay them. There will be recompense. I am enacting my divine right. *Attack*."

Shi Shu nods, hesitantly, then commands the rest of the bridge crew—the demand cascades through them, and a flurry of activity ensues. Targeting computers are spun up. Weapons systems brought online. The tractor beam is spun to readiness. Kartessa looks to Eleodie.

"Do you know what you're doing?"

Eleodie grins like a moon sliver. "No, girl. That's what makes this so interesting. The present is a pair of dice always about to leave my hand, and I never know if it'll come up zero or one, win or lose."

Outside, the void lights up with fire as the attack begins. The Star Destroyers do not have a chance. Soon the New Republic will have a present from his highness, her glory, his wonder, her *luminous magnificence*— the picaroon! The plunderer! The pirate ruler of Wild Space! The glorious knave, Eleodie Marcavanya!

CHAPTER THIRTY-FIVE

THIS IS THE Observatory.

It is one of many scattered across the galaxy. All of them are laboratories, in a sense, and all of them look beyond the galaxy's margins in different directions. At the same time, each is also its own unique entity. Palpatine began establishing the Observatories before the start of the Galactic Empire, infusing each with purpose: Some were meant to house ancient Sith artifacts, others designed to host powerful weapon designs (or the weapons themselves), others still meant as prisons harnessing the lifeforces of those captured within for a variety of strange purposes.

This one, the Jakku Observatory, has its own function.

It is part of the Contingency.

From here, the Observatory appears only to be a bunker mostly buried in the mounding sand. If any would approach, the turrets or the sentinel droids would make swift work of them. It has long been protected here, mostly hidden, only recently emerging, at his command. As Gallius Rax and the transport ship enter the shadow of the Plaintive Hand, approaching the Observatory, he sends another command: this one to power down the turbolasers and the sentinel droid defenses. He sends this command through the sentinel that pilots the ship (for all the sentinels are networked together).

Beyond the Observatory, another shape emerges, because as he powers down the defenses, he also programs the landing dome to rise. And rise it does, bubbling up out of the sand, gently turning as the scree and grit slip free from its rounded surface. The metal dome telescopes open.

It reveals a ship gleaming bright in the dust-filtered sun.

"The *Imperialis,*" Brendol Hux says, leaning forward in the cockpit. Tashu is there with them, and as he sees the ship, he giggles, clapping his hands like a gluttonous child seeing a tray of cakes come out of the oven. Hux has a voice of reverence and confusion as he says, "I . . . thought the Emperor's ship was destroyed."

"It was," Rax answers. "Stolen by a gambler, then scuttled. But it was one of many." As he understands it, all of the Observatories play host to a functional replica of the Emperor's pleasure yacht. The Observatories serve as receptacles for old Sith artifacts, too— and should those artifacts ever need to be moved off-site, the yachts are there for just such a purpose.

Slowly, their transport settles into the well of the valley, easing against the dust-swept stone. The Observatory awaits. From here, it is only a broad door in the side of a dune. The rest lies concealed beneath Jakku.

"I still don't understand what's happening," Hux says.

"This Empire is ended. A new one must begin." *The demesne is clear, the board swept clean,* he thinks. *A new demesne must be made.* "Take your son and the other children. Go to the *Imperialis*. Prep the ship for takeoff."

"How can there be a new Empire?" Brendol blusters. "The one we had is gone. We do not number enough to begin anew—"

"There are others," Tashu says, singsongy.

"Once we had the calculations, we sent another ship ahead."

"Calculations. What calculations? What do you—"

"Brendol, please. Time is fleeting fast, too fast. Go to the ship. I will join you there." And just in case, Rax puts a gently threatening hand on the man's arm. "Understand that you will help be an architect of the future to come. You are a visionary and that is why you are here, alone. This is not a time to test me. This is a time to trust me. Do you trust me?"

The man, red-cheeked and obviously afraid, nods. "I . . . do."

"Good. Now go, go like the skittermouse." To Tashu he says: "Are you ready to fulfill our destiny, Adviser Tashu?"

Tashu licks his teeth and shudders as if experiencing otherworldly pleasure. "All glory to the Contingency. All glory to Palpatine."

"Yes," Rax says, mirroring the same sycophantic smile. "All glory."

It takes both of their handprints to open the door. Tashu on one side, Rax on the other. The scan plates shine around their splayed fingers. Behind the door, a mechanism fires up, groaning and grinding.

The door, gold as the sun, opens slowly, rolling upward.

When they enter, the door closes behind them.

Rax walks ahead of Tashu. He moves forward with a confident stride. The pentagonal hallway descends slowly at a gentle angle. It's formed of burnished metal and black glass, with lines of red light framing every angle. Every ten steps is a pillar holding up the world, preventing the sands from pressing down and swallowing the Observatory whole.

Everything is clean and untouched by the filth of this world. As an irony, Rax runs his hand along the wall, leaving behind the faintest streak of oil and sweat. *There, now the world has left its mark,* he thinks.

No. He is *not* of this world, he tells himself. He has transcended it. Palpatine saw that. Yes, the old man was delusional about the mystical forces that governed the galaxy, giving too much credence to them—he believed that just because *he* had abilities beyond the ken of mortals, all things cleaved to the same power. Which is madness, really. It is the primitive attitude of a creature learning to make fire for the first time, certain that the fire he made was the only power that governed the galaxy.

And yet Palpatine *wasn't* delusional about the state of the galaxy and the role of the Empire. Though he infused it with a great deal of magical foolishness, he was a master tactician, and knew how to play a game so long that the horizon line was actually the starting line.

Palpatine saw something in Rax. A destiny, he called it. Even now, Gallius—Galli, in a way, for he feels oddly young and innocent again, like that Jakku child running across the desert—feels that destiny swelling up inside him. He takes a moment to enjoy it. To feel filled up by it; satiety resonates through him.

But the job is not done. Not yet.

Ahead, the hallway opens up into an eight-sided chamber. In the center of it is a same-shaped bank of computer systems—but not systems like the ones found on a Star Destroyer or even the Death Star. No, these are ancient computational mechanisms from an earlier civilization. From precisely when, Rax cannot say. The Old Republic? The fallen Sith Empire? He knows not and he cares little. Their history is irrelevant.

It is only the present that matters.

Above the computers is the projection of a three-dimensional star chart that matches no known map here in the galaxy. Which makes sense given that it does not chart the known galaxy, does it?

For decades, these computers have been plotting a journey. Outside the known galaxy is an unexplored infinity, Palpatine explained, one closed off by a labyrinth of solar storms, rogue magnetospheres, black holes, gravity wells, and things far stranger. Any who tried to conquer that maze did not survive. The ships were obliterated, or returned to the galaxy devoid of travelers. Communications from those explorers were incomprehensible, either shot through with such static as to make the content useless, or filled with enough inane babble to serve as a perfectly clear sign that the explorer had gone utterly mad out there in isolation. But Palpatine had one in the navy who knew something of the Unknown Regions: Admiral Thrawn, an alien with ice-blue skin who came from beyond the borders of the known galaxy. Palpatine only kept that one around because of what he knew of traversing those deadly interstices. Much of what Thrawn knew went into the computations of this machine.

Palpatine said that this galaxy was to be his, but that it was only one among many. Again that phrase arose: *the unexplored infinity.* This, he noted, was his demesne. The galaxy was his game board.

If he lost this game, the game board was to be broken in half and discarded. A new demesne must then be found.

The computers here have long been searching for a way through the storms and the black spaces. Slowly, surely, they have been putting together a map: a journey into chaos. The Empire has sent probe droids to test the computations as the computers have made them. Many never returned.

But some kept reporting in, pinging the transponder here. Every droid that made it further contributed to the map. And with distance achieved, the computers, through the scanning droids, continued to chart the course and compute the next branches of navigation.

Before Palpatine's demise at the hands of the rebels, the computers finished their calculations, finally finding a way through the unknown. The Emperor was convinced that *something* waited for him out there—some origin of the Force, some dark presence formed of malevolent substance. He said he could feel the waves of it radiating out now that the way was clear. The Emperor called it a signal—conveniently one that only he could hear. Even his greatest enforcer, Vader, seemed oblivious to it, and Vader also claimed mastery over the dark Force, did he not? Rax believed Palpatine had gone mad. What he was "receiving" was nothing more than his own precious wishes broadcast back to himself—an echo of his own devising. He believed that something lay beyond, and so that became a singular obsession. (When you believe in magic, it is easy to see all the universe as evidence of it.)

Now that Palpatine is gone, the original purpose of the Observatory can be maintained. The game is lost. Time to exit and find a new demesne.

The Empire is dead.

But the Empire can live again under Rax.

First, though, preparations must be made. Beyond the map chamber is one more hallway—this one with steps leading down. As Rax passes the computers, he sees on the far side a gift that Palpatine left for him:

It is a broken Shah-tezh board. It lies shattered on

the floor in halves. All around it are the pieces, also broken. Only two pieces remain: the Imperator and the Outcast. He wonders, is that how Palpatine saw him? As the Outcast? This is new. Gallius never knew that. It hits him like a slap to the face. He wants to struggle against it, to rage against the idea that he was some kind of exile at the margins of the Empire . . .

And yet he was, wasn't he? Rax always kept a distance. His role was never to preserve the Empire but to destroy it.

He snatches up both pieces. With a juggle of his fingers he rolls the two figures around in the palm of his hand. Whatever Palpatine thought of him before, he is no longer the Outcast. Rax has become the Imperator.

Gallius pockets both pieces and continues on, humming his favorite cantata as he goes. The hallway ahead is lined with artifacts of the old Sith Empire: a red mask, a white lance, a bloody banner, a holocron so black it seems to consume all the light around it. Between each of the artifacts is a smooth-faced sentinel droid, slumbering in its chamber, ready to be woken if a threat approaches.

Beyond all that is the well. The well is a channel bored through the schist and mantle of Jakku, drilled so deep it touches the center of the world. The well glows with wisps of blue mist winding up through orange firelight. The light pulses and throbs like a living thing. Palpatine told him that once, this world was verdant—overgrown with green and home to oceans. He said that though the surface of the world no longer shows it, the core still has that vital spark of life essence. (And, he added, "That essence disgusts me.")

Tashu gambols down in front of the artifacts, his fingertips dancing along their cases. He mutters to himself, and Rax sees that he's chewed his own lips bloody. "Are you ready?" he asks Palpatine's old adviser.

"I am," Tashu says, turning. His cheeks are wet with tears. His teeth slick with red. "Palpatine lives on. We will find him again out there in the dark. Everything has arranged itself as our Master foretold. All things move toward the great design. The sacrifices have all been made."

Not all of them, Rax thinks.

"You must be clothed in the raiment of darkness," Rax says. "The mantle of the dark side is yours to wear, at least for a time. At least until we can find Palpatine and revivify him, bringing his soul back to flesh anew." This is all a lie, of course. He believes none of it. It is a ruse sold to Tashu. (Lies are like leashes. Tug them just so, and all who believe them will comply.)

And the lunatic believes it because lunatics always believe the things that confirm their view of the galaxy. Tashu's view is that the dark side is all, that Palpatine was the Master not just of the Empire but of everyone and everything, and that through all of this, the Dark Lord will be reborn.

Good. Let him believe that.

Rax helps him carry the lance and the banner. He carefully puts the mask upon the man's head, tightening it with black leather straps and a buckle of old tarnished chromatite. Tashu owns many masks, all of which he believes contain some fragment of the dark side. But never before has he worn one like this: It is a vicious, bestial thing with tusks of coiling black steel and eyes of blood-red kyber crystals. As it snaps against his face, Tashu tightens up, a hungry moan ill contained behind his clenching jaw.

"The final piece," Rax says, handing Tashu the holocron. Even as the man takes it, it seems to leach the light from all around. Tashu goes even paler as he touches it. The veins in his hand stand dark in contrast.

"Yes," Tashu says. One word, short, clipped, ecstatic. His arms stretch out by his sides. His hands shake. "*Yes*. I can feel it. I am a locus of dark energies. All the death and despair of the world is filtering through me. I can feel it on the back of my *tongue*. Captured there like a struggling moth—"

"Then come, let us pray." He interrupts Tashu because if he does not, the man will continue to gabble for minutes, hours, perhaps until both of them have died of old age and gone to dust. Gallius Rax leads Tashu the way a parent leads a child, by the hand. Together they go to the well.

As they approach, a narrow platform extends out, as if sensing their presence. It drifts out over the well: a plank they must walk.

They go out together. Out here, the air is somehow both hot and cold. Warm breath interspersed with wisps of ice.

"Palpatine will be pleased by you," Rax says.

"Yes. He will. And by you, too. We have done it. We have punished the undeservers. We have activated the Contingency. Let us speak a prayer to the darkness, a prayer to all the things that wait—"

"First, my brother, I'd like to ask you something."

"Yes, little Galli?"

"What will you say to him when you see our Master again?"

"I—"

Rax gives him no chance to answer. He pushes Tashu.

The man cartwheels through the mist and the light, spinning, screaming—his body hits the side and slams against the rock, silencing his cries. The body goes and goes until Rax cannot see it anymore.

A few beats of quiet and stillness. One. Two. Three . . .

The world shudders. A fierce growl grumbles up through the bore, and the orange light glows suddenly red—the blue threads of mist turn black. Palpatine was right. The artifacts contain a great deal of energy.

And now they have dropped into the core of this world. With the well open, that energy will vent. So begins the chain reaction that will destroy everything. The planet will soon begin to crack. It shall break apart. It'll swallow the Empire *and* the New Republic fleets and soldiers whole. When it does, it will leave this galaxy to the scavengers and the scum, rotting like a fruit lying forgotten in the dirt. Though an idle thought troubles him: *All fruit, no matter how rotten, can leave behind seeds . . .*

It's time to leave. The *Imperialis* awaits. His destiny calls like a seductive whisper. But then he realizes, he's hearing voices. Real voices. He is not alone in here, not anymore. And one of those voices, he recognizes.

Hello, Sloane, he thinks.

The ground shudders suddenly beneath them, moving hard to the right—Norra nearly loses her footing. Brentin helps to steady her, and she pulls out of his grip, casting him a suspicious look.

"You don't trust me," he says.

"I don't," she says under her breath. *I don't know what's in your head. I don't know if the chip is still controlling you. I don't know why you were with* her *of all people.* He's about to say more, but Sloane interrupts—

"Look," Sloane says, pointing to a bank of octagonal computers. Above them, holoscreens flash red. A diagram shows what looks like a mining bore down through layers of mantle and schist. It's pulsing white. A number sits above it—a percentage, slowly dwindling.

"What am I seeing?" Norra asks.

"I don't know," Sloane answers.

Brentin hurries over to the machine, looking down at a keyboard with a quizzical glance—the keys are triangular, most gold, some silver. He ignores those and instead moves his hand to the holoscreen itself, and when his fingers touch it, it swipes away and fills with scrolling data. "I . . . oh, no."

"What is it?" Norra and Sloane say in unison before giving each other a dirty, dubious look.

"The integrity of the planet has been compromised. Something . . . something is affecting the mantle. A system of tremors causing a cascading failure from the core up. This shaft, this . . . borehole, it's the key to it, a channel focusing the seismic wave. There are baffles here—telescoping vents to close the shaft, but they're on lockdown."

"What does that all mean?" Sloane asks.

"It means this world doesn't have long."

Norra's knees nearly buckle. *Temmin* . . . he's here. Jas, too. Wedge. The whole damn Republic fleet. If Jakku goes, they all go.

"Can you close it?" Norra asks.

"I can try."

"Do that," Sloane barks. "I'm finding Rax. He has to be here somewhere." Her voice sounds threadbare and desperate.

Norra points her blaster at the other woman. "No."

Sloane stares down the barrel of the pistol. "I'm not the enemy here."

"You're *my* enemy. You corrupted my husband. You've brought him on this lunatic's journey. You—"

"What I am is running out of time. Rax is the one behind all of this. Put that pistol down, Norra Wexley. Let me do what I need to do."

Brentin now comes up behind Norra, and she flinches, fearing he's there to attack her—but all he does is say, "Please, Norra."

Her hand shakes so hard she's afraid it might fall off.

Norra lowers the pistol. "Go."

"You could give me the pistol."

"Only way I give you this pistol is by pulling the trigger first."

"Fair enough. I don't need a blaster anyway— I am weapon enough." Sloane nods, as if summoning enough courage to make her last statement true. Then she turns on her heel and walks away, heading down an adjacent hallway. Not once does she look back over her shoulder.

Norra wheels on her husband and hisses at him: "You need to fix this. Brentin, listen very closely. Temmin is here, on Jakku. Your *son*. If you love him, and you love me, and you care at all about the New Republic that you once fought to build, fix this."

Fear and uncertainly flash like lightning in Brentin's eyes, but he nods and in a quiet, firm voice he says: "I will."

She finds him waiting for her. Down a set of steps, past a wall lined with what look to be powered-down droids, Rax waits. An infernal glow rises behind him, with blue embers whirling in the air above.

"Hello, Rax," Sloane says.

It's just her in here with him. She has nothing. No weapon. That damnable Norra Wexley wouldn't lend her a blaster. That awful woman was stubborn as the roots of an old tree. Smart move, admittedly. Sloane thought to simply take it from the woman, but in no world does she believe Brentin Wexley would allow that. And so she tells herself what she told them:

I am weapon enough.

At the very least, she knows they won't be leaving her behind. The shuttle gave up the ghost moments before landing: It was already shot to hell when they took it from the Imperial base, and as the ship settled toward the ground, coming in to land through the blowing sand and whipping dust, the engines gave out, the repulsors failed, and the whole ship thudded dully as it dropped. The panel went dark. The ship died. *There goes our ride,* she thought. Good news was, they didn't have to use the shuttle to blast the doors open. The door wasn't locked. She stepped to it and it opened.

No turbolasers. No defenses at all. An unlocked door. Worry seized her: Was Rax even here? Were they too late?

Now she knows. He's here. This ends.

Rax looks unarmed, as well. She sees no holster at his hip. Only him standing there, shoulders back, chest puffed out in his white naval uniform, a red cape sweeping behind him. *My, he looks pleased with himself,* she thinks. A smug twist to his lips adds further demonstration.

She thinks to punch that smug look right off his face.

"Did you see the show?" Rax asks her.

"I did," she answers. "Was it all for me?"

"No. The whole galaxy was my audience. But you . . ." He kisses the air. "You know more than most. Which means you *understood* it better than almost anybody else."

"I don't understand *any* of it. So why don't you explain it to me?" She holds up both her hands and gives a little shrug. "You're so proud of what you did here. Tell me. What was this all about, Counselor? Or should I call you Galli? Precious little orphan."

That stings him. He tries not to show it, but his lip twitches, his brow flinches. Her barb lands. "I don't have time for this. I am leaving."

Her hands form fists. "Only way out is through me."

"So be it." Rax walks toward her. Slow determination seems to urge him forward, the same determination of a predator stalking its prey—sure-footed, but with an easy, affable gait. Almost as if to say, *Don't worry your little whiskers about me. I won't hurt you, little creature.*

"I will say this," Rax comments as he takes one deliberate step after the next. "You were so close to it. *We* were so close. I always thought you'd be with me here at the end. And here you are." His face goes sour. "Just not how I pictured it."

"You still thought I'd work with you? After Akiva? After *Chandrila*? You threw me into the fire again and again."

"Fire forges some blades." He makes a dismissive gesture with his hands, like someone throwing away a bit of garbage. "And it ruins others."

He's dead ahead of her now. Rax stops walking. He smiles.

"I'm not letting you leave here alive," she says.

"How does this work, then? I don't have a blaster." He tugs back the curtain of his cape to show the void of weapons at either side. "I suppose I should have brought one. You should have, too."

"If wishes were starships—"

He finishes the refrain: "Then farmers would fly."

Sloane pitches forward into the breach, moving fast. Everything has been coming to this moment and she's like a compressed spring coming unsprung—like she's been saving up all that *hatred* and all that *rage,* tamping it down deep, so deep that it's ready to burst out like a scalding geyser. The rage and the hate end at the front of her fist.

Rax isn't a boxer. He hasn't had to fight his own fight since forever—maybe since *never.* He doesn't see the hit coming.

The fist clubs him in the nose. It gives way with a *pop.*

He goes down, and she drops atop him, snarling.

At the computer, Brentin's fingers move hesitantly over the keys. He hits one button and the holoscreen flashes angrily, a pulse of red light filling the room. Brentin curses and closes his eyes, refocusing.

The ground quakes again, sending her heart into her throat. Norra sees the percentage dwindling. Now it's down to 47.

"We should've given her the blaster," Brentin says suddenly.

"What?"

"Sloane. She's alone. And unarmed."

Norra bares her teeth at him, then gestures at him with the weapon. "Brentin, I don't even know which part is you and which part is the chip in your head. Until we get it out, I'll never know. Just turn this thing *off.*"

"I'm sorry," he says, staring down at the keys, his fingers moving frantically. "I'm so sorry for everything."

"Now isn't the time."

"Now might be the only time, Norra. I want you to

know, the man who did those things on Chandrila—it wasn't me."

". . . I know. But I also don't know which man you are now."

"I'm me. It's not the chip."

"So why are you with *her*?" Norra seethes. "She's the *enemy*, Brentin. The one you promised to fight against with tooth and claw when you joined the Rebellion. And now here you are, traveling with her? Maybe that chip in your head scrambled your brain, but she's not your wife."

"She isn't with the Empire anymore."

"Oh. That's *comforting*. I'm sure that erases everything she's done."

"It doesn't. I know it doesn't. But . . ." Her husband utters a wordless moan that devolves into a frustrated growl. The screen suddenly flashes red again and he squeezes both of his hands into fists. "I don't know how to explain it. I don't, okay? All I know is, even if I wasn't in control of myself, I did a bad thing and I want to fix it. Sloane wanted the same thing, I think, and we found ourselves together here with common purpose—"

" '*Together.*' That's great."

"Not like that," he pleads. "Please. I love you. I'm here for you. And for Tem. I wanted to do something *right* to counteract the wrong I'd done. Being on Jakku, it felt good. It felt like justice."

"What do you want to do, Brentin? Go in after her?"

"She needs our help. She's not as bad as you think she is."

"And she's still not any good."

"There's a greater evil in there—"

"Then let her fight it by herself."

*   *   *

Anger and hatred are blinding. Sloane realizes that too late. When she unleashed them, it was like a white flash. It was satisfying and warm. But it blinded her. Rax took the hit and went down, but it was way too easy. Soon as she's on top of him, she sees that glint in his eyes—clever and wary—and she knows she's just been lured into making yet another mistake.

His fist pistons into her side. Right where the ribs never healed, right where Norra shot her back on Chandrila. And the fist—it doesn't hit like a set of hard knuckles. It has a peak to it. A sharpness. Pain hits her there like a lightning strike and she howls. Her eyes are closed for half a second—

And then her head rocks backward as he lurches upward, slamming his forehead into her lower jaw, *bam*. Her teeth dig into her lip. Blood fills her mouth and she falls off him. Stars dance and light smears across her vision. She gags on her own fluids as she crab-walks backward, anguish washing over her like a tide of acid.

Rax is back on his feet and marching toward her. Sloane tries to stand but he drives the nose of his boot into her side. The *same* side. Something gives way. A bone. A rib. She cries out and slumps.

He has something in his hand. Rax gives it a little twirl—

A carving of some kind. A hooded figure.

He moves it back to the palm of his hand, letting the top of it poke through the gap between his knuckles. Playfully, he stabs at the air with that fist, *swish*, and now she knows what hurt so bad when he hit her.

"A piece from a Shah-tezh board," Rax says, his words dripping with satisfaction. He's like someone preening in the mirror. "Hurts, I wager. I saw you favoring that side back at the base, by the way. Seems my instincts were right to hit you there." His haughty smile is suddenly empty of mirth and falls slack on his face. "I really am disappointed it ended this way. You should've been with me now as an ally." Something crosses his face that looks like an epiphany. "You were an outcast, too, in a way. Weren't you? Held at arm's length by an Empire that did not want to know you—"

The ground rumbles. A crack suddenly splits the floor.

"What is happening?" she asks.

"The end of all things," Rax says with a theatrical pout.

She kicks out with a foot, hoping to surprise him and catch him in the knee—he's close now, tantalizingly so, and if she can drop him—

Rax catches her foot and swings her sideways with surprising strength. Her body crashes into one of the pillars. More pain radiates through her in concentric ripples.

"You think I can't fight?" he says with a hook-lipped sneer. His eyes are alive with a mania she has never seen in him before. "As you said, I was an orphan on *this* world. I was a child when I killed my first man, a scavenger who came upon this place and thought he'd found a treasure. I crushed his throat with my *bare hands*. I killed men, beasts, other children. You boxed to win trophies. I fought to save my life and serve my *Emperor*."

Through a bubble of spit and blood, she says: "I don't serve the Emperor. I serve the Empire."

"Your Empire is gone. I have killed it." He tilts his head as if he's listening for something. "You have friends. You aren't alone. Let's call them to us, shall we?"

He drops on top of her, grabbing for her left hand.

She struggles to pry it away, but he presses down with his knee, pushing her shoulder to the floor. He grips her smallest finger on that hand and—

Snap. He levers it backward until it quickly breaks.

Sloane screams.

"Yes. Cry out. The bleat of an animal summoning its pack." He grabs the next finger in. "Again!"

He breaks that one, next.

He hums a song, one swallowed by her pair of screams. Only later will she recognize it for what it is:

The Cantata of Cora Vessora.

Sloane's scream reaches their ears.

The percentage on the holoscreen is down to 33. The walls have begun to split. The floor, too. The tremors do not come erratically—now they are constant, a low-grade rumbling as dust streams down around them.

The war is ongoing inside Norra's heart. Rebels versus Imperials. Freedom versus oppression. But it's more complicated than that. Now there's a war between her and her own husband. Who is he? What has he become? Can they ever be the same again? And then there's the battle over Sloane. Norra wants to leave that woman to her business. Let her win or let her die. Whatever is going on beyond that door is not her business, she tells herself. Let them scrap it out and whoever emerges will either find themselves dragged before a New Republic tribunal, or meet her blaster. (Even that is a war of grave indecision. Again the confrontation of the old dichotomy: justice versus revenge. Justice is of the mind. Revenge is of the heart. Which wins out? Which *deserves* to win?)

Sloane has seized upon revenge. Norra saw that in her.

If she lets her be in there alone, isn't she doing the same?

Doesn't that make her no different from Sloane?

Then: a second scream. Alive with pain.

Blast it all to hell.

She turns away from the computer and raises the pistol. Brentin asks: "What are you doing?"

"I don't know," she responds. It's an honest answer.

"You're helping Sloane."

"Maybe. *No.* I don't know. You stay here."

"I'm getting somewhere—I've closed one of the baffles, I just need to slice through the defenses to get the others."

"Hurry."

Norra marches off toward the sound of Sloane's cries.

Ahead is a long hallway. It descends at an easy angle. Red lights around black metal cast everything in a diabolical glow. Pillars line the side like dark, gleaming guards. Beyond, in the walls, she spies the empty, implacable faces of droids sealed into the walls. It reminds her of the prison ship on Kashyyyk, and she fails to repress a shudder.

Where does this passage go? What awaits at the end? No sign of anything or anyone here. It's eerily quiet. She's about to yell for Sloane—

But then she sees her. The woman is alone on the floor, unconscious, her hair splayed out around her like a spreading puddle. Behind her is a massive pit from which emits a hellish glow. *The borehole,* she thinks.

Sloane lifts her head, casting a bleary eye to her.

"Run," Sloane says, her voice mushy.

The warning comes a moment too late.

Someone steps out from behind one of the pillars. Norra cries out, raising her blaster—but the heel of the man's hand catches her right under the chin, driving up under Norra's jaw so hard her whole head rattles. The dark behind her eyes explodes with light and the man's other hand catches her blaster, twisting it out of her grip handily, so handily in fact that she's shamed by how easily she lost her one and only weapon. She cries out and tries to flee, but—

The blaster cracks her in the head and as she staggers forward onto her hands and knees, she looks over her shoulder to see him raise the weapon. This man in naval whites. This man in his red cape. Gallius Rax. The architect behind everything, if Sloane is to be believed.

Then his gaze flits beyond her—

The sound of running footsteps echoes.

Brentin.

Her husband leaps, slamming into Rax hard. The blaster goes off, but the shot goes wide, smacking into the ceiling above her head. Brentin gets underneath the blaster, wrenching it upward. The two men struggle. It all seems to happen in slow motion. Norra works to stand, dizzied by the blow—but she moves, *has* to move, even though it feels like her brain isn't connected to anything, like her feet are stuck in mud. She throws her body against the wall behind Rax, and she reaches for him—

Even as he kicks out with a boot, knocking Brentin back—

Even as Rax raises the blaster—

Even as she hears herself screaming—

Even as her hands close on his throat from behind, as the blaster goes off, as Brentin staggers back, as a black burning hole blooms in the center of her husband's chest like a dark flower opening to the sun—

Brentin falls backward, clutching at his breastbone.

Rax spins around to meet Norra face-to-face. His visage is a rictus of raw, blistering rage—it is the fury of a fiend trapped in the corner and desperate to claw its way free. He pumps a knee into her stomach. She doubles over but urges herself forward, slamming him into the wall. The pistol swings and cracks her across the cheek and she feels something there give way— a disk in her neck slipping as misery radiates in every direction across her body. She wants to stop. She wants to roll over and give up and plead—*Let me have a moment with my husband, just one, before you kill me.* But that mote of desperation is swallowed in a wave of rage all her own. Norra roars as she grabs the man behind the leg and yanks out—he slams backward and the two of them fall.

The blaster is between them. All hands on it. They struggle. He wrenches her sideways. Her head crashes into the wall, concussed. Her vision starts to slip like a broken gear. In her blurred vision, she sees Brentin there by the wall, holding his chest, staring up at her. His mouth forms words that she can't hear, but she can see.

I love you.

"I love you, too," she says, the words garbled and messy.

She cries out as she summons every molecule of strength she can muster, turning the blaster centimeter by dreadful centimeter toward Rax's chest.

Her finger finds the trigger—

His head slams hard into hers. The blaster goes off. Rax cries out and throws her off him. He pulls himself up as the whole place shakes and shudders and bangs. The man clutches at his shoulder, blood staining his whites. "You shot me," he says, incredulous.

Norra, whimpering, pulls herself toward her husband. His name slips from her lips in a babbled man-tra, *Brentin, Brentin, Brentin,* and she crawls over to him and cradles his head, telling him that he'll be okay, that she'll get him help, that she's survived death so many times she knows he can survive, too. But his eyes are dead as coins and his mouth is slack. Norra cries out. She cradles him. She crumples against him.

I just want to sleep. I just want to be with him again. I'm so sorry, Brentin. So sorry I didn't believe you. So sorry I . . .

Rax stumbles away from her, down the hall, hold-ing his injured shoulder. Norra watches him escape through blurry vision.

No. Come back. I'm not done with you yet . . .

She drags herself off Brentin, crawling like a com-mon cur toward her retreating foe. It's then that her hand bumps into something . . .

The blaster.

He doesn't have it. *She* does.

Gritting her teeth together so hard she fears they might grind down to powder, she raises the pistol from her position on the floor—

Her hand dips and swerves. Her vision smears. Everything is made worse by the shaking. The ground buckles underneath her.

Then a shape moves past her. It's Sloane. The other woman is up on her feet, pursuing Rax now. Through Norra's double—now triple—vision, she watches the two Imperials clash once more, each clumsily brutal-izing the other with fists and kicks. Norra points the pistol at one, then the other, then feels her hand weakening. She doesn't even know if she has the strength to pull the trigger. Sloane cries out, thrown against the wall as Rax uses the wall to pull himself up the steps . . .

She speaks a word. A name.

"Sloane."

The woman turns toward her.

Norra, with the last measure of her strength, spins the blaster across the floor toward the other woman. And unconsciousness takes her away like a swift river.

CHAPTER THIRTY-SIX

SECURITY SPEEDERS HOVER in the space around the Senate tower. Strobing lights throb against the white. Down below, a crowd has gathered, and Sinjir steps into it, pushing past, driven by the dueling forces of grief and anger. He doesn't even know what he's looking for or what he hopes to accomplish—once security forces came and took away Tolwar Wartol, Sinjir had to come here and see it for himself. Perhaps for a vigil. Perhaps as a detective. Perhaps simply as a witness to it all.

It reminds him again of Endor. After it had all happened, with the battle ending and his comrades strewn about, bloodied and defeated—he felt the same sense of dislocation. Like he was no longer connected to anything—a man untethered. *Takask wallask ti dan.* Man without a star.

But now he has a star. Or had, until this.

Ahead, he finds someone joining him—

"Leia," he says.

She cradles her stomach, but it doesn't slow her down. "I should've known they'd make a second attempt on her. They hate her. I should've seen it—how she was at the center of it all." To the crowd, Leia barks, "Move. Move out of my way!" A murmur of awe in her wake.

Ahead, through the crowd, Sinjir sees something impossible.

A specter, surely. A wraith summoned by his own guilt.

He sees her for only a moment, when the security forces around her part—Chancellor Mon Mothma, shrugging a blanket off her shoulders, denying its comfort. *No. It can't be. Can it?* The crowd closes around her again and Sinjir can't see. He thinks to get ahead of Leia to help her part the crowd, but the princess is doing a fine enough job of that on her own, the volume of her voice rising to express her natural gift of command. As everyone moves aside, Sinjir leaps into Leia's wake to follow her. A guard steps in front of him, separating Sinjir from the princess, a sparking baton thrusting toward him—Leia reaches back and twists it from the man's grip. The baton clatters. Two guards move into the fray when—

"Stop!"

Her voice. One word. Tolling like a bell, clear and crisp.

The chancellor steps forward, easing herself between the security peace officer and Sinjir. "He is my adviser," she says, coolly.

"Chancellor. I . . ." Sinjir gasps. "You're alive."

"I am." Her face is a stern, grim mask.

Leia gasps, "Mon." And the two of them melt together in a crushing hug. Leia's head falls to the chancellor's shoulder, and Mon lifts her head back, eyes closed, seeming to savor the moment.

When they pull away from each other, Sinjir asks, "But how? That blast—"

"I wasn't in it. I wasn't here." She must see the confusion on his face, so she answers it: "You made me feel guilty for not buying my own baby gift for a dear friend, remember?" With that, she gives a knowing look to Leia. "I went out on my own. I left Auxi in my place . . ."

That last sentence is a struggle for her to get out. Sadness crosses her face like the shadow from a passing cloud.

"Auxi," Leia asks. "Is she—"

She nods. "Auxi is gone."

Mon says: "That leaves you as my only adviser, Sinjir. And your counsel is needed swiftly." To Leia: "Yours as well, my friend."

Sinjir assures her: "We will find whoever did this, starting now."

"No. Not that. Something else."

"What could possibly be more important?"

She clasps his hands and holds them tight. "Mas Amedda has come out of hiding and wants to sign a cease-fire. He wants to end it. All of it. The Empire is surrendering, and I need the both of you."

CHAPTER THIRTY-SEVEN

THE GROUND IS shaking now hard enough that Rae Sloane is sure the Observatory is going to collapse into the ground, a consumptive fissure swallowing them all. Sloane isn't sure she can do anything about it, but she has to try—she's here, trapped on this world, and what else can be done but try to save it? Woozy, bloodied, and beaten, she follows Rax up the steps.

Blaster in hand.

He looks over his shoulder, a craven fear crossing his face as the mask of confidence falls away. "Get *away*," he seethes, batting at the air with a bloody hand. Sloane shoots him in the back of his right leg.

Gallius Rax—Galli—bugles in pain and falls against the steps. With a groan he pushes himself up on both hands.

She shoots him in the other shoulder. He slumps, sobbing.

Then, as he turns over, his hands up in surrender as he pleads, "Don't, don't, don't, please," she shoots him in the stomach.

Every shot feels perfect. Every shot feels like revenge. Sloane's heard stories about revenge, about how it never really finishes everything, about how it never truly *completes* you, but at this moment, she disbelieves. Because this feels better than anything has ever felt to her.

Rax's hands move to his midriff, where a spreading red stains his raiment. Soon his naval white matches the red cape spilled beneath him.

Unblinking, he stares at her. Mouth gasping. Something wet slides in the back of his throat like a creeping thing.

"You're dying," she tells him. And he is. That much is plain to see. His lips have gone chapped and pale.

"Fellow outcast," he says.

"Yes."

"You serve the Contingency, now."

"I serve no one," she says.

"Listen. *Listen*. There's a ship. Short walk from here." He wheezes. "*Imperialis*. Take it. Hux is there. Others. Use the map—in a data spike in the, the computer. Set a course for the unexplored . . ." He coughs. Flecks of red dot his lips along with bubbles of spit. "Infinity. Already sent a ship ahead. A dreadnought . . . the Emperor's . . ."

It hits her. Of course. Back on Coruscant, looking through the Imperial Archives and taking an accounting of all the ships, one stood out as not being accounted for properly—it was said the New Republic took it down, but no tracking record showed that fate.

"The *Eclipse*," she says.

He nods. "Go to it. Leave this place. Find a new demesne. Start the game over." His teeth clinch together with a vise grip. Through them he keeps talking, babbling now: "Undeserving. I am *undeserving*. Just a skittermouse, not a vworkka. Outcast, always the outcast. Shah-tezh. Cora Vessora. Undeserved . . ."

His head thuds against the step. A line of blood oozes from his nose as the last flash of light goes dark behind his eyes.

Sloane stands. From his hand, she takes something else: the pair of game pieces. Imperator and Outcast. *Mine,* she thinks.

The vibration underneath her wakes her. Norra groans, picking herself up. Her husband is beneath her. Eyes shut, as if sleeping. She pretends that's what it is. *He's just asleep. I'll wake him later. When it's time to go.* She grabs the wall and pulls herself up.

Moving toward the steps, she sees another body there. It's him. Gallius Rax. His red cape pools beneath him like spilled viscera. For him she tells a different story: *He is not asleep. He is dead. Revenge has won the day. Justice has fled into the shadows.*

Nearby, a sound—fingers on keys. The ground suddenly shifts hard and she almost loses her footing. Norra continues up the stairs, one agonizing step at a time. Her gaze follows the sound, the tapping sound, and ahead stands a figure—a bit blurry, but when she blinks the gauzy smear of her vision clarifies. It's Sloane.

The blaster pistol is on the floor between them.

Norra staggers to it and picks it up.

"Sloane," she says, pointing the blaster.

The Imperial—or not, who knows where her loyalties lie anymore—turns toward her, hands by her side. Behind her, the computers project an image of a mechanism: locks and chain-drive banding and telescoping doors. Those are the baffles Brentin was trying to close—but he didn't. He stopped to save her. *No, he stopped to die.*

"Norra Wexley," Sloane says. "You and me, once again. At the end of things."

"Yes." It's all she can say. What else is there? Is any of this even real? Is it all a fever dream? Or is she still lying there on the floor with her husband, asleep, dying, or already dead?

"Brentin. Is he?"

"He's fine," Norra protests, the words so firm and so fierce they serve as a kind of sharp-tongued protest. But she knows he's not. Tears streak down her cheeks and she has to lift her chin to try to deny them. "He's gone," she says, finally, admitting the truth out loud.

"I'm sorry. He was a better traveling companion than I deserved."

"Yes. That's true." Norra swallows hard.

"What are we going to do here?"

"I don't know yet."

"I need to finish what Brentin started and stop this planet from destroying itself. Something has happened in the core. But I can end it. Best I can tell, there are mechanisms that can close the borehole, that can seal off the reaction from heating the mantle and cracking this planet like a geode."

"Oh."

"You should let me do that. Just in case, you should go."

"I don't know where."

"Find your son. Go home. Have a life."

"Easier said than done."

"Easier for you than it will be for me. I have none of those things. I never had a husband or a wife to die in my hands. I never had a child. I had only the Empire and now . . ." Norra doesn't need her to say any more.

"I'm sad for you," Norra says, and she's surprised that she means it.

"I am, too. Are you going to kill me?"

"Brentin said you weren't as bad as I thought you were."

Sloane shrugs. "Damned with faint praise yet again, it seems."

"Aren't we all. Damned, I mean."

"Maybe. Maybe not."

"You go ahead. Save the world. I'm going to leave, now," Norra says, sighing and wiping tears away. The blaster clatters from her hand. "Let's hope Brentin is right and you aren't as bad as I think."

Sloane gives her a small nod. "Good luck, Norra Wexley."

"You too, Grand Admiral Sloane."

Norra turns and goes back down the steps to claim her husband.

Outside, the air is red, choked with dust. Norra tucks her chin and mouth under the collar of her shirt, affording her some small reprieve. Brentin is heavy, but a burden she feels necessary to bear. She intends to take him back to Akiva. Back to where she can bury a body in the salt marshes as is the way of her people. Back to the world where he's not just a memory. Where he can be a face that her son can touch. A body over which Temmin can grieve.

But where? Where will she go?

Again the ground shudders. She staggers, dropping to one knee, then struggling to stand anew.

The shuttle. It's safe there, at least, from the storm. She takes him inside the darkened Imperial ship. She summons as much saliva to her mouth as she can muster (which is very little) and she cleans his cheeks.

Then she tries to start the ship.

No go. It's dead. The engines have failed, and the fuel cells have died trying to give life to this ruined machine.

She is stranded.

She sits in the pilot's seat. She eases Brentin into the

seat next to her. Norra holds his cold, stiff hand. For a time, she sleeps.

The sound of a ship's engine wakes her. She looks out the cockpit viewport and sees through the dust storm a gleaming, shining vessel rise up through the crimson clouds—the yacht moves swiftly and is gone. A hallucination, she thinks. Some dread phantasm to tease her. *Look at the pretty shiny ship. Don't you wish you could be on it?*

Sleep takes her again. Sleep like death, dark and dreamless.

The same sound, a replay of the last, draws her once more out of the deep: ship engines humming. She peers out and sees nothing.

But the scuff of a heel behind her has her lurch to her feet.

Sloane.

"Norra!"

It's not Sloane. It's Jas. Jas, flanked by a tall Kyuzo alien in a broad, domed hat. Jas Emari, her savior. Jas Emari, her ride home.

CHAPTER THIRTY-EIGHT

AN EMPIRE DOES not end all at once, and *this* one, the Galactic Empire that began when Palpatine stole the Old Republic, is no different.

For this empire, it is death by a thousand cuts. A slow bleed that began perhaps not when the first Death Star was destroyed, but very early, when it killed the Jedi to make way for its regime. When a pair of twins—one named Luke, the other named Leia—fell through the cracks, lost to their father and to his dark Master, both of whom were blinded by hate and ego. Other injuries only hastened its demise: the birth of the Rebellion, the death of their first superweapon, the distrust that widened the gap between Vader and the Emperor, and of course the Empire's colossal loss at Endor.

Now an even greater loss at Jakku was the final wound. History would remember that the New Republic was victorious on this day, and that is true. History will forget, however, how in reality this final wound was a self-inflicted one: a contingency plan by a callous, vengeful Emperor who never wanted his Empire in the hands of a successor.

Even still, though the Empire's death comprises a thousand cuts, only one thing makes it official: The signing of a cease-fire, one that accords both the end of combat and the full, unconditional surrender of the Galactic Empire.

Mas Amedda comes out of hiding, rescued (in his account) by a gaggle of Coruscanti *children* who had helped form the backbone of their own resistance movement. He had been held captive by his own people, on order from the usurper, Gallius Rax. Now free, and with Imperial forces destroyed, he was free to sign a meaningful Imperial Instrument of Surrender.

Mon Mothma demands that this take place on Chandrila—the same place that the Empire attacked on Liberation Day. The signing occurs on the crystal cliffs north of Hanna City, under an ancient tintolive tree. The chancellor is flanked by her two advisers: Sinjir Rath Velus, and Hosnian Prime's Sondiv Sella. Princess Leia is present, as well. The signing occurs during the third hour of her labor, though she only tells her husband this after the ceremony is complete—at which point, he hurries her off to the birthing chamber in the heart of Hanna City.

The Empire is surrendered with minimal concession. The Instrument of Surrender informing the Galactic Concordance demands not only that all fighting cease on behalf of the Empire, but also that the Imperial government dissolve immediately. After which Mon Mothma signs a further declaration denoting that all still-living Imperial officials are now categorized as war criminals. Non-combatant functionaries within the Imperial government are given conditional pardons, provided they continue to act by the articles of the Galactic Concordance. Mas Amedda, in return, escapes without such formal censure, though certainly the stigma never leaves him. The media and the history books both brand him as a toady and a lackey and one of the willing—if weak—architects of the Empire. Even still, he is granted a provisional (and powerless) government on Coruscant, left with New Republic overseers who help confirm that he remains as little more than a figurehead, continuing his toothless rule over a troubled world.

After the ceremony is complete, Mon Mothma thanks Sinjir with a bottle of something very expensive: a lachrymead from before the birth of the Empire. Inside the bottle, the liquid—which, if we're being honest, is really just the fermented tears of the sentient bees of the Nem-hive—has a golden glow, like sunlight on the sea. When you shake it, the glow strengthens. "Hope through agitation," Mon Mothma explains. "The light glows stronger when we struggle."

"From before the Empire, you say?" he asks.

"From a better day, yes."

He thanks her. She asks him if he'll drink it.

"No," he says, to his own surprise. "Not today, at least. This feels somehow too special to violate with my crass tongue."

"You've matured," she tells him.

"Just like this wine," he says, with a wink.

The war ends, the Empire dies, but the battle goes on.

Though the cease-fire is signed, the Battle of Jakku still rages. Its forces there refuse to surrender. They fight past the point of sanity. For weeks. Then months. The shattered Imperial remnant has no strategy. Their base is overtaken. The captains of the lingering Imperial fleet use more dramatic and desperate tactics as the battle rages, many trying to mimic the tractor beam snare that served as Agate's final maneuver in this life. A few of those captains, utilizing mysterious coordinates, jump into Unknown Space. It is assumed that their disappearance is tantamount to suicide.

This remnant is like a parasite with its head sunk in

the meat of its own certainty, teeth biting tight. It takes months for the fighting to truly end, months for the New Republic soldiers to round up the captives and count the dead, all that time for the Empire's ghost to catch up with the death of its body and realize that the fight is well and truly over.

Even then, it doesn't stop across the galaxy. Remnants remain. Some hide out, waiting for some savior to come save them. Others go out with spectacular flare-ups of violence and viciousness. But these remnants are few. Gallius Rax did the work of destroying the demesne properly. Those that linger cannot stay long. The rest are prisoners, so many that the New Republic has no idea what to do with them.

On Jakku, the war leaves behind a world of wreckage. Scavengers feast upon the remains. Niima the Hutt emerges even before the fighting is truly over to begin hoarding what she and her people can find. Already a black market forms around the junk and debris—weapons and computers and engines, all littering the sand like the markets of a massive graveyard. Niima sits at the center of this black market like a fat, throbbing tumor diverting blood flow to itself.

The galaxy heals.

The people do, too.

But a grievous injury such as the one caused by the Empire cannot heal without leaving scars behind as a reminder.

Akiva.

The jungle is thick, though the air is thicker. The funeral traditions of the world are many, but this is the one that Norra and her family cleave to: Brentin Wexley's body is wrapped in a gauzy cloth. Friends and family heap him with garlands of hai-ka flowers, which are as orange and as soft as the tail feathers of a fire-bird. Then they sing songs and tell stories over him before sinking him in the salt marsh. The salt will eat the body over a short time, and it will claim him. He may return to Akiva as a child of Akiva—from water they arise, to water they return. Atoms to atoms.

But before the body sinks down, Temmin rushes up to his father and places across him a different honorific—

A metal arm. A *droid* arm. It belonged to Bones, and is the only part of his mechanical friend he was able to rescue from the sands of Jakku. Temmin, trying desperately not to cry, whispers: "Bones, you watch over my dad, okay? Keep him safe." Then he hugs both of them together.

The salt mire takes the body.

Norra falls to the ground, crying, and Temmin holds her for a time as his aunts stand by. When all the others have gone, he helps her stand. They spend a few days with the aunts, and then it's time to go home.

Thanks to a friend who is now apparently a *high-ranking adviser* to the chancellor of the New Republic, Jas Emari not only gets Dengar, Embo, and Jeeta full pardons, she actually manages to get them some money from the New Republic. Not as much as she promised, no. But it's enough to stop them from killing her—*and* enough to convince them to remain formed up as a new crew. Dengar seems particularly pleased by this turn of events. "Times, they are a-changing, my little gompers. We're gonna need to watch each other's backs, eh?"

Even still, she takes some time on Chandrila to herself. She tells her new crew she'll track them down when the time is right.

For now, she says, she has to find somebody else.

The story made its way to her that Jom Barell went to Jakku to save her. Laughable, really, because what? *He's* going to save *her*? Oh, so she can't take care of herself? Jas feels she's proven very well that she has, and so her plan is to go to his apartment, look him dead in the eye (the one eye, since the other is gone), give him a stern lecture on her ability to save *herself* thank-you-very-much, and then kiss him until he can't breathe. But when she gets there, he's not at home.

Someone else is there. A woman. A commando, by the uniform. Jas feels embarrassed, and she stammers an apology—

The woman just says she's here to collect Jom's things.

"Why? Where's he gone?"

"Gone to where we all go," the woman says. Jas still doesn't understand, so the woman spells it out plainly: "He died on Jakku."

It takes too long for Jas to understand. Even when it hits her, it still doesn't *hit* her. The woman says there's a video from the U-wing—and she asks if Jas wants to see it. She doesn't, but she says yes anyway, so she watches it. It's short and choppy—standard for a combat-cam. The ship drops into atmosphere and the SpecForce commandos are hanging near the exit, ready to jump out and join the war even before the damn thing has a chance to land. Jas sees Jom there, and he leans in toward the cam and gives it a wink and a hard nod. "New Republic, *ahuga*—"

And the rest of the commandos, men and women, echo that word:

"AHUGA!"

Some battle cry Jas doesn't understand.

Jom smirks one last time—

From outside the door, from the surface of Jakku,

Jas sees the glint of something. A missile, maybe. Concussive, probably.

None of the others see it. None except Jom. He bellows, "Incoming!"

And then he does the unthinkable. Jom puts his foot down on the lip of the open door, leaping right past the beam cannon placement and out into open air. He stays aloft, pulsing his jetpack—two hard burns of blue energy out the back—and he heads right toward the missile.

The U-wing pivots to port side, lifting up and away from the incoming projectile. As it moves, Jom disappears out of frame—and Jas feels her innards tightening as she inwardly screams that she wants the camera to shift back down again, down, *down*, so she can see him one last time.

Everything goes white and pixilated.

"I . . . I don't understand," Jas says when the vid is over. "He should've mounted that cannon—"

"Would've taken a few seconds to spin up—by then, too late."

"He didn't need to do that."

"He did. And he saved us."

That's all Dayson needs to say.

Jas thanks the woman and leaves. It takes days for her to process it. Days of walking around like she's in someone else's body, days until the truth of the thing hits her with the impact of a wall falling upon her: *He came to save me, and he died in service to that. He followed his heart, and it got him killed.* And then she's left to wonder: Would she make the same choice? Does she have a larger purpose, a greater debt, and is she willing to pay it? Maybe she's the one without a star.

She spends the next week in bed, staring at the ceiling.

*   *   *

War is about loss, yes. But when it ends, joy surges. How could it not? Burying the dead is a somber act, but the celebration that follows confirms that they did not die in vain. They died to make the galaxy free.

And my, does the galaxy celebrate. Not only has the Empire's gauntleted fist let go of the galaxy's neck—it is gone entirely. The oppression is at an end and so the celebrations go for *weeks*. Fireworks on Chandrila. Festivals of food on Nakadia. Nonstop parties in the streets and on the rooftops of Coruscant. And this time, the Empire isn't there to stop it. They do not police these carnivals and festivities. No troopers show up to fire upon the parades or execute protestors. It's just one more sign that the Empire is well and truly gone. The New Republic demonstrates that it is the polar opposite of the Galactic Empire: It *encourages* the celebrations, it holds official revels and pageants and exultations of joy. Wherever the New Republic's light touches, it marks the occasion with a holiday.

Liberation Day is remade into the seven-day Festival of Liberation.

And then, there is the matter of a child.

On the day the Instruments of Surrender are signed, a child is born on Chandrila to Leia Organa and Han Solo. Friends and family gather. Rumors fly about who was there and who was not. Some say that the golden boy, Luke Skywalker, made an appearance and then was gone again, off on some untold mission. Others say his absence was conspicuous. Missing, too, was Solo's copilot, who is said to have finally found his own Wookiee family on Kashyyyk. Stories of the birth range from the dramatic and fortuitous to the utterly inauspicious—one story suggests that the birthing chamber was occupied for three whole days while Leia struggled. Another tells the tale that it was fast and painless: She merely needed to calm herself and meditate to make the moment as untroubled as a mountain lake. Some say the boy was born with a shock of black hair, others that he had a full set of teeth, others still that he was just a baby like any other, sweet one moment, screaming the next, and nestling at his mother as any healthy child does.

What is known is this: The child's name is Ben, and he takes his father's last name, even as Leia keeps only her own family name, Organa.

Han looks into the eyes of his son.

My son.

How the hell did *that* happen? Well, he *knows* how that happened—a night under the stars in the canopy of Endor trees. But in the larger sense, the galaxy is a far stranger place than he figured on if it's letting *him* be a father.

Solo stands in the nursery, alone. The boy, Ben, wriggles and gurgles in the round white bubble of protection that is the infancy cradle. Han leans forward over it, arms crossed on the rail while looking down at the child's chubby face and dark eyes. They regard each other. The child burbles.

While Leia is in the other room taking a shower, Han says in a low voice: "Hey. It's you and me, kid. Whole damn galaxy against us but we'll make it through okay. I'm not always gonna be the best dad— c'mon, I don't know what the hell I'm doing here. I can barely take care of myself. But I'll always keep us pointed in the right direction . . . even if we zig and zag a little to get there. There's your first lesson: Sometimes doing the right thing doesn't mean following a straight line. Sometimes you gotta—" He takes his hand and gestures with it like it's a fish swimming this way and that, left and right and up and down. "Don't tell your mother I said that."

Ben starts to cry. It comes on fast, like a tropical downpour. He's staring up, all innocent, and then it hits, *boom*. The little body tightens up and his mitts make little rubbery fists and punch the air. His white cheeks bloom with red. The sound coming out of him is like a storm siren.

Han winces. Ah, hell. He looks around him like there's gotta be something or someone there to save him—nearby, he finds a small tooka doll that Lando sent over, and he takes it and thrusts it into the air above the boy and wiggles it. "Here. Look. The cat is, ahh. The cat is dancing? Dancing tooka. Come on, kid, you gotta give me something here."

It does nothing to stem the tide of tears.

Han growls, looking around for something else. He's about to yell for Leia—but there she is, coming in through the doorway. "He's, ahh, you know. He's making that sound again."

"He's crying."

"Right. Yeah." Han holds up a finger. "It's not my fault!"

"Han," Leia says, coming over to him, still in her towel. "It's okay. He's a baby. Babies cry. It's how they tell you they want something."

"Oh. Yeah, no, of course. Maybe you could do your—" He mimes his hand floating in the air in an almost religious gesture. Leia has a connection with the kid that he can never have. Like Luke, she has the Force. That's a thing he never used to believe in, but since getting caught up with this group, he's seen a whole lot of strangeness just to believe it's just a bunch

STAR WARS: AFTERMATH: EMPIRE'S END   457

of hooey. Leia can't do what Luke can do and maybe
never will, but she can quiet the kid with but the faintest of gestures. He hates to admit it, but he's jealous of
that. Han will never have that with Ben. They're connected in a way he can't even begin to understand.
"You know. Use the Force."

"Why don't we try something else?"

"A little brandy on his gums?"

"Pick him up," she says.

"Just . . . pick him up?"

"Yes. He's your son. Use your hands. Go on, Han.
Pick him up. He wants to be snuggled."

"I smuggle, not snuggle."

"Han."

He sighs. "Okay! Okay." He stoops down and gingerly reaches for his son. He hoists him up and Ben
twists and turns in his grip. *He's so small.* Han thinks
how easy it would be to break him. Or to drop him.
The boy is vulnerable to everything. And so he does
what feels most natural—he protects the kid by bringing him close to his chest. And just like *that*—

Ben stops crying. The boy nuzzles up against his collarbone. He burps once, his dark eyes pinch shut, and
he's out like a light.

"See?" she says. "You don't need the Force at all."

"But I'll never have what you have with him."

"You don't have to," she says, sweetly. "You will
have your own thing, because you're his father."

Weeks later, Norra's old crew gathers again. Not for
an assignment. They gather because it may be the last
time they see one another for a while. Maybe forever,
given the way things sometimes go. The tavern they
find themselves in is one of Sinjir's favorites, up on the
side of a cliff overlooking the Silver Sea. They gather

to drink, and they drink to Jom, and to Auxi, and to Brentin Wexley, and of course they drink to Mister Bones and tell stories about that mad dancing murderdroid until they're all laughing so hard they're crying. They drink to the Empire and to the New Republic. They drink to Leia and Han and the new baby who surely is keeping them up at nights. ("Squalling grub-monkey," Sinjir calls the boy.)

When they talk of the child, Sinjir adds, as if surprised: "Did you know: The child did not smell bad. Not at all."

Conder laughs and explains, "Sin thought the baby would stink."

"Of course I did. Babies are foul little gobbos, covered in their own infant slime. I expected them to smell sour. Or . . . diapery."

"Oh, Sinjir, no," Norra says, her cheeks blushing with a bit of inebriation from the junipera she's been drinking. "No, no, no. Babies smell wonderful. They smell sweet and fresh and innocent."

"Sounds like you want to eat them," Sinjir says. "Wait, maybe we *should* eat them. Like wriggling little loaves of bread, they are."

Conder drives an elbow under his ribs. He *oof*s.

Norra continues: "Stop it, there's nothing like the smell of a new baby. That little star-child smelled like he was made of clean towels. This one here used to smell so good—" She leans into her son, who of course drinks a sensible jogan-juice. Temmin wrinkles his nose in embarrassment and fails to pull away from his mother as she pinches his cheeks and makes a sound like *wooshy gooshy woo*.

"Mom."

"Oh, relax, Tem. I'm your mother. I'm allowed to embarrass you from time to time. It is my parental right, sacred and omniversal."

"Ugh."

Jas leans back with a scoundrel's ease and clucks her tongue. "I think we're supposed to call him Snap now, isn't that right?"

Again he's embarrassed. Blushing as he does. "That's what the other pilots in Phantom Squadron call me. It's because I can turn like this—" He snaps his fingers, *pow.* Everyone knows it's because of his nervous habit—one shared by his father, once. But no one corrects him on it today.

"Phantom Squadron. More like *Fancy* Squadron," Sinjir says. "Even fancier is this faint dusting of, what is that on your lip and cheek there? Dirt? Choko powder?" He leans forward with a finger to poke at it.

"Ow, hey," Tem says. "I'm growing a beard is all."

"Like Jom," Jas says.

"Like Jom," the rest of them echo. Again they raise their glasses. And again they clink and they drink.

Conder leans forward and says to Temmin: "A mouse droid tells me that the New Republic is setting up a new flight academy on Hosnian Prime. And I hear you'll be a pupil there, is that right?"

"Yeah. It's no big."

"Perhaps you'll actually learn how to fly a ship," Sinjir says with a wink. "You know they're not toys you smash in the ground."

Conder *tsk*s him and says: "Don't let him sass you."

Sinjir makes a face. "I am a sassy bastard. It is my nature."

"Seriously, you should be proud, Temmin," Conder says. "I bet you'll miss your mom, though, huh?"

"About that . . ." Temmin says.

"I'm going with him," Norra says. Eyebrows arch in curiosity, and she answers their unspoken questions with, "Oh, relax. It's not like that, I'm not the dutiful mother unable to let go of her star-pupil son. Wedge

will be the head instructor there, at least to get the
school set up. And he's invited me to teach, too." She
doesn't say anything about how she and Wedge have
been spending considerable time together. It's not romantic. That's what she keeps telling herself, anyway.
The memory of Brentin is still fresh like a burn. It's
too soon to let that fade. She wants to hold on to that
pain as long as she can. "Apparently they think I'm
not too terrible a pilot."

More congratulations go around.

They talk for a while about what they'll all be doing.
The rise of Black Sun and the Red Key leaves Jas looking to pay her way out of her debts—something her
new ragtag crew of bounty hunters can help her accomplish. Sinjir will continue advising the chancellor—
and now the race is on to find a third adviser to help
balance out the constantly bickering pair of Sinjir and
Sondiv Sella. Though Han and Leia aren't here, the two
of them will apparently remain—even though Sinjir
notes the princess is quite keen to get back to helping
those worlds still in thrall to Imperial remnants.

The night goes on and the moon brightens the Silver
Sea. The conversation winds down, and as it happens,
they peel away one by one. Jas says she's off with the
new crew. Sinjir makes a vomit-face as he notes that
he'll be subject to yet another *early-morning meeting,*
which according to him "is an act of torture so vile I
should've been using it as a weapon in my arsenal all
along."

Outside the bar, Sinjir sends Conder on as he and Jas
hang back. A cool wind comes off the sea. Below them,
waves roar against the cliffs. Jas watches Sinjir—there's
something just a little different about him, now. His
shoulders aren't so tight. His angles have softened—

if only a little. It looks as if something has left him: a pressure, a burden, some presence she cannot fully know. It has given him an ease of posture, as if he's found some kind of peace, however strange and temporary it may be.

"Looks like you found your star," Jas says.

"Conder?"

"Not him. Well, *maybe* him—I just mean, you found a life. A purpose. You've been drifting since Endor. You are *takask wallask ti dan* no more, Sinjir."

He leans in and puts an arm around her. "Oh, now, I don't know about that. Without you, I think I'll feel quite lost, indeed."

"You'll be fine. You've gone respectable, remember?"

"Respectable? Bah. I took several steps down on the moral hierarchy going from *Imperial torturer* to *political adviser.*"

"I'm just happy you have purpose."

"Seems we all found our purpose."

She smirks, cocking her head in such a way that her singular ridge of hair flips over, revealing the side of her scalp where the horn spurs were broken off. "I never lost mine."

"But it changed a little, didn't it?"

"Hm. It did. I learned to play well with others, for one." She sighs. "And I learned that perhaps my aunt didn't have it *all* wrong. Maybe I should take more, um, ethical jobs from now on. Nothing wrong with helping people from time to time—as long as there's a bag of credits to go along with it. One must get paid, after all."

"You going to be okay?"

Jas frowns. "What? Because of my debts? I'll be fine. They've chased me for this long and now I have this crew watching my back." She stiffens. "Admittedly, a crew who will probably sell me out as soon as they receive a viable offer to do so, but I will burn that bridge when I get to it."

"No. I mean because of Jom."

Jom. That name sucker-punches her. They've been saying it all night, and it gut-kicks her every time. "Jom and I were never ever going to have a real thing. But we had something foolish and incomplete going on and I was good with that. He was . . ." She tries not to break. She holds it together, if barely. "He was an idiot who liked me more than I liked him and that got him killed."

"That's not your fault."

"No. It's not. It's his. But I still feel bad about it, and I feel worse because there's nothing I can do to balance those scales. That is a debt I can never pay back because there is no one to pay it to."

"Life isn't *all* about debts."

"Life is *only* about debts. You accumulate them. You pay them out. Others gather debts to you and you try to collect in return."

"Your whole life is a ledger?"

"More or less."

He hugs her close. "Your cynicism gives me life, dear Jas."

"The feeling is reciprocal. Regrettably—I have to go."

"We'll see each other again, won't we?"

"I don't know," she answers, and it's an honest answer.

"Fair enough."

He kisses her temple. She holds him for a little while longer, lingering on the cliff as the sea rolls in, bashing against the rocks. And then she goes her way, and he goes his.

* * *

"We'll see them again," Temmin says.

"I know."

"I miss Dad. I miss Bones. They should've been here."

"I know. I miss them, too." She looks to her son. Even now, it's strange to see how he's grown up in this short time since she returned to Akiva. His cheeks are rounder. Hair, bushier. His eyes are a bit darker now, too. Temmin's filled out in his shoulders—when he was a baby, she marveled as he transformed into a toddling thing, and later was floored by the swift transition to the boy he became. Then boy to teenager, and now a teenager to a proper young man. So many changes.

It saddens her at the same time it thrills her.

"We're going to be okay," he says, patting her hand as if sensing her distress. He has a good head on him. Maybe it took a little while to screw it on, no thanks to her. Leaving him on Akiva? Throwing him into a war? *I'm basically the worst mother ever,* she thinks. But they're both alive. And she decides to forgive herself, then, for all the things that happened. Justice and revenge are two warring forces, but for her, she rejects them both. No need anymore to get revenge on herself for what she did, or seek justice and recompense for the kind of mother she's been. Forgiveness for herself comes blooming inside her, bright as a star and warm as the noonday sun. Maybe it's the drink. Maybe it's a night out with friends. But it feels like a great deal of ugliness in her is suddenly washing out to sea. Gone away, goodbye.

"Love you, kiddo," she says to her son.

"Love you, Mom."

"It's past your bedtime, *Snap*."

He snaps his fingers, to demonstrate. "*Or* we could just stay up all night and watch the boats go out to catch fish in the morning."

"Just this once. Then we gotta pack. The Corellian Academy calls."

They stand and they go, not sure whether their adventures have ended or have only just begun.

EPILOGUE

THE UNKNOWN REGIONS

TRAVELING THE ABYSS beyond the known galaxy takes months.

The months for Sloane are hard and lonely. The *Imperialis* is a cold, impeccably designed ship, and she shares it with a pack of wild children and the haggard, haunted remnant of the man named Brendol Hux. The early days of the trip were spent worrying about whether or not one day Hux would rally his vicious orphans to slay her while sleeping. But once she saw that the children listened to Hux's own son—a pale slip of a boy with a tousle of red hair—she went to him and asked young Armitage to make a deal with her. She said to Armitage: "If you're willing to keep me safe from the children, then I will keep you safe from your father. Do we have an accord?"

The boy nodded and said that they did.

And then she found Brendol Hux in his room, and she showed him a swatch of Rax's bloody cape and the data spike containing the map coordinates. She said that she knew Brendol always hated her, and that the feeling was mutual, but if they are to carry forth the banner of the Empire, then they are to be allies, however reluctant.

The oaf made a mistake, then: he came at her. His hands reached for her throat. Even beaten and bruised as she was, it took her no time to hyperextend his knee with a hard kick. As he doubled over, mewling, she grabbed a hank of his messy hair, and she began to beat him. She hit him, punching and kicking the man until he was on the floor, on his knees, whimpering. Sloane told him: "If you ever cross me, I will visit this same violence upon you a hundredfold. Whatever waits for us out here, you're with me. You will not betray me. You will not question me. Do you understand?"

He nodded. Smiling through tears. Blubbering that he was her man.

Then she added, "Your son. Armitage. I know you don't like him. I suspect you hurt him—psychologically or physically, I don't know, and I don't care. You will leave him alone. And you will teach the boy everything that you know. Are we clear?"

More blubbering, more nodding.

That solved that problem.

It did not, however, solve the problem of her loneliness. For the duration of the trip, she remained away from the children, away from Hux. She kept to herself, occupying her time looking at the ship's records—studying its history, its flight time, its communications, its weapons. The ship, like all of Palpatine's yachts, bears the maker-mark of Raith Sienar. It is perhaps unsurprisingly well-fitted with hidden ordnance; most yachts, after all, are not loaded for bear with Umbaran electromagnetic plasma cannons. Also unsurprising is that this ship, given that it's a replica, has had very little flight time. It went from the shipyard over Castell to Jakku, and has remained there for years—going all the way back to when Sienar was a Republic corporation.

What *is* surprising is that, not long after takeoff, the ship transmitted a very small packet of data to a dozen different sources. Ship transmitters, by the look of it. And it takes digging to unlock even this much. Sloane had no one to ask but the strange droid piloting the ship, and so she asked the sentinel, "What did we transmit? And to whom?"

The sentinel answered, "Path coordinates. Sent to Imperials considered loyal."

"Who considered them loyal? Rax?"

"Emperor Palpatine."

"Are you loyal to Palpatine?"

"All sentinels and messengers are programmed to serve his will, even in death."

"Good," she said. Though she was not then, and is not now, sure how good it really is. What waits for them now remains a mystery. *Who* waits—and who will follow in their wake—is an even more troubling conundrum.

And all that assumed they even make it.

The journey through the Unknown Regions has been harrowing. Taking short hyperspace jumps through the chaos has been like navigating a dangerous maze at full speed. But the sentinel assured her the path was safe. They skirted superstorms and saw strange creatures out there in the blackness of the void. They lost system power when a magnetic burst of mysterious origin cascaded through space—but it was only for a few hours, and with power restored they were able to continue on.

It doesn't help that all along her side has ached fiercely. Every morning she checked the old injury, and though the bruise has faded, the ribs look soft and caved in. And even the faintest fluttering touch of her fingertips upon the skin causes her great pain. Something is broken inside. She tells herself she will fix it when they land on the *Eclipse*. If they land on the *Eclipse*.

Truth is, Sloane almost didn't come on this journey.

When she finally shut down the self-destruct mechanism on the Observatory—the one that would have split the world of Jakku in twain, wiping out both the Empire and the New Republic forces—she thought about remaining there on that world. Then she toyed with the idea of following Norra and looking for her own way to the New Republic. Maybe they would imprison her. Maybe they would give her a job. Maybe someone would quietly slit her throat and dump her in the sea. No matter the outcome, at least she would find some purpose, however short.

But then the old ambition came alive once more—a campfire she thought was dark, suddenly glowing once more with a kindled ember. *If there is a chance to rebuild the Empire, shouldn't I take it?* Couldn't she make it better? In her own image? She felt the promise of a frontier nation born of loyalty and order and not given over to the backstabbing and incest of the Empire that Palpatine created and Gallius Rax destroyed. They are pioneers in this space. They are the first outside the charted limits of the galaxy.

She realized: *It can be mine, if only I am willing to take it.*

Soon, they will be at their destination.

And soon, it will be hers to take.

The *Imperialis* glides gleaming around the edges of a geomagnetic storm—at a distance, it looks like threads of hazy light, diaphanous and spectral, emerging from a blue-black cloud and finding one another in the void. The light braiding and twisting.

"There," Brendol Hux says. Hux has cleaned himself up. His hair and beard are trimmed. He's lost some of the paunch he brought with him. Sloane sees what he indicates: in the distance, the lean blade of a Super Star Destroyer dreadnought floats beyond the light and in the black.

She knows that ship.

The *Eclipse*.

To the sentinel droid piloting the *Imperialis* she says, "Take us in. It's time to rejoin with those who came before." She does not fully know who was sent ahead. Hux did not know himself. Is it the original crew of the *Eclipse*? Were the others hand-selected by Palpatine, or by Rax? She cannot say, and she is eager to solve that riddle—and worried about the answer. If those present are loyal to the others, but refuse loyalty to her, then her stewardship of this new Empire will be woefully short. She knows that no matter what, her struggle has not ended. It has only begun, and this worries her considerably.

Her worries are myriad. Will Hux betray her when they join with the others? Who comes after? Do they serve him, or her? Can she be the legacy of Palpatine, or must she always contend with the ghost of Gallius Rax, his presence lingering in those who remain? That man's influence was a virus. Infectious and potentially incurable. Then there comes a question of the children: those bright-eyed monsters. They train every day here on board the ship at the urging of both Brendol and his son Armitage. Armitage has grown more vicious during these months, even for such a small boy.

Sloane likes him. But she worries about him, too.

They could colonize it all.

Their new galaxy will never have known a time without an Empire.

That thrills her.

And, indeed, it worries her, too.

"It's time to start over," she says to Hux. "That is

our first order. To begin again. And to get it right, this time."

"Yes, of course, Grand Admiral. Anything you need. Glory be to Grand Admiral Sloane."

"No," she says. "Glory goes only to the Empire."

My Empire, she thinks.

ACKNOWLEDGMENTS

I think the biggest acknowledgment I need to make is to those architects and dreamers who made this galaxy as real to me as they did to so many others out there over the last (gulp) four decades: George Lucas, Kathleen Kennedy, Leigh Brackett, Irvin Kirshner, Dave Filoni, Timothy Zahn, J. J. Abrams, and soon, Rian Johnson. That's only a spare, cut-down list of the hundreds, even thousands of people who have shaped this galaxy of stories in some way, big or small, over the years.

Thanks, too, to Grand Admiral Editor Elizabeth Schaefer, Vizier Tom Hoeler (who also has a side job as a Huttese translator and songwriter), and Super Secret First Order Literary Agent Stacia Decker.

Read on for the short story

BLADE SQUADRON: JAKKU

BY DAVID J. WILLIAMS AND MARK S. WILLIAMS

This story was originally published in
Star Wars Insider magazine issue #172.

"All available ships, concentrate your fire on the engines of the *Ravager*. Repeat, concentrate on the *engines*—"

Admiral Ackbar's words were still ringing in her ears as Gina Moonsong keyed her comm—

"Okay, Blade Squadron, you heard the man." Moonsong tightened up her squadron's formation as the B-wings swooped in to attack the Super Star Destroyer *Ravager,* flanked on either side by their X-wing escort. She found herself keeping a particularly close eye on the X-wing piloted by Braylen Stramm. Given how much Kuat had depleted their pilots, he'd remained with the squadron; they needed every able-bodied pilot on deck. Officially, their relationship was strictly professional. In reality, though, it was more complicated than ever.

Fanty's voice cut through her reverie: "Fifteen seconds out."

"No TIE fighters, just capital ships." Lieutenant Sandara Li's contralto echoed over the squadron's frequency; she and her wingmate, Johan Volk, rolled in to cover Moonsong's approach. Gina smiled grimly as the *Ravager*'s aft filled her cockpit viewport. To her surprise, there was almost no return fire—the vast ship was beset from too many directions to worry about a small squadron. And there seemed to be some kind of issue with its drive system . . . the craft was shifting course at an unpredictable angle. But that wasn't Moonsong's problem.

Her problem was finding a way to make it even worse.

"Stand by to fire ion cannons. Transmitting targets in three . . . two . . . one. Weapons free! I repeat, weapons free!" The B-wings of Blade Squadron unleashed a withering barrage of fire, scoring multiple hits on the drive systems. Moonsong hung back, allowing her pilots to take their shots and peel away. It wasn't until after Stramm and her wingmate, Fanty, cleared the area that Moonsong started her own attack run. There was an undeniable pleasure in delivering the coup de grâce, and as the squadron commander Gina reveled in it. Moonsong reduced her speed, lined up the engines, and let loose with everything her B-wing had. She was rewarded with orange blossoms of fire and molten debris as the enormous Star Destroyer pitched and heaved. Gina's readouts were going haywire; there was massive EM interference, and what little she could decipher made no sense: Had someone unleashed a *tractor beam* on the Star Destroyer? What was going on? She swerved away but there was nowhere to swerve; all of a sudden the Star Destroyer was losing traction and plunging toward the planet Jakku below.

Leaving Gina right between the two.

She heard Ackbar's voice echoing on override across all channels—

"Soldiers and pilots of the New Republic! The Dreadnought Ravager is down—it falls to Jakku! Beware debris and take cover!"

—and then the admiral's voice was cut off by a sudden explosion that sounded like it was right next to

Moonsong's head. She wasn't sure if she had taken a direct hit from a laser, or if a piece of debris had smashed into her B-wing—but whatever clobbered her had collapsed her shields and knocked out her maneuver drive. She was drifting dead-stick right into the debris field of the crashing Super Star Destroyer. She managed to bring up the auxiliary power, but the readouts told her she was past the point of being able to punch out. She was already in the grip of Jakku's gravity; all she could do was try to redirect her B-wing to bring it in line behind the dying *Ravager* in a desperate attempt to use the giant craft as a heat shield for reentry. All her sensors were now in the red; alarms were warbling right next to her head, and she smelled acrid smoke. But through those alarms she heard a voice:

"Gina! Gina can you hear me!"

She could, but as the comm died, it became clear Stramm couldn't hear her. She wanted to tell him she was sorry, that they should have ditched this whole war and made for some world where no one had ever drawn weapons . . . but now it was too late. The g-forces were hauling her down toward blackout; the prospect loomed before her almost invitingly, like some kind of ultimate solace. But she fought for consciousness—and then stopped fighting gravity; instead, she vectored down and past the *Ravager*. They were well beneath the heat of reentry now; all she had to worry about was surviving the crash—not to mention crashing in a place that didn't promptly get smashed by millions of tons of falling metal. She made some guesses on the fly, used the little power her ship had left to accelerate well past its safety limits, the craft shaking like a leaf in the winds of atmosphere. A vast ceiling of falling metal loomed above. Desert

stretched below. With her last breath of consciousness, she engaged the auto-landing sequence . . .

It was a steady sound; like a drumbeat, or somebody
tapping the inside of Moonsong's skull. As her eyes
opened, she realized that there was some strange-
looking bird pecking at the glass of her cockpit. She
unstrapped herself and activated the emergency explosive, which blew the canopy clear—the bird took off
just in time and flew away with an annoyed squawk.
Moonsong unstrapped herself, pulled herself free of the
wreckage, and stepped out into a wilderness of sand.
She didn't know much about Jakku, nor had she ever
planned on finding out. The place looked like a desolate wasteland. It was a hell of a spot to make a last
stand.

Especially since half the sky was on fire. Miles off
in the distance the huge wreck of the *Ravager* sat like
a fiery mountain spitting plasma-charged steel and
smoke into the air. The sand for miles around had
been turned black from the craft's explosive impact.
Looking back at her wrecked B-wing, Moonsong realized it was a miracle she had survived, but she seriously doubted that was going to remain the case for
long. She pulled off her helmet and thermal gloves before disconnecting the controls for the suit's systems.
She felt more than a little conspicuous in her red flight
suit. She quickly discovered that the B-wing's survival
kit was destroyed, and if you didn't count the signal
flares she carried—which she didn't—then she had absolutely no weapons.

Of course, things could always get worse: The distinc-
tive whine of TIE fighter engines high above brought
her to her feet and running. She ran up the side of a
dune and dived for cover behind a cluster of rocks as

the TIE fighters swooped in, firing wildly and quickly turning what was left of her B-wing into a molten heap of burning scrap. So much for honor among pilots; it seemed that neither the New Republic nor the Empire would be taking prisoners this time. She watched her beloved ship burn and took a deep breath. No comm, water, survival supplies, homing beacon. But heading in the opposite direction of the downed Super Star Destroyer's gigantic funeral pyre seemed like a good start. She folded her lucky flight gloves into her suit and started walking. At least she was still walking . . .

Moonsong was burning with thirst. She estimated she had trudged a good ten or so kilometers from the crash but still had no point of reference to tell her where she was. Darkness was falling fast and she was more than a little concerned about sleeping out in the open. She scurried up the side of a particularly high sand dune and peered down into the valley below—

To find herself looking down at the shattered remnants of an Imperial stormtrooper camp.

Moonsong ran down to the scene of carnage and carefully sifted through the remains of the dead troopers. Whatever had done this had made fast and terrible work of the squad. But Moonsong was intent on turning their bad luck into her good fortune—she went to work scavenging through what was left of their equipment. She found a canteen of water—she didn't care it had belonged to a dead guy, he wouldn't be needing it. As she drank, she unclipped an E-11 blaster and a utility harness—then strapped on the utility belt and unfolded the weapon's stock for maximum stability. She flipped the select fire switch with a degree of satisfaction. Maybe things were looking up.

And then she heard something behind her.

Moonsong spun around to find herself face-to-face with a teenage boy in a torn flight suit.

"Don't shoot!" he said. And then the challenge code: "Thunder!" He looked scared as hell. Moonsong slowly lowered the weapon but kept her finger on the trigger.

"Lightning. Who are you, kid?"

He gave her a crisp salute. "Temmin . . . Temmin Wexley, Phantom Squadron." He didn't look old enough to shave let alone fly an X-wing—and yet here they both were trapped in the same impossible situation. Moonsong allowed herself the ghost of a smile.

"Well, Temmin Wexley: I'm Lieutenant Gina Moonsong, Blade Squadron. Is your comlink still working?"

"Uh . . . no."

"Got a blaster?"

"Sure." Temmin pulled his DH-17 and checked the charge. "I've only got one spare power pack, though."

"What about provisions?"

"Most of my kit was destroyed. I got this, though . . ." Temmin dug deep into a flight suit pocket and pulled out a pair of nutritional supplements. Each bar could sustain a human for up to three days. The downside was the terrible taste. Though at this point Moonsong wasn't complaining.

"Well, at least we won't starve. We've got to link up with the ground forces if we're ever going to get off this rock."

"Yes, si—I mean yes, ma'am—"

"Call me Gina. It's easier."

Moonsong took the first watch while the kid slept. Though that was really just a way to make sure he got some rest, because as soon as he woke, Moonsong skipped her rest and got them on the move instead. She figured they could make some real distance before the sun came back up. The kid seemed sullen and stayed quiet. Moonsong figured a little talking might ease the time and lower the panic factor. Too bad she was terrible at making small talk.

"So, um . . . what happened to the rest of your squadron, kid?"

"They're still up there fighting. But . . . some of them are dead. They were my friends."

"I've lost good friends, too," she said. She touched his hand gently. That was when she got a glimpse of his face in the starlight. "But they're not the only ones on your own mind . . ." It wasn't a question, just a statement. But still he hesitated . . .

"No . . . I mean, yes. I mean, I hope my mom's okay. She's a pilot, too."

"No kidding." Gina paused. "Are you Norra Wexley's kid?"

"She was at the Battle of Endor," said Temmin with something close to awe.

"So was I, actually."

"Yeah, but did you fly a Y-wing into the Death Star and out the other side?"

"That'd be a negative."

"Well, she did!"

"That means she's a survivor," said Gina with a confidence she didn't feel. "Which means you'll see her again. I've got friends I want to see again, too . . ." Moonsong's voice faltered as she thought about Stramm. She decided there and then that if she ever saw his face again she would tell him everything and see where the cards fell.

"Do you hear that?" Temmin asked.

"Hear wh—" But before either of them could react

half a dozen figures popped out from behind a rock with weapons drawn.

One of them called out the challenge: "Thunder!"

Moonsong let out a sigh of relief—they were friendly. "Lightning!"

Weapons lowered as the New Republic soldiers closed around them. One of them recognized Moonsong's rank and gave a perfunctory salute. "Lieutenant, I'm Sergeant Agarne, Third Recon Group."

"You're a sight for sore eyes."

"We don't have much time. Group command is over there. He'll explain everything."

"Copy that. Lead the way." The group double-timed it over a few dunes to a rocky area where a squad of soldiers were digging in.

"Downed pilots to see the group commander," said the sergeant.

"Thank you, Sarge," said a voice from down in the trench. "Do me a favor and double-check our lines of fire again." Agarne gave a curt nod and headed off to check the other soldiers. The group commander climbed out of the trench and faced the two newcomers. Blue eyes shone from within a scarred face.

"I'm Major Ranz," he said.

Moonsong saluted. "Lieutenant Gina Moonsong, commander Blade Squadron. This is pilot Temmin Wexley. If you don't mind us using one of your comlinks, we'll get out of your hair and leave you to do your job, Major."

But Ranz shook his head. "Sorry, Lieutenant, we're under orders to maintain comm silence until we make contact with our target—and even if I could give you a comlink there's so much EMP interference, you'd need a full-blown command-and-control sat uplink to get through all the chaff."

Moonsong shrugged, burying her disappointment.

This was war; nothing went as planned. "What *is* your target?"

Ranz gestured at the scrublands up ahead. "In about thirty minutes, an Imperial supply convoy is going to roll right through that pass. If they're able to reinforce Golga Station, they might be able to mount a counterattack that could make this battle drag on regardless of what happens upstairs."

"A supply convoy." Wexley looked around at the rebel troops. Some of them were wounded. All looked tired. "That sounds like it would be well protected."

"It will be. I expect at least one reinforced company of stormtroopers to be traveling with it."

"Where are the rest of your men?"

"You're looking at them. Yesterday we had a full company."

"You don't honestly think you can take out a heavily armored Imperial supply convoy with a dozen men, do you? That's suicide."

Ranz laughed mirthlessly. "Didn't they say that about taking down the Death Star? Look, we have our orders. You're welcome to some supplies if you want to make a run for it, but we're about a hundred kilometers behind enemy lines with nothing but thousands of angry stormtroopers between here and Base Alpha. It's up to you, Lieutenant."

It wasn't really much of a choice. "Count us in," she said. She glanced at Wexley. "I hope you know how to use that blaster, kid."

Then she turned back to Ranz. "I'd like to suggest a plan," she said.

The six Imperial troop transports skirted across the sands at twenty kilometers per hour. They were unbuttoned, with a single trooper sticking out of the top hatch staffing the craft's main gun. Ranz waited until the very last second and gave the signal.

"Now!" The scouts detonated a jury-rigged cluster of power packs buried in the sand as the second transport passed over it. The ITT rose into the air on a pillar of sand and fire, then flipped over onto its back and split open, spilling supplies and troopers in all directions. The ITT behind it desperately turned, skidding to a halt as it impacted with the wreckage. The lead transport stopped and spun its dorsal turret, spitting cover fire in all directions as the stormtroopers poured out, ready to meet their enemies. The remaining transports pulled into a triangle formation and stopped. On cue, Major Ranz and his New Republic troopers leapt from their spider holes and opened fire on the rear ITTs. Half a dozen rockets turned the rear transports into flaming coffins for the stormtroopers that had yet to disembark—but it didn't take long for the remaining Imperials to form a skirmish line and return fire. They even managed to deploy a heavy-weapons team, which struggled to set up a tripod-mounted blaster cannon. The surviving troopers from the front of the column raced to reinforce the rear and face their attackers . . . just as Ranz had anticipated.

"Now!" he shouted.

Moonsong, Wexley, Sergeant Agarne, and three of the squad popped out of their hiding place at the head of the column and tossed the few remaining antipersonnel grenades they had before running down firing at the few troopers outside the command ITT. Moonsong felt the heated air of near-misses, did her best to forget just how naked and exposed she was to the enemy's fire as she reached the ITT first and yanked a dead stormtrooper out of the smoking cockpit. She smiled as she saw the intact communications gear in the vehicle's dash. But that smile quickly disappeared as she realized the long-range comm dish was damaged.

"Temmin! We're going to have to align the dish manually!"

"I'm on it!" Wexley climbed atop the vehicle, pulled out his multitool, and quickly unscrewed the fitting that held the dish in place. An explosion went off nearby and Wexley fell from the ITT like he'd been hit by shrapnel; Moonsong somehow managed to focus anyway, keying up the coded channel to fighter command that piped her voice in directly to Admiral Ackbar's command ship *Home One*. Third Recon Group had no such access, but Moonsong did—and she had managed to persuade Ranz that even if the letter of his orders stipulated they couldn't break comm silence until contact with the enemy had been made, well . . . that still meant that once contact had occurred, any and all signaling was just fine. It was a technicality, maybe, but it was one that might yet save all their lives. Sergeant Agarne poked his head in as blasterfire strafed their position.

"Pick up the pace, Lieutenant! They're onto us and we can't hold them off for much longer!" Moonsong climbed out of the cab firing wildly as she made her way to the wounded Wexley.

"Okay, trooper, up and at them!" she shouted at Wexley. "I haven't given you permission to kick off!" She was relieved to see that he hadn't been hit—the blast had merely stunned him. He groaned as Moonsong pulled him to his feet and helped him limp off toward the nearest dune for cover. The stormtroopers had finished setting up their tripod cannon, and proceeded to pour fire on the New Republic positions behind them while the bulk of the Imperials started a flanking maneuver. That was when Moonsong heard a massive boom, followed by an enormous plume of smoke rising from where the major's position used to be. She realized he must have detonated the remaining explosives in an effort to stop the stormtroopers from overrunning his position. A few remaining New Republic troopers who had assisted with the assault on the lead ITT fell back and rallied around Moonsong's position. Sergeant Agarne fell in next to her and slapped a fresh pack into his blaster rifle.

"All right, you lot: Set your blasters on single shot and watch your aim. The only way we're getting out of this is if we conserve our ammo."

"You really think we're getting out of this?" someone muttered. That was when the unmistakable sound of fighter engines overhead drew Moonsong's attention— up in the sky diving out of the sun were the familiar shapes of TIE fighters streaking toward them. On their first pass, their deadly laserfire raked the area, killing most of the remaining troopers in Ranz's element as well as a few stormtroopers too close to what was left of his position.

"It's over!" shouted one of the rebels. "They've got us . . . we've got to surrender!"

"I seriously doubt these guys take prisoners," said Moonsong. She stood up and raised her rifle to her shoulder; if this was it, she figured she would go down fighting. "Okay, you want some of this? Come and get—" but even as she said the words, the TIE fighter suddenly exploded, followed by the next one in formation, and then the next . . . until finally the only fighter craft in the sky were B-wings diving down and strafing the ITTs. Snubfighter laserfire kicked up huge plumes of smoke and sand; the stormtroopers broke formation and scattered in all directions. The second pass of the B-wings finished most of them off. The rest ran into the desert. Moonsong waved to the sky as Blade Squadron sped past, waggling their wings and rolling in salute to the survivors on the ground. She wasn't surprised to see Stramm's marking emblazoned on the lead fighter. She stepped over to where Wexley was kneeling.

"What's happening?" he said, looking up at her.

"We're going home," she said. "Your mother will be proud."

She knelt beside him with a hand on his shoulder while the fighters that made up Blade Squadron landed all around them. Stramm stepped out and walked over to them.

"I see you've got a new friend," he said.

"This is Temmin," said Moonsong. "Temmin, this is Braylen."

"Good to meet you," said Stramm. He took Gina's hand. "You gave me quite a scare," he said. "Don't do it again, okay?"

"Hey, I thought you weren't going to try to give me any more orders."

They looked at each other for a moment, and then both started laughing. "I wouldn't dream of it," he said. Just before things turned awkward, she pulled him in and kissed him. She felt more than a little dazed—it seemed surreal that the sands of Jakku hadn't claimed her. As to what came next—well, she would just have to see.

Read on for an excerpt from the
highly anticipated novel:

STAR WARS
THRAWN

BY TIMOTHY ZAHN

Published by Del Rey Books

All beings begin their lives with hopes and aspirations. Among these aspirations is the desire that there will be a straight path to those goals.

It is seldom so. Perhaps never.

Sometimes the turns are of one's own volition, as one's thoughts and goals change over time. But more often the turns are mandated by outside forces.

It was so with me. The memory is vivid, unsullied by age: the five admirals rising from their chairs as I am escorted into the chamber. The decision of the Ascendancy has been made, and they are here to deliver it.

None of them is happy with the decision. I can read that in their faces. But they are officers and servants of the Chiss, and they will carry out their orders. Protocol alone demands that.

The word is as I expected.

Exile.

The planet has already been chosen. The admirals will assemble the equipment necessary to ensure that solitude does not quickly become death from predators or the elements.

I am led away. Once again, my path has turned.

Where it will lead, I cannot say.

ELI HAD ALMOST managed to convince himself that the group would merely be meeting with some Palace official when they were ushered past a pair of red-robed and red-helmeted Imperial Guards into the emperor's throne room.

Even more than Coruscant itself, the holos and vids Eli had seen of Emperor Palpatine paled in comparison with the real thing.

At first glance the emperor didn't seem like much. He was dressed in a plain brown hooded robe, with no ornamentation or glitz of any sort. His throne, while massive, was solid black and very simple, again with no ostentation about it, raised a mere four steps above the floor. In fact, the darkness of his robe made him almost disappear from sight into the black of the throne.

It was as the group drew closer that the eeriness began.

The first was the emperor's face. The holos and vids always showed him as a dignified, older man, aged somewhat with the experience of life and the cares of leadership. But the holos were wrong. The face beneath the hood was *old,* and creased with a hundred deep wrinkles.

Not ordinary wrinkles, either, the kind Eli's grandparents had earned from years under the open sky. These creases were less like age and more like scars or burn tissue.

The histories stated that the Jedi traitors' last attempt to seize power had been an attack on thenchancellor Palpatine. The histories hadn't mentioned that his victory over the assassins had come at such a terrible cost.

Perhaps that was also what had happened to his eyes.

A shiver ran up Eli's back. The eyes were bright and intelligent, all-knowing and utterly powerful. But they were . . . strange. Unique. Disturbing. Damaged, perhaps, by the same treachery that had ravaged his face?

Intelligence, knowledge, power. And, even more than with Thrawn, a sense of complete mastery over everything around him.

The emperor watched in silence as the party walked toward him. Parck led the way, Barris and Eli behind him, followed by Thrawn and the trooper and stormtrooper witnesses. The guard contingent Parck had brought remained outside the door, six of the Imperial Guards having taken over their escort duty.

It seemed to take forever to reach the throne. Eli wondered how close they would be permitted to approach, and how Captain Parck would know when he had reached that point. The question was answered as Parck came to within five meters and the two Imperial Guards at the foot of the steps glided to positions directly in front of him. Parck stopped, the rest of them following suit, and waited.

And waited.

It was probably only five seconds. But to Eli it felt like a medium-size eternity. The entire throne room was utterly still, utterly silent. The only sound was the thudding of his pulse in his ears, the only movement the shaking of his arms in his sleeves.

"Captain Parck," the emperor said at last, his gravelly voice neutral. "I'm told you bring me a gift."

Eli winced. A *gift*? For the Chiss of the stories, that would have been a deadly insult. Thrawn was behind him, and he didn't dare turn around, but he could imagine the expression on that proud face.

"I do, Your Majesty," Parck said, bowing low. "A warrior reportedly of a race known as the Chiss."

"Indeed," the emperor said, his voice going even drier. "And what, pray tell, would you have me do with him?"

"If I may, Your Majesty." Thrawn spoke up before Parck could answer. "I am not merely a gift. I am also a resource. One you have never seen the like of before, and may never see again. You would do well to utilize me."

"Would I?" the emperor sounded amused. "Certainly you're a resource of unlimited confidence. What exactly do you offer, Chiss?"

"As a start, I offer information," Thrawn said. If he was offended, Eli couldn't hear it in his voice. "There are threats lurking in the Unknown Regions, threats that will someday find your empire. I am familiar with many of them."

"I will learn of them soon enough on my own," the emperor countered placidly. "Can you offer anything more?"

"Perhaps you will learn of them in time to defeat them," Thrawn said. "Perhaps you will not. What more do I offer? I offer my military skill. You could utilize that skill in making plans to seek out and eliminate these dangers."

"These threats you speak of," the emperor said, "I presume they're not simply threats to my empire?"

"No, Your Majesty," Thrawn said. "They are also threats to my people."

"And you seek to eliminate all such threats to your people?"

"I do."

The emperor's yellowish eyes seemed to glitter. "And you wish the help of my empire?"

"Your assistance would be welcome."

"You wish me to assist people who exiled you?" the emperor said. "Or was Captain Parck incorrect?"

"He spoke correctly," Thrawn said. "I was indeed exiled."

"Yet you still seek to protect them. Why?"

"Because they are my people."

"And if they withhold their gratitude and refuse to accept you back? What then?"

There was a slight pause, and Eli had the eerie sense that Thrawn was giving the emperor one of those small smiles he was so good at. "I do not need their permission to protect them, Your Majesty. Nor do I expect their thanks."

"I've seen others with your sense of nobility," the emperor said. "Most fell by the wayside when their naive selflessness collided with the real world."

"I have *faced* the real world, as you call it."

"You have indeed," the emperor said. "What exactly do you wish from my empire?"

"A state of mutual gain," Thrawn said. "I offer my knowledge and skill to you now in exchange for your consideration to my people in the future."

"And when that future comes, what if I refuse to grant that consideration?"

"Then I will have gambled and lost," Thrawn said calmly. "But I have until that time to convince you that my goals and yours do indeed coincide."

"Interesting," the emperor murmured. "Tell me. If

you served the empire, yet a threat arose against your people, where would your loyalties lie? Which of us would command your allegiance?"

"I see no conflict in the sharing of information."

"I'm not speaking of information," the emperor said. "I'm speaking of service."

There was a short pause. "If I were to serve the empire, you would command my allegiance."

"What guarantee do you offer?"

"My word is my guarantee," Thrawn said. "Perhaps your servant can speak to the strength of that vow."

"My servant?" the emperor asked, his eyes flicking to Parck.

"I do not refer to Captain Parck," Thrawn said. "I speak of another. Perhaps I assumed incorrectly that he was your servant. Yet he always spoke highly of Chancellor Palpatine."

The emperor leaned forward a little, his yellowish eyes glittering. "And his name?"

"Skywalker," Thrawn said. "Anakin Skywalker."